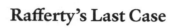

Rafferty's Last Case

Rafferty's Last Case

A
MINNESOTA
MYSTERY
Featuring
SHERLOCK
HOLMES

LARRY MILLETT

University of Minnesota Press
Minneapolis
London

Published by the University of Minnesota Press
111 Third Avenue South, Suite 290
Minneapolis, MN 55401-2520
http://www.upress.umn.edu

ISBN 978-1-5179-1311-3 (hc)
ISBN 978-1-5179-1312-0 (pb)

Library of Congress record available at https://lccn.loc.gov/2021061578

Printed in the United States of America on acid-free paper

The University of Minnesota is an equal-opportunity educator and employer.

30 29 28 27 26 25 24 23 22   10 9 8 7 6 5 4 3 2 1

Contents

Book V. Endgame at the Ryan

Prologue

A Knife to the Back

When the darkness of forever beckons, there is no time to waste. Using nearly his last reserves of energy, Shadwell Rafferty rolled over, pain tearing at his body like a sharp-clawed beast, so that he could face the end with his eyes looking toward the heavens. He took a deep breath, aware there would be very few more, and listened to the old grandfather clock across the room as it ticked away his final moments. He wondered if God would appear, the Great Invisibility made manifest at last, but he saw no immediate sign of a divine presence. Perhaps it was just as well, he thought. Life was a mystery and death should be, too.

Truth was, Rafferty had been ready for his day of departure for a long time, only not in the way it was happening. He'd hoped to go peacefully, a few friends at his bedside, a few choice closing words, and then a quiet slip into the unknown. Instead, he was alone, in agony, blood gushing from a deep knife wound to his upper back as death began to press down on him like a heavy stone.

The attack had come just as Rafferty, returning from a meeting with a murderer, stepped into the study of his apartment at the Ryan Hotel in downtown St. Paul. It happened so suddenly and with such force that Rafferty crashed to the floor without ever seeing his assailant's face. As he fell, he heard loud knocking at his door and a voice calling his name. He cried out for help but received no response.

Rafferty was all but certain who had attacked him. A bloodied knife, which Rafferty recognized as one given to him years ago as a gift, lay on the floor beside him as if to confirm his impending demise. Rafferty knew why the vicious, desperate attack had occurred. He'd just made a startling discovery, one so shocking it had entirely changed his thinking about the murder case that had obsessed him for more than a month.

He'd been investigating the murder of twenty-five-year-old Daniel St. Aubin, and the case had led Rafferty down a twisting path into the bleak presence of pure evil. From the start, he'd known there were five prime suspects. The five Ps, Rafferty called them, for the suspects were a policeman, a poet, a priest, and two politicians. Rafferty had interviewed each of them, looking for clues that might point him to the killer. But the truth had eluded Rafferty until just before the man with the knife came to silence him forever.

Rafferty had kept meticulous notes as he puzzled through the case. Hours earlier, sitting at the big mahogany desk that formed the centerpiece of his study, he'd typed up his latest thoughts about St. Aubin's killer. Rafferty had made many such notes during his investigation, all deposited in a manila folder atop his desk next to his trusty Underwood typewriter. The killer undoubtedly had found the notes and would, of course, destroy them. But Rafferty had taken precautions, and the killer was mistaken if he thought he would get away with his crimes.

Rafferty had another reason to believe his death would not go unavenged. Two extraordinary men had arrived recently in Chicago, amid much publicity, and they would be shocked to learn of Rafferty's fate. He was sure they would come to St. Paul, if they could, to investigate his murder.

Light now began turning to darkness, thought and life itself at their last extremities. Wondering for the final time at the majesty and misery of the world, Rafferty searched once again for a glimpse of light that might guide him into a new, perhaps better place. He had for years given up on God, or perhaps it was the other way around, and he blamed the hard, cold Jesuits of Boston for his apostasy. With their measureless disgust for sinful mankind, they had driven faith from his heart at a young age, and he'd long doubted it would ever return. But in the past few years he'd begun to see strange glimmers, lamps flickering in the darkness, and faith had reemerged like a tiny flower growing out of stony ground.

Rafferty began to see a faint glow of possibility in the air around him. Was it a promise from the heavens or a mere mirage? Rafferty didn't know, but as he prepared to cross over, he reached into his shirt pocket for a scrap of paper with a telephone number on it. The number would be a vital clue if—

Suddenly, a flood of memories and images began roaring through his head, like a movie shown at ultrahigh speed. The rush ended as abruptly as it had begun, followed by a flash of light, and then ineffable calm. He felt at peace as the scrap of paper fell from his hand. So it was that on the twenty-first day of January 1928, at just past six in the evening, Shadwell Rafferty took his final breath.

Book I

A Body, a Funeral, a Promise

1

"Are You Here?"

George Washington Thomas, Rafferty's longtime business partner and closest friend, found the body and paid a price for his discovery. He and Rafferty had planned to meet at six for dinner at the hotel café. A man of large appetite, Rafferty was rarely late for a meal, and when he hadn't shown up by quarter past six, Thomas grew concerned. He went up to Rafferty's second-floor apartment and knocked on the door three times while calling out Rafferty's name. There was no answer. Worried that Rafferty had fallen or even suffered a heart attack, Thomas fished out his key to the apartment and opened the door.

When he awoke ten minutes later, feeling as though he'd been struck by a highballing express train, Thomas staggered to his feet and tried to collect his senses. A bloody knot on the back of his head told him what had happened. He'd been sapped from behind as soon as he stepped into the apartment. He had no idea who had ambushed him or why. But as his mind cleared, his thoughts turned to Rafferty. Had he been attacked as well?

"Are you here, Shad?" Thomas called out. Silence. A dark wave of dread flowed over Thomas. Something felt terribly wrong. He checked Rafferty's bedroom. No one there. Then Thomas went into the study and experienced the most terrible shock of his life.

Rafferty lay prone on the carpet in front of his desk, blood pooling around his right shoulder. His eyes were fixed and wide open. Two objects—a folded piece of paper and a blood-smeared knife— lay next to his body. His jacket and pants pockets were turned inside out, as though someone had searched through them.

Tears streaming down his cheeks, Thomas tried to revive Rafferty but it was useless. He had known for some time that Rafferty was failing and that death could not be far away. But bloody murder? No, that was not how Shad deserved to meet his end. Thomas felt not only the depths of grief but also seething anger. He intended to find the man who had taken Shad's life, before the police did if possible, and send him straight to hell.

The murder weapon, a bowie knife with a six-inch blade and inlaid walnut handle, looked identical to one Rafferty had owned for years. The scrap of paper next to Rafferty's right hand was a more tantalizing clue. Thomas bent down and carefully unfolded it to reveal a telephone number—Gar 2030—written in Rafferty's hand. Thomas recognized it as a local number from the Garfield exchange area in downtown St. Paul.

Thomas debated what to do about the phone number. It clearly was an important piece of evidence, but could the police be trusted with it? He already suspected Rafferty's murder might somehow be connected to the St. Aubin investigation and a possible police cover-up, in which case the clue might vanish if the coppers got their hands on it. Better safe than sorry, Thomas thought. He refolded the scrap of paper and slipped it into one of his shoes.

Rafferty often carried a derringer for protection but Thomas didn't find it on his body. Had the killer taken it? Or had Rafferty, believing he was safe in his apartment, been unarmed when he was attacked? Rafferty's billfold was also missing and presumably stolen.

Another question soon occurred to Thomas. Where were Rafferty's notes on the St. Aubin case? They should have been in a folder he usually kept on his desk or in one of the drawers. Thomas made a quick search but didn't find the folder. He wondered if the killer had taken it before making his escape. Perhaps it had even been his prime target all along.

Thomas decided to look around the rest of the apartment before calling the police. His first stop was a curio cabinet in the front parlor where Rafferty displayed his bowie knife in a tooled leather sheath. One look at the empty sheath confirmed that Rafferty had been murdered with his own knife.

It wasn't long before Thomas came upon an oddity. Resting on a small side table in the parlor were two guns. One was an old single-shot Stevens pocket rifle Rafferty had used to good effect many years earlier during the Secret Alliance affair in Minneapolis. Thomas had hardly seen it since then. Now, here it was, loaded with a .32-caliber round. Next to it was a more modern weapon from Rafferty's gun collection—a .45-caliber Colt automatic pistol. It too was loaded.

Thomas knew that Rafferty never left guns lying around for fear of a mishap. Instead, he stored all of his weapons in a heavy safe in his bedroom. Thomas went into the bedroom to inspect the safe. It was locked and showed no signs of tampering. So why were there two guns out in the parlor? Had Rafferty simply forgotten about them? It didn't seem likely.

What seemed more likely to Thomas was that the police couldn't be trusted with the weapons, since they were famously light-fingered when it came to guns recovered from crime scenes. Thomas had the combination to Rafferty's gun safe, so he put the guns there. For all he knew, they could prove to be a vital clue.

Thomas desperately wanted to spend more time hunting through the rest of the apartment but thought better of it, at least for the time being. Questions would be raised if he waited too long before notifying the police. Using the phone on the desk, he placed a call to police headquarters.

When the law arrived, Thomas gave a full statement. His head was still aching but no one offered him medical attention. Instead, the police—led by Chief of Detectives Jackson Grimshaw, a powerful bull of a man—treated him as a suspect despite the nasty bump on his head. But after an hour of questioning, and a search of his person, Grimshaw let Thomas go for lack of any evidence against him.

Thomas hung around the Ryan's lobby with the intention of returning to Rafferty's apartment once the police left. He sent a telegram to Chicago, praying it would bring powerful forces to bear on his beloved friend's murder. Then he turned his attention to the telephone number left next to the body. He put a call through to the number, which turned out to be an answering service.

"To whom do you wish to speak?" the woman on the other end of the line asked.

Thomas didn't know, so he improvised. "Maybe I have the wrong number," he said. "Do you answer phones for several people?"

"There are fifteen customers who use this service, sir."

"Could you tell me who they are?"

"Sir, that would not be possible. If you don't know the party you wish to speak to, I can't be of help. Good night."

AFTER THE POLICE CLEARED OUT, Thomas returned to Rafferty's apartment. The coppers had tossed the place, leaving behind a mess. Thomas began a careful search of his own. He wasn't sure what he was looking for but wondered if the police, who were no geniuses, had missed some vital bit of evidence.

Thomas found himself in tears again as he sifted through the remains of Rafferty's life. Fortunately, the police had left most of Rafferty's memorabilia undisturbed. The Congressional Medal of Honor he'd won at Gettysburg with the First Minnesota Regiment still occupied a prominent place in the curio cabinet. So too did a photograph of Rafferty's older brother, Seamus, who'd also enlisted with the Minnesota Regiment and died a few months after Gettysburg on an obscure Virginia battlefield. There were many items as well from Rafferty and Thomas's saloon, which had operated for nearly thirty-five years on the ground floor of the Ryan. Coasters, pickle jars, beer mugs, shot glasses, a wooden tap handle, prized bottles of bourbon—it was all there, every piece a wondrous invitation to reminiscence.

Other prizes were scattered randomly around the apartment. There was a trophy northern pike Rafferty had landed at Lake Osakis, stuffed and mounted on a wall behind his desk; a menu chalkboard signed by Teddy Roosevelt during a stop at the saloon in 1901; and an elaborate hookah won in a poker game from a man who claimed to be the son of a Turkish sultan but who was in fact a flimflam artist from Detroit.

Rafferty kept his most cherished heirlooms on a fireplace mantle in the parlor. The greatest treasure was a picture of his wife, Mary, who'd died in childbirth just a year after their wedding, their baby boy gone too, along with a big piece of Rafferty's heart. Another of Rafferty's favorites was a group photograph of the First Minnesota in 1861 as they gathered at Fort Snelling before marching off to war. How young he looked then, Thomas thought, and how terrible that regiment's fate.

Not all of the pictures spoke to tragedy and loss. Many memorialized happier occasions, and one in particular brought a smile to Thomas's face. It was a poster-sized blowup of a photograph showing Rafferty, Sherlock Holmes, Dr. John Watson, James J. Hill, and Thomas in 1896 after the conclusion of the legendary ice palace case. Rafferty and Holmes had formed an enduring friendship during the case, and now murder had ended it.

It was just before midnight by the time Thomas finally headed home on the Selby Avenue streetcar. He was heartbroken and tired, grief coursing like some horrible sickness through his blood. Even so, he had cause for hope. Help, he believed, might soon be on the way.

WHEN THOMAS REACHED HOME, he broke the bad news to his wife, Pats, and they cried for a while in each other's arms. Pats finally nodded off at three in the morning, too exhausted for more tears, but Thomas couldn't sleep. His mind racing, he went back over every detail of Rafferty's murder. It had been staged to look like a burglary, but the theft of Rafferty's notes from the St. Aubin case strongly suggested otherwise. No random burglar would have been interested in the notes. Nor would any self-respecting thief have left the two guns behind.

Thomas had assisted Rafferty during much of the St. Aubin investigation and knew the case well. It had been a challenge to solve because St. Aubin turned out to be a criminal of a particularly vicious sort, which meant that any number of people might want to see him dead. But a vital clue provided by St. Aubin's mother allowed Rafferty to narrow his search for the killer to five prime suspects. Had one of them also killed Rafferty because he was getting too close to the truth? Thomas thought it very possible. But which one?

Jackson Grimshaw, the policeman in charge of investigating both Rafferty's murder and that of Daniel St. Aubin, was the first suspect. Thomas knew Grimshaw all too well. He was a broad-shouldered man in his forties, with a hard, impassive face dominated by a curling mustache that lodged above his lips like a small, fur-bearing animal. He was a dangerous character—he'd shot and killed at least two men, supposedly in the line of duty—and was known for roughing up anyone who got in his way.

The detective also had a reputation as the police department's chief cover-up artist, able to make criminal matters vanish, for a price, if the accused was someone of wealth and influence. Grimshaw's work, often performed on behalf of the mayor of St. Paul or other powerful politicians, did not go unrewarded, and he lived well beyond a detective's pay grade in a fine house just off Summit

Avenue. Rafferty regarded Grimshaw as "the dirtiest of the dirty coppers," but that didn't necessarily make him the murderer.

Suspect number two was Bertram Abbey, the poet. Before young Scott Fitzgerald came along, Abbey had been St. Paul's leading literary figure, a dashing man who in 1919 had earned a Columbia University Poetry Prize for a lengthy opus called "The Body of the Poet." The prize was supposedly a big deal, although Thomas wasn't much for poetry and knew little about it. Later, Abbey had turned to writing mystery novels, at least one of which became a best seller, or so Thomas had heard.

Thomas didn't know Abbey personally but had seen him a few times. Invariably dressed in a mauve-colored suit, an ascot, and a slouch hat decorated with a feather, he enjoyed cruising around in a bright red Hupmobile coupe, if for no other reason than to draw attention to himself. Born to wealth, Abbey lived in a Summit Avenue mansion. Although he'd been married for a time, he was reputed to harbor a taste for young men and usually kept at least one handsome servant in his employ. Abbey hardly seemed the murdering kind, but as Rafferty liked to say, "Any man will kill if it is the only way to save his own miserable hide."

The third and to Thomas's mind most unlikely suspect was the priest, Monsignor Pierre Denis, rector of the St. Paul Cathedral. Rafferty had long been an agnostic, allowing only that if "there were some proud drinkers among the angels," he might consider eternity in the Elysian Fields. Yet for many years he'd lit a candle every week at the cathedral in memory of his long-lost wife and son. During one of those visits he'd met Monsignor Denis and had "a nice long talk about God and other ethereal topics," as he later told Thomas, and in so doing Rafferty reopened the door to faith.

Rafferty and Denis met occasionally for lunch at the Ryan's café, and Thomas sometimes joined them. The monsignor was about fifty, tall and gaunt, with thinning hair, a narrow face, and piercing blue eyes. He was "crazed with religion" in Thomas's jaundiced view, but Rafferty seemed to enjoy his company and also respected his intellect. The newspapers described Denis as "Archbishop Austin Dowling's right-hand man" and noted he was also "well-versed in the art of politics at city hall." The monsignor was thus firmly connected to the two great sources of power in St. Paul. But could he really be a murderer?

The fourth and fifth suspects were politicians—Mayor Richard O'Donnell and his chief aide and adviser, Montgomery Meeks. Thomas didn't know either man very well. The mayor, in his second term, seemed to be a classic politician. Born to an old St. Paul family and trained as a lawyer, he was tall and silver-haired and spoke in a sonorous voice "smooth as flowing honey," or so a newspaper columnist had once written.

O'Donnell had won office by proclaiming the need to return to what he called "old-fashioned morality." Yet as far as Thomas could tell, the mayor also believed in old-fashioned politics. Despite his high-toned manner, O'Donnell headed a formidable political machine that raked in regular "contributions" as the price of doing business with the city, especially its police. "He is just another grifter in a fancy suit," Rafferty had once said of him. Yet it was a big step up from graft and corruption to murder, and Thomas found it hard to believe the mayor could have been involved in St. Aubin's death.

Meeks, the final suspect, was an even slicker operator than his boss. Known simply as Monty, he possessed superb political instincts, a quick wit, and a nimble mind. He enjoyed the mayor's full trust and was an expert at handling delicate problems that required a smooth touch. One newspaper article described him as St. Paul's "fixer-in-chief, a man who gets things done where others have failed." Thomas recalled a particularly vivid conversation with Rafferty regarding Meeks. "He is a very clever fellow, the fox who thinks he can outfox all the other foxes. But I am inclined to think he may be nothing more than a common street magician in the end. Sleight of hand will only get a man so far." Thomas didn't really know Meeks beyond his reputation as a political schemer. Even so, murder seemed a stretch for such a man.

Five suspects. Many questions. Few answers. Thomas thought it was going to be a hard business to bore down to the hidden truth and flush out a killer.

"HAVE YOU SEEN THE NEWS?" the first man asked, a copy of the *Pioneer Press* on the table in front of him.

"What news?" came the reply on the other end of the phone line.

"News that isn't good for us," the man said before revealing what the newspaper had reported.

"Is that a fact?" said the other man. "I didn't even know he's still alive. He must be ninety by now."

"More like in his seventies, I'd say, and still going strong by all accounts. Didn't you follow that big case of his in England a year or so back?"

"No, why should I care? Besides, if he's in England, how did he get here so fast?"

"You should read more, my friend. He was in Chicago for a lecture tour. Once he gets here and starts digging into Rafferty's murder, he's going to be trouble. Big, big trouble."

"I don't see how. Everything's been taken care of."

"Has it? Nothing is ever airtight, and he has a way of finding things out. It's what he does."

"Well, we can take care of him if we have to."

"Yes, we could, and then what? The whole damn world will want to know what happened to him, that's what. We have to be smart about this."

"So what's your plan?"

"I'm working on it. The first step will be to try to figure out what he knows and what he doesn't. We'll go from there. People think he's God, but he isn't. Trust me, we'll deal with him one way or another."

2
"It Is the Darkest of Days"

[From "Murder in St. Paul," a manuscript by Dr. John Watson left behind after his death]

On the evening of January 21, 1928, Sherlock Holmes delivered his third and final lecture on the "Art of Detection" to a spellbound audience at the Auditorium in Chicago. We had been touring in America since the first of the year, a trip undertaken after the success of my most recent collection of tales celebrating Holmes's exploits. Chicago was our final stop.

When Holmes finished his lecture, we returned to the lobby of the Palmer House, where we were staying. A telegram awaited us. Holmes read it, and his face turned ashen.

"What is it, Holmes?"

Wordlessly, he handed me the message, which said, "Shad has been murdered. It is the darkest of days. Come to St. Paul if you can. The funeral will be Wednesday. G. W. Thomas."

"My God! How can this be?"

"I do not know," Holmes said, rising from his chair. "But I intend to find out. Let us see if there is a night train to St. Paul."

So began an extraordinary case, which would test Holmes's genius to the utmost. Rafferty's murder, we soon discovered, was but one chapter in a tragic saga rife with cruelty, deceit, and death. We also discovered, as Rafferty had, that powerful men in St. Paul were prepared to cover up the terrible truth at any cost.

WE FOUND AN OVERNIGHT TRAIN on the Burlington Route, and as we hurtled north through the darkness I found myself thinking about Rafferty. He'd called us on the day of our arrival in Chicago, and it had been wonderful to hear his voice again. He told us his health was poor and so he couldn't travel to join us. But we were able to reminisce at some length about our many adventures together over the years. Rafferty also mentioned a new investigation he had taken up in St. Paul but provided few details.

By this time, it had been nearly eight years since we'd seen Rafferty in person, during the case of the Eisendorf Enigma in southern Minnesota. But he'd corresponded on occasion, usually to report on some interesting new case which occupied his attention. His most recent letter had made clear his health was failing, and yet he never complained and instead seemed to take a sly amusement in his own descent into what he called "the pit of old age." Of course, Holmes and I were hardly young either, and so it was easy enough to commiserate with our friend.

Thinking of Rafferty and the Eisendorf case, I could not help but reflect on all that had happened since we had seen him in 1920 in that cursed little village shadowed by high bluffs. The case marked a profound turning point in Holmes's life and career, coming at a time when I and the world believed his days as a consulting detective were over. He'd announced his retirement in the early years of the century and moved to the solitude of an estate in Sussex, where he became an unlikely beekeeper. His lonely house on the South Downs seemed to suit him well enough. With no distractions he had ample time to pursue his interests in chemistry and writing. He produced several notable monographs, including one devoted to the interpretation of blood stains, which has proved invaluable to Scotland Yard and police agencies throughout the world.

Yet Holmes ultimately grew weary of his isolation and began to yearn for a return to a more active life. At about this time, however, he began to experience a significant health problem in the form of persistent shortness of breath, and so I recommended in 1920 that he travel to the Mayo Clinic in Minnesota to seek treatment. His condition turned out to be emphysema, brought on by decades of smoking, and there was no cure. But he was told that giving up tobacco would be the only sure way to keep his condition from deteriorating. By a heroic effort of will, he managed to do so, and I account it a remarkable achievement given the hold tobacco had on him for so long.

Following the Eisendorf affair, which nearly cost him his life as he pursued an old nemesis, Holmes made the fateful decision to "permanently retire from retirement," as he put it. He soon undertook a series of secret investigations at the behest of His Majesty's government, and so remained largely out of the public eye. But in 1926 his dazzling solution to the murder of young Laura Pemberly in London thrust him once again into the limelight. The next year, I presented some of our much earlier adventures in a collection called *The Case-Book of Sherlock Holmes*, and so began what I can only regard as a kind of Holmes mania among the public.

This popular enthusiasm for Holmes led the famed promoter William Atherton to offer him a very large sum of money to undertake a series of lectures across Europe and the United States. The tour proved to be a triumph, Holmes speaking to rapt audiences wherever we went. By the time we reached the end of the tour in Chicago, Holmes and I were very much looking forward to returning home. Then came the sickening news of Rafferty's murder.

Now we had only memories of Rafferty. All through the night, as we raced toward St. Paul, Holmes and I shared stories of our many grand adventures with him. What a great and good friend he was! And how sad to know he had met such a terrible end!

WE REACHED ST. PAUL at half-past nine in the morning of the twenty-second. Rafferty's old friend and associate George Washington Thomas met us at the new Union Depot, which proved to be much grander than the cramped old station we'd become accustomed to on our earlier visits. It was a great pleasure to see Thomas once again. He is a tall, slender Negro, somewhere in his seventies, but still sharp of mind and quick of movement.

"Welcome," he said, giving us both vigorous handshakes. "I trust you traveled well."

"As well as can be expected under such terrible circumstances," Holmes replied. "As you said, these are dark days."

Thomas shook his head slowly and his shoulders slumped. I saw he had begun to cry. I stepped forward and patted Thomas on the shoulder. "It will be all right," I said.

"This is indeed a time for tears but also for action," Holmes said with a touch of sternness. "You must tell us everything you know about Mr. Rafferty's murder."

Thomas wiped away his tears and his head snapped back up. "You're right, Mr. Holmes. Once we get to the hotel, I'll fill you in. I've booked rooms for you at the Ryan, where Shad lived and where he was murdered. I'm sure you remember it."

The name did indeed summon up many memories. We'd stayed at the hotel during the ice palace affair and had spent more than a few hours in Rafferty's famed drinking establishment there. I remembered in particular that awful night when Rafferty, incensed by the wanton killing of his beloved bulldog, vented his fury with such force it required the strength of four men, including Holmes and myself, to restrain him from taking murderous revenge against John J. O'Connor, then the city's chief of police. Yet many wonderful incidents also came to mind, for Rafferty was a man with a rollicking sense of humor and an irrepressible love of life, as well as a brilliant detective in his own unorthodox way. That he was dead now seemed utterly impossible, as though some great glimmering star had suddenly gone dark.

During our short cab ride to the hotel, I was reminded once again that January in Minnesota can be remarkably frigid. "Don't think it will reach zero today," Thomas observed. "'A bit nippy' is how Shad would have described it. Of course, he had plenty of padding to keep him warm."

The hotel was much as I remembered it—a busy pile of red brick and white stone, its walls animated by numerous bays and balconies culminating at the roofline in an unpruned abundance of towers, turrets, and pinnacles. "It possesses a mad gothic style unknown to the cathedral builders of old, and I highly doubt it will go down as a monument for the ages," Rafferty once told me. He also explained how the unlikely structure had been built at a cost of one million dollars by a silver mining magnate from Nevada named Dennis Ryan, who "arrived in St. Paul at a time when he could conveniently be separated from his fortune by the usual hoodlums in charge of civic affairs."

Rafferty loved the hotel, where he lived for decades in an apartment above his famed saloon, and he viewed it as the true heart of St. Paul. By 1928, however, Holmes and I found the Ryan looking rather the worse for wear, and a much newer hotel—called simply The St. Paul—had drawn away much of its business. Even so, the Ryan's long skylit lobby proved inviting enough, as did our worn but neatly kept rooms.

After we'd settled in, having agreed to meet Thomas within the hour for breakfast, Holmes ordered a copy of the city's morning newspaper, the *Pioneer Press*. On a normal day, the front page undoubtedly would have featured an interview with the daring explorer Richard Byrd, who was in St. Paul touting his plan to fly over the South Pole. But the intrepid aviator was pushed aside by the news of Rafferty's murder, which was bannered across the front page. A lengthy story reported all that was known about the crime, while another article reviewed Rafferty's storied life. I was surprised to see that a box inserted in the main story announced our "pending arrival" in St. Paul.

"I imagine Mr. Thomas told the newspaper of our plans," Holmes said as he pored over the main story. He took particular note of the following paragraphs:

Chief of Detectives Jackson Grimshaw stated last night he is convinced Rafferty was stabbed to death by a thief who had broken into his apartment.

"We learned of several recent thefts from rooms at the Ryan, so we know a thief has been on the hotel premises," Grimshaw said. "We think Rafferty was killed when he surprised the intruder. When we find the thief, we will have our murderer."

However, Grimshaw noted that hotel thieves are known to go from city to city plying their trade. "I doubt the man who committed this crime is still in St. Paul," he said. "But I am confident we will track him down in the end."

Grimshaw also stated he "has no reason to believe" Rafferty's murder was in any way connected to the death last month of Daniel St. Aubin, scion of a prominent Summit Avenue family. Rafferty had been investigating the death and had strongly suggested St. Aubin was murdered, despite an official coroner's verdict of suicide.

"St. Aubin's death has never been suspicious to the police, and I fear Rafferty was on a misguided mission," Grimshaw said. "But his murder is certainly a great tragedy, and we will do everything in our power to find the person responsible."

"Well, what do think?" Holmes asked after I'd read the story.

"It's obvious the police already have a theory as to what happened."

"Yes, and it is lazy theory at best. It is easy to blame a crime on some unknown thief, thereby absolving the police of any duty to ferret out the real truth. I do not expect we will have much cooperation from the police. It is just as well. The police are more often an impediment than an asset when it comes to a proper criminal investigation."

It became fully clear just how much of an impediment Grimshaw might be after we met Thomas at the hotel's café for breakfast. He said Rafferty had been convinced that Grimshaw and other authorities had conspired to cover up the true cause of St. Aubin's death.

"The coroner's office officially ruled it a suicide, but Shad was suspicious right from the start," Thomas said. "He knew it was murder through and through. In fact, he thought Grimshaw himself might have done the deed or knew who did."

Thomas then told us everything he knew about the circumstances of Rafferty's death. He also provided a full account of the St. Aubin case and the five prime suspects Rafferty had identified. One detail was particularly striking. Thomas said that Rafferty, on the day of his murder, had telephoned to report an "astounding development" in the case. Unfortunately, Rafferty didn't reveal what he had learned but promised to share the information with Thomas later at dinner. Before that could happen, Rafferty was dead.

"I only wish I had pressed Shad to tell me what he knew," Thomas said. "Things might have turned out differently."

"Do not blame yourself," Holmes said. "What might have been is of no use to what must be. You did nothing wrong. It is the murderer who must be held to account."

Thomas then told us about a most intriguing clue he'd found by Rafferty's body and deliberately hidden from the police. He produced a small piece of paper with a telephone number written on it. "The writing is definitely Shad's. I'm guessing he must have taken it out of one of his pockets just before he died. I'm sure he was trying to tell us something."

Thomas said the telephone number, Garfield 2030, was for an answering service with multiple clients. "But I don't know who the clients are or which of them Shad might have been interested in."

"And I take it you were unfamiliar with the number before last night?"

"That's right, Mr. Holmes. Shad never mentioned it to me, so I figure it was something he'd come across very recently."

"Perhaps it related to that astounding development he spoke of. We shall look into it shortly. In the meantime, Mr. Thomas, tell us more about the suspects in the St. Aubin case."

Thomas did so, describing each of the men in considerable detail, beginning with Grimshaw. He concluded by stating, "I'm ninety-nine percent sure one of them also murdered Shad."

"That may well be," Holmes said. "However, we cannot be as a blinkered horse, seeing only a narrow path before us. We must keep our eyes open to all possibilities."

AFTER BREAKFAST, we went up to Rafferty's apartment. Holmes made a close study of the door lock before we entered the apartment, which looked as though it had been struck by a violent windstorm. The floors were littered with paper, notebooks, and a miscellany of other items. Drawers and cabinets had been rifled through, books pulled down from their shelves, storage boxes overturned, and clothes removed from closets.

"The police don't go about their business delicately," Thomas said.

"Clearly, they were very thorough," Holmes said. "Yet we know Mr. Rafferty's notes on the St. Aubin case were already gone from his desk, presumably taken by the murderer, before the police arrived. Do you have any idea, Mr. Thomas, what else the police may have been looking for?"

"No, but I didn't notice anything missing except for the notes when I looked around here last night after the coppers left. There was one funny thing, however."

Thomas then went to a safe in the bedroom and removed two guns. One was a Colt automatic pistol. The other was a peculiar weapon with a barrel perhaps ten inches long. Thomas identified this second one as a pocket rifle belonging to Rafferty and said, "I found these last night on that table by the door, both fully loaded. It's strange because Shad hadn't used the pocket rifle or the Colt .45 for years. I can't figure why he'd have left them out unless he was getting ready for trouble."

Holmes said, "Perhaps he was. But before we delve into the mystery of the two guns, tell us more about the notes Mr. Rafferty kept regarding the St. Aubin case. I gather Mr. Rafferty was meticulous about recording his observations and ideas."

"I don't know if *meticulous* would be the right word, but he did his best to maintain good notes when he was investigating a case. He used to keep pretty much everything in his head because he had an amazing memory. But as he got older he realized he had to start putting things down on paper—clues he found, people he interviewed, theories he was considering, that sort of stuff. And I know he typed up a lot of notes about St. Aubin because he referred to them all the time."

"And you said Mr. Rafferty kept the notes in his study?"

"Yes. They would have been in a folder on his desk or in one of the drawers. I'll show you."

The apartment consisted of five rooms—a parlor, a study, a bedroom, a small kitchen, and a bath. Thomas led us into the study, where he'd found Rafferty's body. A dark crimson stain on the oriental rug marked the spot where our friend had spent his dying moments. It was a melancholy sight, and I hoped Rafferty had not suffered unduly.

Files and notebooks were strewn all around a large desk in the middle of the study. The desk's drawers were open, as were those of a nearby file cabinet. The police obviously had gone through all the drawers and left anything they didn't want on the floor. Holmes gathered up the discarded documents and quickly scanned them but found nothing of value. He then turned his attention to the desk. Its expansive top was bare save for an Underwood typewriter and a tray of paper.

Holmes examined the typewriter and remarked at once that its ribbon was missing. "I do not imagine Mr. Rafferty made a habit of typing without a ribbon," he said. "Someone obviously removed it."

"I didn't even notice that," Thomas said. "But why would the killer take the ribbon?"

"Because it shows the machine's key strikes and therefore might have told us what Mr. Rafferty had most recently typed. Of course, it is also possible the police took it as evidence, although I rather doubt that. What we can say for certain is that it was no burglar who murdered Mr. Rafferty, as the police claim. A burglar would have had no reason to take the ribbon."

Holmes now searched the desk drawers, one of which contained a package of carbon paper along with pens, pencils, paper clips, and other small items.

"Did Mr. Rafferty make a habit of using carbon paper when he typed?" Holmes asked Thomas.

"Sometimes. If he thought something was important, he'd usually make a copy."

"Where would he keep those copies?"

"I don't really know. Probably in that file cabinet."

But the cabinet's three drawers were empty, and there were no carbon duplicates among the documents scattered on the floor.

Holmes surveyed the scene for a few more moments, then said, "You are right, Mr. Thomas, in thinking the killer took all of Mr. Rafferty's notes pertaining to the St. Aubin case. But I wonder if he found any carbon copies. We shall have to see about that. Now, what about the murder weapon? You told us the knife belonged to Mr. Rafferty. Where was it usually kept?"

"In the curio cabinet in the parlor."

The study, with its blood and memories, began to feel oppressive, and I was relieved when Holmes went out to look at the cabinet. He inspected the sheath where the knife had been kept and used his magnifying glass to look for fingerprints. Then he said, "It is instructive that the killer used a knife from this cabinet. Finding it here amid so many other objects would have taken some effort, and yet he had it in hand when he accosted Mr. Rafferty. It suggests he knew in advance where the knife was kept. If so, Mr. Rafferty's murder was a premeditated crime and not the random act of a burglar, as the police seem wont to believe."

After Holmes had made an exhaustive examination of the apartment, we took seats around Rafferty's small kitchen table, where a half-eaten piece of toast on a small plate reminded us of our lost friend.

"He always had his toast here in the morning," Thomas said softly. "I guess I'll have to clean up the place."

"Yes, but that will have to wait," Holmes said, looking at Thomas. "We must focus on what happened here last night. You told us Mr. Rafferty was stabbed from behind and so had no chance to defend himself. And we know the attack must have occurred not long before you arrived on the scene and were struck down yourself."

"That's right. I came up because he was late for our dinner."

"Yet Mr. Rafferty was always very prompt about meeting you for dinner, was he not?"

"Yes."

"But he was unaccountably late last night. Why? Several possibilities come to mind. The first is that the killer was someone Mr. Rafferty knew, quite possibly one of the suspects you mentioned. The killer paid a call on Mr. Rafferty, who admitted him to the apartment. They perhaps talked for a time before entering the study, and then as Mr. Rafferty turned around he was suddenly attacked, with no opportunity to defend himself. What do you think of that possibility, Mr. Thomas?"

Thomas shook his head and said forthrightly, "No offense, Mr. Holmes, but I think little of it."

"Why is that?"

"In the first place, how did the killer manage to get his hands on the knife without Shad seeing him? Also, Shad was nobody's fool. Remember, he told me he was close to solving the case. He wouldn't have let any of the suspects into the apartment without being very careful. At a minimum, he would have armed himself, by which I mean he'd have a gun on his person, not just sitting on the table. And if he thought the man could be the killer, he would never have turned his back on him."

"I agree. Here is another possibility: what if the man had a gun, accosted Mr. Rafferty outside the apartment door, and forced him to go inside?"

"I suppose that's possible, Mr. Holmes. But I knew Shad as well as anyone, and if a man with a gun told him to turn around, he just wouldn't do it. He always said if you turned your back to a man pointing a gun at you, you were asking to be shot. No, even in his condition, he would have had it out with the man right then and there. Besides, if the man had a gun, why would he have stabbed Shad?"

Holmes smiled and said, "I must concur. I am very much inclined to favor a third possibility, which is that the killer lay in wait here for Mr. Rafferty, who had gone out for some reason before his planned dinner with you. That could explain the two guns. Perhaps he had them with him when he went out, then set them down after his return, only to be ambushed in his study."

"I guess that makes sense," Thomas said, "but I still wonder why he would have taken along that old pocket rifle. It's not much good unless you're shooting at a distance, and it's hard to conceal."

"True, it is peculiar. But there is a much bigger question, which is where Mr. Rafferty went before he came back here. Wherever it was, he must have felt he was in danger. Otherwise, there would have been no need for all the weaponry. And given Mr. Rafferty's infirmities, I do not think he would have gone far. Is it possible he had a meeting with someone here in the hotel?"

"Could be, I suppose, but where?"

"That is what we shall have to find out. Incidentally, did you find Mr. Rafferty's wallet?"

"No. Either the killer took it or the cops did when they searched the place. Shad usually kept it in a drawer in the same table where the guns are. My guess is that if the cops grabbed it, they just wanted the money. Shad usually carried a hundred dollars or so around with him."

"The police may have had another reason for taking it," Holmes said.

"So that the murder would look like a robbery," I offered.

"Watson, you have become a first-class detective in your old age. Yes, that is the reason. If true, it suggests the police were in some manner a party to Mr. Rafferty's murder, and I need not tell you what difficulties that could present for our investigation."

"You are right, Mr. Holmes, but I must warn you: Big Jack Grimshaw is a hard customer and not a man you want as your enemy," Thomas said.

"Doubtlessly not, but if so, we shall do what we must," Holmes said. "We may make many enemies before this business is done. Now then, let us go back to the matter of how the killer entered the apartment, assuming he was lying in wait for Mr. Rafferty. I have carefully examined the door lock, for which I found a key hanging on a hook in the kitchen. Do you know if Mr. Rafferty had any other keys to the apartment?"

"No, it was just that one. I had another. If he accidentally locked himself out, he could always get a passkey from the front desk."

"I see. And did he make a habit of keeping the key on the hook?"

"Yes. He'd hang it up first thing when he returned to the apartment. That way he'd always know where it was."

"Now, as for the door lock itself, it is an old but very intricate model made by Mallory and Wheeler, a Connecticut firm I believe is now out of business. May I ask, Mr. Thomas, when this hotel was built?"

"That's easy. We opened our saloon on the ground floor in 1885, when the hotel was brand new."

"I thought as much. As it so happens, Mallory and Wheeler locks from that era are difficult to pick because they require a very special sort of tool. I doubt there are many people alive today, in St. Paul or anywhere else, who would have such an instrument readily at hand."

"So you're suggesting whoever entered the apartment must have been a skilled locksmith, is that it?" I asked.

"Possibly. However, I saw no evidence of tampering around the lock. I strongly doubt anyone tried to force it. All of which suggests the murderer had a key to the apartment, used a hotel passkey, or gained possession of one or the other in some fashion. Mr. Thomas, did anyone beside you and Mr. Rafferty have a key to the apartment?"

"No."

"Then we shall have to explore in more detail how the killer gained access. But for the moment let us return to the clue Mr. Rafferty left for us with his dying breath. I should like to try that telephone number. We must regard the number, in a way, as Mr. Rafferty's last will and testament. He clearly wanted to convey something of the utmost importance about his investigation into the St. Aubin affair."

We went back into the study and Holmes picked up the phone there. "Garfield twenty thirty," he told the operator. After a long pause, Holmes hung up. "There was no answer. It is undoubtedly an after-hours answering service, and that may be significant."

"How so?"

Holmes answered with a question of his own. "You have just such a service, do you not, Watson?"

"Yes, for emergencies when I am out of the office."

"Precisely. Professional men—especially doctors—tend to use an answering service."

"So do you think Shad was trying to reach a doctor?" Thomas asked.

"Possibly. Do you know the name of Mr. Rafferty's physician?"

Thomas did and passed the name on to us.

Holmes said, "Good. Now all we need is a list of the answering service's clients."

"They wouldn't give a list to me," Thomas noted.

"Then I shall have to be very persuasive," Holmes said with a smile. "I am rather good at that. Another idea has occurred to me. You mentioned Mr. Rafferty kept few valuables here in the apartment. Yet he must have had some items he wished to store in an absolutely safe place, am I correct?"

"Oh my God," Thomas said, "how could I have forgotten? You're right, Mr. Holmes. Shad had a safe-deposit box at the First National Bank."

"Ah, I thought as much. Yet I have found no key for such a box anywhere in this apartment. Would Mr. Rafferty have kept it on his person?"

"I don't think so, but I can't say for sure."

"I fear then that the police have it and will try to open the box as soon as possible. However, that may require a court order. If the police do gain access to the box, I doubt we will ever know what they found."

"That's not true, Mr. Holmes," Thomas said. "We can get there first. You see, I'm also signed in on the account and have a second key."

"Mr. Thomas, you are a man of many wonders. We must go to the bank as soon as it opens."

WE WERE AT THE FIRST NATIONAL BANK, located only two blocks from our hotel, at nine o'clock sharp on Monday morning. Thomas signed in with his key at the safety deposit vault and went with a guard to retrieve Rafferty's box. Holmes and I then retired to a small private room to wait.

"What do you think we'll find?" I asked Holmes, who was nervously pacing about the room, which was equipped with two chairs and a table.

"Most likely, we will find nothing of importance. But there is a chance—"

Before Holmes could finish his thought, Thomas arrived with the safe-deposit box. He set the metal box, which was quite long and deep, on the table and said, "You can do the honors, Mr. Holmes. The last time I opened it there wasn't much inside. Just some legal documents, a few gold coins, those sorts of things."

But when Holmes opened the box, a revelation awaited us. The coins and legal papers were there but so too was a file folder containing dozens of carbon copies of documents. Holmes thumbed through them with his usual facility, his excitement growing from one page to the next.

"Mr. Rafferty has bequeathed us a gift," he finally announced. "These are his files from the St. Aubin case and they look to be quite thorough. The last entry is dated January eighteenth, three days before Mr. Rafferty was murdered. It is as if he had a premonition of his death and the possible destruction of his work, and so he made sure to keep copies of his notes in a safe place. I shall give these files my full attention when we return to the Ryan. Now, Mr. Thomas, I have one more request of you this morning. Will you show us the exact spot where Daniel St. Aubin's body was found?"

"That's easy enough. Just follow me."

Thomas led us to an alley along the north side of the Ryan, which separated it from another large building. It was a bleak place, hemmed in by high brick walls, and it served as a conduit for the bitter winter winds. Thomas stopped about halfway down the alley and said, "It was right about here. Shad said St. Aubin was a bloody mess, half his face blown away."

The alley was paved in rough cobblestones, which were blanketed in a mantle of ice and slush, and I struggled to keep my footing. After looking up and down the alley, Holmes said, "It is not hard to see why Mr. Rafferty suspected murder from the very beginning. This would be a most peculiar place to commit suicide. It is neither entirely private nor public. Better to leap off a prominent bridge if Mr. St. Aubin intended to make a statement. And if he wanted privacy in his final moment, this is hardly the ideal locale."

"That's just what Shad thought," Thomas said.

Only a few feet from where St. Aubin had died, a steel door led into the hotel from an inset loading dock. Holmes went to the door and tried the knob. The door was locked.

"Most interesting," he said before we left Thomas and returned to the warmth of our rooms.

Holmes spent the remainder of the day studying Rafferty's notes, giving careful attention to even the most minute detail. When he had pored over every last document, he said, "We must take great care with the treasure Mr. Rafferty has left us. It is possible the police found the key to his safe-deposit box and will obtain a court order allowing them to open it, if they have not done so already. They will find the box empty, of course, and they will quickly learn who removed the contents. It will then be only a matter of time before our rooms are searched, and I have no doubt they will appropriate the notes if they find them."

"Well then, we should keep them in the hotel safe," I said.

"No, the police might find a way to gain access to it under some pretext. I have a better idea."

Holmes had already spent some time exploring the hotel. He'd found an unused janitor's closet two floors above our room, and I went with him as he hid the notes there behind a collection of old paint cans. This precaution quickly proved its worth, for our rooms were indeed searched, to no great effect, just days after our arrival.

After we had stowed away Rafferty's notes for safekeeping, Holmes placed a call to Garfield 2030 at seven o'clock, and this time the call was answered as I listened in on the conversation.

"Answering service," said a woman's voice.

"This is Sherlock Holmes. With whom am I speaking?"

"Is this a joke?"

"No, it is an extremely serious matter. I am in need of information regarding the murder of Mr. Shadwell Rafferty, and I am certain you will want to assist in any way you can."

Holmes's voice and manner were so commanding that the woman, who identified herself as Dorothy Flynn, said she would be pleased to help such a famous detective. "I've read all of your stories. Are they really true?"

"For the most part," Holmes said, looking at me, "although Dr. Watson is not above an occasional fancy. Now then, Miss Flynn, I require a list of your clients. As I understand it, there are seventeen."

"That's correct."

"I assume they are mostly professional people."

"Wow, I can see why you're so famous. How did you know?"

"A simple deduction. I also assume you keep a record of all the calls into your office."

"Sure. We log in everything. Somebody special you're looking for?"

"Perhaps. I should like to see that call record as well as your client list. Where are you located?"

She gave an address in a downtown office building a short distance from the Ryan.

"Excellent," said Holmes. "We will be there within the hour."

We found Dorothy Flynn in a small office on the third floor of the Guardian Building. She was a heavyset, dark-haired woman in her forties, and she was very excited to see us.

"My God, I can't believe this. You look just like the picture I saw in the paper, Mr. Holmes, only maybe not as tall."

Although Holmes had given no interviews to the press since our arrival in St. Paul, a newspaper photographer stationed in the Ryan's lobby had snapped a picture of us.

"It seems I am not larger than life after all," Holmes said with a wry smile. "Now, let us see what you have for us, Miss Flynn."

She had prepared a client list for us but said the call logs had to stay in the office because no copies were available. Holmes went through the logs for the past several months but found no calls from Rafferty or any other person with whom we were familiar. He also noted that some callers left no names.

Miss Flynn explained that this happened quite frequently. "When people find out we're an answering service, sometimes they just hang up without leaving a message."

After autographing a notebook for Miss Flynn, who stated she would cherish our signatures for the rest of her life, we returned to Holmes's room at the Ryan. Holmes went over the client list at once.

"We have seven doctors, two dentists, two plumbers, two bail bondsmen, and four organizations: the Amherst H. Wilder Charity, the American Birth Control League, the Society for the Poor, and the Emergency Relief Fund. As you can see, Watson, Mr. Rafferty's personal physician is not on the list."

"Perhaps he simply wanted to leave a message with one of the doctors about some information he was looking for."

"Perhaps. We shall have to check with every individual and organization on this list to find out which of them Mr. Rafferty may have contacted, or tried to. That task can wait, however. I shall retire early tonight, Watson. Mr. Rafferty's funeral is tomorrow, and I have a eulogy to prepare."

3

"I Give You My Promise"

Rafferty's funeral, perhaps inevitably, was held at the St. Paul Cathedral, which towered over the city much as Rafferty had in his prime. The cathedral had been the dream of Archbishop John Ireland, who rightly saw it as his crowning achievement. It had taken a decade to build after Ireland found a superb site high on St. Anthony Hill above the city's crowded downtown. He hired a French-born architect named Emmanuel Masqueray to design his dream, and the Frenchman did not err on the side of under statement. When the cathedral opened in 1915, its gigantic dome dominated the city, a testament to the power of faith as well as the archbishop's fundraising abilities.

Rafferty, whose opinions occasionally extended into the realm of architecture, was inclined to think the new cathedral was "too big for its britches," as he once told Thomas. He found it rather cold and overwhelming, and preferred the simple old downtown church it had replaced. But he still came to the new cathedral weekly to light his votive candle, and he had first encountered Monsignor Pierre Denis while performing that sacred duty. They struck up an un- likely friendship, talking of God and hope and the shape of things to come. Although Rafferty professed skepticism about the workings of divine providence, Denis believed his friend was at bottom a man of faith. And so he insisted Rafferty's final send-off should be a full funeral mass at the cathedral.

Patrick O'Halloran, a good Irishman and better mortician, was called on to embalm Rafferty's body, and he performed all the under- taking magic he could. He dressed Rafferty in a loud red jacket that

Thomas insisted on, slicked back what remained of Rafferty's wild outcropping of gray hair, smoothed his unruly beard, placed a rosary in his folded hands, and pronounced him "a fine-looking corpse, ready for all to see." At nine-thirty on the morning of Tuesday, January 24, a hearse brought Rafferty to the cathedral. Visitation was set to begin at ten, with the funeral at two in the afternoon.

Thomas had wanted the wake to be held where good liquor and tall tales of Rafferty's many adventures could flow in equal measure, but no large hall was readily available on such short notice, and so he agreed to the visitation at the cathedral, which could easily accommodate three thousand souls under its dome. But Thomas also arranged for a "real wake," as it is called, to be held on the following Saturday at a popular downtown speakeasy.

The morning dawned clear and cold, the wind cutting like a scythe through even the heaviest clothes, but it did not deter the crowds that poured in from every corner of St. Paul to pay their respects. Despite O'Halloran's efforts, Rafferty still looked dead as could be, and Thomas couldn't bear the sight. Instead, he slipped into a pew well away from the coffin, greeting people he knew as they came by to have a last look at Rafferty and say a prayer for his soul, wherever it might be. The funeral service, however, would be the main event, not the least because of the riveting news that Sherlock Holmes himself intended to deliver a eulogy.

Most funerals, unless they involve some figure of universal renown or perhaps disrepute, are displays of social class. The rich and powerful are sent off to a new investment opportunity by those of their own class, as are the poor. But Rafferty had led an unusual life. He knew the plush paneled rooms of Summit Avenue and had been a particular friend of James J. Hill, as rugged a character in his own way as Rafferty, albeit much richer. Yet Rafferty was equally at home among the saloons, pool halls, gambling dens, and other low dives of the city, and his list of acquaintances included more criminals than stockbrokers. So it was that his funeral presented many peculiar sights.

Louis J. Hill, successor to his father's business empire, sat only a row of pews away from another Louis, better known as "Fingers" McGee, regarded as one of the city's ablest pickpockets. Nearby were Ordways and Livingstons and Herseys and Mannheimers, all prominent members of the city's wealthy merchant class, while not far behind them sat plumbers and beer vendors and retired cops and the occasional woman of the night. Rafferty, lying gray and still in his coffin, had managed to bring them together, if ever so briefly, to hear of his life and contemplate the grating mystery of his death.

Near the back of the church stood another extraordinary figure, this one very much alive. Long and lank and dressed in a dark suit of the finest wool, Sherlock Holmes could not be missed. His bearing, it would later be said by one and all, was regal and commanding as he took in the scene with his sharp gray eyes. Mourners entering the church gazed on him with a sense of awe. Sherlock Holmes in the flesh! And was that his friend and the chronicler of his many legendary adventures, Dr. John Watson, standing beside him? It must be, everyone agreed, and what a splendid pair they were!

Holmes and Watson had arrived an hour before the funeral mass was to begin. After saying a brief farewell to Rafferty, whose bier had been placed by the communion rail in front of the altar, they'd moved to an inconspicuous vantage point at the rear of the church. From there, Holmes could see for himself all of the suspects in Rafferty's murder, and his sharp eyes missed nothing as the mourners began to gather.

[From "Murder in St. Paul"]

Holmes and I left the Ryan Hotel directly after lunch to attend the funeral services for Rafferty, which were to be held at the new

Catholic cathedral situated on a bluff above the business portion of the city. Holmes had insisted we leave early, not only so that we could have a last opportunity to see Rafferty, but for a reason he regarded as even more pressing.

"The prime suspects in Mr. Rafferty's murder will be at the funeral," he said as we rode in a bright yellow cab up to the cathedral.

"How do you know they will be there?"

"Oh, they will be there, Watson. They could hardly afford not to attend."

It was almost one o'clock when we reached the cathedral, our cab dropping us off along a side avenue just as a streetcar emerged from a tunnel coming up from downtown. I had a vague recollection of some wild incident in the tunnel Rafferty had once told us about but could not conjure up the details. The cathedral, meanwhile, presented an impressive spectacle. It is high, gray, and rather forbidding, a mass of granite culminating in a dome worthy of London's own St. Paul's. Inside, however, the huge church proved to be curiously bare, with walls of simple white brick.

We had just enough time to have our last look at Rafferty, as the coffin was to be closed in preparation for the two o'clock funeral mass. Holmes is the least sentimental man about death I know. To him, it is largely of clinical interest, as demonstrated by his meticulous study of the decomposition of corpses, which is today used by police throughout the world to help fix the time of death in certain homicides. Still, I could sense Holmes was moved by the sight of our old friend, now at peace forever.

Thomas, who had arrived earlier, joined us at the bier as we paid our final respects. As we were about to return to our pews, we encountered Monsignor Pierre Denis, who was to preside over the funeral services. He was a tall, gaunt man with chiseled features, and I saw something of Holmes in his appearance. We introduced ourselves, and Holmes said, "It is a hard day for us, Monsignor, and no doubt for you as well. I understand you and Mr. Rafferty were close friends."

"I am not sure I could say that, Mr. Holmes, but we were certainly acquaintances. He was a most extraordinary man in every way."

"Indeed, and he was working to the very end to solve a most difficult murder case. By chance did you happen to know the victim in that case, Daniel St. Aubin?"

A hint of suspicion flashed in the monsignor's cold gray eyes. "I knew him only in death, I'm afraid. I officiated at his funeral as a favor to Muriel—his mother, that is. She's a parishioner here at the cathedral. As for poor Daniel, he was not much of a churchgoer."

"Ah, I see. It sounds as though Mr. St. Aubin was quite harried in his final days. Indeed, it seems he fell into trouble with the wrong people."

"Is that so? I wouldn't know about that. Now, if you will excuse me, I must attend to the other mourners. It has been a pleasure meeting such a great man as yourself, Mr. Holmes."

"I suppose you have formed an impression of the monsignor," I said to Holmes as we moved back toward the rear of the church.

"Yes, there is in his eyes the hard glint of the zealot, but there is a certain worldliness evident as well. I have no doubt he is a complicated man."

We soon found a spot where we could take in the entire sweep of the church, which is arranged in a cross-shaped plan under the dome. The church had already begun to fill up, and it was expected that the long rows of pews would be fully occupied by the time the services began. We had already met Monsignor Denis, and Thomas was prepared to point out the other suspects as they arrived.

At one-thirty Bertram Abbey entered the church by one of the side doors. Attired in a startling mauve suit—no mourning black for him—he moved easily through the crowd and appeared to be on familiar terms with many of its more refined members. With him was a young man of almost Apollonian beauty. Thomas had told us of persistent rumors regarding the poet and his affection for young men. I do not believe it would be indelicate to note that Holmes, having come up through the English public schools, was acquainted with men of Abbey's kind and found nothing especially novel or shocking about his supposed predilection. But it naturally gave rise to speculation as the exact nature of Abbey's relationship with St. Aubin.

Abbey saw us at the rear and came up to introduce himself, leaving his companion to stake out a seat for the service. "I must say this is a supreme honor. Sherlock Holmes and his great chronicler, Dr. John Watson! It is too bad we meet under such tragic circumstances. I know you were great friends of Mr. Rafferty."

"Indeed we were," Holmes replied. "Did you also know him well?"

"Only in passing. But I think it fair to say he was a legend here in St. Paul. The crowd before us attests to that. Well, I will not keep the two of you. But I look forward to talking with you again, if the opportunity arises."

"I have no doubt it will," Holmes said.

Mayor Richard O'Donnell and his aide, Montgomery Meeks, were the next to appear. The mayor was a tall, silver-haired man in his fifties with chiseled features. Dressed in a beautifully tailored black suit, he had an imposing presence and was soon surrounded by other mourners. He shook their hands and murmured condolences before he and Meeks broke free and approached us.

Meeks was also a striking figure, with a bright face, sandy hair combed to one side, and blue eyes that flashed and glinted as though possessed of some secret source of illumination. His every manner, from the eager lunging pace of his gait to the way his whole body seemed to galvanize with a sudden burst of energy when he spotted Holmes, conveyed a sense of volatility and restless intelligence.

"Ah, Mr. Sherlock Holmes," he said, walking up to us without a hint of hesitation. "My name is Montgomery Meeks, but you may call me Monty, and this is the mayor of our fair city, the Honorable Richard O'Donnell. The mayor, I'm sure, feels as honored to meet you as I do."

"That is most certainly true," said O'Donnell, who was perhaps ten years older than his assistant and seemed to be of a more reserved character.

"Thank you," said Holmes. "Of course, Dr. Watson is with me and I imagine you already know Mr. Thomas."

"Yes, a fine member of our Negro community," the mayor said before quickly turning his attention back to Holmes. "Mr. Rafferty was a remarkable man and much loved in our city. The ice palace case, I can safely say, is now something of a local legend."

"Yes, it was a singular affair in many respects," Holmes said. "And what about you, Mr. Meeks? Did you have many dealings with our departed friend?"

"Of course. Who didn't in St. Paul? Mr. Rafferty was a wonderful man and quite the detective in his spare time, although no match for you, I'm sure."

"In my experience, Mr. Rafferty was a match for any man," Holmes said. "And, of course, he was working on a case at the time of his murder."

"Yes, that St. Aubin business," Meeks said. "He apparently thought it was—"

"That has nothing to with why we are here today," O'Donnell said sharply. "Come now, Monty, we should be moving along. My apologies, Mr. Holmes, but a mayor's job is to see and be seen on occasions such as this, and so we must attend to the mourners and give what comfort we can."

"I understand. Do not hesitate to do your duty."

As we watched them walk away down the center aisle, stopping at almost every row of pews to greet someone, Holmes said, "The mayor, it seems, does not wish to talk about the St. Aubin case. As for Mr. Meeks, he has voracious eyes, and I very much sense that he would like nothing better than to match wits with me. I shall give him that opportunity."

Just before the mass began, we moved to the front pews, where seats had been reserved for us. An usher tried to turn Thomas away, but Holmes made it clear he was to sit with us and bore down on the usher with such a withering stare that the poor man quickly acquiesced.

As Monsignor Denis emerged from the sacristy, Thomas gave Holmes a nudge and directed his attention to a large rock of a man who had squeezed his way in at the end of our row.

"That is Grimshaw," Thomas whispered. "He is trouble in every way."

The policeman did indeed look to be the kind of man who would relish battle at a moment's notice. He was broad shouldered and big chested, with a short neck supporting a bullet-like head unadorned by hair except for an expansive mustache. He appeared to be about forty-five. I suddenly caught his eye as he turned to look at us, and there was in his baleful gaze something disturbing and unholy.

The cathedral's organist, who had been playing low, mournful music for many minutes, abruptly went silent as Monsignor Denis emerged from the sacristy. "Let us pray," he began in a strong, clear voice, and we did.

I will not recount all the details of the funeral mass, which lasted for nearly two hours, in large measure because so many eulogists wished to speak. Louis Hill offered some wise, consoling words, as did Mayor O'Donnell, who said Rafferty's name would enter that "immortal list of men good and true who fought for truth and justice," adding "and he poured a fine drink, too." Denis also spoke movingly about how Rafferty had begun "to move back to God" in his final years and now would "surely be in the Lord's sheltering arms."

Thomas was among the last to speak, recalling his long friendship with Rafferty and their many adventures together. But it was a terrible time for him, and he could barely get through his speech, fighting backs tears the whole way. "Shad was the finest, bravest, most honorable man I ever knew," he concluded. "Life without him will not be good or fair or beautiful."

And then a hushed silence fell upon the mourners as Holmes strode up to the pulpit to deliver the final eulogy. His speech was brief but all who heard would undoubtedly remember it for years to come.

"What can we say about Mr. Shadwell Rafferty?" he began. "We can say that he was remarkable in every way, but we all know that already. He did not merely occupy the world, as so many men do, but illuminated it, day after day, by his shining presence. He was a barkeep, a detective, a fisherman of great repute, a friend to anyone in need, an enemy to all who would do evil. He was my friend and yours, and we shall miss him until our own dying days."

Holmes paused for what seemed like many seconds, and when he resumed there was in his voice something as hard and deep as the very bedrock of the earth.

"But there is now an injustice that must be righted, for Mr. Rafferty and for us all. His life was taken, with cruel and duplicitous brutality, before the heavens could fairly claim him. I believe the man who murdered our friend is here now, a devil among us."

The cathedral in an instant turned dead silent, as though some unseen force had caused the mourners to lose their breath. Then Holmes delivered his final words, and they struck like thunder: "I give you my promise. I will find the man who murdered Shadwell Rafferty if it is the last thing I ever do."

Book II

Rafferty Investigates

4

"Was That a Gunshot?"

There was a time in St. Paul when people saw no shame in committing public suicide. Everyone remembered the case of Tollefson, the tanner on Indiana Avenue, who swallowed rat poison, then wandered across the Wabasha Street Bridge, his face a frightful mask of pain, before he finally hoisted himself up on the old iron railing and leaped—"grateful for release," or so the newspapers said—into the swirling waters of the Mississippi. Then, too, there was McGinty, a once-prominent real estate broker gone to drink and dereliction, who was found hanging one Sunday afternoon in the atrium of the Globe Building, where he maintained an office. The note attached to his shabby suitcoat said simply, "I have had enough."

But in the champagne days of 1927, society then being greatly advanced, suicide was considered a private affair, best accomplished far away from the public eye. The newspapers, which had once delighted in recounting every last detail of a well-staged act of self-destruction, were generally content to let tortured souls leave the world in peace, free from the indecorous glare of publicity. Nonetheless, a few suicides were so strange and so pregnant with mystery that they could not be ignored.

So it was that the newspapers felt compelled to report the apparent suicide of a young man from a prominent Summit Avenue family found dead one chill December evening near the busy corner of Seventh and Robert Streets, close by the city's great department stores and the mighty old Ryan Hotel. His name was Daniel St. Aubin, and the circumstances of his death, in an alley, were just peculiar enough to attract publicity. But what the newspapers didn't report, at least initially, was that one of St. Paul's most venerated residents discovered the body.

Approaching his eighty-fifth year, Shadwell Rafferty was all but certain there would be no eighty-sixth. He had come to think of himself as the shuffling remnant of a man, a gray ghost held together by tenuous sinews of pain and memory. His heart was failing, his knees creaked and buckled like an old flight of wooden stairs, his hips were all but frozen by arthritis, cataracts clouded his eyes. And yet, by one of those fine cruelties nature inflicts upon the old, Rafferty's mind was as sharp as ever, thereby allowing him to contemplate the disaster his body had become.

Still, he arose each morning in a state of grateful amazement, for his long life had been the story of bullets somehow dodged. He thought back often to Gettysburg, where his regiment, the fabled First Minnesota, had made its doomed charge into a thousand screaming rebels. Death had whistled through the air all around him that day, and yet neither shot nor shell had touched him. There had been many other dangerous adventures in the years that followed, but somehow he was always the man left standing.

But no one escapes the tenacious grasp of time, and Rafferty had made careful preparations for the end. He'd paid off the last of his debts and made his will, which would deliver the bulk of his modest estate to George Washington Thomas. Still, Rafferty was not the sort to wait around idly for death to sashay through the door, and he did his best to stay active.

He was out of the saloon business thanks to Prohibition—in Rafferty's view just about the stupidest idea in human history. Had he been younger at the time, he would have opened a speakeasy somewhere, but by 1920 he was too old to think of starting all over again. Instead, he'd embarked on a minor new career as an adviser to the city's numerous bootleggers, his connections at city hall helping to assure the police would not interfere with what Rafferty saw as a noble endeavor.

Like his old friend Sherlock Holmes, Rafferty had also continued to find occasional work as a consulting detective. But Rafferty's manifold infirmities meant that he operated largely as an oracle, to be consulted when all other avenues of inquiry had failed. The Buddha of the Ryan Hotel, Thomas called him, prompting Rafferty to reply, "Well, I do not claim to possess that exalted figure's wisdom, but I believe I have a bigger belly!"

Mostly, however, Rafferty was content to let the days move at their own pace, even if the tempo always seemed to be accelerating. The clock, he knew, was his enemy, eager to sweep him out of the world, but he refused to be rushed. He read, listened to the radio, went on occasional Sunday drives with Thomas, who'd acquired a well-used Model T, and visited other friends to talk about days past, the afflictions of old age, and whatever else came to mind. But most of his dearest friends were dead and Rafferty often found himself alone, left with the sense he had lived too long, like an ancient turtle locked in its shell, gazing out over an empty sea.

Yet Rafferty never gave in to despondency—life even in its waning days remained for him a vital adventure—and despite his failing body, he would not allow himself to succumb to inertia. Almost every evening after his meal at the Ryan's dining room, he took a constitutional, if only for a few blocks. So it was that on the night of Friday, December 16, Rafferty emerged from the hotel just after seven. Bundled up in a fur coat, cane in hand, he pushed his protesting body out onto the sidewalk.

He said hello to Dilly Brown, one of the hotel's longtime doormen, then turned north on Robert Street. Quite a few people were about, most of them coming or going to the department stores— the Emporium, the Golden Rule, and Mannheimer Brothers—all within a block of the hotel. With Christmas looming, the stores were open late, their windows aglow like lighthouses guiding shoppers safely to their destinations. It was cold, though not especially so for early December, and Rafferty took in a deep breath of the crisp air. Better than being dead, he thought, as he made his way up Robert, moving as slowly as an old schooner in slack winds.

He was just coming up on a block-long alley that separated the hotel from a large office building when he heard a gunshot. Rafferty's hearing wasn't as sharp as it once had been, but he'd been around guns all of his life, and he was certain the shot had come from a pistol. He did his best to hurry up to the alley, which was illuminated by a single lamp mounted on the back wall of the hotel.

What Rafferty saw next would, in the end, prove to be the death of him. Halfway down the alley in the lamp's pool of light lay a motionless body. Just as Rafferty spotted the body he saw a pair of dark figures running down the alley near its far end at Jackson Street. The figures—men, judging by their size—disappeared around the corner before Rafferty could get a good look at them.

"Was that a gunshot?" asked a man who had come up beside Rafferty.

"It was surely that," Rafferty said. "It looks like someone's been hit. Go get that copper directing traffic up on Seventh."

Rafferty turned into the alley and hobbled up to the body sprawled on the rough stone pavers. The body was that of a young man who lay on his back, his legs and arms spread out, as though he had wafted down from the heavens. His face, or what was left of it, was a bloody mess. A bullet had torn a jagged hole through his chin and jaw before crashing through his brain. Next to the man's right hand was a short-barreled revolver that looked to Rafferty's dimming eyes like an old Colt, probably from the nineteenth century. One corner of the gun's wooden grip was chipped away, suggesting the weapon had received hard use.

Rafferty felt a wave of sadness tinged with doubt. What would possess someone so young to take his own life? Or had he in fact been murdered? Rafferty studied the body while he waited for the police. The victim hardly looked destitute. He was handsomely dressed in a gray tweed overcoat, dark wool slacks, and black leather gloves. The coat was unbuttoned, revealing a gray vest from which a gold watch chain dangled. Curiously, the coat's two pockets were turned out, as though someone had rifled through them. A fur hat of high quality had tumbled off the man's head as he fell, and it lay marooned in the expanding pool of blood around his shattered skull.

"What have we got here?" a voice asked. Rafferty turned around to see the tall, broad form of Officer Michael Gregson, who regularly directed traffic in the vicinity. Rafferty knew him well. "Why, Shad, I couldn't tell at first it was you. Ain't you getting a little old for gunplay?"

"I am but this is none of my doing, Greg. It's very likely someone shot this poor fellow."

"Did they now?" Gregson said, bending down to take a better look at the body. "Why, I'd say he shot himself. The gun's right there."

"Oh, I doubt that. Why would he bother to turn out his coat pockets before shooting himself? Besides, I caught a glimpse of two men in the alley. They were running away. That's highly suspicious, don't you think?"

"Well, maybe it was just a couple of fellows who happened to come upon the body and were too scared to stick around once they saw what happened," said Gregson, who had never struck Rafferty as an Aristotelian intellect.

"And before they left, they turned out his pockets but didn't bother to take his fancy gold watch? No, Greg, that doesn't make sense."

"So you say. What did these other fellows look like?"

"I don't know. They were far away and gone in a flash. But something's wrong here. Why would anyone choose to commit suicide in an alley like this? And why were those men running away?"

Gregson scratched the back of his head and said, "Well, Shad, I guess we'll just have to let the detectives sort it all out."

"That's what I'm afraid of. Before they arrive, how about you take a look through the young man's pants pockets? Maybe we can learn something. Check first for a wallet. If he was robbed—"

"Oh no, I'm not doing that. The big dicks would skin me alive if they found out. No, you just stay here while I go to the call box. And don't you touch nothing."

"Right," Rafferty said and watched as Gregson double-timed back down the alley.

The nearest police call box was half a block away at Seventh Street, so Rafferty knew Gregson wouldn't be gone for long. In his prime, Rafferty would have taken advantage of Gregson's brief absence to inspect the dead man's pockets. But now, getting down on one knee was about as easy as swimming the English Channel, and all Rafferty could do was stare at the body and wonder at the waste of a young life.

"The dicks are on their way," Gregson said when he returned. "You going to wait for them?"

Rafferty felt the chill of the night seeping like icy water through his heavy coat. "No, it's too cold out here for an old man to be standing around. I'll head back to the Ryan. The fellows from the detective squad know where to find me."

As RAFFERTY SETTLED BACK into the comfy warmth of his apartment, two men not far away talked briefly on the telephone.

"It's done," the first man said, "and everybody will think he killed himself."

"Good," said the second man. "I take it he didn't make it to the Golden Rule."

"No. We got him in that alley next to the Ryan. No witnesses. All very neat and tidy, just the way you wanted it."

"And did you find what we're looking for?"

"No, he didn't have nothing on him."

"Damn. We have to find the goods."

"Could be he was just bluffing."

"I assure you, he wasn't bluffing. Now, what about our assistant?"

"He did what he was supposed to. Are you sure he won't talk?"

"And expose himself? Not a chance. We're in the clear for now, but we have to find St. Aubin's stash."

"I'll keep looking. It'll turn up."

"It had better, my friend, or we're all in big trouble."

To Rafferty's surprise, no police detectives came to interview him that evening. He wasn't sure why until he read the *Pioneer Press* the next afternoon. Under the heading "Downtown Suicide," a story reported that the dead young man in the alley was "Daniel R. St. Aubin, 25, of the well-known hardware wholesaling family." The story included an interview with Jackson Grimshaw, who claimed to have information regarding St. Aubin's state of mind before he supposedly killed himself. Rafferty found three paragraphs especially interesting:

Chief of Detectives Jackson Grimshaw stated that St. Aubin may have been despondent over a failed love relationship, according to evidence found at his apartment.

"Unfortunately, acts of self-destruction are not uncommon when young lovers experience a breakup or some other disappointment," Grimshaw stated. "We think this was the case with St. Aubin."

Grimshaw, however, could not account for why St. Aubin took his life where he did. "We may never know what led him to that alley," he said.

Rafferty doubted whether Grimshaw knew anything about young love or love of any other kind. And just what was the "evidence" of despondency supposedly found in St. Aubin's apartment? Rafferty also noted that the story made no mention of the men he'd seen running from the alley, even though Grimshaw must have learned about them from Officer Gregson.

By the time Rafferty finished the story, his wise old nose was itching. The whole business just didn't smell right. If St. Aubin's death was a suicide, it was a very strange one, and yet the police seemed uncommonly eager to put the case to rest without bothering to make a thorough investigation.

After mulling over the situation, Rafferty decided to telephone a reporter he knew at St. Paul's afternoon paper, the *Dispatch*. He told the reporter how he'd found the body and that he thought St. Aubin's death was suspicious. The story about Rafferty's doubts made the early-afternoon edition of the newspaper. Not long thereafter, Jackson Grimshaw came looking for Rafferty.

LIKE MANY OTHER CITIZENS of St. Paul, Rafferty had little confidence in the police. To be sure, there were plenty of good officers in the department, but a foul odor of corruption had hung about its doings for years. Vice of all kinds flourished in the city—gambling dens, brothels, and speakeasies did a booming business—even as big crooks like Dan Hogan, known to be one of the nation's leading fences and a reliable launderer of money, operated with impunity. The police turned a blind eye to most of it, although they put on a show of launching largely ineffective raids every now and then. Rafferty's old nemesis, John J. O'Connor, who as chief of police allowed gangsters to run loose in the city so long as they committed no violent crimes within the municipal boundaries, had died a few years earlier, but the department's new leadership showed no inclination to adopt honesty as a governing policy.

Jackson Grimshaw was known to be especially corrupt, but his close connections to the city's political leadership made him untouchable. It also made him free to operate as he pleased. Intimidating people was his specialty, and Rafferty figured he'd try to do just that after reading the story in the *Dispatch*.

It was just after four when Grimshaw pounded on Rafferty's door. "Open up," he yelled, "or I'll knock the goddamn door down."

Rafferty cracked open the door and peered out at Grimshaw. "Well now, isn't this a pleasant surprise. Have you come for afternoon tea, Big Jack?"

Grimshaw shouldered his way inside, ready for a confrontation, only to see a double-barreled derringer pointed at his chest. "You best be careful, Big Jack. This old Remington of mine has an unpredictable trigger and I would hate to see a mishap occur. Did I ever tell you about the time I accidentally shot a man in his privates? It must have been very painful for the poor fellow."

"What's this? Are you threatening an officer of the law?"

"No, I am merely taking precautions. You'll be wanting to talk about the death of Daniel St. Aubin, I imagine. Have a seat and you can talk all you want."

"Don't shoot yourself with that thing," Grimshaw said, stepping past Rafferty into the apartment. "Quite a dump you've got here, but I suppose it's as good a place as any for an old man to die."

"Ah, and I'm sure you'd like to help me along," Rafferty said as Grimshaw sat down on a frayed settee. Rafferty, still holding the derringer, took a seat across from him. "Speak your piece, Big Jack, and then feel free to leave."

"Yeah, I'll speak my piece all right. Why are you sticking your fat old nose in this St. Aubin business? What do you care about him? He shot himself. A great shame, I'm sure, but it happens all the time."

"Do you really think so? Tell me, why didn't you come around last night to interview me? I could have told you it didn't look like suicide."

"Why in hell would I interview you? There was no need. The gun was right by his hand. You saw it there and so did Gregson. Ballistics will prove soon enough it was the weapon he used. The whole thing is as clear as day. It was a suicide, plain and simple."

"Was it? What about St. Aubin's coat pockets? Why were they turned out?"

"Who knows? Maybe he was looking for something. Maybe he just liked to walk around that way. It don't matter."

"And what of the men I saw in the alley, running away?"

"What of them? I know what you told Gregson. You can't describe the men. You can't say what they were doing there. You can't in fact say a goddamn thing about them. It's just a coincidence, nothing more. "

"For a detective, you seem curiously incurious, Big Jack. I'm of a mind there is more to all of this than you say."

"You're in fantasy land. Nothing's going on except some young fellow blew his brains out. An open-and-shut case, that's what it is."

"I see. So there'll be no real investigation. By the way, what's the evidence you supposedly found that St. Aubin was despondent over a love affair?"

"That's none of your business. You're supposed to be smart, Rafferty, but it don't look that way to me. Spouting nonsense to the papers just makes a fool of you. And like they say, there's no fool like an old fool. So why don't you just be a nice old fellow and enjoy what little time you have left instead of meddling in things that don't concern you? Besides, a man of your age is very frail. Why, a simple fall could kill you."

"Yes, I suppose it could. Then again, even the young and strong can fall if they are not careful."

Grimshaw offered an icy smile and rose from his seat. "I'll be going now, Rafferty, but don't forget what I said."

"I do not put much stock in the words of a liar," Rafferty said, "and I know you to be one, Big Jack."

The red cape had been waved, and the bull responded. "To hell with you. If it's trouble you want, you'll get it," Grimshaw said, walking toward the door. "Watch your back, old man, watch your back."

"I will take that as wise counsel," Rafferty said as Grimshaw stomped out, slamming the door behind him so hard the entire apartment shook.

THE UNPLEASANT ENCOUNTER with Grimshaw fortified Rafferty's suspicions that Daniel St. Aubin had not committed suicide. Rafferty, however, had no plans to investigate the case on his own. He was old and tired and didn't need the trouble, or so he told himself. But his curiosity wasn't easily satisfied, and he couldn't help wondering why Grimshaw was so eager to be done with the matter. What was the detective afraid of? Perhaps, Rafferty thought, it had something to do with the St. Aubin family's wealth and influence.

Rafferty didn't know the family well. He'd met Daniel's father, George St. Aubin, once or twice over the years. He'd been a partner, and a very wealthy one, in a wholesaling firm that supplied hardware stores all around the Midwest. The elder St. Aubin had died quite young some years before, but his company was still going strong. Presumably, Daniel St. Aubin had also worked for the firm, although Rafferty didn't know that for a fact.

Rafferty wasn't aware of any scandal attached to the family. George St. Aubin had struck Rafferty as a typical merchant prince, business always on his mind, and he'd never been actively involved in civic affairs. His wife, as far as Rafferty knew, was still alive, but he didn't recall ever meeting her.

And yet the scion of the family now lay dead, shot in an alley under suspicious circumstances, and the police were insisting it was a clear-cut case of suicide. Had the family pressured the police to treat the death in that way? If so, why? It didn't make sense to

Rafferty. Uncertain how to proceed, and feeling the effects of a bad cold, Rafferty spent a quiet weekend as the St. Aubin case gradually retreated to the back of his mind. Monday was also a time of rest, Rafferty barely emerging from his sickbed. He was feeling better by Tuesday, which brought an unexpected visitor.

THE WOMAN KNOCKED on Rafferty's door at ten in the morning. She was tall and thin, perhaps a year or two past fifty, with a long, narrow face and a nose as sharp as the point of a pencil. Her gray eyes were large and probing. She wore an expensive fur coat, its dark mass offset by the string of pearls around her delicate neck. A rich woman, Rafferty thought, and possessed of that unfailing certitude only great wealth affords.

"You are Mr. Rafferty, I presume," she said. "May I come in? I wish to speak to you."

Rafferty, who had only minutes before climbed out of bed and was still wearing his pajamas beneath a long red robe, gave a slight bow and said, "Certainly, ma'am. Please make yourself at home. I could make some coffee if you'd like. And if you need to hang up your coat—"

"No, I am fine," the woman said as she took a seat on the same settee Grimshaw had occupied a few days earlier. She looked around the apartment with evident disfavor. "I must say I have seen tidier places."

"I suppose you have. I'm an old bachelor, ma'am, and I fear housekeeping is not among my chief virtues. Now, perhaps you might tell me who you are and why you've come to see me."

"It is about my son, Daniel St. Aubin. Someone murdered him and the police intend to do nothing about it. I read your comments in the *Dispatch*. Moreover, I am told by Mr. Louis Hill, who is a friend of the family, that you are man who could be of help to me. Is that so?" The woman definitely knew how to get to the point.

Rafferty hedged. "It is possible, but first let me offer my condolences. It must be a terrible time for you."

"It is. Danny was my only child and now he is gone forever. I want justice, Mr. Rafferty, nothing more, nothing less."

"As do we all," Rafferty murmured, "but in your son's case—"

Mrs. St. Aubin cut him off. "I have learned from the police that you found my son's body? Is that correct?"

"Yes. It was purely by chance."

"Do you believe he committed suicide?"

"I have my doubts."

"Why?"

Rafferty began to feel as though he were in court being cross-examined by a relentless attorney. He told Mrs. St. Aubin about her son's turned-out coat pockets and the men he'd seen fleeing from the alley, adding, "I don't know if the men were involved in your son's death, but their presence raises questions the police seem unwilling to ask."

"So I have come to understand. There is a cover-up going on, Mr. Rafferty, and someone has to get to the bottom of it. You see, I am absolutely certain Danny was murdered."

"May I ask what makes you so certain?"

"This," she said, removing an envelope from her purse. Inside was a letter, which she handed to Rafferty. "Danny wrote this to me last week. At the time, I did not give it much credence, knowing my son as I do. But now I see that I was wrong. You may read it, aloud if you wish."

Postmarked December 9, it read:

Mother,

I am a writing to tell you I have come upon some troubles, which may put my life in jeopardy. The precise nature of these troubles need not concern you. Suffice it to say there are powerful men in this city who are deeply unhappy with me. Perhaps even unhappy enough to do me in. If that happens, I am hoping you will see fit to seek justice on my behalf, even if I have been a rotten son and you a rotten mother. Perhaps we deserved each other all along.

Be that as it may, should you learn I've been killed, no matter what the circumstances, do not deal with the police, who are thoroughly dishonest. A detective named Jackson Grimshaw has been especially rotten to me and has threatened my life. But there are four others you should know about: Bert Abbey the fag poet, the mayor and his assistant, Monty Meeks, and that priest at the cathedral, Monsignor Denis. They all have reasons to detest me, and you should consider them all suspects in the event of my untimely demise.

However, if things work out as I expect they will, I'll be fine, and my glorious existence will continue. Meanwhile, don't worry. I won't be asking you for any more money, so the great St. Aubin fortune is in no danger.

I would send my love, but what would be the point?

Your Faithless Son,
Danny

Rafferty was struck by the letter's sheer strangeness. St. Aubin was offering advance clues to his own murder, should it occur. Equally peculiar was the letter's abrasive tone. Clearly, St. Aubin and his mother had not been on good terms.

"A most remarkable letter," Rafferty finally said. "I've never seen the likes of it. I take it you have not shown it to the police?"

"Of course not. I am no fool."

"I would never think otherwise, Mrs. St. Aubin. Do you have any idea what your son could have done that led to his murder?"

"Possibly, but as you can tell by the letter, Danny and I were hardly close. In fact, he despised me. The problem was with him, I assure you. Danny was always a difficult boy, selfish and uncaring, and he became even more so after his father died."

"You mean your husband, George? That was quite a few years ago, wasn't it?"

"Fifteen to be exact. Danny was only ten at the time. It happened very suddenly, and I believe Danny was deeply affected, although he never showed it. Afterwards, he became all but impossible to deal with. I had high hopes for him but he never showed a whit of ambition or any desire to work hard. Instead, he preferred a life of idleness and dissipation. He even informed me once that he aspired to be a writer, as though that were a worthwhile occupation. Because of his behavior, I was forced to cut him off from any allowance some years ago. He has been on his own since then."

"I see. Now, you indicated, if I heard you right, that you might know why he was killed."

"It pains me to say this, but he may have been involved in a criminal scheme of some kind."

"What makes you think so?"

"It is only a guess, as I have no specific knowledge as to what he was doing. But I have heard rumors—very nasty rumors—about him. I can tell you no more than that. The rumors may well be false."

"And this criminal scheme you mention, you have no knowledge as to what it was?"

"None whatsoever."

"Well, it must have been something big enough to entangle your son with the powerful men he mentions in his letter."

"So it would seem."

"What about the men he named? Do they have any strong relationship to him or you?"

"Not that I am aware of. I will say Bert Abbey is known to me, but we are by no means bosom friends. I believe Danny may even have attended one or two of those silly Saturday salons he holds at the University Club. And of course I know Monsignor Denis, since I attend mass at the cathedral. Danny certainly knew of him but beyond that I cannot tell you much. I talked with that horrible Detective Grimshaw after Danny's death, but he was not the least bit helpful or sympathetic. I am not sure how Danny would have come in contact with him. As for Mr. Meeks, I do not recall ever meeting him, and I have no idea how he might have been acquainted with Danny."

"When was the last time you spoke with your son and did you have any inkling he was heading for trouble?"

"It was in late October, I believe. He came looking for money, which is all he ever really wanted from me, but I would have none of it. He dropped a few hints then that he might be in some kind of trouble, but he did not act as though it was anything really serious."

"Did he go into any details?"

"No, and there was certainly no mention of any criminal endeavor. Danny was not one to share much about his life with me or anyone else, as far as I know."

"Is it possible his problem involved a girl rather than some crime? The police have suggested a broken love affair as the possible cause of his supposed suicide."

"That is pure nonsense, a fairy tale. I do not think Danny ever really loved any girl or would become despondent about being jilted. It was not love he was after."

"Ah, I understand. Is it possible he had been intimate with her and—"

"Knocked her up?"

"You surprise me," Rafferty said with a smile.

"Sex, Mr. Rafferty, is as much the business of the world as anything else, and there is no point being coy about it. However,

Danny said nothing about a girl when we talked. Now, there is one other thing you should know about. Danny lived at the Piedmont Apartments, and I went there yesterday to reclaim family memorabilia, jewelry, and the like. The building superintendent told me the police searched Danny's apartment Friday night. It must have been right after his murder. I found the apartment to be in shambles. Drawers and cabinets were open, cushions removed from chairs, clothes strewn all over the floor. It was quite appalling."

"That's interesting. Any thoughts as to what the police were looking for?"

"No. Danny had a few items of value, such as some jewelry and gold coins, but they had not been touched. But I did make an interesting discovery. Danny had set up a small darkroom in the apartment, but I did not find a single photograph or any film. I thought that was odd. The police must have taken it all."

"What kind of pictures did Danny shoot?"

"I have no idea, but he seems to have been a serious photographer. There was an expensive new Leica camera in the apartment as well as equipment of some kind in the darkroom."

"Are you sure the photos weren't kept somewhere else in the apartment?"

"I am a thorough woman, Mr. Rafferty. There were no photographs."

"Then I will take your word on it. Let us assume, therefore, that the police made off with the pictures. The question is why. Perhaps the photos were incriminating in some way and that is why Grimshaw and his men took them."

"Perhaps, but that is not my chief concern at the moment. It is Danny's murder that preoccupies me. Now, will you investigate it? I am all too aware he was not a good person, but he was my son and no one deserves to be murdered in cold blood. Naturally, I will pay for your time and expense. And I will also give you this," she said, removing a three-by-five-inch photograph from her purse and handing it to Rafferty.

The photo showed an exceptionally good-looking young man with dark hair and strong, sensuous features. He was smiling but not with mirth. It was, Rafferty thought, more of a cynical smirk.

"Danny," Mrs. St. Aubin said. "Taken early this year. Wasn't he handsome?"

"Indeed he was."

That sultry face had been reduced to a bloody mass of pulp and bone when Rafferty found the body, and the sight of St. Aubin in that bleak alley, the life blasted out of him in an instant, was an image Rafferty couldn't shake from his mind. Now, his mother wanted the hard solace of justice, whatever that might be, and Rafferty felt he couldn't refuse her.

"All right, I will look into the case. I can make no promises, but if your son was indeed murdered, I will do my best to find out who took his life."

"Very well, I will put my faith in you," Mrs. St. Aubin said as she once again dug into her purse. She extracted some cash and an elegantly printed business card, which she handed to Rafferty. It identified her as Muriel St. Aubin of 286 Summit Avenue and also listed her telephone number. Rafferty in turn found one of his cards and gave it to her.

"I shall look forward to receiving regular reports," she said before handing two crisp fifty dollar bills to Rafferty. "I trust this will be sufficient as an initial payment."

"It will do just fine," Rafferty said, happy to see the money, which would be a nice addition to his thinning bank account.

He managed to pull himself out of his chair to escort Mrs. St. Aubin to the door. "Perhaps by next weekend I will have something to report to you."

"I would expect nothing less," she said and hurried off down the hallway.

RAFFERTY LAUNCHED HIS INVESTIGATION the next morning by trying to answer a fundamental question: how had St. Aubin ended up in the alley where he met his demise? Assuming it wasn't a place he'd chosen to commit suicide, why had he gone into the alley? Was he lured there on a pretext? Did his killer chase him into the alley and corner him there? Or had he come to the alley on his own, perhaps to meet someone? If so, for what reason?

Hoping to find some answers, Rafferty began by phoning Thomas to tell him what he'd learned from Mrs. St. Aubin and to ask for help.

"That's quite a story," Thomas said. "But do you really want to get involved in it?"

"I've been sitting around for months with little to do, Wash, and I do not find the idleness pleasing. I might as well occupy my mind with something. So I've agreed to take the case. You can be of help, if you're up to it."

"Of course I am. What do you need?"

"I'm thinking some legwork is in order, but my days of pounding the pavement are over. A few inquiries will do the trick. You know most of the shop owners and clerks around the hotel as well as I do. Pay them a visit, if you would, and find out if anybody recalls seeing St. Aubin on the night he died. Ask, too, if they saw Grimshaw or any of the other four suspects. While you're at it, make sure to talk to Dilly Brown. He was the hotel doorman on duty that night. Maybe we'll get lucky."

"I'll get right on it. Anything else you need?"

"Come to think of it, why don't you have a talk with Benny Nussbaum? He has some of the best eyes in St. Paul."

Rafferty had lived in the Ryan for decades and knew all of the street vendors in the vicinity. One in particular, a "newsboy" named Benny Nussbaum, was a fixture. He'd worked the busy corner of Seventh and Robert Streets for years, hawking newspapers morning and night from a small stand, and little escaped his attention.

"I'll talk to Benny right away," Thomas said. "Maybe he saw St. Aubin that night."

"It would be grand if he did, Wash. We will have to learn a great many things from a great many people if we ever hope to get to the bottom of this business."

5

"We Are Entering Deep and Dangerous Waters"

Benny Nussbaum wasn't at his usual stand when Thomas went looking for him that afternoon. But Thomas soon found him nearby at a hole-in-the-wall diner where he usually ate lunch. An elfin man in his fifties with big brown eyes and a long graying beard, Nussbaum had always reminded Thomas of a downsized biblical prophet, even if his news did not come from on high.

"Hello, Benny," Thomas said as he took the stool next to Nussbaum. "How are you doing these days?"

"The best I can say is that I'm still sucking air. How about you?"

"I'm fine."

"And Shad?"

"He's hanging in there."

"That's good to hear. I'm having egg salad for the millionth time, I think. Care to join me?"

"Egg salad it is," Thomas said and put in his order. "As it so happens, Benny, Shad is looking for some information and asked me to talk to you. Let me show you something."

Thomas got out the photo of Danny St. Aubin and set it on the counter. "Do you recognize this fellow?"

Nussbaum looked carefully at the photo and said, "Sure, that's the guy who shot himself the other day. St. Aubin's his name, right? His mug was in the papers. It was a funny thing."

"What do you mean?"

"Well, I saw him that night, you know, when he did the deed. Him and another guy. Sure didn't think he'd go off and kill himself."

"Shad thinks he didn't."

"No kidding. Somebody did him in?"

"Looks that way. Now, you said you saw him with another man. When and where was this?"

"Right on my corner. It must have been around half past six, give or take. St. Aubin came up to my stand and hung around for a few minutes, and pretty soon the other guy showed up."

"What happened next?"

"They talked for a while, I guess. Then St. Aubin handed the other guy an envelope, one of those manila things, and the guy left."

"What did St. Aubin do after that?"

"Not sure. I got kind of busy and I didn't see him again."

"What did the man St. Aubin met look like?"

"He was young. Blond hair, as I recall. Kind of a pretty boy, if you know what I mean."

"How old would you say he was?"

"Maybe eighteen or so."

"Did you notice anything else about him?"

"Not really. I wasn't paying all that close attention."

"Benny, you've been a big help," Thomas said. "Can I ask you about a few other people you might have seen that night?"

"Sure."

Thomas mentioned Abbey, Meeks, O'Donnell, and Monsignor Denis. Nussbaum said he hadn't seen the mayor and didn't know the others by sight.

"What about Jackson Grimshaw?" Thomas asked.

"The big dick? Oh yeah, I know him. Saw him that night, as a matter of fact."

"When was that?"

"Oh, about six. He bought a *Dispatch* and some chewing gum. Got back three cents in change and kept it. He always does. A real cheapskate, that one."

"Did you see where he went?"

"East on Seventh, I think, but I'm not positive."

When Thomas's egg salad sandwich arrived, he picked at it briefly, then put a ten-dollar bill next to the plate.

"My treat, Benny," he said, "and if you stop by the restaurant this evening, Pats will serve you up some real food, on the house."

"Are we talking chicken gumbo?"

"We are."

"I'll be there," Nussbaum said. "That wife of yours, she's something."

"Yes, she is," Thomas agreed. "She most certainly is."

WASH THOMAS HAD MARRIED late in life after "a long career in tomcatting," as Rafferty once put it. In Patricia Brown, a high-spirited and beautiful woman everyone called Pats, he found genuine love for the first time. After the saloon he and Rafferty co-owned had been closed by Prohibition, Thomas and his new wife opened a restaurant along Rondo Avenue in the heart of St. Paul's small but vibrant Black community.

The place, called Pats Chicken Delight, occupied the front portion of an old house where Thomas and his wife lived. They'd done their best to spruce up the restaurant with potted palms, fresh flowers on every table, and photographs of old St. Paul street scenes on the freshly painted walls. But as with any successful eatery, it was the food that mattered, and the restaurant quickly built up a loyal customer base of all colors.

Pats was a marvel in the kitchen, and her signature dish—a chicken gumbo with many mysterious ingredients—sold out every day. Her buttery biscuits, which packed enough calories to satisfy a lumberjack, were equally popular. Thomas served as host and maître d' supervising a small staff of efficient waiters that included several men who'd gained their expertise serving travelers aboard the North Coast Limited on its long run to Seattle. Operating the restaurant entailed long hours, but Thomas didn't mind. He'd always been a hard worker and he liked being around his wife all day, because in her radiant presence the blues had no chance.

AFTER HIS LUNCH WITH NUSSBAUM, Thomas went back to the Ryan to tell Rafferty what he'd learned. Dilly Brown was on duty in front of the hotel, and Thomas stopped to talked with the doorman. What Brown had to say came as a stunning surprise, and Thomas was eager to share the news when he arrived at Rafferty's apartment.

"I just talked to Dilly Brown," he said after he took a seat on one of Rafferty's ancient upholstered side chairs. "He told me he saw St. Aubin outside the hotel the night he was killed. It was just before seven. St. Aubin was standing around, smoking a cigarette, like he was waiting for somebody."

"Well, that's an intriguing bit of news. Did this somebody ever show up?"

"Not that Dilly saw. But get this: St. Aubin actually spoke to Dilly. You'll never guess what he said."

"Ah, Wash, you are tantalizing me now. What did he say?"

"St. Aubin asked Dilly if he knew Monsignor Pierre Denis by sight."

Rafferty gave a low snort and said, "And here I thought I was too old to be surprised. I guess I must abandon that claim now. How did Dilly respond?"

"He just shrugged and said he didn't know the monsignor. St. Aubin said, 'All right, I was just curious,' or something like that and then left. That's about all Dilly could tell me."

"Did Dilly say which direction St. Aubin went?"

"He's not sure. He got busy hailing a cab. But he thinks St. Aubin might have walked up toward Seventh."

"Is Dilly positive it was St. Aubin he spoke to?"

"He is. He saw his picture the next day in the papers."

"What about the shooting? Did Dilly hear anything?"

"Afraid not. He was actually in the lobby when it happened."

"Well, what are we to make of this, Wash?"

"Sounds like maybe St. Aubin was planning to meet Monsignor Denis at the hotel."

"So it does. What I'm wondering now is if they met in the alley instead."

"Could be. Anyway, I've got some more news to report. I talked to Benny."

After Thomas recounted his conversation with Nussbaum, Rafferty said, "So now we have more mysteries to occupy our attention. Who was this other fellow and what was in the envelope? And what was Grimshaw doing in the vicinity? We have wandered into puzzle land, Wash, and the pieces are scattered all over the place. It will be hard putting it back together, especially if Big Jack and the police are involved. The coppers have a lot of practice hiding things."

"And you have a lot of practice finding out things. I'll bet on you over Grimshaw, or anybody else for that matter, any time."

"I appreciate the vote of confidence, Wash, but I fear we are entering deep and dangerous waters. We will have to be very careful from now on."

6

"I Took Him up to the Sixth Floor"

When Rafferty was murdered, Thomas felt as though something vital had been ripped out of his body, leaving a gaping hole in its place. He also felt the sharp sting of regret, believing he'd made a big mistake by taking a trip to Savannah, Georgia, in the midst of the St. Aubin investigation. Thomas had worried about leaving Rafferty alone, especially after learning that Rafferty believed he was being followed by the police. But Rafferty had dismissed Thomas's concerns and insisted he'd be fine on his own for a while.

And so Thomas and Pats had greeted 1928 by boarding a train for Savannah, where Thomas's sister owned a small house in the Black section of the city. Savannah was rigorously segregated, with Jim Crow in command, which meant that Thomas, like it or not, had to tread carefully. The shaded streets and squares where he and Pats took their daily walks rested, he knew, on the ugly foundations of the slave trade, and sometimes he felt the weight of all those tortured and abused souls oppressing him. As the son of slaves, Thomas detested the awful history of the place, but he had to admit it was wonderful to escape the deep freeze of Minnesota.

Yet all during his time in Savannah he felt a gnawing unease he'd never experienced before, and it centered on Rafferty. As the days went by, Thomas, who talked occasionally with Rafferty long distance, could not dampen his sense of disquiet. He and Pats had originally planned to stay for three weeks, but after two Thomas was so anxious that Pats told him there was nothing to do except return to St. Paul.

On the long train ride back, Thomas found himself reminiscing about his friendship with Rafferty. They'd first met after the Civil War in Nevada, drawn there by the silver riches of the fabled Comstock Lode. They didn't find a fortune but they did become close friends. Thomas, who'd lived through the terrible New York draft riots of 1863 in which largely Irish mobs hunted down and murdered Blacks, liked to say that Rafferty was the "first Irishman I met who did not seem interested in killing me."

By the 1870s Rafferty's mining days were done and he decided to return to St. Paul. Thomas went with him. Rafferty took a job on the city's police force while Thomas found work as a short-order cook. Then, in the early 1880s, Dennis Ryan relocated from Nevada to St. Paul and used some of his fortune to build the grand hotel that bore his name. With the help of a generous loan from Ryan, Rafferty and Thomas joined forces to open a saloon in the new hotel in 1885.

Thomas helped Rafferty tend bar and also did some cooking. Always good with figures, he handled all the books, since Rafferty was a notoriously awful accountant. The saloon proved to be a success from the start, drawing in customers from all walks of life, and by 1895 the *Pioneer Press* dubbed it "St. Paul's premier drinking establishment." Meanwhile, Rafferty was also becoming noted for his work as a detective, and Thomas was rarely far from his side.

They ran the bar together until the morons in Washington inexplicably concluded that America needed to go dry. But what a time of it he and Rafferty had enjoyed! Thomas wouldn't have exchanged those years for anything on Earth. It had been a marvelous life for him, better than any he could have hoped for given the bleak circumstances of his birth to a family of slaves in Virginia. He still felt a sense of amazement at all he'd experienced, including being on a case with the likes of Sherlock Holmes.

The anxiety Thomas had experienced in Savannah dissipated as soon as he and Pats arrived back in St. Paul on January eighteenth. He intended to watch over Rafferty and help protect him as the

Danny St. Aubin case neared its denouement. Then, just days later, the unthinkable had happened and Thomas knew his life would never be the same.

Pats had finally convinced him he couldn't have prevented Rafferty's murder, even if they had never gone to Savannah.

"Feeling guilty and moping around won't do you no good," she told him, and Thomas knew she was right. Regret was like ashes in a fireplace, and poking them around accomplished nothing. Securing justice for Rafferty, on the other hand, would require Thomas to be a man on fire, burning for the truth. And one way or the other, he intended to have justice, if it was the last thing he ever did.

THE ARRIVAL OF HOLMES and Dr. Watson buoyed Thomas's spirits, even though he sometimes thought the famed duo, despite being unfailingly polite in his presence, viewed him as inferior because of his skin color. He recalled how Holmes had told him once he was a "fine Negro gentleman," in a way that somehow suggested he was a rarity among his race. Thomas would have been happier if Holmes had simply called him a "fine gentleman" and left it at that.

To be sure, Holmes's occasionally condescending manner was nothing like the overt prejudice Thomas had dealt with his entire life, which had begun in slavery in Virginia. He'd been called all the usual names, but he was a fighter and any man who dared insult him soon learned there would be a cost. Yet even the most high-minded white people almost always betrayed some slight hesitation when he shook their hands, as though they feared his dark skin might rub off on them and resist all efforts to wash away.

Rafferty had been different in that regard from the start of their long friendship, and Thomas often wondered how the big Irishman had managed to grow up in Boston, a city seething with racial animosity, without being poisoned by all the usual hatreds. Rafferty himself rarely spoke of the subject, but Thomas gleaned from many conversations over the years that Rafferty's service in the Civil War had deeply affected his feelings toward African Americans. Slavery in its real, tortured flesh became an abomination to him, even as many of his fellow soldiers voiced nothing but contempt for the camp followers and newly minted freemen who trailed after the Army of the Potomac. Or maybe, Thomas thought, it was simply that Rafferty, for all his rugged strength, had been one of those rare souls born with a pure heart free of all toxins.

Thomas had no objections to Holmes taking charge of the investigation into Rafferty's murder. The great detective was indeed a dazzling man, with powers of observation and deduction beyond those of most mere mortals, and he was also relentless. He would hunt down Rafferty's killer or die in the effort.

Yet Holmes, for all of his genius, didn't know St. Paul the way Thomas did. Thomas also had his own secret army to help him in the campaign to uncover Rafferty's murderer. Although St. Paul had African American doctors and lawyers and teachers, much of the city's Black population still toiled at lesser jobs as janitors, garbage collectors, short-order cooks, dishwashers, and elevator operators, or if they were fortunate, worked for better wages as porters or waiters for the railroads. Thomas knew these men and women, who were largely invisible to the white world but who had eyes and ears and saw and heard many things. He made it his mission to talk to these invisible observers, and he found his first big clue, not surprisingly, at the Ryan Hotel.

THE DAY AFTER RAFFERTY'S FUNERAL, Thomas had returned to the hotel early in the evening to nose around. A majority of the hotel's elevator operators, maids, and kitchen workers were Black. Thomas questioned as many of them as he could, asking if they'd seen anything unusual on the night of Rafferty's murder. But he drew a blank until he spoke with a night elevator operator named

Henry Johnson, who'd worked at the hotel for many years. Johnson knew everybody and was a regular bloodhound when it came to sniffing out the secret, scandalous couplings that occurred regularly within the Ryan's old walls. Johnson usually took a break around ten in a small back room reserved for employees, and that's where Thomas found him.

"How's my handsome fellow?" Thomas asked as he came up behind Johnson, who was eating a sandwich at a table in the break room. Although well into his sixties with silver-flecked hair to prove it, Johnson looked much younger, and he was indeed a handsome man in his hotel livery, which included a sharp maroon jacket with gold epaulets and brass buttons.

He turned around and smiled. "Well, if this don't beat all! Wash Thomas in his full glory. Little late for you, ain't it?"

"It is," Thomas admitted. "I don't keep the sort of night hours I used to now that I'm a married man."

"Oh yes, you liked to prance all night with the ladies back in the day, you surely did." There was a pause, then Johnson said, "I suppose this is about Shad. A bad thing, Wash, a bad thing. He was a good man."

Thomas nodded and took a seat. "He surely was. But I'm thinking you might be able to help out, Henry. Were you on duty the night Shad was murdered?"

"Sure. I start my shift at three and go until midnight."

"Did you see Shad that night?"

"Twice. I took him up to the sixth floor about half past four and then back down to two around six."

"Did he say what his business on six was?"

"No, but I figured he must be meeting somebody up there."

Thomas tried to remember if Rafferty knew anyone on the sixth floor but didn't think he did. "Are there any apartments up there?"

"No, just overnight rooms."

"Do you remember ever taking Shad up to that floor before?"

"Can't say that I do."

"How did he seem to you when he got into the elevator?"

"All right, I guess. He was holding his left arm kind of funny, though, like he was trying to keep something from falling out of his coat."

"Did you see what it was?"

"No."

"Did Shad say anything to you?"

"Just the usual chitchat. 'How are you doing?' That sort of stuff."

"Was he with anybody?"

"No."

"Did you notice if he was carrying anything. Papers or a book or something like that?"

"He had a folder."

"Like a manila folder?"

"Right. I could see it had some papers in it."

"Now, you said you saw him again around six?"

"Uh-huh. I took him back down to his apartment on two."

"Did he still have the folder with him?"

"I think so."

"Did he say what he'd been doing up on six?"

"No, he just nodded when I said hello. But he did look a mite distracted, like he had something on his mind."

Something, Thomas thought, that would get him killed within minutes.

Johnson had little else to offer. On a long shot, Thomas asked if Johnson had seen any of the suspects in the case other than Grimshaw at the hotel that night. He hadn't. However, he pointed out that hotel visitors, especially those with furtive intentions, often climbed the stairs rather than ringing for an elevator. "Less chance of being seen that way, you know, if they're visiting a lady."

Thomas had one more idea. He'd taken along a photo of St. Aubin and showed it to Johnson. "Did you ever see this young fellow in the hotel?"

Johnson gave the picture a good look before he shook his head. "Can't say he looks familiar."

Thomas thanked Johnson with a five-dollar bill, then headed up to Holmes's room on the third floor to report on what he'd discovered.

7

"There Is Still Much We Must Learn"

[From "Murder in St. Paul"]

Sherlock Holmes always preferred to conduct an investigation as "cleanly as possible," as he liked to put it. By this he meant that relying on information gathered by others, particularly the police, could be of more hindrance than help.

"I must cut my own way through the rough seas," he once told me. "Being in another ship's wake can prove treacherous in the long run."

Yet in the case of Rafferty's murder, Holmes understood from the beginning that he would have to adjust his tactics in light of the discovery of Rafferty's duplicate case file.

"Inspector Lestrade, may he rest in peace, was a good enough fellow in his own way, but he often veered off course and so I could not afford to follow him," Holmes noted. "But it is different with Mr. Rafferty. We have his case files and we have Mr. Thomas's testimony and we know both can be absolutely relied upon. Our task therefore will not be to chart an entirely new course, but to perfect the one Mr. Rafferty set. He learned much but we are in a position to learn even more, as Mr. Thomas demonstrated to me last night."

This was the first I had heard of their meeting. It was now just after eight in the morning and I realized, by Holmes's haggard expression, that he had been up most of the night. "Mr. Thomas must have come by quite late," I said.

"Yes, you were firmly in the embrace of Morpheus. In any event, Mr. Thomas gained some most intriguing information from one of the night lift operators here, a man called Henry Johnson."

THE OPERATOR'S ACCOUNT, I agreed, was quite fascinating. I told Holmes I was particularly struck by what Johnson had reported regarding the manner in which Rafferty held his left arm.

"Yes, it is a salient detail, and Mr. Thomas and I agreed that in all likelihood Mr. Rafferty was squeezing that long-barreled pocket rifle under his arm. Presumably, he also carried the pistol we found in his apartment. This strongly suggests he went to the sixth floor to meet someone he considered to be very dangerous."

"And the folder he took along must have been his notes on the St. Aubin case."

"So it would seem. What remains to be discovered is with whom he met."

"Wouldn't the hotel registry provide a clue?"

"Perhaps, but registries do not always contain real names. It is also possible Mr. Rafferty met someone who was not a hotel guest. We must have a look at the sixth floor."

THE RYAN IS A LARGE HOTEL, advertising hundreds of rooms and apartments, and searching an entire floor presented no easy task. But Holmes was insistent, and after breakfast we went up to the sixth floor to see what we could find.

"What exactly are we looking for?" I asked Holmes.

"A vacant room. Let us do some door knocking, Watson."

We split up and knocked on every room door. This accomplished little other than to rouse a dozen or so guests, several of whom, Holmes later reported, recognized him at once and sought his autograph. One man even asked for advice about how to entrap his cheating wife. I was about to write off our mission as a failure when Holmes summoned me to a dead-end hallway at a far corner of the floor. He showed me a heavy metal door with a glass window marked "Stairway."

"I found this by the stairway door," he said, showing me a red, black, and gold cigar band that bore the name Daily Habit.

Although it had been nearly eight years since we'd seen Rafferty alive, Holmes's phenomenal memory, in which even the most minute and obscure details are subject to instant recall, came to the fore. "It is the same brand Mr. Rafferty was smoking when we last saw him in Eisendorf."

"I cannot believe you remember that."

"Nothing is ever discarded from my mind, Watson. You should know that by now."

"But it must be a common sort of cigar," I said. "Anyone could have left the band here."

"True enough, but have a look at the room across from the stairway. It's the only unlocked room I found. I wonder why."

"There is always the obvious possibility someone forget to lock it."

"The obvious, Watson, is too often a disappointment, and I prefer not to be disappointed today," Holmes replied as he led me into the room, which was identified by a number over its door as 652.

It was no luxury accommodation. The furnishings consisted of a spartan bed and bed stand, a small writing desk, two slatted wooden chairs positioned haphazardly near the door, and a threadbare carpet displaying several unwholesome-looking stains. Two yellowing prints, both depicting forest scenes, decorated the beige walls. A large closet was filled with lamps, small tables, chairs, and other dusty items that obviously had been stored there for some time. I also noted that the room was very cold.

Holmes went to a radiator beneath the only window and found it barely warm to the touch. "The heat is clearly insufficient, and I doubt this room is ever rented. The bed does not appear to have been used of late, as evidenced by a large spider web behind it. And yet someone has been here fairly recently."

"How do you know that?"

"The chairs, Watson. Why are they in the middle of the room? Indentations in the carpet indicate their normal placement. One was at the desk and the other next to the radiator. However, drag marks, which remain faintly visible in the carpet, show that both were moved out through the door and into the hallway at some point."

"That is very curious," I admitted.

We went back out to the hall, where Holmes paused to look down its length. "I should say it is a good forty feet to the point where this hall turns at a ninety-degree angle to meet the main corridor where the lifts are located. Would you agree?"

"Yes, that looks about right. But of what importance is that?"

"It may explain why Mr. Rafferty armed himself as he did," Holmes said but would not elaborate on the point. "In any case, I believe this is where Mr. Rafferty met someone just before he was murdered. But who was that person and how was the meeting arranged? Did the person call him and invite him up to this location? Or was it a meeting place Mr. Rafferty selected, knowing the hotel as well as he did?"

"It's certainly an out-of-the-way place," I said. "It doesn't look as though many guests stay in this part of the hotel."

"I suspect that is due to the lack of heat. I knocked on every door along this hall and received no answers. Mr. Rafferty and whoever he met here were all but certain of being undisturbed. In that regard, it was a risky move on Mr. Rafferty's part."

"Which explains why he brought along two guns."

"Precisely. Think of the situation, Watson. Mr. Rafferty, as we know from his notes, was close to solving the St. Aubin murder. He may in fact have identified the murderer at last. The fact he was so heavily armed leaves no doubt he believed he was about to meet a dangerous person. It was very probably the murderer."

"Do you have any idea whom Mr. Rafferty might have met?" I asked as we waited for a lift to take us down to our rooms.

"It is too early to say, Watson. There is still much we must learn."

JUST AS HOLMES AND I had divided our forces to search the sixth floor, so it was that we went separate ways in the afternoon in hopes of gaining new information. Holmes asked me to begin contacting the answering service customers to see which of them Rafferty may have been trying to reach just before his death.

"While you are going about your business, I intend to give more study to Mr. Rafferty's notes," Holmes said. "He was murdered before he could write down an account of the meeting in room 652, but I suspect a clue lurks somewhere in his notes, if I am wise enough to spot it."

Contacting the names and organizations on the list provided by Miss Flynn at the answering service occupied me for many hours. My work, however, proved futile. No one I talked with had been in contact with Rafferty or knew of any reason why he would have wanted to reach them.

Holmes finally emerged from his room at seven and we went downstairs for dinner. He was in one of his quiet moods and our meal was accomplished largely in silence. On the way back to our rooms, Holmes stopped at the hotel's front desk to speak with the night clerk.

The clerk was a rotund man in his forties with thinning brown hair, wire-rim glasses, and watery blue eyes. "How can I be of help to you gentlemen?" he asked, giving no indication he recognized Holmes.

"You may help by answering some questions. Were you on duty the night Mr. Rafferty was murdered?"

"No, the fact is I'm brand new. Just started this evening."

"I see. Who would have been at the front desk that night?"

"Which night was that again?"

"January twenty-first," Holmes said with some impatience.

"Well, let me look, sir. I have a work schedule. Ah, here it is. Donald Hobbs is who you're looking for. He works Fridays through Tuesdays. I assume he'll be here tomorrow night if you wish to speak with him."

Holmes nodded and said, "Thank you. We will indeed talk with Mr. Hobbs. Now, I should like to inspect your register for January twenty-first."

"Oh, I am afraid I couldn't do that, sir."

"Why is that?"

"Hotel policy. I am not permitted to allow unknown persons to inspect the register. It's a matter of security. I'm sure you understand."

I could scarcely believe what I was hearing. "Do you know to whom you are speaking?" I fairly shouted at the clerk. "This is Sherlock Holmes."

"Ah, you cannot fool me," the clerk said. "Everyone knows he's a fictional character."

Holmes has always been a master at dealing with rude functionaries, and I assumed he would deliver an expert tongue-lashing to the clerk. Instead, he smiled and said, "You may be right, sir, for I am indeed Dr. Watson's creation, at least as far as the greater world is concerned. In any event, we will deal with the register another time."

As we went up to our rooms, I said, "That clerk was absolutely insufferable and you should have—"

"Drawn and quartered him and tossed his entrails out on the street?"

"You are being ridiculous, Holmes. But you certainly should have made a scene and demanded to see the register."

"Had I done so, Watson, word would quickly have spread among the hotel staff that I had mistreated, even abused one of their own, and then what? Would we ever receive their full cooperation? Perhaps not. The register can wait. We shall see it soon enough."

LATER THAT EVENING, I found myself in an uncharacteristically restless mood, sleep eluding me, and I went to see Holmes in his room. He was propped up on his bed, Rafferty's notes in hand. The reading glasses he sometimes used rested atop his head, and so I knew he had been thinking. For some reason, I began to recall our old flat on Baker Street, Holmes lost in a cloud of tobacco smoke or playing his violin as he considered some knotty problem. Now, there was no tobacco and he had largely abandoned the violin. Yet in other ways nothing had changed, for Holmes remained the perfect thinking machine, and I had no doubt he would carry the day and find Rafferty's murderer.

"I see you're still pondering Mr. Rafferty's notes," I said. "Any new insights?"

"Perhaps. However, there is something you must see, Watson. It arrived less than an hour ago."

Holmes handed me a telegram, which had come from Chicago. It read: FIND OUT WHAT REALLY HAPPENED TO MARGARET O'DONNELL AND YOU WILL FIND YOUR MURDERER. A FRIEND.

"Well, that's certainly strange. Who is this Margaret O'Donnell?"

"Surely you remember, Watson. We saw her name at Calvary Cemetery."

So we had, and memories of Rafferty's burial services there came rushing back.

AFTER THE FUNERAL, we had joined a long procession of cars going out to the cemetery, which occupied large grounds in the western part of the city. In summer the cemetery might have been a pleasant enough place to dwell in eternity, but in the unforgiving whites and grays of winter it seemed to be desolation itself, snow blanketing the frozen earth and barren trees stabbing at the sky. We learned from Thomas, who rode with us in a large sedan provided by the mortuary, that Rafferty had owned a grave site at Calvary for years and would be buried next to his wife and son.

Although a few hefty granite monuments erected by wealthy families rose above the cemetery's undulating ground, most of the grave markers were simple affairs, wedged flat into the earth like the bodies below them. Just such a marker was all that Rafferty had wanted. Thomas told us he had yet to call the monument company to cut and inscribe Rafferty's grave marker, which would be made of dark Minnesota granite.

Rafferty himself had never taken much interest in what the marker might say. Still, there had to be something suitable on Rafferty's grave, and Thomas said he thought long and hard before coming up with what he considered to be an appropriate inscription. "It will read, 'Shadwell James Rafferty, 1843–1928, soldier, bartender, seeker of the truth.' What do you think?"

"The words are appropriate," Holmes said, "and say all that needs to be said."

The procession ended at a spot beneath a tall oak tree, and we left our cars to walk through a hard crust of snow toward the grave site, where Monsignor Pierre Denis was waiting. To my surprise, I saw rising nearby a tall gray granite tombstone inscribed with the name "St. Aubin." Upon making inquiries, we learned it was indeed the grave of the murdered young man and his father.

Once we reached Rafferty's gravesite, I experienced that sense of absolute finality that imbues all burial grounds. The death of a man such as Shadwell Rafferty always seems inconceivable at first, but then the moment arrives when the coffin drops into the earth and the impossible becomes real. However, we learned there would be no immediate interment, as the ground was frozen solid to a depth of several feet. Rafferty would be buried only when the earth had thawed enough for the gravediggers to do their doleful work.

Even so, Monsignor Denis conducted a short service at the gravesite as Holmes, Thomas, and I huddled in the biting cold with a hundred or more fellow mourners. After the final blessing had been delivered, we returned to our car, grateful to be out of the cold. Holmes struck up a conversation with the driver, a silver-haired man well practiced in the art of looking funereal.

"I noticed that Daniel St. Aubin's grave is not far from Mr. Rafferty's. Were you at his services as well?"

"I was, Mr. Holmes. It was a small affair, just the mother and a few others. The monsignor did the honors. I guess he knows the family."

"The monsignor, I imagine, knows many of St. Paul's prominent Catholic families."

"He does. In fact, he's a good friend of the mayor, from what I hear. Presided over his daughter's funeral just last month. I was here for those services, too. That was a very sad business, Mr. Holmes. The poor girl was just seventeen. I never did find out what she died of. In fact, her headstone is just up there on the right."

I confess I did not pay a great deal of attention to the driver's remarks, for Rafferty was still very much on my mind. But I did look out the window as we passed the tall headstone inscribed with the name Margaret Mary O'Donnell.

NOW, HOLMES WAS IN RECEIPT of an anonymous telegram suggesting the girl's death was somehow linked to our murder investigation.

"Who do you suppose sent it?" I asked Holmes, who stared up at the ceiling, hands behind his head.

"One possibility comes immediately to mind, but I cannot be certain. I have already sent a telegram to Chicago to make certain inquiries. We must take the message seriously. Our unknown friend may be pointing us to a vital aspect of the case that has not previously come to our attention. Or, he may simply be trying to lead us down a blind alley. What I do know, Watson, is that we are squarely in the middle of a very difficult investigation. In rereading Mr. Rafferty's notes, I have been struck by how often he remarked upon the complexity of the St. Aubin affair. Indeed, he likened it to going down a road with so many branches he could never be certain he was on the right path. And now, it seems, yet another branch has been added to the road."

"So what do you propose to do?"

"I propose to keep on working. Behind all that has happened here, beginning with Mr. St. Aubin's murder, I believe there is a single motive force, a person at once cunning and ruthless whose true nature is hidden to the world. But I have made it the business of my life to find such people, who are never quite as clever as they think they are."

Book III

Suspects and Clues

8

The Blackmailer

When Daniel St. Aubin was ten, he lured a four-year-old cousin to the attic of the family mansion on Summit Avenue, telling him they were going to have some "great fun." Layered with dust and filled with a jumble of strange objects, the attic was Danny's private place, a refuge where he could be free, if only for a little while, from the watchful eyes of his nanny. He'd spent much of his childhood there, rummaging through boxes of old photos and heirlooms of every kind and inventing stories about all of them. "The Secret St. Aubin Show," he called it, and it belonged to him and no one else.

His little cousin's name was Roy, and Danny hated him. He was always wiping his snotty nose with his sleeve, and he'd break out into tears when Danny hit him or called him stupid, which in Danny's view he was. Once they'd climbed up the long flight of steps to the attic and shut the door behind them, Danny led Roy toward an old toy chest lodged in a far corner under the roof beams. "There's a nice red fire truck inside," he told him. "Just follow me."

It was summer and the attic was oppressively hot, but Roy didn't seem to mind. "Fwire twuck," he said. "Wed Fwire twuck."

"That's right, Roy," Danny said. "You'll like it. But it's dark over there, so you'll have to reach inside to find it."

"Fwire twuck," Roy repeated.

They reached the wooden chest, which was pushed up against a low wall and entangled in spiderwebs. "It's right in there," Danny said, opening the lid. When Roy leaned over for a look, Danny came up from behind and shoved him into the chest, then slammed down the lid and sat on it.

At first Roy thought it was just a game of hide-in-the-box. But he soon began to panic. "Out, out," he cried, pushing up on the lid with his hands and knees.

Danny didn't budge, and the more he heard Roy struggle, the better he liked it. Other people's suffering had never affected him, and why should it? Would Roy care if he suffered? Danny had a stash of root beer barrels in his pants pocket. He took one out and popped it into his mouth, savoring the sweetness. Roy was becoming hysterical now, screaming and wailing, but Danny ignored him. The candy was all that mattered.

By the time Mrs. Blodgett, the nanny, came up to the attic in search of the boys, Roy was gasping for air. "Danny, stop it!" she yelled, dragging him off the chest to rescue Roy, who emerged from his tiny prison with a look of utter terror on his tearstained face.

"Why did you do that, Danny?" she scolded, then swatted him on the behind. "Don't you know you could have hurt Roy?"

"We were just playing," Danny said calmly. "I thought we were having fun."

Afterward, Roy's mother never let him play with Danny again. She also told her sister, Muriel, that Danny was deeply disturbed and should be seen by a doctor. Muriel St. Aubin, however, dismissed the episode as a childhood prank and assured her sister that Danny had meant no harm. Even so, Danny's father, who had never taken much interest in him, delivered a stern lecture. Danny donned the mask of sincerity that was to serve him well throughout his short life and apologized for his rude behavior. A few months later, when his father died of a massive coronary at dinner, dropping from his chair as though he'd been shot with a high-powered rifle, Danny did his best to look crestfallen, but in truth he didn't feel a thing.

As Danny grew older, there were more incidents—a squirrel trapped in the yard and skinned alive, a rough game of doctor with a ten-year-old girl, money stolen from Mrs. Blodgett's purse—and

Muriel St. Aubin finally had to admit something wasn't quite right about her only child. She took him to a doctor, a big bearded man with an ugly mole on his cheek, and Danny claimed he'd simply acted out because of his father's death. "He's just a little angry," the doctor later told Muriel. "The poor boy wishes his father were still alive. He'll grow out of it."

He didn't. He had his first taste of alcohol at age twelve, began sampling marijuana a year later, and lost his virginity to a prostitute when he fifteen. His reputation was such that St. Paul Academy wouldn't have him, so his mother enrolled him at Central High School. He was by then an exceptionally handsome young man, intelligent and well-spoken, and he had already become a master at manipulating other people. He made friends easily and used them for whatever he needed, and even his teachers were charmed by his wit and physical grace.

A young English teacher found him particularly attractive, and just after his seventeenth birthday he slept with her. He enjoyed the sex but saw it as a means to an end. He assumed the teacher, who was just twenty-four and at the start of her career, would not want their sexual liaison to become public knowledge. She was stunned when he put the matter before her, but she eventually agreed to pay him a hundred dollars for his silence. It was his first successful blackmail scheme, and he found it to be a delicious experience.

His mother, however, continued to believe against all odds that he was a good boy at heart, and when he turned eighteen, she insisted he go to work as a clerk at St. Aubin and Gervais, the wholesale hardware firm in which his father had been a partner. It would be his chance, she said, to learn the family business from the ground up and make something of himself. Honest work had never appealed to Danny, but his mother threatened to cut off his allowance for good if he didn't comply with her wishes, and so he'd agreed to her plan.

Later, he would recall with a kind of stomach-churning distaste his imprisonment as a clerk in the grim, high-ceilinged offices of St. Aubin and Gervais. He wrote up orders for shovels and wood screws and light bulbs and a thousand other things, and the work was so exquisitely tedious that every day behind his desk seemed to last a century. It was only at night that he managed to really live, frequenting speakeasies and gambling dens and hiring the services of prostitutes whenever he could.

After three months of torture, trapped in a drab little world of drab little people who failed to understand how completely they were wasting their lives, Danny walked out and informed his mother he'd never work at St. Aubin and Gervais again. A big row followed, during which Muriel made a spectacle of disowning him.

"You've never been a good son to me," she told him, "and now you're going to find out that the real world is a harsh place. You're foolish and ignorant, Danny, but one day, when you are out of money, you'll come back, begging for forgiveness. Then we shall see."

But Muriel didn't know her son any better than anyone else did. Danny actually had a plan, and learning other people's secrets would become the business of his life.

ONCE HIS MOTHER CUT HIM OFF from the family fortune, St. Aubin launched his career as a professional blackmailer. It was slow going at first, and he took a few odd jobs to support himself while he cultivated sources and learned how to extract information from them. The gamblers, touts, and bootleggers he hung out with were especially helpful because they knew many fascinating things. St. Aubin also insinuated himself into the wealthy young Summit Avenue social set. It was a fast crowd, full of carefree fools who liked to drink and party and gossip. Sometimes, the gossip was about their parents or other rich relatives, and St. Aubin always listened carefully.

One night St. Aubin went to St. Paul's most notorious gentlemen's club, just to see if any opportunities presented themselves. He had no homosexual leanings but thought that men who did might well pay up so as not to have their secret lives revealed. It turned out to be a shrewd move. Several older men hit on him immediately. Among them was a prominent lawyer hailed by one and all as a devoted family man. St. Aubin pretended to be sexually interested in the lawyer and promised to meet him later at a nearby hotel.

Their rendezvous did not turn out to be what the lawyer expected. There was no sex, but Danny managed to take a surreptitious photograph of the half-dressed lawyer and then demanded hush money. He left the hotel with two hundred dollars in his pocket. By the time St. Aubin was through with him, the lawyer had paid out a thousand dollars.

Watching people squirm gave St. Aubin deep pleasure, and as he built his blackmailing business he found plenty of targets. Gay men were lucrative, and so too were the bored Summit Avenue housewives he occasionally bedded. Along the way he sometimes uncovered what he called bonus secrets, involving everything from financial chicanery to infidelity, and he exploited whatever information he could. One of the most shocking revelations involved his own mother, but he concluded that the iron-willed Muriel wouldn't stand for blackmail, so he filed the secret away, thinking it might come in handy someday down the road.

As he expanded his business, St. Aubin honed his photographic skills, equipping himself with a state-of-the-art Leica 35mm camera. He used fast film so he could photograph in low light, and he set up a dark room in his apartment to develop the negatives. Cheating husbands became one of his specialties, and St. Aubin sometimes spent days following a mark, waiting for the moment the man met his lover. One good photo of the rendezvous was usually all St. Aubin needed to earn a nice payday.

Like every good businessman, St. Aubin kept meticulous records in the form of files organized by name. By late in 1927, there were almost fifty names in his files. At first, St. Aubin kept the file in his apartment, but he soon realized that would be a bad idea if the police came looking for him one day. So he moved the files to an unused hall closet at the Piedmont, using a key he'd stolen from the head janitor's office.

St. Aubin was clever about how he did business and knew when to turn off the faucet that poured money into his wallet. He'd learned that blackmail victims would only pay so much before rebelling and threatening to go to the police, no matter the consequences. So he'd gotten in the habit of offering his marks an installment plan—three payments, usually totaling around a thousand dollars—and no more. It worked, and he managed to operate with impunity for years.

In his best year, St. Aubin extorted more than ten thousand dollars from people with something to hide. It was more than enough to live well, but he couldn't seem to keep money in his pocket. He liked to gamble and drink and buy expensive clothes, and he found himself constantly short of cash. He also began to run out of victims. Word of his activities had gradually gotten around, and he became too notorious in St. Paul for his own good. The well was beginning to run dry. Then, in late 1927, St. Aubin stumbled upon the opportunity of a lifetime.

IT HAD HAPPENED IN NOVEMBER, at a notorious party house just off Summit Avenue that often attracted underage drinkers. Margaret O'Donnell was among the drinkers, and from the moment St. Aubin saw her, he began planning a seduction. She was incredibly beautiful, he thought, yet obviously vulnerable, with the haunted eyes of a lost child. He introduced himself as a successful businessman, gazed at her in the manner of a saint contemplating the glories of heaven, and made it clear he viewed her as the most magnificent young woman he'd ever met.

But his finely tuned performance, designed to get her into bed with him that very night, did not have the expected result. "You just want to screw me," she said with a kind of grim disgust. "Why are all of you men such liars?"

The cruelty and manipulation at the heart of St. Aubin's life were built on a foundation of shrewdness when it came to reading people. He could, when it suited him, don the guise of a sympathetic friend, and so he did with Margaret.

"You sound terribly bitter," he said. "Something awful must be bothering you. You'll find I'm a good listener and not the bad fellow you seem to think I am."

As the night wore on and Margaret shared in the alcohol being passed around, she began to open up to St. Aubin, who gave the impression of taking in her every word as though she possessed uncanny wisdom. Her tale of woe at first did not seem especially interesting. She was pregnant, which meant nothing to St. Aubin. Girls got knocked up every day. But the more she talked, the more obvious it became that she'd been impregnated against her will, and not by some pimply-faced teenage boy. It was an older man, she told him, who'd drugged and then assaulted her.

"I want to make him pay," she said. "He thinks I'm stupid but I'm not. I won't be quiet unless he keeps his promises. All of them!"

St. Aubin pressed her to name the man. She refused at first, saying she still expected him to "do the right thing and be a real man." By two o'clock in the morning she was hopelessly drunk, and St. Aubin agreed to drive her home. Margaret talked incoherently for much of the way, but just before she slipped off to sleep she mumbled the name of the man who had impregnated her. It was a stunning revelation, and St. Aubin knew at once it could make him a rich man.

9

"I Must Warn You to Be Careful"

Declan Patrick Morrissey—"Dec" to everyone who knew him—ran a large downtown pool hall where hardly anyone played billiards. Gambling and drinking were the establishment's real activities. Thirsty St. Paulites from all walks of life frequented the place, which was widely regarded as the city's finest speakeasy. Morrissey, known for his ornate speaking style and encyclopedic knowledge of bawdy limericks, was also a prime attraction.

While not tending to the needs of drinkers, Morrissey pursued a sideline as henchman-in-chief for "Dapper" Dan Hogan, the city's reigning crime boss. Although Hogan would within a year be blown to pieces by a bomb that detonated when he started his car, in 1927 he remained the undisputed czar of the local underworld. Rafferty was acquainted with Hogan and had no doubt he'd know something about the Danny St. Aubin case. Rafferty knew Morrissey much better, however, and thought he'd be just as good a source of information as his boss. So on the Friday before Christmas, Rafferty hobbled over to Morrissey's establishment for a talk.

Rafferty had once been something of a regular at the place but had visited less frequently of late because of his troubles getting around. Morrissey operated what Rafferty called "a good, clean joint." He tolerated no fighting or cursing or prostitutes and served fine Canadian whiskey, Cuban rum, and several liqueurs of his own devising, along with the best beer available in the city.

Black-haired and hazel-eyed, Morrissey was short but powerfully built and a formidable character. He carried a silver-plated pistol and kept a beautifully engraved Italian shotgun beneath the bar to discourage unruliness. It was rumored he'd once shot a man in Chicago in a dispute over some young beauty, but all he ever told Rafferty about the affair was that "sometimes the application of a bullet in the right place is the only way to resolve a problem."

The pool hall, which bore no name since virtually everything that went on within its walls was illegal, occupied a cavernous space in the basement of the gleaming Hamm Building, which had been erected only a few years earlier by William Hamm, whose family brewery had long been the largest in the city. The building was therefore a suitable place for a speakeasy. It was also rumored that the crisp lager beer Morrissey served came from a small but well-financed brewery run by former Hamm employees on the city's East Side.

Morrissey's business attracted little police attention thanks to large monthly contributions to the patrolmen's benevolent fund, but in 1926 the feds had raided the place and hauled Morrissey off to court on the usual charges of making and serving liquor. A jury in St. Paul duly weighed the clear and convincing evidence in the case and concluded it somehow wasn't quite clear or convincing enough and promptly acquitted Morrissey. A day later he reopened his establishment.

Rafferty found the place doing a brisk business and spotted a county judge, a police captain, and several lawyers among the imbibers lined up at a long oak bar decorated with back mirrors, paintings of naked ladies cavorting among fauns, and a large sign that read MILK, SODA, JUICE, COFFEE. PLEASE DRINK RESPONSIBLY. Morrissey wasn't at the bar so Rafferty went to a small back office to find him. A wide-shouldered bruiser with an incomplete set of teeth and a .45 automatic holstered on his hip guarded the office to protect against any disturbances, such as the arrival of assassins from a competing gang. The bruiser didn't recognize Rafferty but cracked open the door and said, "Boss, there's some codger out here named Rafferty who says he knows you."

Morrissey was out the door in a flash and gave the bodyguard a withering stare before pumping Rafferty's hand. "By God, Shad, it's been awhile. How are you?"

"Well, I am not quite at death's door, Dec, but I can see it clearly from where I stand. In the meantime, I'm still at the detecting business and I'm thinking there might be a thing or two you can help me with."

"Then come on in and I'll see what I can do." Morrissey turned to the bodyguard and said, "Dumbass, fetch a beer and be quick about it."

The beer soon arrived, cold and crisp as a winter morning, and Rafferty, who had taken a seat across from Morrissey's desk, enjoyed a long, satisfying draught. "Ah, Dec, I can only hope that when all the Prohibitionists go to Hell, which a just God will surely demand, they will be forced to bathe in vats of red-hot beer for eternity."

"Amen to that. Now then, my friend, how can I be of help?"

"It's about Danny St. Aubin. What do you know about the young man and his death?"

Morrissey shot his guest an alarming look and said, "Word around town is that St. Aubin didn't kill himself, but as to what really happened, well now, that's one of those profound mysteries best left to the heavens, where angels cavort and no devils sing, if you catch my drift. My earnest advice, which I offer without charge, is to leave the whole business alone."

"I appreciate your wise counsel, but I've made certain promises to St. Aubin's mother, and I intend to keep them if I can. Just tell me what you know. Anything will be of help."

Morrissey went over to a small bar in one corner of the office. He poured a finger of whiskey and said, "Care for a chaser?"

"No. I fear old age has rendered whiskey more often than not disagreeable to me. It is surely Satan's work, but I must live with it. Come now, Dec, let me hear what you know."

"All right, I'll pass on a tasty morsel or two for your delectation. I can tell you that the consensus among my sources, who are many and varied, is that St. Aubin got on the wrong side of powerful people and paid the price."

"Which people?"

"The mayor of our fair city, for one. In fact, I am told His Honor only recently sent Big Jack Grimshaw out to provide some moral instruction to the young man."

"With his fists, no doubt."

"Yes, I fear Big Jack is not a gentle teacher. Apparently the lad took quite a beating."

"When was this?"

"A couple of weeks ago."

"What was the mayor so upset about?"

"That, I fear, is beyond the ken of a humble man such as myself. However, I can tell you that St. Aubin didn't have a savory reputation. From what I've been told, he was in the blackmail racket. He made a habit of getting the goods on some of our most distinguished citizens, especially those swells up on Summit Avenue, and they supposedly shelled out plenty of dough to keep him quiet."

"Ah, and who are these swells you speak of?"

"I can name no names. For some reason, I am rarely invited to the soirees and cotillions up there, even though I am a well-regarded master of the Irish jig. In any case, you and I both know blackmailing is a fine way to get yourself killed."

"And you think that's why Danny St. Aubin was murdered?"

"Could be. But the little birds who sing in the night have gone mostly quiet when it comes to young Mr. St. Aubin. The fix is in and it's closed tight as a miser's purse. Whatever happened to him, you're going to have a time of it finding out."

"Well, nothing is easy when you're as old as I am, Dec, but I am bound to give it a try. Now then, what else do you know?"

"Well, I hear St. Aubin liked guys more than girls, if you catch my drift."

This revelation came as a surprise to Rafferty. "How do you know that?"

Morrissey shrugged and said, "Rumor has it he was chummy with that Abbey fellow—you know, the poet—who's a well-practiced sodomite, from what I'm told. Besides, I heard from Billy Baer, who runs that club for poofs up on St. Peter Street, that he saw St. Aubin there on more than one occasion. Apparently, some of the older gentlemen there found him to be a regular Apollo."

Rafferty wasn't sure what to make of the claim that St. Aubin was a homosexual. But even if he was, did that fact have anything to do with his death? Rafferty recalled what had happened on the night of St. Aubin's murder, when he'd asked the Ryan's doorman whether he knew Monsignor Denis by sight. Was it possible St. Aubin had been involved in a sexual relationship with the priest? Rafferty put the question to Morrissey.

"Now that would shake up all those black robes at the chancery office, wouldn't it?" Morrissey said. "Oh yes, a fine scandal that would be! Alas, I cannot say I have any evidence of it. The monsignor doesn't do his drinking here, so I don't really know the man."

"Fair enough," Rafferty said. "Has anything else wormed its way into your eager ears?"

"That's about all, Shad. But there is one more thing: I must warn you to be careful. The big boys over at city hall won't be happy if they think you're onto something. You push them and they'll push back—hard. Big Jack in particular is not a man to be toying with."

"The two of us have already had a nice little talk. The thing is, Dec, I'm too old to worry about getting into trouble. It will find me soon enough, no matter what."

"Well, I wish you luck, and I believe you'll need it. This city is full of secrets, and they will not be found out easily."

Rafferty leaned back in his chair and drained the last of his beer. Another glass would have tasted just fine but he decided against it. He hoisted himself out of his chair and shook Morrissey's hand.

"You have been a great help, Dec, as I knew you'd be. I may call on you again if need be."

"Any time, Shad. My door is always open to you."

RAFFERTY CALLED MRS. ST. AUBIN on Christmas Eve and provided a bowdlerized account of his conversation with Morrissey, making no reference to the claim that Danny was homosexual. That revelation, if true, wasn't something Mrs. St. Aubin needed to hear at the moment, or so Rafferty reasoned. But he did mention her son's reputation as a blackmailer and asked if she knew of anyone he may have been extorting money from.

"No," she said quickly and firmly.

A bit too firmly, Rafferty thought. "Are you certain? I've been told Danny may have blackmailed a number of wealthy people on Summit Avenue."

"Is that so? Well, you will have to ask them about it, won't you?"

"It appears I will. What about Mayor O'Donnell? Can you think of any reason why he may have been angry enough at Danny to have him beaten up?"

"I know nothing about that. I do not move in the mayor's circles and do not count him as a friend. But I find it hard to believe he would be involved in such a thing."

"Perhaps, but I can tell you that Detective Grimshaw supposedly administered the beating. Danny never mentioned it to you?"

"No. As I said earlier, my son and I were not in regular communication."

Mrs. St. Aubin, Rafferty was finding out, did not qualify as the most helpful client he'd ever had. "All right, I'll keep on digging, Mrs. Aubin. I'll be in contact again when I know more."

"Of course you will," she said and hung up.

FOR MANY YEARS, Rafferty spent Christmas Day at his saloon, which he threw open to anyone in need of holiday cheer. He offered free food and drinks, and the event became an institution in St. Paul, always attracting big crowds. But with his beloved saloon lost to Prohibition, Rafferty had been forced to make other Christmas plans.

It had been a lonely time for the first few years, with no companion other than Rafferty's old bulldog, Sherlock the Fourth. But the dog had died in 1922, and after that Rafferty didn't feel up to caring for an animal anymore. Rafferty had no family in St. Paul, nor did he enjoy a steady relationship of any kind. Although his wife had been dead for decades, he'd never given serious thought to remarrying. A heart, he believed, could only be given fully once, and he had given his to Mary. The wound of her death had never completely healed, and there were long nights when it still hurt.

Still, Rafferty had enjoyed the company of a number of wonderful women over the years. One of them—Majesty Burke, who was involved in the Secret Alliance case—had come close to stealing his heart, but then she'd been taken away in the Spanish flu pandemic, and Rafferty was alone once again. On some days Rafferty tumbled into a deep pit of dark thoughts and lost dreams, all hope seemingly gone.

Wash Thomas always found a way to bring Rafferty out of his blue fog and back into the light. This was especially true during the holidays. After Wash married Pats and opened their restaurant, Rafferty inaugurated a new Christmas tradition with them. As Rafferty had done with his saloon, Wash and Pats opened their place on Christmas, serving free meals to needy folks in the surrounding Rondo neighborhood, and Rafferty always helped out as much as he could.

On what would be Rafferty's last Christmas, he arose at nine o'clock, donned his gaudiest red jacket along with a matching stocking cap, and took a taxi up to the restaurant. He peeled potatoes and performed other kitchen chores, then assisted in serving food when the restaurant opened at noon. It was a long but rewarding day, and by the time he sat down with Wash and Pats to enjoy a private Christmas dinner, he was in a good mood, his aches and pains temporarily assigned to limbo. Roast turkey with stuffing, mashed potatoes, wax beans, and cranberry sauce were on the menu, followed by apple and pumpkin pies, and after they'd all overeaten without shame, Rafferty was in an even better mood.

Although the feast was wonderful, it had the feeling of a last supper for Rafferty, who knew his body was breaking down. He'd been experiencing heart palpitations and bouts of angina from which the nitroglycerin prescribed by his doctor provided only limited relief, and he wasn't sure how much longer he could last. Still, he tried to suppress such doom-laden thoughts and do his best to stay positive.

"You have outdone yourself, Pats," he said as they enjoyed coffee and cordials. "It was a meal much too good for a king. I believe I will never have to eat again."

"Oh, you will. You've got plenty of meat on those old bones of yours. I just wish I could put some on this man of mine," she said, reaching for her husband's hand. "He's way too skinny."

"Wash is a miracle," Rafferty said. "I think food turns to dust in his belly, which is why he never seems to gain a pound."

"No, it's all the exercise I get running around for you," Thomas said with a grin. "I tell you, Pats, Shad's got me on the move all the time with this St. Aubin business."

"Well, you'll get your rest soon," Rafferty said. "When are you going down to Georgia to see your family?"

"Pats and I plan to leave on January second. But I'm a little worried, Shad. I don't know if I should leave you alone here, what with everything that's going on, not to mention your health. Why don't you come along? The warm weather would do you good."

"No, traveling doesn't suit me anymore, and don't worry, I'll be fine here. Besides, I'm getting more and more interested in the St. Aubin case. It's like a good mystery tale, and I just keep turning the pages to see what will happen next."

As it turned out, the tale would have many more twists in the days ahead.

10

"We Must Dig and Dig"

[From "Murder in St. Paul"]

The notes Rafferty left behind in his bank box were of the greatest interest to Holmes, and he pored over them at every available opportunity with the exacting attention of a biblical scholar. I too read the notes, which seemed quite random, like loose change tossed in a jar whenever Rafferty thought to empty his pockets. Some notes were typewritten, others penned on stationery or a scrap of paper in Rafferty's distinctive hand. A few items were dated but most were not. Holmes did his best to organize the notes, dividing them into five sections, one for each of the prime suspects.

By the Saturday after Rafferty's funeral, Holmes pronounced himself satisfied that he had gleaned everything of value from the notes. We were in his room, the newly organized documents laid out before us, and Holmes was in a mood to talk. Although he had triumphed over his addiction to tobacco, he had found no other calming agent for his busy mind than constant movement, and so he paced the room as he spoke.

"Now begins the real work," he said. "We must dig and dig like patient miners, uncovering one layer of rock after another until we find the precious ore. Mr. Rafferty's case file is extremely useful, but it does not provide a treasure map on which the proverbial X marks the spot. His life was cut short before he could fill in that final element."

"He must have come very close to doing so, according to what Thomas has told us."

"That astounding development he spoke of to Mr. Thomas just before he was murdered does indeed suggest he was on the verge of identifying Daniel St. Aubin's killer. Unfortunately, if he put his suspicions on paper, we have no record of it, since he did not have enough time to put copies of his last set of notes in his bank box."

"So the murderer has them."

"Or the police. In either case, the notes are gone, and we are left with many questions. Even so, we can be certain of at least two things, based on Mr. Rafferty's investigation. The first is that Daniel St. Aubin did not die by his own hand. His death was carefully staged to look like a suicide, by parties unknown. The second is that Mr. Rafferty's murder is related in some way to that of Mr. St. Aubin. We have two interconnected murders, and so we must follow a double scent, as it were."

"So how do you propose to proceed? Are we to investigate both murders at once?"

"Yes, I do not see that we have any other choice. There is also a third matter to consider, which is the death of Margaret O'Donnell. The anonymous telegram from Chicago urged us to look into her death. I have already made a few inquiries, and they lead me to believe the telegram came from her brother, Paul."

"What makes you think so?"

"I placed a call to a man called Declan Morrissey, who runs the pool hall where Mr. Rafferty's wake will be held tonight. His name came up frequently in Mr. Rafferty's notes as a reliable source of information. Mr. Morrissey told me about Paul O'Donnell, who seems to be a rather pathetic character and who apparently is in Chicago at the moment. We shall learn more about him tonight, since I intend to speak at some length to Mr. Morrissey. He also may be able to offer some insight into Margaret O'Donnell's death, the cause of which seems to be a great secret."

"It's rare for a seventeen-year-old to die so suddenly in this day and age," I noted. "Perhaps it was an accident of some kind."

"Perhaps. There must be a death certificate on file. First thing Monday, Watson, I would like you to find that certificate."

"I'm sure Thomas would know where it's filed."

"Excellent. In the meantime, I intend to talk with Mrs. St. Aubin. It has occurred to me that her son, who was by all accounts strikingly handsome, could have had a relationship with the O'Donnell girl."

"But wasn't Mr. Rafferty told he was more interested in men than women?"

"Yes, by Mr. Morrissey, in fact. But the evidence to that effect is mere hearsay. On the other hand, if Mr. St. Aubin did indeed have some involvement with the O'Donnell girl, it would add a new dimension to our case. Perhaps he and the mayor's daughter were as Romeo and Juliet, star-crossed lovers who came all too quickly to their ends."

Mrs. St. Aubin, as it turned out, could not immediately be reached. We learned she had gone to New York, where she was staying at the Waldorf Astoria. Holmes left a message for her at the hotel. She hadn't returned his call by seven that evening, when Holmes and I went out to attend Rafferty's second wake, which proved to be far more lively than his first.

I WAS NOT PREPARED for the astonishing scene that greeted us when we arrived at Morrissey's cavernous basement pool hall. A pulsating throng packed the establishment in a loud buzz of voices and an ever-thickening pall of tobacco smoke. When we met Thomas at the door, Pats by his side, he told me he'd counted nearly three hundred visitors thus far.

"Are any of our prime suspects in attendance?" Holmes asked as he surveyed the crowd.

"The mayor came by but didn't stay for long. Haven't seen any of the others."

Thomas told us the crowd consisted largely of "regular folks" but also included lawyers, doctors, businessmen, bankers, and members of the clergy. A few criminals were also on hand, certain well-known pickpockets among them. However, Thomas said he'd warned the "light-fingered gentlemen" that if they tried to ply their trade amid such a juicy array of marks, Morrissey's enforcers would teach them a memorable lesson.

As we talked, the crowd began to grow quiet. Heads turned, voices dropped to whispers, and even the four aproned bartenders serving the multitudes suddenly became statues. Then a mighty burst of applause thundered through the pool hall.

"That's for you, Mr. Holmes," Thomas said. "Sounds like you've got everybody's attention."

This was indeed the case, and when the applause died down a number of mourners rushed forward to commune with Holmes, whose universal renown made him like a magnet in a great pile of metal shavings. It was then that our old friend Louis Hill came to the rescue. Attired in a beautiful tailored wool suit fit for a king, he appeared at the door and greeted us warmly. The richest man in St. Paul and perhaps all of the Northwest then paused for a moment, looked out upon the merrymakers like the Pope eyeing his faithful flock, and said in a booming voice, "Carry on, ladies and gentleman, carry on! The next round is on me!" Amid wild cheers, the crowd, packed so tightly that there was scarcely room to move, resumed its merrymaking, and thereby gave Holmes and me some breathing room.

As the crowd moved like a thirsty herd toward the bar, a man whom Thomas identified as a "longtime county judge" mounted a makeshift podium and announced over the din that the time had come "to tell tall tales about our late, beloved friend." Pounding a gavel he'd brought along, the judge managed to quiet the crowd. The stories that followed were outlandish but also richly amusing.

One involved the time Rafferty wedged his massive torso into a catch basin to save a stranded dog, only to require rescue by the fire department when he became stuck. Another concerned his claim that he'd caught a pike weighing "a hundred pounds if it weighed an ounce" at Lake Osakis, only to have the alleged lunker wiggle free at the last moment. Yet a third centered on a brawl at Rafferty's saloon during which he'd single-handedly ejected three burly lumberjacks looking for liquor and trouble. The story grew ever more embellished in the telling until the lumberjacks formed a veritable army of ax-wielding woodsmen. The judge concluded by raising a glass "to the one and only Shadwell Rafferty" as the crowd roared its approval.

Holmes and I thoroughly enjoyed the stories and could well have added many of our own. However, the haze of smoke smothering the hall began to greatly irritate Holmes's emphysema, and he was all but gasping for air by the time Thomas directed us to Declan Morrisscy, the proprietor of the establishment. He took one look at Holmes and said, "You appear to be a man in need of better air. Come along and we'll talk."

Morrissey turned out to be an intriguing character. Short and muscular, he had the sort of eyes that can freeze a man, but there was also an inviting warmth to his manner. After telling us to call him "Dec," he ushered us into his private office, which was blessedly free of smoke. Thomas, meanwhile, returned to his unofficial duties as doorman.

"A drink for either of you gentlemen?" Morrissey asked after we pulled up two side chairs next to his desk.

"A brandy would be most excellent," Holmes said. "Dr. Watson, I'm sure, would not be averse to a touch of Scotch."

"Your wish is my command," Morrissey said and poured our drinks from a small but amply stocked bar near his desk. The Scotch proved to be superb, and I could tell that Holmes also found his brandy more than satisfactory. "Now, then, what can I do for the most famous detective in the world?"

"I have only a few questions," Holmes said. "I know Mr. Rafferty spoke to you at some length last month while investigating the St. Aubin case. His notes in that regard are quite thorough. It was you, I believe, who first alerted him to Mr. St. Aubin's activities as a blackmailer."

"I did, but there wasn't much I could tell him about that. Not exactly my bailiwick, if you know what I mean. Doesn't matter to me if some Summit Avenue swell gets caught with his pants down. Still, a man in my line of work needs to stay alert, so naturally I hear many things."

"I have no doubt you do. What have you heard about the mayor's late daughter? Please tell me all you know of her and her death."

"Well, I can tell you she was a gorgeous girl, and boys must have hovered around her like the proverbial bees in search of the sweet nectar of love. Oh yes, she was a beauty! Now, some say she might have been a bit 'loose,' but beyond that I know little about her. As to how she died, as I told Shad, that is a secret worthy of the pharaoh's tombs. The mayor knows, of course, but as he and I are hardly bosom friends, I remain in the Stygian darkness when it comes to his daughter's fate. Naturally, there have been rumors. I cannot attest to their accuracy, but—"

Holmes jumped in. "Rumor is the rough, mealy stuff of human intercourse, Mr. Morrissey, and I never discount it. What do these rumors say?"

"Well, there are a number of them, as you might expect. One says she was pregnant and died in childbirth. Another holds that she ran away from home and that a mishap of some kind took her life. There is also a theory she committed suicide after her father banned her from ever seeing her lover again."

"Could Daniel St. Aubin have been that lover?"

"Ah, that's an interesting thought, Mr. Holmes, but I've heard St. Aubin was not exactly a ladies' man."

"So you told Mr. Rafferty. But as your only evidence for this is that he once visited a certain gentlemen's club, let's assume for a moment that he might have been attracted to Miss O'Donnell."

"Fair enough. If he wasn't a poof and had a pulse, he would have sought her favor, I'm sure. As to whether or not he reached the promised land, I cannot say. From what I know of him, however, he was just the sort of fast-talking scoundrel who might have gotten her with child."

"According to Mr. Rafferty, you said Detective Jackson Grimshaw delivered a beating to Mr. St. Aubin, possibly on orders from the mayor. Could it have been because Mr. St. Aubin had impregnated her?"

"I suppose so, but try proving it. The mayor has a nice way of distancing himself from the dirty work that goes on in our fair city. As for Big Jack, he's just a brute with a badge, and he does what the big boys tell him to do. He threatened me once a few years ago but backed off after I told him, in the nicest possible way, that if he laid a hand on me, he'd die in an unfortunate accident within twenty-four hours. He knew I'm as good as my word, and he hasn't bothered me since."

Holmes smiled and said, "You do not strike me as a man who would easily give in to threats, Mr. Morrissey. Now, when I spoke to you briefly on the telephone this afternoon, you told me a little about Paul O'Donnell, Margaret's brother. Please describe him to me in more detail, if you would."

"What can I say about Paulie except that he's a lost soul? Never got along with his father and never really amounted to anything.

He's a big drinker and it'll do him in before his time. As I told you over the phone, the last I heard he was making his living as a gambler and card shark in Chicago."

"I have already contacted the police there to see if they can find him. I have reason to believe he sent me a telegram regarding his sister's death, which he clearly views as suspicious. Yet he did not put his name on the telegram. I wonder why. And if he truly believes his sister met with foul play, why has he not come back to St. Paul to make his concerns known?"

Morrissey said, "That's just the way Paulie operates. He doesn't want to get involved in anything or tied down or made to explain himself. Paulie's a traveler, except he's on the fast train to nowhere. He inherited a load of money from his grandfather and has been drinking it away ever since. The mayor has long since disowned him, from what I understand. Anyway, he's a sad case. He took a dive from the Robert Street Bridge a couple of years ago, but they fished him out of the river with only a few bruises to show for his effort. A regular miracle, I guess, although a man who bungles his own suicide is hardly to be admired, in my book."

"Even so, he could have strong feelings for his sister."

"I suppose so. But he won't be easy to find. Like I said, he's always on the move, and I don't think he's been in St. Paul for quite a while. Maybe he's in Chicago, or he could be roaming the Kirghiz Steppe for all I know."

"If you do by chance learn of his whereabouts, please let me know at once. I have but one more question. What have you heard regarding the police investigation into Mr. Rafferty's murder? I suspect Detective Grimshaw will somehow fail to discover any useful clues."

"A very good guess, Mr. Holmes. Big Jack will do whatever it takes to smother the truth and please his masters. It burns me to the bottom of my toes what happened to Shad, and if you need any help, Mr. Holmes, you just ask. I have capable men who are at your disposal, no questions asked."

"Thank you. The time may indeed come when I avail myself of your offer."

"Well, I wish you luck, Mr. Holmes. You and Dr. Watson are in for a rough time of it. Once the fix is in here, it closes like the jaws of a vice, and Hercules himself would be hard-pressed to pry it open."

"Prying things open is my specialty," Holmes said as we rose from our chairs, "for I have found the mind is the strongest power of all. You have been most helpful, Mr. Morrissey, and I wish you a pleasant evening."

WHEN WE RETURNED TO THE RYAN, at around ten o'clock, we stopped at the front desk, where Holmes struck up a conversation with Donald Hobbs, the night clerk who had been on duty the night Rafferty was murdered. Hobbs was a thin, bespectacled man in his late twenties, and he appeared stunned that Sherlock Holmes would deign to speak to him.

"I usually start at six but I came on at four that afternoon to cover for a fellow who had to leave early," Hobbs said. "It's a night I'll never forget. Still can't believe someone murdered Mr. Rafferty. What a terrible thing! He was a legend in this city and a fine gentleman in every way. I just can't—"

Holmes cut him short. "Yes, we all agree on that point. Now, Mr. Hobbs, I imagine you spoke to the police after Mr. Rafferty's murder."

"Of course. I told them everything I knew."

"No doubt. Whom did you speak to from the police?"

"It was that big detective, Grimshaw. A bunch of other cops arrived first and then he showed up to take charge. I don't mind telling you he's a scary sort of fellow. Wouldn't want to cross him, I can tell you that."

"Had you ever seen or talked to Mr. Grimshaw before that night?"

"A few times. The Ryan is a very respectable hotel, but now and then some criminal unknown to us rents a room and the police come looking for him."

"And when that happens, do the police request the criminal's room key?"

"Sometimes. But usually we just go up with the cops and knock on the door. If there's no answer, we open it for them."

"Am I right in assuming there is also a master key, which can be employed to access all the rooms and apartments?"

"Yes. Actually, there are six as far as I know. The head of building maintenance has three that are used mostly by our cleaning people. Two more are kept here in a strongbox beneath the desk, and there's another one in the main hotel safe."

Holmes rubbed his chin, then pivoted to a new subject. "Before the night of Mr. Rafferty's murder, when was the last time you encountered Detective Grimshaw here?"

"Just a few days earlier. I think it was on Thursday."

"The nineteenth?"

"That sounds right. Grimshaw came to the desk just after I started my shift at six and said he needed to check on a guest."

Holmes's ears almost literally perked up, like a hound being summoned to the hunt. "Did he ask for a specific room key?"

"He didn't, and it was kind of strange. He wanted a master key, so I had to give him one. I told him I could go up with him but he said no. It was just, 'Give me the key and be quick about it.' He wasn't the least bit friendly."

"And I take it he didn't say which room he was going to?"

"No, but I saw him heading toward the steps, so it was probably a room on the lower floors."

"When did he return the key?"

"He wasn't gone for very long, as I recall. Maybe fifteen minutes or so. He just dropped off the key and left."

"Mr. Hobbs, you are a most observant man. Do you recall, by the way, whether Mr. Rafferty would have been in his apartment at that time?"

"Oh, I doubt it. He was pretty punctual about eating dinner at six in the café."

Rafferty's apartment, as we well knew, was on the second floor. Had Grimshaw gone there two days before Rafferty's murder? Holmes would say later that he suspected Grimshaw had done just that, probably with the intent of searching it.

Holmes said, "Let me ask you about something else, Mr. Hobbs. Are you familiar with room 652 here?"

"Sure, that's up in the east wing, but it's vacant now. The heat isn't very good in that part of the hotel, so we don't book the rooms up there in winter."

"Do you know of anything special about 652?"

"Can't say that I do. Why?"

"Apparently, that room was left unlocked. Any idea why that would be the case?"

"Boy, I really can't say. It should have been locked like all the others."

"To your knowledge, did Mr. Rafferty ever have occasion to use the room?"

"No. I mean, why would he want to go up there?"

"A good question, Mr. Hobbs. Are you aware of anyone—a frequent hotel guest, say, or an employee—who has made a habit of using that room?"

"Never heard of such a thing."

"And I imagine you wouldn't know if Mr. Rafferty or anyone else was in the room shortly before his murder."

"That's correct."

A hotel guest now came up to report a problem of some kind. The matter occupied Hobbs for several minutes while Holmes, not the most patient of men, tapped his fingers on the desk. When the clerk returned his attention to us, Holmes said, "Let us continue with what happened on the night of Mr. Rafferty's murder. Did you see him that evening?"

"I don't believe so. The desk was busy, so I probably missed him. But I did see that Negro friend of his come in, and the next thing you know the cops are here and that's when I found out what happened."

"Before the police arrived, did anything at all unusual happen that night? A ruckus of any kind? An unexpected guest or visitor? Something out of the ordinary you or another staff member might have noticed?"

Hobbs removed his spectacles and rubbed his forehead. After a good deal of massaging, he said, "No, nothing really stands out. It was just business as usual."

"You have been most helpful, Mr. Hobbs. Now, I should like to examine your hotel register for the day of Mr. Rafferty's murder. I know of the hotel's policy in this regard, but as this is a matter of murder, I am confident you will make an exception. And do you not agree, Dr. Watson, that Mr. Hobbs will play an important role in your account of this case?"

"It could not be otherwise," I averred.

Hobbs succumbed to these blandishments and, after making sure none of his superiors was in the vicinity, showed us the register. The list of guests who'd booked a room on January 21 was not long and one signature immediately caught Holmes's attention. It began with an ornate capital *B* followed by an *A* and then tailed off into an illegible scrawl.

"Whose signature is this?" Holmes asked.

For the first time, Hobbs appeared hesitant. "Well, I didn't check that person in, so—"

"But you know who he is, do you not? Come now, Mr. Hobbs, speak up."

"I don't want to get in trouble."

"You will not," Holmes said. "I shall personally vouch for you if necessary."

"All right, it's Bertram Abbey."

We knew from a brief mention in Rafferty's notes that Abbey was reputed to have occasional assignations at the hotel, and Holmes immediately pressed the point.

"I presume Mr. Abbey was meeting someone in his room. A lover perhaps?"

Hobbs looked as embarrassed as if he'd just stumbled into a colony of nudists. "Well, I don't know about that. It's his business, after all."

"So it is. Does Mr. Abbey regularly book a room here?"

"I'm not sure. I've seen him a few times, that's all. But as to who he might have been with, I can't say. I don't pry into the private activities of our guests."

Holmes showed Hobbs a photograph of Daniel St. Aubin and asked, "By any chance, did you ever see Mr. Abbey with this man?"

"That's the fellow who shot himself in the alley, isn't it? His picture was all over the papers. I don't recall ever seeing him here."

"Were you working the night he died?"

"No, I was off, so I'm afraid I can't tell you much about it."

"A commendable policy," said Holmes. He then asked whether Hobbs had seen Mayor O'Donnell, Montgomery Meeks, or Monsignor Pierre Denis at the hotel prior to Rafferty's murder.

"Didn't see the mayor. He's here a lot for banquets and such and always stops by the desk to say hello. As to the other two, I wouldn't know them by sight, so I couldn't really say if they were here. I did see a priest, though."

These words galvanized Holmes, who asked Hobbs to describe

the priest. It was quickly established that he bore a striking resemblance to Monsignor Pierre Denis.

"What time did the priest come into the hotel?"

"It was just before five, I think. It wasn't too long after I came on duty."

"Did you speak with him?"

"Briefly. I asked if I could be of help and he said no, he was just going up to visit one of his parishioners who lives here and was quite ill."

"I take it he didn't mention the parishioner by name?"

"No."

"Did the priest go up the stairs or take an elevator."

"The stairs, as I recall."

"Did you see him again when he left?"

"No. With all the hullabaloo about Mr. Rafferty, I sort of lost track of who was coming and going. Sorry."

"Very well. That will be all for now. You have been most helpful, Mr. Hobbs. Here is something for your time."

Hobbs had a broad smile on his face and a twenty-dollar bill in his hand when we finally went up to our rooms for some much-needed rest.

THE NEXT MORNING, I went to Holmes's room at ten and found him engrossed in the newspapers.

"Mr. Rafferty's death remains in the news, although it has already been consigned to the back pages, where Detective Grimshaw offers ever more ornate fictions. He claims the burglar supposedly responsible for Mr. Rafferty's death has been traced to New Jersey, but an arrest has yet to be made."

"And never will be, I presume."

"Yes, the detective will doubtlessly report soon that the mythical burglar has gone to Timbuktu, joined the Bedouins, and vanished into the Sahara. I am also—"

The telephone jangled and Holmes immediately took the call. "Yes, yes, put her on," he said, then whispered to me, "Mrs. St. Aubin, from New York."

I listened in on the conversation. It was instantly apparent from Mrs. St. Aubin's firm, imperious voice that she was not intimidated by speaking to a man as famous as Holmes.

"I am glad you have taken over my son's case," she began. "Perhaps you can ensure that justice is done."

"I am also investigating Mr. Rafferty's murder, which I believe is connected to that of your son."

"Yes, it is most unfortunate what happened to Mr. Rafferty, especially as I hired him, but then again he knew the risks of his occupation. Now, what is it you want from me?"

"I have a few questions about your son. Do you know if he was involved in any manner with Margaret O'Donnell, the mayor's daughter?"

"I am not aware of that, but I suppose it is possible."

"What can you tell me about her?"

"I did not know her personally, but she had a reputation as being a fast girl."

"In what way?"

"Oh, come now, Mr. Holmes, you know perfectly well what I mean. From what I have been told, the girl was a little hussy who slept around, drank and smoked, and left nothing but trouble in her wake."

"All right, then I will be direct. Do you know if your son might have impregnated her?"

"I have no such knowledge. However, it would hardly be surprising if she found herself in that condition. I am not in the business of passing on rumors, Mr. Holmes, but I can tell you I have heard on good authority she was sent to the House of the Good Shepherd."

"What sort of place is that?"

"It's a school and convent run by nuns, who take in troubled and in some cases pregnant girls sent there by their families or the courts. Apparently, Margaret was there for a time last year."

"When was that?"

"I believe it was shortly before she died in early December."

"Her death at such a young age must have come as quite a shock to her family and friends. What did she die of?"

"I really cannot say. No one seems to want to talk about it, and in any case it is none of my business. Now, do you have anything useful to ask of me?" she said with some asperity.

"I do not ask useless questions," Holmes retorted, "but I sometimes receive useless answers. Now, I believe you indicated to Mr. Rafferty that you knew little or nothing of your son's activities as an extortionist, is that correct?"

"Yes. If Danny was engaged in any criminal acts, which have yet to be proven, he hardly would have confided them to me."

"But you had suspicions, did you not?"

"Perhaps, but that is all."

"You also told Mr. Rafferty you went to your son's apartment after his death and found it had been ransacked by the police. You stated you made a thorough search but found no documents or photographs that could have been used for purposes of blackmail."

"Yes, there was nothing like that."

"Had you ever been to his apartment before then?"

"No, I was not invited."

"I find it interesting he had a darkroom in the apartment. Did he ever show you any of his work?"

"No, he did not. Now, I have an appointment to keep, Mr. Holmes, so please move along, if you would. I do not have all the time in the world."

"No one does," Holmes said, and then began quizzing Mrs. St.

Aubin about the remarkable letter her son had written a month before his murder. When Holmes asked about the suspects named in the letter, Mrs. St. Aubin at first merely repeated what she had told Rafferty. However, by means of skillful questioning Holmes was able to tease out a few new morsels regarding Bertram Abbey.

"I understand your son attended Mr. Abbey's salons. Did he do so quite frequently?"

"I don't really know."

"Did you ever go to one, perhaps out of mere curiosity?"

"Yes, and it was a waste of time. There was a lot of talk about love and death and other pointless musings."

Holmes now asked a surprising question. "Were you by chance the only woman at the salon that day?"

"Why do you ask? Of what interest could that be?"

"I ask because it may be important. Please answer the question."

"Very well. Yes, I was the only woman there. Otherwise it was mostly young men who seemed quite enchanted with Mr. Abbey's nonsense."

"And was your son enchanted?"

"He wasn't there that day, so I couldn't tell you."

I now began to see the ultimate destination of Holmes's inquiry, and I wondered how Mrs. St. Aubin would respond to what was certain to be an indelicate question.

Holmes forged ahead until the dreaded query came: "Do you have any reason to believe, Mrs. St. Aubin, that your son was perhaps more interested in men than women?"

Her reaction was swift and fierce. "That is ridiculous. How dare you make such a suggestion!" She hung up before Holmes could respond.

"I appear to have made a new enemy," Holmes said, "but that is the problem with the truth, Watson. Sometimes it is the one thing people cannot abide."

"So you think St. Aubin did indeed have an attraction to other men?"

"I have my doubts. I am more inclined to think that sex was for him simply another weapon to be used for purposes of blackmail. But perhaps Mr. Abbey will be able to enlighten us on this matter when the time comes."

AT ELEVEN, THOMAS JOINED US for a late breakfast of pancakes, sausages, and eggs in the Ryan's café. Holmes picked at his meal, which consisted of two poached eggs and little else, while filling Thomas in on our conversations with Declan Morrissey, Donald Hobbs, and Mrs. St. Aubin. Thomas took particular interest in what we had learned from Hobbs about Bertram Abbey. "I can't believe it's just a coincidence he was right here the night Shad was murdered."

"I agree. However, Detective Grimshaw has my immediate attention. He is the only one of the five suspects in Mr. St. Aubin's death, and therefore Mr. Rafferty's as well, who had easy access to a master key to this hotel. He must therefore be regarded as a prime suspect, whether acting on his own or at someone else's behest. We will speak to him tomorrow, if possible, and see what he has to tell us."

"It won't be much," Thomas said. "He'll never admit to anything."

"I do not expect him to. But the lies men tell often provide the best avenue to the truth, and I am most curious to hear what the detective will have to say. In the meantime, there is also the question of how Margaret O'Donnell fits into the puzzle. Even the exceptionally well-informed Mr. Morrissey does not know the circumstances of her death."

"The death certificate must have been filed with the county recorder by now," Thomas noted.

"Good. Watson intends to look for it tomorrow."

"If for some reason it's not there, we must demand the truth from her father," I said.

"Yes, but will he tell us the truth? The cause of his daughter's death remains a closely held secret, and he is the person who slammed the door shut and locked it in order to hide what occurred. His son, on the other hand, seems eager to open it."

"Are you certain he sent that telegram, Holmes?"

"I do not know who else it could be from. But since it was sent from Chicago, there is a chance he is still there. Do you remember Sergeant Logan of the Chicago police? We met him during my speaking engagement there."

"Of course. He seemed like a stout fellow."

"So he did. He is in receipt of the telegram I sent a few days ago. If anyone can track down Paul O'Donnell in Chicago, he can."

11

The Policeman

It was said of Jackson Grimshaw that he came out of the cradle hard as granite and ready for a fight. He was born to a laundress and her drunken, no-account husband in the Badlands, an impoverished corner of the city just north of downtown. Regarded as St. Paul's chief incubator of crime, the Badlands occupied the slopes of a steep hill incised with crooked dirt streets that wound past a ramshackle collection of hand-built cottages, most of which had never seen a coat of paint. There were few lamps along the narrow, winding streets, and after dark no respectable man or woman would think of venturing out into such a dangerous place.

Grimshaw fought his way out of the Badlands. The youngest of five children, he was big and muscular even as a boy, and by age ten he'd taken charge of his own gang of petty thieves, who learned to fear his fists and fierce temper. His mother died when he was eleven, and an older sister took charge of the family, since their father was rarely around. When he did appear, he was drunk and beat the children for no other reason than he seemed to enjoy it. But Grimshaw, known as Big Jack to his gang, grew stronger by the year, and on his fourteenth birthday he knocked his father out cold in a fight. When the old man woke up, Grimshaw told him to leave and promised to kill him if he ever came back. He didn't and died a few years later in a brawl in one of the dives down on Washington Street.

By age sixteen, Grimshaw was the family breadwinner, operating a successful burglary ring that hit dozens of homes and businesses around the city. Clever and streetwise, he also became his own fence, selling off the gang's loot to a variety of disreputable customers. He was arrested several times on suspicion of one crime or another, but the police could never make the charges stick, largely because Grimshaw's fellow hoodlums knew that testifying against him would be an extremely unwise thing to do.

Grimshaw seemed destined to pursue a life of crime for years to come until an incident two days before his twenty-first birthday caused him to reconsider. He'd set up burglary with a man named Joe Corcoran, who was a skilled safecracker. Corcoran was also known to be short-tempered and volatile. The burglary, at a Summit Avenue mansion, produced a windfall in the form of five thousand dollars in cash discovered in a safe.

When the time came to split the proceeds at Corcoran's apartment, he demanded four thousand for his work, since he had opened the safe. Grimshaw insisted on a fifty-fifty split, as had been agreed on in advance. An argument ensued, during which Grimshaw knocked Corcoran to the floor. As Grimshaw turned to leave with his share of the proceeds, Corcoran got to his feet, drew out a pistol, and fired point-blank at the back of Grimshaw's head. All Grimshaw heard was the click of the trigger.

The misfire saved Grimshaw's life and cost Corcoran his. Grimshaw spun around, grabbed the gun, and used it to beat Corcoran over the head until he was senseless. Soon thereafter, he stopped breathing. Grimshaw took the remaining twenty-five hundred dollars and left. Since it was the first time he'd worked with Corcoran, Grimshaw never became a suspect in the perfunctory police investigation that followed.

But the incident left Grimshaw badly shaken and led him to reassess his life and his ambitions. He was making decent money and lived in a first-class apartment building, yet he also realized that his criminal career had become a walk on a wavering tightrope. The police were nosing around, members of his own gang were growing restive and loose-lipped, and unpredictable characters like

Corcoran would always pose a threat. Grimshaw came to the conclusion he would either end up dead or in prison unless he found a better way to make a living.

Grimshaw had come to know, and pay off, numerous policemen over the years. The cops in his view were much like he was, except that when they beat somebody it wasn't considered a crime. So it was that he began to think a career in law enforcement, which offered manifold opportunities for graft, might serve him better than his precarious occupation as a criminal. Despite his shady past, Grimshaw had no trouble signing on with the force, especially after he paid a generous "recruiting fee" to a police captain of his acquaintance.

He began as a patrolman, a job that offered paltry wages. However, Grimshaw earned a good supplemental income from shopkeepers who paid him by the month to shovel out the criminal muck that bedeviled them. His ability to instill fear in the low criminal classes became legendary, and it was remarked that any precinct he patrolled was as clean of mischief as Eden itself before the snake appeared. At age twenty-seven Grimshaw became the youngest man in the department's history to be promoted to the rank of detective. In this job, too, he excelled, for he knew the workings of crime as well as any criminal. He also knew how to extract information from a recalcitrant suspect without leaving any marks of his handiwork.

Always out for the main chance, Grimshaw rapidly mastered the politics of both the department and city hall, and over time he found ways to make himself useful to those in power. His initial work along these lines occurred when an alderman who spoke eloquently of the need for public decency was robbed and beaten in a notorious brothel. Grimshaw stepped in to cover up the affair even as he hunted down the criminals, retrieved the stolen goods, and suggested in the strongest possible terms that the miscreants leave St. Paul for good. The alderman was most grateful, bestowing on Grimshaw a token of his appreciation in the form of two one-hundred-dollar bills. Before long, Grimshaw was called on to handle other imbroglios threatening men of high standing, and in each case his labors were amply rewarded.

He also cultivated the local press by feeding reporters a steady diet of sensational crime news while skillfully suppressing any stories that might embarrass his powerful overlords at city hall. Reporters, he knew, were lazy by nature but needed constant fuel to stoke their editors' insatiable demand for copy. Grimshaw became so expert at this work that local crime reporters came to rely on him for news, with the understanding that publishing the wrong kind of story would result in a permanent Siberian exile from his good graces.

Grimshaw was quickly elevated to chief of detectives, and in this capacity his influence—and wealth—grew substantially. The handsome emoluments of his work allowed him to purchase a fine house just off Summit Avenue, and within a year he had also acquired a wife. A timid bird of a woman attentive to his every command, she bore him two sons who would later remember their childhoods as more terrifying than anything else. Yet Grimshaw liked to keep up appearances, and he and his cowering family were often seen at Sunday mass at the cathedral. Afterwards, Grimshaw liked to stop and chat with Monsignor Denis, on the theory that in St. Paul it never hurt to look like a good Catholic.

As part of his promotion to chief of detectives, Grimshaw was awarded his own office at city hall. The official explanation was that he had been assigned to serve as the mayor's bodyguard, although he was in fact rarely seen with O'Donnell. A better explanation for Grimshaw's presence in city hall was that the mayor wished to keep him close at hand, since the detective knew a great many secrets. Exactly how the mayor's daughter had died was among these secrets. But there were others as well, involving Meeks, Abbey, and even Monsignor Denis. St. Aubin's supposed suicide, it was hoped, would bury all of these secrets for good.

As 1927 drew to a close, Grimshaw had every reason to believe his career offered boundless potential. He had set his sights on becoming chief of police and was assured by his masters at city hall that the job would be his one day. There was only one problem, and it had a name: Rafferty. Grimshaw had created what he thought was a perfect cover-up of St. Aubin's death until that old man began sniffing around.

GRIMSHAW WAS IRRITATED by Rafferty's meddling in the St. Aubin case. He knew of the old man's reputation as a first-rate detective. He also knew Rafferty couldn't be intimidated. But what would be the best way to keep him at bay? A week or so after St. Aubin's death, Grimshaw picked up his phone and placed a call. It was time to seek some advice.

"Are you alone?" he asked when a man answered.

"Yes, we can talk freely. What's going on?"

Grimshaw described his interview with Rafferty and said, "The old man thinks he's onto something, but I don't know if he'll be a problem. He's feeble, for one thing, and he ain't got a shred of proof linking you or me to this business."

"And we must keep it that way. You have to be especially careful. You got rid of the gun, didn't you?"

"Sure. They'll have to dredge the Mississippi to find it."

"And what about that fellow who had the gun? Delray, wasn't that his name?"

"Yeah, and he's as gone as the gun."

"Good. With luck, we have Rafferty boxed out. But don't underestimate him. He's clever and he knows this city as well as anyone alive. He has sources everywhere and he'll use them. And, of course, there's still one big loose end."

"St. Aubin's blackmail stuff. I know. But I don't see why you should worry. The photos we found didn't have nothing to do with you."

"True, but whatever documents he managed to collect might tell a different story. Are you absolutely sure there were no files in his apartment?"

"Sure I'm sure. We know how to toss a place. Didn't find a safety deposit key either, or any key that might go with a locker. Maybe he just kept everything in his head."

"Unlikely. A blackmailer needs documents. We know he had photos, so he must have had other little goodies squirreled away somewhere. Have you checked with his friends? Could he have left the stuff with one of them?"

"We've been asking around, but it don't seem like he had many friends. He was kind of a loner. But we'll keep looking."

"You do that. By the way, who's Rafferty working for? He must have a client. Otherwise, why would he bother to get involved?"

"Yeah, that makes sense. But I don't know who hired him."

"My guess is that it was St. Aubin's mother, and we can't afford to take her lightly. Her pocketbook is deep and she has influence at city hall. If she hired Rafferty, it must be because she doesn't believe her son killed himself. Remind me what she said when you talked with her."

"She questioned the suicide story right away and said it couldn't be true."

"Did she say why?"

"She just claimed he wasn't the kind of person who'd kill himself, but people say that about suicides all the time."

"Yet now she's gone out and hired Rafferty, and that tells me she has more than vague suspicions. I wonder what she knows."

"Maybe that rotten son of hers told her the whole story, about his blackmailing and all of that."

"Maybe, but somehow I doubt it. In any case, we have an ace in the hole and we can use it if we have to. Where are you keeping St. Aubin's stash of photos?"

"Don't worry, they're safe with me."

"Make sure they are. You never know when they might prove useful. I think we're in good shape overall, but keep an eye on Rafferty. If he gets too close to the truth, you'll have to deal with him."

"It will be my pleasure," Grimshaw said.

After he hung up, Grimshaw felt everything was under control. True, he'd told one lie to the man on the phone. That antique Thunderer revolver wasn't in the Mississippi. It was in a safe at Grimshaw's home, along with other old weapons he collected. The Thunderer was a real rarity and with a little repair work to the stock it could be sold, once the St. Aubin case was forgotten, for a handsome price.

Still, it had been a piece of bad luck that Rafferty found the body. He was too smart to be fooled by the suicide story. But what could he do other than whine to the newspapers? Not much, Grimshaw thought. Then, speak of the devil, Rafferty showed up a few days after Christmas to ask some tough new questions. Dealing with him, it seemed, was going to be much harder than Grimshaw thought.

12

"You Are Sniffing at the Clouds"

Shadwell Rafferty knew as well as anyone that ferreting out the truth in St. Paul, especially in matters involving city hall, was never an easy proposition. The city's notoriously tangled streets reflected its culture, which followed old tribal lines all but indecipherable to outsiders. Rafferty had grown up in Boston, another place fabled for its crooked streets and inscrutable politics, and so he'd found himself right at home in St. Paul, where there was a city within a city, a hidden realm of crossings and connections. Rafferty intended to venture into these secret byways as he investigated Daniel St. Aubin's murder.

Rafferty made plans to interrogate all five of the chief suspects, beginning with Grimshaw. Whether on his own or at another's bidding, the detective had orchestrated a classic police cover-up after St. Aubin's demise, or so Rafferty believed. But he knew Grimshaw would never reveal a shred of the truth unless somehow forced into a corner, and to do that Rafferty would have to come armed with incriminating information when he spoke to the detective.

There was one man, Rafferty thought, who just might have such information. His name was Louis Peltier and he was the police department's captain of patrol. Peltier was a descendant of one of the old French Canadian families who'd founded St. Paul, and the city and its secrets were deep in his blood. More important, he was known to detest Grimshaw, whose ugly temperament and political maneuverings had endeared him to very few of his fellow officers.

Two days after Christmas Rafferty phoned Peltier and suggested they meet for lunch at the Carling Café, a popular downtown eatery. Peltier readily agreed. He and Rafferty were old friends, going back to the time fifteen years earlier when they'd worked together to capture the infamous West End rapist, who had assaulted a dozen women before he was finally revealed to be a neighborhood druggist with a wife and three children.

Peltier was waiting when Rafferty arrived at the café, which was laid out in the manner of a Gothic hall, complete with a vaulted plaster ceiling supported by fake hammer beams. Waitresses in rustic outfits apparently inspired by an old Dutch painting moved efficiently among diners seated in wide, high-backed booths along the walls. Peltier was in one of the booths, munching on a sesame seed breadstick, and rose to greet Rafferty.

"Well, Shad, I see you are moving a bit slowly these days," he said as Rafferty settled into the booth after much maneuvering.

"I have officially become a snail," Rafferty said, "albeit a very large one. But you still look young and nimble, Louie. Tell me your secret so I can take it happily to the grave."

"Never have seconds and always stay active," Peltier said with a smile. A slender, compact man in his sixties, Peltier appeared to have heeded his own counsel, for he looked much younger than his years. He sported a fine thatch of brownish white hair and a carefully tended Vandyke beard, and his blue eyes were lively.

"Ah, if only I had followed that advice, I might not be the outsized wreck you see before you," Rafferty said. "Then again, a life without seconds. . . . Well, it would not have suited a man of my appetites."

They chatted for a time about the old days, ordered beer and sandwiches, and finally got down to business.

"I am investigating the death of Danny St. Aubin," Rafferty said, "and I have reason to suspect Jackson Grimshaw is connected to it."

"Is that so? What do you suspect?"

"That Grimshaw is covering up the young man's murder and may even have had a part in it."

"The coroner, if I'm not mistaken, has ruled it a suicide."

"The coroner, I am reliably informed, also believes the Pope is a Lutheran. Come now, Louie, this whole business with St. Aubin is emitting a foul odor, and you and I both know it. Remember, I found his body and I saw two men running from the scene. The suicide was staged, the gun that killed him put in his hand. I am sure of it. You know how things are done here, Louie. Grimshaw works for the big men at city hall. Someone must have ordered a cover-up. The question is why."

Two beef sandwiches with all the trimmings arrived, and when the waitress left, Peltier said, "Officially, I have no involvement in the St. Aubin case. Officially, I know nothing. Officially, I have heard nothing. Do you agree?"

"I do. You are a veritable temple of ignorance, as far as I can tell."

In Rafferty's experience, Peltier had always been a man of few but well-chosen words and he was now. "I assume you know St. Aubin was suspected of being a very nasty character," Peltier said.

"Yes, I have heard talk he was a blackmailer but I have few details. Tell me more, if you would."

"Word has it St. Aubin was very proficient in that line of work and made a good living at it. Apparently, he hit up some well-known citizens who'd been indiscreet in one way or another. Nothing was ever proved against him because his marks didn't want to talk. Even so, if you're a blackmailer, you have lots of enemies."

"Who was he supposedly extorting money from?"

"Don't know. His victims, as I said, had good reasons to keep their traps shut. But if somebody got tired of paying up, maybe they decided to take care of the problem once and for all."

"It has been mentioned to me that no less a figure than the

mayor of this city may have been involved with St. Aubin," said Rafferty.

"I have nothing to say about the mayor."

"Ah, you are a wise man, Louie. Now, I assume, Grimshaw knows St. Aubin was a blackmailer."

"I do not see how he couldn't."

"Was Big Jack investigating the young man in that regard?"

"Possibly."

"So you don't know for sure?"

"I can't say for sure."

"Hah, there's a difference, isn't there? I understand your reticence, Louie. Big teeth are chomping around the city and a man doesn't want to get caught in them."

"No, a man does not," Peltier said with a grin.

"All right, I do not wish to see you masticated and spit out on the street, so I will pursue the point no further. Now, what else can you tell me about St. Aubin's death?"

"Three things. First, there's the gun that killed him. It's an old .41 caliber Colt revolver called a Thunderer. Second, word is that Grimshaw knows the gun very well because he took it off a burglar some time ago and never turned it into the property room. Third, the burglar's name is Frank Delray. You might want to speak to him, if you can find him."

"Any idea where he might be?"

Peltier shrugged. "As I said, I'm not on the case."

"True enough," Rafferty said, picking up half of his sandwich. "Well then, let's eat. I'm hungry."

BACK IN HIS APARTMENT after lunch, Rafferty considered his next step. Peltier had confirmed Declan Morrissey's claim that St. Aubin was a blackmailer. But if the police were covering up the murder and the blackmailing that had led to it, Rafferty faced a huge challenge in trying to solve the case. The fact that one of the chief suspects, Jackson Grimshaw, was also the police officer in charge of investigating St. Aubin's murder made matters doubly difficult. How could Rafferty hope to break open the case with so many forces arrayed against him and with time running out on his own clock? Yet he knew he couldn't quit. The case absorbed him, and the more he thought about it the less time he spent contemplating the ultimate mystery of his impending extinction.

Rafferty decided to put the blackmail angle on hold for a while and instead dig into the more palpable matter of the revolver found by St. Aubin's body. That evening, after enjoying an afternoon nap, Rafferty phoned Declan Morrissey. Did he know of a burglar named Frank Delray and where he might be found? The answer came an hour later. Delray's last known address was on Central Terrace, near the State Capitol.

THE NEXT MORNING Rafferty took a taxi up to the address Morrissey had provided and told the driver to wait for him. Despite its elegant-sounding name and its location just blocks from the white marble splendor of the capitol, Central Terrace was hardly a tony precinct. The short street offered a seedy collection of old, brick rowhouses and sagging Victorian homes subdivided into cheap sleeping rooms. Numerous vacant lots adorned with piles of trash and clumps of dirty snow did not enhance the ambience. Frank Delray's residence formed the central unit of a decrepit brick rowhouse free from all traces of architectural ambition. A heavy wooden door, its broken window infilled with cardboard, served as the entrance to the Delray homestead, and Rafferty gave it a good hard knock.

A woman—stout, fortyish, with a broad lumpy face and close-set brown eyes—answered, opening the door halfway and eyeing Rafferty as she might a salesman peddling worthless trinkets.

"Who are you?" she demanded.

"My name is Rafferty and I am wondering if Frank Delray might be at home."

The woman snorted with the gusto of a horse. "Fat chance of that. I haven't seen him in days. What do you want with him, anyway?"

"I just had a few questions I wished to ask," Rafferty said, reaching into his coat pocket and extracting a ten-dollar bill. "But perhaps you could help. I'd gladly pay for your time. May I come in?"

The woman, who was wearing a tattered red shift and nothing underneath by the look of it, examined the bill and said, "My time is very valuable, you know."

Rafferty found another ten-spot in his pocket. "I'm sure it is. Would this help?"

"All right, come in, but first the money."

Rafferty handed over the two bills and stepped inside. The apartment was just as he imagined it would be—cracked plaster walls, rotting pine floors, threadbare furnishings, and no evidence that either of its occupants believed in the virtue of good housekeeping.

Rafferty brushed aside several items of clothing and found a seat on a stained brown sofa. The woman sat across from him. "Like I said, Frank's gone," she offered. "So what do you want?"

"I take it I have the pleasure of speaking to Mrs. Delray," Rafferty said.

"Yeah, I'm the lucky lady who married the swine, and look what it got me. The lap of luxury, as they say. Now, get to the point, will you? I ain't got all day."

In fact, all day seemed to be the extent of what she had, but Rafferty didn't press the point. He'd come to ask about the revolver, but he was intrigued to learn that Delray had recently vanished.

"You can begin by telling me what happened to your husband. You say he's gone. When did he leave?"

"Monday before last. Only he didn't exactly leave. A couple of coppers came to the door and took him away. Said they needed to question him about something or other. That's the last I seen of him."

"Is he in jail?"

"No, I checked, don't ask me why. But he's not there. I guess he just decided to take a hike and leave me here to fend for myself. Well, good riddance, I say. He never did nothing for me except cause trouble."

"He made his living as a burglar, is that right?"

"I wouldn't know. I'm an honest woman."

"Yes, I'm sure you are. Now, I have a few more questions, and they're very important. So important I might be persuaded to part with another twenty dollars if you can answer them."

The prospect of doubling her haul clearly intrigued Mrs. Delray, who leaned forward as though eager to smell the cash Rafferty was withdrawing from his pocket. "Okay, ask."

"Your husband once owned an old revolver. I'm sure you must have seen it. I would like you to describe it to me."

She paused, apparently unsure whether an answer might incriminate her in some wrongdoing. Still, the money beckoned.

"Maybe I seen it, but I never touched it. I don't like guns."

"I understand. When might you have seen it?"

"It was a while ago."

"Ah, Mrs. Delray, I'm sure you can be more precise than that. I'd hate to see that twenty dollars stay in my pocket, where it will do you no good."

Mrs. Delray closed her eyes, apparently in hopes of stimulating her memory. After a few seconds, she said, "Come to think of it, I'm pretty sure it was in October around the time of my birthday, which he forgot about like he always does, until I reminded him. Anyways, he was playing around with the gun and said maybe he'd give it to me as a present. As if I'd want it."

"Do you know where he got it?"

"No."

"All right, so you saw the gun. What did it look like? Did it have a long barrel or a short barrel?"

"It was short."

"Two or three inches?"

"That's right."

"What color was it?"

"Silver."

So far so good, Rafferty thought. The gun he'd seen by Danny St. Aubin's body was nickel-plated with a short barrel. "What about the grip, the handle where the gun is held in the hand? What was it made of?"

"Some sort of wood, I think."

Now came the key question. "Did you notice anything in particular about the grip? Was it in perfect shape or was it perhaps damaged in some way?"

Mrs. Delray thought hard, twenty dollars hanging in the balance. "There was a small corner missing," she finally said.

"A corner of the wood?"

"Yes, on the lower part."

"Lower left or lower right?"

Another moment's thought. "Lower left."

Rafferty exhaled a deep breath. There could be no doubt now that the gun Jackson Grimshaw had supposedly confiscated from Frank Delray and the gun that had killed Daniel St. Aubin were one and the same.

"What happened to the gun?" Rafferty asked.

"The cops took it."

"How do you know that?"

"Frank told me. A couple of dicks came here to ask him about something or other and they found the gun. I wasn't here, or I would've told them to go to hell. I don't like the cops. They're the biggest criminals in town, if you ask me."

"Many would agree with you, Mrs. Delray. When did the police take your husband in for questioning and confiscate the gun?"

"Right around the first of November. I was visiting my sister up in Duluth for a couple of days. She's got a nice house, not a dump like this. When I got back, Frank was still hopping mad about the cops taking the gun. I guess he thought he could have sold it for good money."

"Did he identify the police officers who took it?"

"I think I did hear a name but I can't remember."

"Was it Grimshaw?"

"Could have been, but maybe if you—"

"No, the well has run dry," Rafferty said, lifting himself up from the sofa. He handed Mrs. Delray the additional twenty dollars he'd promised but no more. "I thank you for your help. I can show myself out."

"Sure," she said, adding, "You never said why you're interested in Frank and that gun."

"I have my reasons, but the less you know about this business, the better off you are. However, if I do happen to locate your husband, I'll let you know."

"Don't bother," she said. "If he's dead and buried, I'll be fine."

As he walked out the door, Rafferty suspected her wish might already have been granted. But even if Delray was dead, Rafferty thought the gun might still have a story to tell. The police, presumably in the person of Jackson Grimshaw, had confiscated the revolver less than two months before St. Aubin was killed with it. Where had it been kept during that time? Rafferty didn't know, but if he could somehow prove it was in Grimshaw's possession, then the police claim that St. Aubin committed suicide would come undone.

BACK IN THE TAXI Rafferty instructed the driver to drop him off at police headquarters and once again wait. The department, which was officially known as the Bureau of Police even though nobody called it that, occupied a pair of nondescript brick buildings on Third Street a few blocks from city hall. Rafferty stepped into the dingy lobby, which offered battleship-gray paint, dark oak benches scuffed by years of hard use, and dirty windows that admitted light with great reluctance. A sense of melancholy and decay suffused the room, as though all the crimes reported within its walls had settled over everything like toxic dust. The desk sergeant, who had the weary eyes of an old bloodhound and who viewed Rafferty and the entire world suspiciously, asked what he wanted.

"The property room," Rafferty said.

"That's off-limits to the general public," the sergeant said before doing a slow double take. "Wait a minute, ain't you that Rafferty fellow I seen in the newspapers?"

"In the flesh."

"You're looking into that St. Aubin business, right?"

"That I am. I've been hired to investigate it, which is why I need to look at some evidence in the property room."

"All right, it's in the basement. But be quick about it. You ain't supposed to be down there."

"I won't be long," Rafferty said. The building had no elevator, so Rafferty had to make his way down a long set of steps, an arduous process. His hips were aching badly by the time he reached the property room, which was manned by a white-haired cop who'd been assigned the job because he was too old to work the streets. His name was Mike McMorrow, and Rafferty had met him a few times before.

"Mike, it's been a while, and as I remember the last time I saw you was back when you were patrolling a beat over at Seven Corners."

"Thank God those days are over. At least it's warm in here year-round. I imagine you're looking for something."

"I'd like to see that old revolver Danny St. Aubin supposedly shot himself with. I'm investigating the case as a private matter."

"Sorry, I can't show it to you," McMorrow said.

"Why is that?" Rafferty asked, thinking he was about to be hit up for a bribe.

"Because it ain't here."

"It wasn't turned in as evidence?"

"Nope."

"Where is it then?"

McMorrow shrugged. "Don't ask me. All I know is I ain't seen it."

"What about any other evidence in the case?"

"Same story. Nothing got turned in here."

"Kind of strange, don't you think?"

"I've been a cop for thirty years," McMorrow said. "Nothing seems strange to me no more."

When Rafferty returned to his taxi, he told the driver to take him to the county jail. Rafferty's business there was brief. Then he made his last stop of the day, at city hall.

JACKSON GRIMSHAW'S OFFICE was on the second floor of the city hall and county courthouse, a grimy old Victorian monument soon to be replaced by a new Art Deco building nearby. Grimshaw wasn't in his office when Rafferty arrived, but a passing secretary in the hallway said he'd be back shortly. Rafferty planted himself on a creaking wooden chair across from Grimshaw's desk, thinking how odd it was that the detective had a private office at city hall. No one else in the police department, not even the chief, enjoyed that privilege, as far as Rafferty knew. Grimshaw clearly was a special case.

"What do you want?" Grimshaw asked sharply when he walked in and saw Rafferty.

"Why, it is the pleasure of your company I seek, Big Jack, along with a little information."

"I got no time for that. Feel free to leave. I will not stop you."

"I think I'll stay a while," Rafferty said, "for there are some peculiar things we need to discuss regarding the death of Danny St. Aubin."

"There ain't nothing to discuss. It's an open-and-shut case of suicide."

"Ah, I doubt that very much. The suicide story you're peddling doesn't make sense. Take that .41 caliber revolver you say Danny used to shoot himself. A highly unusual weapon, wouldn't you agree? I can't recall ever seeing another Thunderer of that type in all my years. It's a wonder how Danny happened to possess such an antique. Have you learned how he obtained it?"

"What the hell difference does that make? There are old revolvers to be found at every pawn shop in the city."

"True, but Danny wasn't poor. If he felt need of a weapon, he could have purchased a much better one. No, you and I both know where that revolver came from. You liberated it from the well-known burglar Frank Delray and then tucked it away just in case you'd find a use for it someday, which you did."

"You are hallucinating, Rafferty. You should see a doctor."

"Well, I am most grateful for the medical advice, and yet the fact is, you were seen with that very same revolver not long before Danny was killed. From what I hear, you even mentioned what a fine old weapon it was. Perhaps you are the one who should consult a doctor, Big Jack, since your memory seems to be failing you."

Rafferty in fact hadn't talked to anyone who saw Grimshaw with the gun, but he tossed out the false claim in hopes it would produce a telling reaction. It did.

"No one saw me with that revolver," Grimshaw shot back. "You can't prove a thing."

An interesting answer, Rafferty thought, because Grimshaw didn't deny having the gun, only that he hadn't been seen with it.

"I've heard more convincing denials than that," Rafferty said, "but the truth will come out. It always does. By the way, where's the revolver now? It should be under lock and key in the police property room, shouldn't it? Yet it's not there for some reason. I imagine it's stirring up the bottom of the Mississippi as we speak, attended by curious catfish."

Grimshaw's eyes narrowed and he sat up slightly in his chair. "I see you're looking for trouble, and you'll get it if you ain't careful."

"And I will be ready for it if it comes, Big Jack. Now, speaking of things that seem to have gone missing, I'm wondering what happened to those photos you confiscated from Danny's apartment. I hear they're very incriminating. Anybody we know caught in embarrassing circumstances?"

Rafferty, who had no idea what photos, if any, St. Aubin had in his darkroom, was once again tossing out bait in hopes Grimshaw would bite.

"You're dreaming again. We didn't find no pictures."

"Really? Danny was apparently quite the photographer and yet you didn't find a single example of his work? Somebody got their hands on the photos. Sure it wasn't you and your boys?"

"Yeah, I'm sure. Maybe the janitor got them. Why don't you file a report? Our burglary squad will give it their full attention."

"No doubt. But here's what I'm thinking. You gathered up those photos to protect certain influential people. People Danny was blackmailing. They're probably what got him murdered."

"You are sniffing at the clouds," Grimshaw said, "and all you have is vapor."

"It's not vapor, Big Jack. What I'm sniffing at has a foul odor. It reeks of murder and corruption and cover-up, and you're not going to get away with it. The bills will come due in one way or another. Incidentally, where is Frank Delray these days? I understand he was arrested recently and yet no one seems to know where he is."

"I don't concern myself with the likes of Delray. Make inquiries at the jail if you are looking for him."

"I have. The jail has no record he was booked."

"Maybe he's on vacation in sunny Florida."

"Or perhaps he's in a much colder, darker place. Perhaps you even put him there."

"I have done nothing with Delray, and you cannot prove otherwise."

"You are probably right, and in any case Delray means nothing to you. But our esteemed Mayor O'Donnell is a different story. You're his man and you do his dirty work, as everyone knows. And Danny St. Aubin was a problem for the mayor, wasn't he? A big enough problem that you had to teach him a little lesson."

"You should be writing dime novels, Rafferty, as you seem to like inventing things."

"I didn't invent the witness who saw you close by Danny the night he was murdered. Did you do the deed yourself, Big Jack, as favor to your masters?"

Grimshaw stood up and pounded a fist on his desk with such force that a tray of paper tumbled to the floor. "Do not push your luck, Rafferty, or you will regret it. Now, for the last time, get out of my office and don't come back."

Rafferty got to his feet and said, "I know the kind of man you are, Big Jack, and I know what you have done. It is only a matter of time before the game is up for you."

"You're the one running out of time," Grimshaw shouted as Rafferty went out the door.

LATER THAT DAY, ensconced in his study with a glass of lager produced by Hamm's supposedly retired brewmaster, Rafferty typed up accounts of his interviews with Mrs. Delray and Grimshaw. In a day or two, he'd deposit the carbon copies in his safe-deposit box. He'd never before taken such extreme precautions with his notes, but something told him he should do so now. A kind of low rumble was coursing through his bones and he knew what it foretold. If he did die soon, his notes would be vulnerable to theft, by the police if no one else. Better to be safe, he thought and put his trust in the First National Bank.

13

"The Mystery Deepens"

[From "Murder in St. Paul"]

Holmes was up unusually early on Monday, hounding me awake and then hovering nearby like an impatient genie while I dressed.

"I have been thinking a great deal about Daniel St. Aubin," he announced. "Mr. Rafferty's investigation leaves little doubt that the young man was St. Paul's very own version of Charles Augustus Milverton."

The mere mention of Milverton—"the king of blackmailers," as Holmes once called him—brought back many memories of a case that had been one of the most singular of Holmes's career.

"And I take it you believe that St. Aubin, like Milverton, met his death at the hands of one of his victims."

"It would seem so. But which victim pulled the trigger or hired someone to do the deed? I shall be curious to see what that great police detective Jackson Grimshaw has to say about it. And if you would be so kind, Watson, as to finish your needlessly prolonged dressing ritual, we shall speak with Grimshaw later this morning."

"It is not a ritual," I protested, searching for a suitable tie to go with my jacket and shirt. "But I see no reason why I should go wandering about like some disheveled bohemian."

"I doubt you will ever be mistaken as such. But while you complete your elaborate costume, here is a question for you: what do you think about the revolver that was found next to Mr. St. Aubin's body?"

"Well, we know it once belonged to that burglar. What was his name?"

"Delray. Frank Delray. We also know Mr. Delray may well be dead and that the weapon itself has disappeared."

"Rafferty thought it was at the bottom of the river, as I recall."

"Yes, and for once Mr. Rafferty may have been wrong."

"Why do you say that?"

"While you were otherwise occupied yesterday, I called Louis Peltier, Mr. Rafferty's old friend on the police force. We talked at some length, mostly about Jackson Grimshaw."

"I see. And what did you learn?"

"Several things, the most interesting of which is that Detective Grimshaw is a well-known gun collector."

"And you think—"

"That Grimshaw may have kept the revolver to add to his collection? It is a fair possibility. It would be a foolish mistake on his part, and yet I have found that collectors tend to be obsessed about what they collect. If the detective is such a person, then we may have an opportunity to retrieve the weapon. In any event, we shall have to learn more, and I think Mr. Morrissey at the speakeasy is just the man to help us."

"How so?"

"He knows many people, and I have no doubt professional burglars are among his acquaintances."

Holmes and I had resorted to burglary during the Milverton case and now he appeared to be contemplating another such adventure. "So am I to assume you are plotting a break-in?" I asked.

"Perhaps. I have always believed, Watson, that burglary, if properly undertaken, can sometimes be very useful."

WE HAD BEEN INFORMED that Grimshaw was usually in his office before noon, and as Holmes believed in the value of surprise, he did not phone ahead to schedule an appointment. The city hall and county courthouse where Grimshaw maintained his office took up the better part of a downtown block and was conspicuous for its buff-colored limestone walls and ungainly proportions. We found Grimshaw's office at the end of a long corridor on the second floor. It was just a few doors down from the mayor's office, a proximity Holmes remarked upon.

"It appears the mayor likes to keep Grimshaw nearby," he said, "perhaps with good reason."

The door to Grimshaw's office was ajar and we walked in unannounced. The detective was seated at his desk, cleaning a large revolver. "I am Sherlock Holmes," my friend announced, "and this is Dr. Watson."

I was struck by how spartan the office was. The walls were bereft of art and the only bookshelf was bare. I saw no personal items such as family photographs or other memorabilia. The top of Grimshaw's desk was clean save for a typewriter, a tray of paper, and a small bottle. We had entered the lair of a man who had little use for either paperwork or sentiment.

Grimshaw gazed balefully at us, slipped the pistol into a desk drawer, and said, "I know who you are." He made no effort to stand up and shake our hands, his rude manner leaving little doubt he was not pleased by our presence. Nor did he invite us to sit down, but we took seats nonetheless on a pair of wobbly wooden chairs across from his desk. Grimshaw wore a black suitcoat over a patterned gray vest, but even in such attire the power of his upper body was evident due to his broad shoulders and massive chest. His cruel gray eyes, which took us in with a hard glare, told the story of his life. He said, "If this is about Rafferty—"

"It is, and many other things," Holmes interjected. "But first let me wish you a speedy recovery from your unfortunate illness."

Grimshaw looked at Holmes with evident amazement. "I don't see how—"

"An elementary deduction, detective. That apothecary bottle on your desk contains a substance that looks very much like milk of magnesia. It is often prescribed after a bout of intestinal distress. Some bad fish perhaps?"

Grimshaw, his mouth agape, stared at Holmes in disbelief before muttering, "I don't eat fish."

"How unfortunate. Incidentally, why were your men following Mr. Rafferty before his murder?"

Holmes's abrupt change of subject caught Grimshaw off guard. He appeared ready to make an immediate reply but thought better of it. He shook his head, leaned back in his chair, and said, "I have no idea what you're talking about."

"I see. Any thoughts as to who might have been following Mr. Rafferty, if not the police?"

"I wouldn't know. Maybe it's something you'll have to investigate, being the great detective that you are."

"Perhaps so," Holmes said evenly. "Indeed, there are many other curious features about our friend's murder. Take his apartment, for example. You and your officers, I'm sure, searched it."

"So what?"

"What did you find?"

"Nothing of consequence. Just a lot of old junk."

"You found no notes of any kind relating to Mr. Rafferty's investigation into Daniel St. Aubin's death?"

"Nope."

"You are aware, are you not, that Mr. Rafferty kept such notes and that they were taken by the man who killed him?"

"How would I know that?"

"I believe Mr. George Thomas told you about the notes when you interviewed him."

"Not that I recall. Besides, you can't trust the colored. They lie all the time."

"I see. Mr. Thomas cannot be trusted simply because of his race?

You, on the other hand, would never tell a lie. What a noble fellow you must be! However, if Mr. Thomas did not mention any notes, as you claim, then why did you and your men turn Mr. Rafferty's apartment inside out? What were you looking for?"

"It was just a routine search for evidence, that's all."

"So you were merely adhering to your 'routine' by all but destroying the apartment in search of nothing in particular, is that the case? It strikes me as a rather wasteful practice, detective. Tell me this then: have you even bothered to make any inquiries about Mr. Rafferty's notes? They could well be the reason why he was murdered."

"Says you. I ain't got no evidence of that. Listen, I'm a busy man. If you—"

"I rather wonder how busy you really are," Holmes interjected. "It has been nine days since Mr. Rafferty's murder, and yet there seem to be no new developments in the case, judging from what I read in the newspapers."

"The newspapers don't know nothing. We're working on the case, but there ain't much to go on. We can't snatch leads out of thin air like those geniuses in detective stories. We figure the murder was committed by a professional hotel thief who's already moved on to another city."

"An interesting theory, detective, but unfortunately one that is not in accord with the facts of the case. For example, the knife used to kill Mr. Rafferty is a curious business. It was hardly a weapon of convenience. The knife was at the back of a shelf in a curio cabinet, and yet the killer had time enough to find it, take it with him, and then employ it to murder Mr. Rafferty. Would not a simple burglar have brought along his own weapon in case of trouble?"

"I guess you'd have to ask the burglar that, wouldn't you?"

"Yes, perhaps I would. Were there any fingerprints on the knife?"

"None that we found."

"Then I presume you would not object if I inspected the knife myself."

"It's evidence in a murder case, and we don't let it out of our sight. You can get a court order if you want to look at it, but you won't find nothing."

"How helpful you are, detective," Holmes said in a way that left no doubt he meant exactly the opposite. "Let us return to your theory that a burglar committed the crime. Why do you suppose this alleged thief made off with the ribbon from Mr. Rafferty's typewriter?"

"I don't know what you're talking about."

"I think you do. The ribbon was taken because it would show what Mr. Rafferty had most recently typed in regard to the St. Aubin case. The killer did not want that information to be known. Or perhaps you and your fellow officers confiscated the ribbon. If so, I should like to examine it."

"We ain't got no ribbon. Who's to say there even was one in the typewriter?"

"A typewriter is of no use without one, but as you seem uninterested in the matter, let us move on. How did the thief you postulate gain entrance to Mr. Rafferty's apartment?"

Grimshaw shrugged and said, "Maybe he picked the lock. Maybe he stole the room key. Maybe Rafferty left the door open. It don't matter, the way I see it. The killer got inside, Rafferty surprised him, and out came the knife."

"I doubt he picked the lock," Holmes said, "and the key to Mr. Rafferty's apartment is accounted for. Nor is it at all likely Mr. Rafferty would have left his door unlocked. On the other hand, if someone had access to one of the hotel's master keys, he could easily have slipped inside the apartment and ambushed Mr. Rafferty."

"What are you getting at?"

"Just this: I am reliably informed you took the unusual step of demanding a master key from the Ryan Hotel's front desk just two days before Mr. Rafferty's murder. What did you want? If you wished to enter a particular room, you could have obtained that room key from the desk."

"I was conducting an investigation, which ain't none of your business."

"I beg to differ, detective. I submit you sought out that master key because you wished to search Mr. Rafferty's apartment while he was at dinner. I imagine you were looking for his notes on the St. Aubin case, to see what he knew. You also could have taken a wax impression of the key and had a duplicate made, for later use."

"Well, ain't that a sweet fairy tale. I will read it to my kiddies this evening."

"Yes, I am sure they will find it fascinating. And while you are at it, you might tell the children how with such a key, you could enter the hotel from the back alley where Mr. St. Aubin died and go up to any floor on the freight elevator without being seen by the front desk clerk."

"Yeah, well, I ain't got a key like that, so what's the point? Now, you and the doctor must have better things to do than sit here and waste my time. There's nothing more I can tell you."

"We shall leave when we are ready," Holmes said, his eyes fixed on Grimshaw. "You see, I believe Mr. Rafferty was no random victim. He was targeted because he threatened to expose the truth behind the murder of Daniel St. Aubin."

Grimshaw received this statement without any visible change to his adamantine features. He said, "St. Aubin committed suicide. The case is closed."

"Is it? You are aware, of course, that Mr. St. Aubin was a blackmailer, an occupation that can be quite hazardous."

"Am I? He had no criminal record, as far as I know. As I said, he obviously killed himself. The gun was right there by his body."

"Ah yes, the gun. It has gone missing, I understand. Where do you suppose it is?"

"I couldn't say. I gave instructions to turn it in, but somebody must have filched it from the property room over at headquarters. Naturally, we're working day and night to identify the responsible party. You'll be the first to know if we find the gun."

"How kind of you. What about the fatal bullet? Was it matched to the gun with a ballistics test?"

"Why would we bother with that? It was obvious enough what happened. Or maybe you're just too much of a genius to see the obvious."

I found Grimshaw's contempt and sarcasm to be quite disgusting, but Holmes responded to the detective's provocation with nothing more than a bemused smile. He said, "The obvious, I have found, is sometimes merely a disguise to hide the truth. But I must say, things do seem to disappear in the presence of the police here, do they not? Take Mr. Rafferty's wallet, for instance. It wasn't on his body. Where did it go?"

"For such a great detective, you don't seem so smart. The killer took it."

"Yes, the murderer could have taken the wallet, but why would he have done so if it was only the money he wanted?"

"I can't say. I'll ask him when we find him."

"I am sure you will. Now, since we are on the topic of disappearances, there is also the matter of the well-known burglar Mr. Frank Delray. He once possessed the missing revolver, which you by an amazing coincidence confiscated well before Mr. St. Aubin's alleged suicide."

"That ain't true."

"We shall see about that. And what of Mr. Delray himself? He seems to have vanished after being arrested by members of your department. It is quite a curious coincidence."

"Crooks of his kind go on the lam all the time when things get too hot for them. He could be anywhere."

"I doubt that very much. I have it on good authority that Mr. Delray was murdered under color of law and that his remains reside in a secluded place not far from St. Paul."

Holmes's bold statement surprised me, for I had seen nothing substantive in Rafferty's notes regarding Delray's possible fate. Only afterwards did Holmes reveal he had concocted the story of Delray's burial to test Grimshaw reaction.

And react Grimshaw did, for apprehension, which the eyes cannot hide, flickered across his features. But he admitted to nothing. "Well, Mr. Holmes, if you know where this Delray fellow is, I suggest you go right ahead and dig him up."

"A capital idea. I may do so when the appropriate time comes. But let us go back to Daniel St. Aubin. Did you have any dealings with him before he died?"

"No, why would I?"

"So you were not the man who delivered a savage beating to him as a warning?"

"Who told you that? It's a lie."

"Is it? I wonder. Your recall of all manner of events seems to be extremely limited. It must be a curse for a detective of your stature to possess so poor a memory."

His cheeks reddening, Grimshaw stood up and walked around his desk toward us, like a battleship maneuvering to line up its guns. "You are a very clever fellow, ain't you, Mr. Holmes?" he said, his voice full of menace. "But you are in my city now, and you best be careful about making wild allegations. You will find yourself in great trouble if you keep it up."

At this tense moment, the mayor's assistant, Montgomery Meeks, walked into the office. His big, eager eyes swept the room before he turned his attention to Holmes. "Why Mr. Holmes and

Dr. Watson, how nice to see you again! I trust I am not interrupting something. I can come back later."

"No need to," Grimshaw said. "I was just leaving. The two of them are all yours and you're welcome to them." And with that, he stalked out of the office.

"Looks like you and Grimshaw had a bit of a row," Meeks said. "The detective is a gruff fellow but good-hearted, I assure you."

"He is quite effective at hiding the latter quality," Holmes said. "Still, we had a most interesting conversation. Tell me, does he do a great deal of work for the mayor?"

"Oh, now and then he is called on to help with delicate matters, but it is not a regular occurrence."

"And yet the detective has his office here rather than at police headquarters? Why is that?"

"If you must know, he headed a special investigation some years back and needed to work out of city hall for a time. And then, he somehow ended up staying here. Inertia, I fear, is the curse of every bureaucracy. Well, I should be going. Duty calls. I'm sure we'll talk again. Have a pleasant day, gentlemen."

Once Meeks had gone, Holmes said, "He is quite the smooth operator, and it is always hard to know what to make of such a man. Detective Grimshaw, on the other hand, is a straightforward brute, but not a stupid one. He has low animal cunning and he is operating on grounds intimately familiar to him, as we are not. We must heed his advice and be very careful."

Before leaving the city hall and courthouse we paid a visit to the county recorder's office, where we hoped to find Margaret O'Donnell's death certificate. But a clerk, who seemed discomfited by our request, informed us that the certificate had not yet been filed.

"Is that the usual case?" Holmes asked. "The girl has been dead for nearly two months."

"All I can say is that it can take a while for a death certificate to be filed. It just depends on when the doctor gets around to it."

"And who was the doctor in Miss O'Donnell's case?"

"I'm sure I wouldn't know. Now, is there anything else I can help you with?"

There wasn't, and after we left Holmes remarked, "The mystery deepens, Watson, and it is more important than ever that we locate Paul O'Donnell. He must speak for his sister if no one else will."

"WE ARE IN NEED of a girlfriend," Holmes announced, much to my surprise, when I stopped by his room that afternoon.

"A girlfriend? Come now, Holmes, you are talking nonsense. I am a married man—"

"Yes, Watson, I know, and I am pleased you have found marital bliss, if such a thing can be said to exist. However, it is not the two of us I have been thinking about. It is Margaret O'Donnell who occupies my mind. And she is why we need a girlfriend."

"I'm afraid I don't follow you."

"Then let me explain. I have decided it is too early to confront the mayor about his daughter. He has orchestrated the campaign to hide the cause of her death, and he will continue to do so unless we possess specific evidence which will force him to speak the truth."

"And how do we obtain such evidence?"

"That is where a girlfriend enters the picture. Whatever happened to Miss O'Donnell cannot be a secret to everyone in St. Paul. There must be a friend in whom she confided. It may take Sergeant Logan in Chicago some time to track down Paul O'Donnell, if indeed he can. Therefore, a girlfriend is our best hope at the moment. Margaret was only seventeen, and a girl of that age invariably has at least one friend with whom she is very close. We must locate that friend and talk to her."

"And how do we do that?"

"By finding out where Miss O'Donnell went to school."

THOMAS MET US for breakfast the next morning, which was the last day of January. Outside, the temperature had once again plunged below zero, but the Ryan's café was warm and inviting. We found a quiet corner table well away from the other diners, and Holmes shared with Thomas what we had learned thus far. He concluded with an account of our contentious interview with Grimshaw.

"No surprise there," Thomas said. "Grimshaw is a hard man and mean as they come. Do not take his threats lightly."

"We shall not," Holmes said. "Yet I cannot bring myself to believe Grimshaw is a great plotter of any kind. He is a bullet but someone else—someone who possesses a far more supple intellect than the detective—is pointing the gun. That person must be our ultimate target. But first there is much work to be done. Mr. Thomas, you can be of immediate help. I would like you to look into Margaret O'Don-nell's death. You have sources in this city we do not, and perhaps one of them can tell you something of value."

"I can do that," Thomas said, "but it is a well-kept secret from what I know."

"Indeed it is, but there are many avenues that might lead us to the truth. What do you know of the Summit School here in St. Paul?"

Holmes had already made inquiries and learned that Margaret O'Donnell was enrolled there at the time of her death. The school was said to be an expensive private institution patronized by the city's wealthy families.

"I know a little about the place," Thomas told us. "Shad and I once investigated the case of a girl there who disappeared during the middle of the school day. It was feared she'd been abducted, but Shad had his doubts. As usual, Shad was right. She'd actually run off with her boyfriend, and before long we found the two of them shacked up in a vacant house not three blocks from the school. Anyway, all the big families on Summit Avenue send their girls there to make proper ladies of them, but I guess it doesn't always work out that way, does it?"

"So it would seem. I should like to visit the school. Is it far?"

"No, it's just a ways out on Goodrich Avenue. A taxi will have you there in fifteen minutes."

AFTER BREAKFAST, Holmes placed a call to the school's headmistress and explained in a most convincing fashion that he had long been interested in new approaches to the education of young women. Would it be asking too much for us to stop by in the afternoon and observe firsthand the workings of an institution as excellent as the Summit School? It would be no trouble at all, he was assured.

A taxi delivered us to the school, which occupied a handsome brick building in a pleasant neighborhood of newer houses along streets lined with young trees. The headmistress, a dark-haired woman of indeterminate age but with a very determined demeanor, was named Sarah Converse. She met us at the school's front door.

"The girls are quite excited, Mr. Holmes, to see you in person," she said. "They will convene at two in the auditorium, and I am sure they will be most attentive to what you can tell them of your adventurous life as so ably recorded by Dr. Watson."

I doubt Holmes had planned on giving a talk, but as he needed Miss Converse's cooperation, he said he would be pleased to do so. "Before I speak, I should like to have a look at your beautiful school. I am particularly interested in your library. I imagine it is very up-to-date in every respect."

"Most certainly. I will show you the way."

The library was on the second floor, and Holmes marveled over it as though it was one of the wonders of the world. "I spent many days in the library at my school," he said. "In fact, I still have a photograph of the library in our yearbook. I suppose you put out a yearbook here as well. I would enjoy seeing a copy of the most recent one, if it is readily available."

"Of course," Miss Converse said. "This year's book will not be out until May but let me show you last year's."

She went to a low shelf and retrieved a book with a bright red cover titled *The Spar, 1927*. Holmes made a show of inspecting the book, slowly thumbing through it while delivering frequent compliments as to its remarkable excellence. The last section of the book was devoted to photographs of all the students, and there Holmes found what he was looking for.

"How sad," he said abruptly. "How very sad."

Miss Converse was taken by surprise. "Is something wrong, Mr. Holmes?"

"No, it is just that I noticed a picture of Margaret O'Donnell. She was the mayor's daughter, was she not, and died at a very tender age? It must have been a tragic story."

"Yes, it was."

"Did some terrible illness befall her? An infection of some kind? Or was it an auto accident perhaps?"

Holmes's questions met with a stony stare from the headmistress, who said, "Margaret was away at the time. I do not know the circumstances of her death."

"Ah, I see. Still, the funeral must have been difficult for all of her classmates. The young are always surprised by death, especially when someone their own age is suddenly taken away."

"The funeral was private. Now, let us speak of it no more. The girls are gathering and are eager to hear from you and Dr. Watson."

After regaling the school's students with dramatic stories of our adventures, not all of them without embellishment, we thanked Miss Converse, who called a taxi for us.

"Well, I am not sure we learned anything useful," I noted as we settled into the taxi.

"To the contrary, Watson. We now know there was a private funeral for Margaret O'Donnell. That is most unusual and serves to underscore just how much secrecy enveloped her death. The yearbook I inspected in the school library also offered much of value. As I paged through it, I saw a photograph of Margaret O'Donnell rehearsing for a school play. A girl was with her, and the two of them had their arms around each other's shoulders in the unmistakable manner of close friends. The other girl was identified as Missy Forsyth, and I intend to speak with her as soon as possible."

14

The Poet

Bertram Abbey began life with a silver spoon in his mouth and was certain in his own mind that he had never allowed it to tarnish, even if others might disagree. The silver came from his father, Edmund, a structural engineer and entrepreneur who in the late 1890s found treasure in concrete. He developed a new type of cylindrical grain elevator that was stronger and more efficient than the wood or tile varieties of old. By 1910 versions of Abbey's New Patent Elevator, as it was called, stood like monuments to some unknown deity in farm towns all across the Midwest. And as the grain flowed into these towering structures, so too did the dollars into Edmund Abbey's pocket.

He'd spent most of his career in Minneapolis, working for the Pillsburys and other flour-milling nabobs, but as his fortune grew he moved to St. Paul because there was a particularly large and hideous mansion on Summit Avenue that for some inexplicable reason enchanted him. The house, said to be twenty thousand square feet if not more, dated to the 1880s and had originally been built for a New Englander who arrived early in St. Paul and grabbed all the swag he could from a new world in the making.

The house, if not the finest on Summit, was the tallest, sporting a round tower almost as high as one of Abbey's elevators. The brick walls teemed with wildly overscaled ornament that suggested, if nothing else, that the architect knew how to run up his fee. Within was a maze of tall-ceilinged rooms decorated with faded murals and parquet floors, culminating in a lavish two-story-high library where Bertram, an only child, spent much of his youth.

His father, a huge bearded man who paid little attention to his appearance or to his son, dropped dead of a stroke when Bertram was sixteen. His mother, Florence, suddenly possessed of millions to spend on her own, sold the business and occupied herself shopping, drinking, and entertaining handsome young men. She became a scandalous figure in St. Paul yet remained popular because she knew how to throw an excellent party. It was at one of these galas that she accidentally swallowed a toothpick, which perforated her colon. Infection and death followed.

So it was that Bertram, at the ripe age of twenty-two, found himself in possession of a fortune, a mansion, and the opportunity to do whatever he wanted. Since money was no object, he became a poet. After producing two collections of verse destined to sink like lead weights into the ocean deeps of obscurity, he suddenly burst onto the national scene at age thirty-one with "The Body of the Poet." One critic described the prizewinning poem—a long, intricately rhymed epic about postwar ennui and many other things—as a "surprisingly gleeful ode to gloom." Although its almost singsong cadences weren't to everyone's taste, the poem was mysterious and quotable, and it became a minor sensation when it was published in book form in 1919. The poem was also filled with allusions, not always subtle, to Bertram's secret sexuality.

He'd known since he was fifteen that he wanted to be with men, but he was wise enough never to mention this discomfiting reality to his parents. At eighteen he was sent off to Harvard, and there he found willing partners and the reassuring knowledge that he was far from alone. But when he returned home, he discovered that St. Paul's conservative upper-crust society wasn't welcoming to men of his kind.

As a cover, he established himself in the public eye as a blazing heterosexual out for bedroom conquests, and over the years he recruited several female companions who were perfectly willing to take his money in exchange for performing in the great charade. He even married one of them, thereby cementing his heterosexual bona fides. The prearranged divorce that followed a few months later claimed "incompatibility" as the cause of the breakup, and the wife-in-name-only was more than happy to depart with a generous settlement. In the meantime, Abbey frequented the city's underground network of clubs, bars, and meeting places where he and his male friends could gather with relative impunity.

Abbey hired young men he met to work at his mansion, tending the grounds, cooking, and serving as in-house staff. But he also made a point of engaging attractive female maids to bolster the fiction he was just another randy playboy. The maids were strictly day workers, while the young men understood their tasks might include overnight bedroom duty. Although there was much whispering about Abbey's true sexual tastes, he always kept up proper appearances, and because he was brilliant and charming and handsome and rich and a poet of great distinction, he quickly rose to prominent position in St. Paul society.

"The Body of the Poet" propelled Abbey into the role of St. Paul's literary lion in residence. His reign, however, was short-lived. Two years later, a young man who'd grown up within blocks of Abbey's mansion published a blockbuster novel called *This Side of Paradise*. Critics swooned over it and its precocious twenty-three-year-old author, F. Scott Fitzgerald. Abbey read the book and decided he had to meet Fitzgerald, who had just married a whirlwind of a woman named Zelda and who liked to party. He found Fitzgerald and Zelda drinking one night at the Commodore Hotel and tried to strike up a conversation. It did not go well. Fitzgerald was unaware of Abbey's poetry and showed little interest in learning about it. A drunken argument ensued, and Abbey left in a rage. A few months later, Scott and Zelda moved away from St. Paul for good, and Abbey never saw them again.

But Abbey kept on reading, and when the *The Great Gatsby* appeared in 1925, he was stunned. It was purer poetry than he'd ever written or ever could write, and it left him profoundly unsettled. New poets were also coming to the fore, their works far more technically and intellectually challenging than his, and he knew it. He stopped writing poetry, a gift gone with his youth, and quickly remade himself into a mystery novelist.

Under the pen name Benedict Braxton, which he thought sounded both English and distinguished, Abbey published his inaugural mystery, *The Summit of Death*, in 1927, and it became an instant bestseller. The book featured a high-born, gossipy, but oh-so-clever detective named Vincent St. Germain, who was drawn into an intricate murder case involving St. Paul's high society, a world Abbey knew intimately. "I am writing *Gatsby* without the art, but I am making much more money than that little prick Fitzgerald," he told a friend.

Abbey greatly enjoyed his newfound career. He redecorated his mansion into what he described as a "Victorian hothouse," hired more young assistants, bought several sports cars, and spent a few delightful weeks every winter in Key West. And with his literary career revived and Fitzgerald out of the picture, Abbey reclaimed his position as St. Paul's leading man of letters.

SEVERAL YEARS AFTER "The Body of the Poet" made his name as a writer, Abbey launched what he called the Saturday Literary Salon at the posh University Club on Summit Avenue. He invited friends, socialites, local dignitaries, and aspiring writers and offered them wine, cheese, readings, and the promise of dazzling conversation. It was at one such salon in 1926 that he first encountered Daniel St. Aubin, who had literary aspirations.

Abbey found the young blackmailer to be gloriously beautiful, possessing a fine physique, long black hair, dark flaring eyes, and features that might have been chiseled by Michelangelo. The fact that he was rumored to be a blackmailer made him even more dangerously attractive, and Abbey began working at once to insinuate St. Aubin into his inner circle. St. Aubin had written several stories, which Abbey encouraged him to read at the salon. Centering on the activities of a thoroughly despicable extortionist, the stories were clumsy and poorly written. Even so, Abbey praised them profusely.

Abbey hoped to lure St. Aubin into his bed, and after a salon session he suggested a one-on-one meeting at his mansion to talk further. But when Abbey proposed the private meeting, St. Aubin told him, "I don't care much for fags, Bert, if that's what you're getting at, so I won't be going to your little love nest. But maybe someday I'll get in touch and when I do, you won't like it."

After that shocking statement, St. Aubin never attended another salon, and Abbey assumed he'd never see him again. But Abbey did find a use for St. Aubin as the model for a handsomely disreputable character in *The Summit of Death*. Abbey was basking in the glow of rave reviews and booming sales one November afternoon when a letter delivered in the mail suddenly upended his life.

Hand printed on cheap stationery, the anonymous letter read:

DEAR FAG, DO YOU KNOW HOW OLD JOHNNY BOY IS? OF COURSE YOU DO. THE POLICE AND NEWSPAPERS WILL BE INFORMED UNLESS YOU PAY UP. OTHERWISE, GOOD LUCK IN PRISON, YOU BUGGER. INSTRUCTIONS TO FOLLOW.

P. S. I KNOW YOUR OTHER SECRET. IT WILL COST YOU MORE WHEN THE TIME COMES.

A photograph was included with the letter, and Abbey could not believe what it showed. A great hole opened in Abbey's gut as he read the letter and stared at the photograph. He felt himself reeling.

Was his life about to come crashing down? It seemed all too likely.

Abbey quickly realized the letter must have come from Daniel St. Aubin, whose reputation as a blackmailer had only grown since their first encounter more than a year earlier. But how had St. Aubin obtained the photograph? And how did he know about Johnny Boy? Johnny Riordan was one of Abbey's house assistants and claimed to be nineteen years old. Abbey suspected he was younger than that but had made no inquiries to resolve the question. Was he in fact underage, as St. Aubin implied?

Abbey tried to calm himself and think. His first task was to wring the truth out of Johnny. It took some serious browbeating before Johnny admitted he was sixteen but would be seventeen in just two weeks. Wonderful. The hole in Abbey's gut grew larger. Now what? Think this through, Abbey told himself, trying to fight off panic. It would have to be proved, he knew, that he and Johnny had actually had sex. Abbey would deny it, of course. What about Johnny? Abbey wasn't sure. The kid was wise beyond his years and a well-practiced maneuverer. He just might talk to the police if he saw something in it for him.

And if Johnny did start blabbing, Abbey would be in for it. The authorities in St. Paul generally tolerated homosexuals if they went about their business discreetly, but an adult man having sex with someone under eighteen, male or female, was statutory rape. If Abbey was hauled up on such a charge, regardless of its outcome, he knew he was finished. No publisher would touch his books, his friends would desert him, and he'd instantly become the pariah of Summit Avenue.

Abbey made an immediate decision. He gave Johnny five hundred dollars in cash and instructed him to pack up and take the first available train to Chicago and from there go on to New Orleans. "You deserve a vacation," he told him. "I'll make all the hotel arrangements. I know a little place in the French Quarter you'll really

like." Johnny had no objections. New Orleans in November promised to be much nicer than St. Paul.

Two days later, another anonymous letter arrived at Abbey's
mansion. It instructed him to leave five thousand dollars in cash in a
bag along an isolated stretch of Water Street on the city's West Side.
The drop-off was to be made the next night at eleven o'clock. NO
POLICE, NO TRICKS, OR YOU WILL BE DONE, the letter concluded.

At first, Abbey wasn't sure what to do, but before long he had an
idea. There was one man, Montgomery Meeks, who just might be
able to fix his problem, and he was just a phone call away.

ABBEY HAD FIRST AVAILED HIMSELF of Meeks's skill as a fixer a
year or so earlier in a dispute over a wealthy stockbroker's building
plans. The broker bought a long-vacant lot next to Abbey's mansion
and then unveiled plans to fill it with a large but severe new house,
designed in the latest modern style. Abbey regarded the proposed
house as an abomination, as did some of his neighbors.

Conveniently ignoring the fact that his own mansion was widely
viewed as an architectural monstrosity, Abbey vowed to stop the
project. He hired a lawyer but was advised that nothing in the city's
zoning code prohibited the broker from building the house he had
in mind. Believing his money and influence would count for something at city hall, Abbey appealed directly to the mayor's office, and
that's when Meeks came to the rescue.

The mayor's assistant turned out to be very accommodating. The
zoning code, he informed Abbey, was a flexible document capable
of multiple interpretations. He also noted that the city's zoning
board relied on recommendations from its staff of bureaucrats in
complicated cases such as Abbey's. Meeks went on to say that these
bureaucrats were notoriously slow to act without the aid of a well-
timed push. Or as Meeks put it, "The wheels of government need a
little grease to move forward."

Abbey understood perfectly. He applied a thousand dollars' worth of grease to something called the St. Paul Public Affairs Foundation, which was in fact a private slush fund Meeks maintained with the mayor's full knowledge for a wide variety of underhanded purposes. Several weeks later the zoning board voted down the broker's project for violating several obscure technicalities.

The dispute over the house had occurred as Abbey was beginning work on *The Summit of Death*. Abbey found Meeks so enchantingly devious that he wrote him into the novel as a character named Morgan Mattson who maneuvered his way through the plot, which included several racy bedroom episodes, with unseemly gusto. Meeks, of course, recognized himself in the story and told Abbey, "You have made me into a reprobate, and I must say I greatly enjoy being thought of in that way." It was an odd remark, and Abbey couldn't quite tell whether Meeks was joking or was genuinely pleased to be depicted as an amoral cad.

"I've got a big problem," Abbey said when he contacted Meeks to explain the spot he was in with the blackmail demand. "I'm hoping you can help me."

"Who do you think sent the stuff?" Meeks asked.

"Daniel St. Aubin. I don't see how it could have been anyone else. The allegation I'm involved with a juvenile is absolutely false, of course."

"Of course," Meeks murmured, sounding unconvinced by Abbey's protestations of innocence. "What about the photo? What does it show?"

"I would rather not say. But it, too, could be a source of embarrassment. The question is, should I pay St. Aubin?"

"If you pay once, you will keep on paying," Meeks said.

"But if he goes to the police with this material, I could be ruined. Then there's the newspapers. What if they run a story?"

Meeks scoffed at the idea. "The newspapers, Mr. Abbey, exist to feed pablum to the masses and protect the rich and influential from embarrassment. It's a fine arrangement all the way around. I'll handle the newspapers. And the police will take care of St. Aubin. He's in need of some serious adult discipline. In the meantime, if you would care to make a donation to our municipal foundation, that would be wonderful."

"What sort of donation did you have in mind?"

"Oh, I'll leave that to you. I'm sure you'll want to open your purse wide for such a good cause."

After some thought, and considering the gravity of the matter, Abbey sent in a donation of two thousand dollars. If St. Aubin could be silenced for good, Abbey thought, it would be money well spent.

THE NEXT DAY Jackson Grimshaw appeared at Abbey's front door and flashed his badge. Abbey wasn't expecting him but understood the purpose of his visit. He led Grimshaw into a paneled library warmed by a huge fireplace and closed the door behind them. How wonderful, he thought, I'm meeting with a policeman come to clean my dirty laundry.

Grimshaw wasn't much for small talk. "Show me the letters," he demanded.

"Certainly," Abbey said, instantly aware he was in the presence of a terrible man. Everything about Grimshaw was hard and cold, and he seemed to Abbey like a big, sharp-edged slab of stone somehow come to life. "Would you like anything to drink first?"

"No, just the letters. And that photo."

"I can't show you the photograph."

"Why? You want out of this mess, don't you?"

"I do. However, I've already destroyed the photograph." In fact, Abbey still had the shocking image but couldn't bear the thought of the police or anyone else looking at it.

"That wasn't smart, Mr. Poet. The blackmailer will have more than one print, that you can be sure of. All right then, hand over the letters, or did you destroy them, too?"

"No, I have them."

Abbey retrieved the letters and gave them to Grimshaw, who read them slowly, as though every word was a mystery.

"So who's this Johnny Boy?" he asked.

"He works for me. His name is Johnny Riordan. He's a fine young man. I don't know why—"

Grimshaw cut him off. "How old is he?"

"Nineteen," Abbey lied.

"Is that so?" Grimshaw said with a grunt. "You buggering him?"

Abbey tried to sound appalled. "Of course not. How could you suggest such a thing? He's merely one of my house servants."

Grimshaw's dead eyes contained nothing except a black sheen of disbelief. "Well, ain't that swell. Is this servant of yours around?"

"No, I'm afraid not. He left a few days ago. I think he said he was going to Detroit to see his family. I gather it was some sort of emergency."

"I'm sure it was. Nice to see you're not entirely stupid, Mr. Poet. I suppose there's no telling how long Riordan might be gone."

"He didn't say."

"Then you'd better hope it's for a long time. In fact, maybe you should persuade him to stay in Detroit or wherever the hell he is permanently. That might be a good thing for both of you."

"Yes, it might," Abbey agreed.

"So I understand you think a guy named Danny St. Aubin is trying to pull off this business, is that right?"

"It is."

"I'd ask you how he got his fingers around your throat, but it really don't matter. So here's the deal. Forget about that drop-off tonight. I'll have a nice little talk with St. Aubin. I'm sure I can convince him as to the error of his ways. I'm told he has rooms at the Piedmont, is that right?"

"Yes, he has an apartment there."

"All right. I'll find him."

Grimshaw stood up, looked around, and said, "What do you do with all these books?"

"I read them."

"Waste of time, if you ask me. Now, I happen to be soliciting donations to the Police Patrolmen's Benevolent Fund. I think two hundred would help the cause, don't you?"

After Grimshaw left with four fifty-dollar bills in hand, Abbey burned the letters from St. Aubin in the fireplace. He hoped his troubles would disappear with them. As for Grimshaw, the man was a brute, but a brute who could be bought, and Abbey thought the detective might just be an ally worth cultivating.

THAT NIGHT, as St. Aubin emerged from his apartment at the Piedmont, Grimshaw lay in wait. He came up behind St. Aubin, hit him with a sap, and dragged him into an alley. By the time Grimshaw was finished, St. Aubin had a broken nose, swollen lips, a black eye, and a bruise on his stomach the size of a concrete block.

"No more of this blackmail crap or I'll be back to see you," Grimshaw told St. Aubin as he straddled him. "Do you understand, you filthy bugger?"

His mouth filling with blood, St. Aubin stared up at Grimshaw's vicious face and nodded.

"Good. Just remember what I said. Your stupid life depends on it."

Grimshaw reported back to Meeks the following morning on the success of his mission and also called Abbey with the news.

"St. Aubin won't cause no more problems," he told Abbey.

Grimshaw, it turned out, was wrong.

15

"You Are Being Insolent"

Shadwell Rafferty rang in 1928 by going to bed early on New Year's Eve and leaving any merrymaking to his dreams. He had dinner on New Year's Day with a few old friends, and on the morning of January 2 he saw Wash and Pats Thomas off to Savannah. Then he settled in for a long bout of reading. He wanted to know more about Bertram Abbey and began by wading into "The Body of the Poet."

Rafferty's taste in poetry ran toward the likes of Robert Service, whose ballads of the Yukon gold rush and barroom brawls struck close to home. Although Rafferty had never been to the Yukon, he'd mined silver in Nevada and also knew more than a little about saloons and their fractious clientele. The sort of highbrow poetry Bertram Abbey wrote was, on the other hand, all but a foreign language to Rafferty. With its intricate ruminations on the meaning of something or other, "The Body of the Poet" struck Rafferty as a form of high-minded dithering, and he could barely get through it.

Still, Rafferty found one extremely interesting stanza in "The Body of the Poet." It read, "The poet is a man of lies. / He's seldom what he seems. / He heaves up words to neutralize / The poison of his dreams." Were the lines an admission that Abbey had a secret, somehow toxic life? Or was he just engaging in the usual poetic license? Rafferty wasn't sure, but if nothing else the lines suggested that Abbey would be a devious man to deal with.

Rafferty found Abbey's mystery novel to be far more entertaining than his poetry. *The Summit of Death* was fast-paced, highly enjoyable, and featured elaborately planned acts of mayhem of a sort rarely, if ever, found in real life. Set on mythical Longview

Avenue in what Abbey described as a "decaying old Midwestern city of no great repute," the novel offered a particularly interesting cast of characters who appeared to be based on real-life people from St. Paul.

The flamboyant detective Vincent St. Germain, a rich man-about-town who spoke in perfectly crafted sentences, was clearly a stand-in for Abbey himself. There was also a certain Father Laurent who bore a suspicious resemblance to Monsignor Pierre Denis. The rough and ready Sergeant Sam Stryker, who assisted St. Germain by cracking the occasional skull, had to be Grimshaw. Likewise, a wily political operator named Morgan Mattson was almost certainly modeled on Montgomery Meeks.

But it was a character named William Kent, depicted as "a perfect young Apollo," who really drew Rafferty in. Abbey lavished long passages of all but erotic prose on the character, who was described as "twenty-five years of age, blond, blue-eyed, with all the fleeting fairness of youth." Kent's angelic appearance, however, belied his true nature. He turned out to be a cunning blackmailer who "took the devil's own pleasure" in taunting his unfortunate victims. But justice was ultimately served when one of Kent's would-be victims shot him, immured his corpse behind a basement wall, and then celebrated with "a glass of Amontillado and a toast to Edgar Allan Poe."

Although Kent wasn't a physical match for the dark-haired Danny St. Aubin, Rafferty suspected they were one in the same. And it could hardly be a coincidence that Kent, like St. Aubin, was a blackmailer.

AFTER COMPLETING HIS SELF-IMPOSED reading assignment four days into the new year, Rafferty called Louis Peltier at the police department. Rafferty had been wondering whether Danny St. Aubin could have found a way to blackmail Abbey. One idea came to mind.

"A quick question, Louie. Have the police, to your knowledge, ever received any complaints about Bertram Abbey?"

"What kind of complaints?"

"Well, I have been told he prefers men to women. If some of them were underage—"

"Yeah, yeah, I see where you're going. Again, this is a conversation we never had, agreed?"

"My word on it."

"Okay, I can tell you there's a rumor floating around that our friend Grimshaw did a big fix job for Abbey. Apparently, Abbey got some sort of a blackmail letter back in November, but Grimshaw took care of the problem."

"Did St. Aubin send the letter?"

"Don't know."

"What did the blackmailer threaten to expose?"

"Again, I don't know, but you can guess. I'm told there was even a compromising photo."

"A photo of Abbey with a boy?"

"I'm not sure. I haven't seen it. You should have a talk with Margo Sartell. Word has it she took the picture. Do you know her?"

"Ah, the lovely Miss Sartell. We've met."

Sartell was a longtime photographer in St. Paul who'd once worked for the *Dispatch* and *Pioneer Press*. Of late she'd been employed by detective agencies. Catching unfaithful spouses in the act was her specialty, or so Rafferty had heard.

"Did you think Grimshaw got his hand on the photo?"

"Can't say. It's not like the two of us commune over coffee and doughnuts every morning. Anyway, that's all I know, Shad. Now remember—"

"Ah, Louie, my memory is terrible. What were we just talking about? I don't seem to recall a word of it."

Rafferty's next call went to Muriel St. Aubin. He wanted to ask her the same questions he'd put to Peltier, albeit in a more round-about fashion. Rafferty had kept her informed about the progress of his investigation, which admittedly wasn't moving forward at a dizzying pace, and he knew she was growing impatient. When he reached her, she said, "I presume you are calling to tell me you don't know anything more but hope to learn something of consequence one of these days, is that it?"

Rafferty ignored the sarcasm and said, "No, I'm calling with a question for you regarding Danny and Bertram Abbey. Did your son ever mention that he might have learned something incriminating about Mr. Abbey?"

"You mean that he's queer? That's hardly a secret."

"No, it would have been something beyond that. Perhaps something that might have deeply embarrassed Mr. Abbey or even exposed him to criminal charges. I'm told Danny may have taken a photograph of some kind he intended to use for purposes of blackmail."

"What kind of photograph?" Mrs. St Aubin asked, a sudden note of urgency in her voice.

Rafferty said, "I don't know. I have not seen it. Would you have any idea?"

"Of course not. Why would you even ask such a thing? As I have told you, Danny did not confide in me."

"My apologies, Mrs. St. Aubin, if I have offended you. I am merely trying to get at the truth. Let us move on, if you don't mind. Can you tell me if Danny knew any of the young men who work for Abbey? I've been told there are quite a few."

"His little harem, you mean? It's possible Danny might have known some of them. But if you're saying my son—"

"No, I'm not suggesting any kind of intimate relationship. I'm just trying to figure out if Danny was acquainted with anyone in Abbey's household who might have passed on incriminating information."

"Strange that you should ask. I received a phone call just before Danny's murder from a man who was trying to reach him. The man sounded quite young and I quizzed him a bit, since his name was unfamiliar to me. He said he'd met Danny at one of Abbey's Saturday salons. He also said he'd worked for Abbey once but was now out on his own. He seemed very nice, so I gave him Danny's address at the Piedmont."

"What was the caller's name?"

"It was Johnny somebody. I'll think of it in a second."

"Did he say why he wanted to reach Danny?"

"All he said was that it was a very important matter, or words to that effect, and he needed to talk to Danny as soon as possible. He . . . wait . . . Johnny Riordan, that was his name."

"I see. And do you know where he can be reached?"

"How would I know that? Come now, Mr. Rafferty, just what are you getting at?"

"I'm not sure, Mrs. St. Aubin, but I would like to have a chat with this Riordan fellow. It's possible he knows something about your son's murder."

"Well then, I suggest you find him, Mr. Rafferty, and see what he has to say. Good afternoon," she added, then hung up.

The abrupt dismissal hardly surprised Rafferty. Mrs. St. Aubin, he'd found, was a difficult woman, imperious as a queen behind her fortress of wealth. And yet she'd sounded anxious when Rafferty brought up the blackmail photograph her son had supposedly possessed. What had caused her alarm? Rafferty wasn't sure, but he began to suspect Mrs. St. Aubin knew more about her late son's business than she was letting on.

More curious than ever about the photograph, Rafferty decided the time had come to speak to the woman who took it. He placed a call to Margo Sartell's studio, hoping she'd be willing to cooperate. There was no answer, so he made a note to call her again later.

RAFFERTY HAD EXCELLENT SOURCES among the servant class along Summit Avenue, and he started making inquiries about Riordan. After numerous phone calls, he learned that Riordan, who was a popular figure among his cohorts, had left St. Paul in mid-November. A house maid who'd befriended Riordan said he told her he was going to New Orleans on a long vacation, courtesy of his employer, Bertram Abbey. That was the last time she'd seen Riordan.

"By the way, how old would you say Johnny is?" Rafferty asked.

"Oh, he's still just a boy," the maid said. "Sixteen or seventeen maybe."

This was interesting news, and it led Rafferty to a speculative syllogism. Riordan was underage and Abbey had seduced him. Riordan knew St. Aubin and told him about his relationship with Abbey. Therefore, that relationship formed the basis of St. Aubin's attempt at blackmail. It all made perfect sense, except for one problem. Rafferty had zero proof any of it was true.

If he wanted to prove his theory, he needed to find Riordan. But first, he'd see what Bertram Abbey had to say for himself. Although he'd heard plenty of stories about the poet-turned-novelist's flamboyant lifestyle, Rafferty had never actually met Abbey. What would be the best way to approach him?

Rafferty suspected Abbey wouldn't agree to a meeting unless a motivation—fear usually worked—was provided. So he phoned Abbey, introduced himself, explained how he was investigating Danny's death, and then said, "A matter of blackmail has come to my attention. It may be nothing or it may be of great importance. I'm sure you would like to clear up the questions I have. Otherwise, awful rumors might begin to spread, and I would hate to see that happen."

THE STRATEGY WORKED, and the next afternoon Rafferty arrived at the doorstep of Abbey's rambling mansion, which had always reminded him of some mad king's fairy-tale castle. A young butler escorted Rafferty into a library well stocked with beautifully bound books. Rafferty found a chair next to the fireplace and warmed himself for several minutes before Abbey swept into the room.

"A pleasure to meet you," he said as he glided over to a long red divan and took a seat.

"Likewise," Rafferty said, taking a long look at Abbey, who cut quite a figure. He wore a precisely tailored mauve suit, a perfectly starched white shirt, and tasseled black loafers gleaming with a new coat of polish. He was not a big man, but Rafferty saw at once that he had a gymnast's taut body, suggesting he took regular exercise. His features were dainty except for large, slate-gray eyes set well apart, and his light brown hair was whipped up into a rather ridiculous pompadour. Rafferty had expected to find a fop, but Abbey didn't really come across that way despite his fussy attire. There was steel in his eyes, which took in Rafferty with a steady gaze.

He said, "I have heard all about you, Mr. Rafferty, and your many remarkable adventures with Sherlock Holmes. Now that we've met and I see what a fine fellow you are, I am thinking I should put you in my next book, as a fictional character of course. Let's see, what would I name you? What about Riley O'Rourke? How does that sound?"

"Very Irish, and I'd certainly be flattered to work on a case with Vincent St. Germain."

"Ah, so am I to take it you've read my poor scribblings?"

"I have. Your mighty poem was too much for me, I confess, but the mystery tale is most intriguing and very well done. I'm sure my friends Mr. Holmes and Dr. Watson would agree."

"Well, that would be high praise indeed. However, you're not here to discuss my literary efforts, are you? Over the phone you mentioned something about blackmail, but I'm truly in the dark as to why you brought up that subject in connection with me."

"I am too old to take the roundabout, Mr. Abbey, so I will drive straight through to the point and save us both some time. You see, I read *The Summit of Death*, and I believe the young blackmailer in that book, William Kent, is based directly on a young man named Daniel St. Aubin, who as you know died recently under mysterious circumstances. I have been told that Danny at some point tried to blackmail you. Is that true?"

Abbey appeared put out by the question. "Oh, really, Mr. Rafferty, don't tell me you believe that old canard that everything an author puts in a book must be based on some fact or incident in his own life. I write fiction, which means I make things up. It is quite ridiculous to contend that because there is young blackmailer in my novel I therefore must have been blackmailed by a similar sort of person."

"So the police never investigated a blackmail scheme in which you were the target?"

"Of course not."

Although Rafferty had only his friend Peltier's word, which was pure hearsay, that there had indeed been such an investigation, he spoke as though it was a well-established fact. "Come now, Mr. Abbey, we both know you received a letter from Danny St. Aubin that threatened you in some way. There was also a compromising photo. Naturally, this was most upsetting, so you brought the matter to the attention of Detective Jackson Grimshaw."

"I have never met Mr. Grimshaw," Abbey insisted.

"I find that hard to believe. In fact, a witness saw you and the detective together down at city hall one afternoon."

There was no such witness, but Rafferty hoped Abbey might be tricked into a revealing denial. Abbey didn't fall for the ruse. Instead, he abruptly rose to his feet and said, "That is a flat-out lie, Mr. Rafferty, and I believe there is nothing more to say. I am deeply offended by your wild allegations, which have no basis in fact. Let me show you to the door."

"Well now, I was just getting comfortable by this nice fire, but if you insist, I will leave," Rafferty said. "However, I am an old locomotive on slippery rails and it takes me a while to build up momentum. Give me a moment if you would."

While Abbey looked on impatiently, Rafferty staged a slow scene of hoisting himself out of his chair with the help of his cane. Meanwhile, he kept on talking. "Incidentally, how did you get Grimshaw to take care of your problem? I imagine money changed hands. And what did Danny have on you? Something to do with Johnny Riordan and that compromising photo, I suppose."

"You are being insolent," Abbey said. His body stiffened and anger flashed in his eyes. "Now, please leave at once and do not come back."

"As you wish," Rafferty said, "but you will find I am not easily gotten rid of, especially when it's murder I'm investigating."

Rafferty shuffled out into the home's huge front hallway, where a wide flight of steps framed by railings carved into fantastic swirling shapes ascended to the second floor. Patterned red wallpaper was everywhere, offset by lush peach and ivory furnishings in the Louis XIV style. The place felt like a bordello to Rafferty, although no madam was in sight.

At the front door, with Abbey eager to usher him out into the cold, Rafferty said, "I do wonder what has happened to young Mr. Riordan. You sent him off to New Orleans. Why would you do that? Were you worried about statutory rape charges?"

"Out," Abbey said and slammed the door.

Rafferty stood for a moment on the stoop, aware his impertinent questions had put fear in Abbey's heart. But what next? How could Rafferty turn his suspicions into hard evidence that Abbey had not only committed a sex crime but may even have murdered Danny St. Aubin to cover it up?

As he pondered these weighty questions, Rafferty suddenly realized he had no immediate way of getting home. The nearest street-car line was blocks away, there were no public phones nearby to call a cab, and the temperature was barely above zero. Rafferty looked out and saw a black sedan idling nearby. A burly man in a heavy winter coat and wide-brimmed hat was behind the wheel. A cop, Rafferty assumed, keeping tabs on him at Grimshaw's behest.

Rafferty limped out to the curb and gave the cop a wave, thinking he might as well ask him for a ride. But just then, luck came his way in the form of a taxi driven by a cabbie Rafferty knew. He hailed a ride and headed back to the Ryan, thinking about how he might locate Johnny Riordan, if he were alive. Rafferty would soon discover that Riordan was indeed alive and surprisingly close at hand.

ONCE RAFFERTY WAS GONE, Abbey made three quick phone calls, to Grimshaw, Meeks, and Denis. The message in each case was the same. Rafferty, he said, was closing in on the truth, and that could lead to ugly consequences for all of them. Something, Abbey said, would have to be done about the old man.

Book IV

More Suspects, More Questions

16

"She Is a Woman Who Makes Arrangements"

January had been a terrible month for Wash Thomas. It had seemed full of promise when he and Pats headed off to Savannah. Then had come days of worry as Rafferty, alone in St. Paul, pursued his increasingly fraught investigation into Daniel St. Aubin's death. When he returned in mid-January to be at Rafferty's side, Thomas had thought everything would work out. They would solve the St. Aubin case as they had so many others, working perfectly in tandem. But it wasn't to be, and when Rafferty was murdered, Thomas felt as though some bitter poison had been injected straight into his heart.

With loving support from Pats, Thomas had slowly recovered his equilibrium, and as January turned to February, he began to believe in hope again. There was no bringing Rafferty back, but there was good reason to think his murderer would be found. Sherlock Holmes seemed to be making progress every day, pushing and prodding and examining every feature of the crime as only he could. At the same time, Thomas was bringing his own particular genius to the investigation. He knew St. Paul in a way Holmes and Watson never could and he became their inside man, digging into places beyond their reach.

So it was that on February first, a day after his breakfast with Holmes and Watson, Thomas took on the assignment of looking into the tantalizing mystery of Margaret O'Donnell's death. While Holmes made inquiries at Margaret's school, Thomas concentrated on her father. Thomas knew all too well that he faced a difficult task. The mayor had constructed a fortress of secrecy around the circumstances of his daughter's demise, and it had no obvious means of entry. But was there a hairline crack in the wall or some other tiny opening that might lead inside? Thomas thought the mayor's house servants might be a potential source of information, especially if one or more of them was Black. But both the maid and cook at O'Donnell's home turned out to be white, and they quickly made it clear they wanted nothing to do with Thomas.

Had he been white, Thomas could have gone next to various city hall officials—aldermen, commissioners, judges, head clerks—and sounded them out, but he knew that would be futile. They'd have no interest in answering questions from an uppity Black man. So he started digging elsewhere, in the bowels of city hall, talking to elevator operators, janitors, backroom clerks, and night watchmen. Somebody, he reasoned, had to have heard something. But no one had, and the fortress remained invulnerable.

Then, as Thomas headed back to his restaurant, weary after a day of fruitless inquiries, he thought of one other person, a lawyer named Marcus Jefferson, who might know something about the mayor and his dead daughter. Jefferson was one of the few Black lawyers in Minnesota. Like Thomas, Jefferson had been involved in civil rights campaigns, and he'd represented numerous Black men dragged into court on bogus charges. He was not only a crackerjack attorney but also a man with an ear to all that was going on in St. Paul. And since he was regularly at the city hall and county courthouse on legal business, he just might know something about Margaret O'Donnell's death.

Jefferson's office was in the front room of his residence on Selby Avenue, along the streetcar line Thomas always took home, and so it was easy for him to stop by for a talk. The office, as Thomas knew from previous visits, was essentially a paper storehouse, piled high with stacks of legal documents arranged according to some arcane system known only to Jefferson. In the middle of it all was a vast mahogany desk where Jefferson, a graying man in his late forties whose intellect and stomach were both more than ample, sat like the king of a dead forest.

"Wash, it's always good to see you," Jefferson said as Thomas stepped into the well-organized mess. "So how have you been since Shad's death?"

"I will be honest with you, Marc, it's been a bad time, but I'm getting by. That's why I've come to see you. I'm working with Sherlock Holmes and Dr. Watson to find Shad's killer."

"Well now, that's something, isn't it? Tell me, what's Holmes really like? He must be a difficult and demanding man to work with."

"He is, but he has always been fair with me, and that is all I can ask. And he is every bit as smart as Dr. Watson makes him out to be in those stories of his. Anyway, if you don't mind, I have a few questions for you."

Thomas explained why the fate of Margaret O'Donnell might be tied in some way to Rafferty's murder, then said, "Her death is a complete mystery. The girl is dead and buried at seventeen, and no one will say what happened. Have you heard anything about the cause of her death beyond the usual wild rumors?"

Jefferson gave Thomas a strange look, as though the mere question was cause for grave concern. "I have heard something," he finally said, "but if I tell you, it cannot come back to me."

"It won't, and you know my word is good."

"All right, I trust you. Have you ever heard of a woman named Bertha Coddington?"

"No. Who is she?"

"She is a woman who makes arrangements," Jefferson said. "Very delicate arrangements for girls who find themselves in a family way and are not happy about it."

Thomas understood at once. "So she refers the girls to doctors who can end their pregnancies."

"Yes. But as I'm sure you're aware, abortion is illegal in Minnesota and most other places, so of necessity Mrs. Coddington operates, shall we say, in the shadows."

"And you think Margaret O'Donnell used this Coddington woman's services?"

"It has been bruited about, but I don't know it for a fact. What I do know is that a botched abortion can be fatal to the mother. However, I must emphasize that I have no direct knowledge as to what might have happened to the O'Donnell girl. There may never have been an abortion, and for all I know the girl died in some other way."

"I understand. Where does this Mrs. Coddington have her offices?"

"I'm not sure. In fact, that may not even be her real name."

"How is she reached then?"

Jefferson opened a drawer in his desk and removed a cigar box filled with business cards. "It's here somewhere," he said, pawing through the cards. "I've referred a few young ladies to her over the years. Ah, here it is."

Thomas looked at the card and felt a moment of triumph. Bertha Coddington's phone number was Garfield 2030.

"You look like you've seen a ghost," Jefferson remarked as Thomas stared at the business card.

"No, but maybe I've found one."

Thomas rushed back to the restaurant, where Pats was hard at work in the kitchen, and told her he'd help out as soon as he could. But first he called the answering service. He couldn't conceal his impatience as he waited for the call to go through.

"My goodness, Wash, you're fidgeting like a little boy who has to pee," Pats said. "What's going on?"

"Tell you in a minute," Thomas said just as he was connected to the answering service.

But any hope he had of speaking to Bertha Coddington was soon dashed. The service only took messages for her and the operator said she couldn't be reached directly.

"But you must have her number," Thomas protested.

"We don't," the operator said with a tone of indifferent finality. "So, do you wish to leave a message?"

"Not now," Thomas said and hung up.

After telling Pats what had caused his excitement, Thomas placed another call—this one to Sherlock Holmes at the Ryan Hotel—and delivered a full report about what he'd just learned.

"What did Mr. Holmes say?" Pats asked after Thomas had completed the call.

"He said I'd done a marvelous job. Imagine that! He also told me he's going to be talking soon to that poet fellow, Abbey. I bet that will be interesting."

"I suppose so, but right now I could use—"

"Some help," Thomas said as he peeked out past the kitchen door into the dining room. "Looks like we've got a full house."

"I know, and it's a full house with plenty of empty stomachs," Pats said. "Now, Mr. George Washington Thomas, you need to get to work."

BERTRAM ABBEY FELT NERVOUS and irritated, although hardly surprised, after he hung up the phone on the morning of February 2. Sherlock Holmes had called to request a meeting, and Abbey had agreed, suggesting dinner at his mansion that evening. But what exactly did the legendary detective want and, more important, what did he already know? Enlisting local authorities to cover up his activities had been easy enough for Abbey. Outwitting Sherlock Holmes would be quite another matter.

Despite his worries, Abbey believed he could handle Holmes. Abbey didn't see how Holmes could dig up any real evidence tying him to the murders of St. Aubin and Rafferty. As for St. Aubin's blackmailing efforts, Abbey was reasonably sure he could finesse the situation if need be. A potential sex scandal, after all, was a minor matter compared to murder, and with Grimshaw and Meeks and perhaps even the mayor himself in his corner, Abbey believed he was in no great danger. Johnny Riordan had also been taken care of—Abbey hadn't heard from him in more than two months—and it seemed highly unlikely Holmes could have tracked him down.

Still, Abbey knew a bloodhound like Holmes, who could detect even the faintest whiff of wrongdoing, would be relentless in pursuing Rafferty's killer. And there was always the possibility that Holmes had uncovered where he was the night Rafferty was murdered. That would require some explaining, and Abbey had rehearsed an answer just in case. Satisfied he was ready for Holmes, he went into the kitchen to discuss the dinner menu with his cook.

17

"How Old Do You Suppose He Is?"

[From "Murder in St. Paul"]

By February 2, we had been in St. Paul for nearly a fortnight, and the day brought two significant developments in our murder investigation. The first came about as a result of excellent detective work on Thomas's part. He had learned that a woman named Bertha Coddington, who possibly arranged abortions among other services, was connected to the answering-service telephone number found next to Rafferty's body. Thomas, however, had been unable to reach Mrs. Coddington in person, a circumstance that Holmes found most interesting.

"It is a regular cloak-and-dagger business with Mrs. Coddington, who seems to operate in the shadows," Holmes remarked. "I have examined telephone directories for both St. Paul and Minneapolis, and neither includes anyone by the name of Coddington. It is possible the name is an alias. Even so, we can deduce from her line of work that she must be connected with the American Birth Control League, which is one of the answering service's clients."

Holmes contacted the league's offices in St. Paul to ask about Mrs. Coddington, but he was rebuffed at every turn when he spoke to the director. She claimed to know nothing of a Bertha Coddington and stated most emphatically that the league did not arrange abortions. Moreover, the names of clients—if indeed Margaret O'Donnell was among them—were kept in the strictest confidence. The call ended with Holmes in a state of extreme frustration.

"It seems as though the league is covering up for the woman," I noted.

"Perhaps," Holmes said. "But if she is arranging abortions, which are illegal, she may be working on her own, without the league's knowledge. The question, of course, is whether she arranged an abortion for Margaret O'Donnell. That might well explain the secrecy surrounding the girl's death. In any case, we must find out what Mrs. Coddington—or whatever her real name may be—knows."

Holmes then tried another tack. He placed a call to Declan Morrissey, who was known to be acquainted with every element of St. Paul's criminal underground. Had he by chance ever heard of Bertha Coddington?

Morrissey said he had. "I am given to understand she arranges certain services for young ladies who have unfortunately sampled the apple and lost their place in paradise, if you catch my drift, Mr. Holmes."

"And how would I reach her?"

"Ah now, that I could not say, although I have been told Coddington is in fact a pseudonym. As to her real name and where she might be plying her irreligious trade, I fear I am at a loss. But I suspect she is not here in St. Paul, for I would almost surely know more of her if such was the case."

"Well, we have learned something," Holmes said when he concluded the call. "Coddington must indeed be an alias, and that will make her doubly difficult to locate."

Holmes finally decided to place a call to the answering service in hopes of speaking to the elusive Mrs. Coddington. He represented himself as the father of a sixteen-year-old girl who had "gotten herself in a family way." He also mentioned that Marcus Jefferson had recommended her as someone who might be of help.

While we awaited a return call, Holmes asked me to contact local physicians to see if one of them might have referred the mayor or his daughter to Mrs. Coddington. But I made no headway, and several doctors chided me for even asking about her.

What we did not know at the time was that the woman who called herself Bertha Coddington had been tipped off about our investigation. The man who passed on this information also told her it would be very unwise of her to deal with anyone she didn't know. Mrs. Coddington took the advice to heart, and so we never received a call back from her.

As the hours passed with no word from Mrs. Coddington, Holmes turned his attention to another mystery figure—Johnny Riordan.

"It is imperative we find him," Holmes said, "and I have put the redoubtable Mr. Thomas on the job."

We had learned about Riordan and his relationship with Abbey from Rafferty's notes. Rafferty had been able to establish three other salient facts about Riordan: that he knew Daniel St. Aubin, that he may have assisted in various blackmail schemes, and that he had come back north to Minneapolis following a short stay in New Orleans. But the Minneapolis police had given little effort to finding him despite a request from Holmes to do so.

"I have already asked much of Mr. Thomas, and I do not like placing yet another burden on his shoulders, but he is our invaluable man. If anyone can locate Mr. Riordan, he can. I believe Mr. Riordan is the wild card in this business, and he may have a great deal to tell us once we find him."

"Grimshaw is also looking for him, is he not?"

"Yes, and Mr. Rafferty had great fears what would happen if the detective got to Mr. Riordan first. He would be a dead man, and there would be yet another cover-up."

Over a late lunch at the Ryan's café, Holmes had more news to report. "I have been on the telephone with Sergeant Logan and he confirmed Paul O'Donnell has been in Chicago. However, he checked out of a hotel there yesterday, with luggage. The good sergeant is now canvassing the railroads to see where Mr. O'Donnell might be headed. In the meantime, we have a date for dinner."

"With whom?"

"Bertram Abbey. I also spoke to him and he extended the invitation. It will be an excellent opportunity to quiz him. We know from Mr. Rafferty's notes that he had a motive to murder Mr. St. Aubin, who attempted to blackmail him, possibly over his involvement with Johnny Riordan. And of course, we also know that on the night of Mr. Rafferty's murder, Mr. Abbey stayed here at the Ryan and presumably met a man for an assignation."

I knew whom Holmes believed that man to be but pointed out he had no proof a tryst had actually taken place that night.

"Perhaps, but we have irrefutable evidence of a previous assignation here, and it is not illogical to think that the two of them might have met again, perhaps even to plot Mr. Rafferty's murder. However, I do not intend to raise the matter with Mr. Abbey tonight. As you know, Watson, it is always wise to save some ammunition for a later time, when your opponent believes you have run out."

"Well, Abbey has much to explain. I will be curious what he has to say."

"As will I. However, it will not be easy to elicit the truth from him. A man of his kind must of necessity be a practiced liar. In any event, we have work to do before dinner. Classes at the Summit School dismiss at three o'clock, and we need to be there when that happens."

AT THE APPOINTED HOUR we took a taxi up to the school and told the driver to wait for us. The day was unusually mild, and we walked over to the school's entrance just before three to observe the students as they poured out. Missy Forsyth emerged in the middle of the pack and Holmes recognized her instantly from the yearbook picture he'd seen two days earlier.

"Ah, you must be Miss Forsyth," he said. "Could we talk for a moment?"

She was slender, black-haired, and lively, but not strikingly beautiful in the manner of her friend, Margaret O'Donnell. "Oh goodness," she said, "Sherlock Holmes! I don't believe it. I heard your talk Tuesday, but I never thought, you know, that I'd meet you in person like this."

"Well, now you have, and I must say it is a pleasure to meet you as well. Are you walking home? Dr. Watson and I would be happy to accompany you."

"Yes, I live just two blocks away. But I can't imagine what you would want to talk to me about."

"It's about Margaret O'Donnell. I understand she was a good friend of yours," Holmes said as we crossed the street, where I indicated to our cab driver we would return shortly.

The girl stopped and performed the sign of the cross, as though blessing her memories. "Oh, poor, poor Maggie. It's so sad. I'll never, ever forget her. I promised that to myself. How did you know we were friends?"

Holmes smiled and said, "My dear Miss Forsyth, I am Sherlock Holmes and knowing things is my business. What kind of girl was Maggie?"

"She was really nice but I guess you could say she was kind of wild. She liked to have fun. And she was oh so pretty! The boys couldn't stay away," the girl added in a rueful tone. Young men obviously hadn't paid nearly as much attention to her.

"Was one of those admirers Daniel St. Aubin?"

"Gee, Mr. Holmes, I can see why you're so famous. Yes, she saw Danny for a while, although you could hardly call him a boyfriend, if you know what I mean."

"You mean he was much older than the boys she usually saw?"

"Yes. He must have been thirty. That's awfully old!"

"Ancient," Holmes agreed. "Did she go out with him frequently?"

"No, she wasn't going steady with him or anything like that. Besides, it was supposed to be a secret. She knew if her dad found out she'd be in big trouble."

"And did he find out?"

"I think so, because one day she just sort of disappeared and nobody at school saw her again until we found out she was, you know, in heaven. And then Danny shot himself. It's a very sad story."

Holmes agreed that it was, then asked several perfunctory questions, all the while telling the girl how helpful she was and thereby winning her over. Finally came the question I knew would culminate his inquiry.

"Maggie's death is indeed quite a mystery and certainly a terrible tragedy. How did she die?"

The girl stopped once more, slowly shook her head, and said, "Oh, Mr. Holmes, I wish I knew. All I know is that she went away and then in no time she was dead."

"Do you have any idea at all where she went before her death?"

"I . . . I . . . well, I don't know for a fact."

Her hesitation gave her away. She knew something but was reluctant to tell us.

Holmes said, "This is very important, Miss Forsyth. You must tell us what you know, or the truth will never come out about your friend. You owe it to her memory to speak up, and you may be perfectly assured whatever you say will be held in the strictest confidence."

"Okay, I guess, but I don't know for sure. There were rumors she went to Good Shepherd."

"Yes, I have heard that. I understood it is an institution which takes in troubled girls. What sort of trouble was Maggie in?"

"Well, you know, the thing that can a happen if a girl isn't careful."

I now spoke up. "She was pregnant, in other words."

Miss Forsyth stammered, "Well . . . I . . . it could be, but girls do go there for other reasons, I'm sure."

"No doubt, but it is Maggie we are interested in," Holmes said rather severely. "Did she tell you she was pregnant?"

"I can't say."

"Why not?"

"I was sworn to secrecy, Mr. Holmes. I can't tell you."

"Your loyalty is admirable, Miss Forsyth, but Maggie is dead. Her secret does not matter to her anymore."

"Well, it matters to me," the girl insisted.

"Of course it does. But did you know that when secrets are whispered they remain secrets? Go ahead, just whisper into my ear, Miss Forsyth, and the secret will be safe."

Holmes bent his head down beside hers, and to my surprise she began whispering into his ear. When she was done, Holmes said, "Yes, that must have been a difficult situation for poor Maggie. Do you suppose Mr. St. Aubin was aware of her circumstances?"

"I don't know, I really don't. Anyway, here's where I live," the girl said, nodding toward a white clapboard house behind a picket fence of the same color. "I have to go in now. I don't think I can answer any more questions. Just promise me you won't say anything bad about Maggie to anybody."

"You have our word," Holmes said.

As we returned to the Ryan in our cab, Holmes told me that Margaret O'Donnell had indeed confided to her friend Miss Forsyth that she believed she was pregnant. However, she didn't say who had fathered the child.

"St. Aubin must have been the father," I said.

"That is possible, but we must not leap to conclusions, Watson. There is still much we do not know."

Holmes spent the rest of the afternoon reading Bertram Abbey's mystery novel, a copy of which he had obtained from a local bookstore, while I went through the daily newspapers. I found nary a word about Rafferty's murder or our investigation, but it would not be long before Holmes and I were once again making headlines.

Abbey's mansion was a rather hideous affair, a pile of blood-red brick adorned with huge splotches of swirling orange terra-cotta, which erupted from the walls like outsized carbuncles. Jutting out from one corner was a tower almost as tall as a lighthouse, its uppermost chamber aglow as though guiding us to the mansion. A high hedge penetrated by a broad iron gate surrounded the home, which was set well back from Summit Avenue at the edge of the bluffs overlooking downtown.

On our cab ride up to the mansion, we passed the vast sandstone fortress once occupied by James J. Hill. My thoughts at once went back to our first meeting with the Empire Builder, in August 1894, and of the many adventures that followed in pursuit of the arsonist known as the Red Demon. How long ago that seemed!

Holmes noticed too and remarked, "Mr. Hill was a most extraordinary man and an honorable friend. I sometimes think he should still be there in his mighty house, seated by a fire in the study, reading a book and making great plans. But of course there is no defeating time."

My friend uttered these gloomy sentiments as the cab driver turned into the driveway of Abbey's mansion and deposited us at the front stoop. A young man in perfectly starched red, white, and gold livery greeted us at the door and led us into an elaborately furnished parlor lined with windows providing a magnificent view of the city and the broad valley of the Mississippi. Abbey, who was seated on a cream-colored couch with thick, rounded armrests, stood up at once and came over to greet us.

"Ah, what a signal occasion this is," he said as he shook our hands. "Sherlock Holmes and Dr. John Watson in the flesh! I am honored, sirs, to be in your presence. Please, sit down."

Although Abbey was about forty years of age, he had a gymnast's agile body and he radiated a sense of youthful energy. Everything about his manner was sharp and lively. He spoke quickly, moved quickly, and was obviously quick of mind. After we had settled in with strongly alcoholic aperitifs brought by another liveried servant, the conversation turned to Abbey himself and his achievements as a writer.

"I must confess I have not read your poetry, Mr. Abbey, but I found your mystery novel to be quite brilliant," Holmes said. "No less an authority than Dr. Watson has said so, and I should not doubt he's learned a few authorial tricks from reading it."

This was not true—all I knew about Abbey's novel was what I'd read in Rafferty's notes—but I said, "Very true, very true. Your mystery is indeed excellent."

"Why, I am flattered," Abbey said, "but you must know I think of it as a mere trifle."

"To the contrary," said Holmes, "*The Summit of Death* is quite instructive. Our friend Mr. Rafferty was convinced it offered some remarkable insights into the nature of Daniel St. Aubin, a practiced blackmailer whom I believe you knew."

"I am afraid Mr. Rafferty, may he rest in peace, was mistaken. He thought the fictional William Kent was based on Daniel St. Aubin, but such was not the case. My fictional characters are garments spun from the wool of many sheep."

"I see. But you were well acquainted with Mr. St. Aubin, were you not?"

"'Well acquainted' overstates the case, Mr. Holmes. St. Aubin attended a few of my salons and read some stories, which I'm afraid were not very good. Then he stopped coming, and that was the last

I saw of him. Moreover, he most certainly never tried to blackmail me, nor would he have any ammunition, as it were, to do so. I have not led a blameless life, Mr. Holmes—who has?—but I have done nothing of which I am ashamed."

Abbey uttered these words with smooth conviction, and if he was lying, he was very good at it. Holmes, who displayed no reaction to Abbey's assertions, pressed ahead.

"And yet I am reliably informed the police opened an investigation into a letter you received which made certain threats."

"There was no such letter. I fear you have been hearing unfounded rumors."

"So you know of no police investigation into the matter under the direction of Detective Jackson Grimshaw?"

"No. I have heard of Grimshaw, but I have never met him. I believe he has a reputation as something of a brute."

"His reputation is well deserved," Holmes said. "Perhaps it is fortunate you have never encountered him."

Although I thought Holmes might next turn to the subject of Johnny Riordan, he instead posed only a few more general questions before we were summoned to dinner.

Our meal, presented in a long dining room decorated with fading murals depicting frontier scenes of Indians, settlers, and cavalrymen, was superb. Abbey's cook, whom he described as a "talented young fellow I stole from the kitchen of the Waldorf Astoria in New York," included broiled whitefish, three kinds of potatoes, and fresh steamed vegetables from a greenhouse on the property, all accompanied by a superb French Chardonnay. Holmes, never a gourmand and often uninterested in eating at all, made no comment on the excellent fare. But once our dessert of glazed fruit tarts had been served and coffee poured, Holmes resumed his close questioning of our host.

"Were you by chance at the Ryan Hotel on the night Mr. Rafferty was killed?"

Holmes no doubt expected a denial from our host, but instead Abbey said, "Yes, I was there. It was a mere coincidence, of course."

"I see. What brought you to the hotel?"

"It was a private matter. I occasionally book a room at the Ryan when I wish to spend time with a favorite friend away from all the prying eyes here."

"Who was this friend?"

"Mr. Holmes, I am surprised you would ask. A true gentleman does not reveal such things."

"How noble of you," Holmes said but did not press the point, in keeping with his earlier statement to me about saving some ammunition for another time.

Holmes then tried a ruse in the hope Abbey might make a damaging admission. "During your stay at the Ryan that night, I have reason to believe you encountered Mr. Rafferty. Indeed, someone saw you knocking on the door of his apartment."

Abbey, however, admitted to nothing. "That is not true, Mr. Holmes, and I suspect this supposed witness of yours is a phantasm. The fact is, I wasn't even aware Mr. Rafferty resided at the hotel until I read the newspapers the next day. What a terrible thing his murder was! Do you have any clues as to the killer's identity?"

"Several," Holmes said. "Now, may I ask in which room at the hotel you stayed that night?"

"There is a corner suite on the third floor, number 320, that I usually check into."

"I see. And you were in the room all night?"

"Yes."

"So you never went up to the sixth floor?"

Abbey looked genuinely baffled. "Why would I do that?"

"Perhaps to meet someone."

"Sorry, Mr. Holmes, but that's simply not true."

"By the way, what time did your anonymous friend join you in your suite?"

Abbey gave an exaggerated shrug, let out a deep sigh, and raised his arms as though appealing for divine intervention.

"Mr. Holmes, I know you wish to investigate Mr. Rafferty's murder to the fullest extent, and I am happy to be of any help I can, but does it really matter what time my friend arrived or when he left?"

"It does if you should find yourself in need of an alibi."

"And why would I need an alibi?"

"You were in the hotel, just one floor above Mr. Rafferty's apartment, on the night he was killed. You were also acquainted with, and possibly blackmailed by, a young man whose murder Mr. Rafferty was investigating. Both circumstances are suspicious. Surely, as a writer of mysteries, you must know what that means."

"Ah, so I am regarded as a suspect. How intriguing. But the simple fact of the matter is that I had nothing to do with Mr. Rafferty's murder and would have had no reason whatsoever to kill him, or anyone else for that matter."

"I make no accusations, Mr. Abbey. I am merely exploring possibilities, much as your detective Vincent St. Germain would do if he were on the case. I am sure you understand. Indeed, I have but a few more questions. Were you interviewed by the police on the night of Mr. Rafferty's death?"

"No. I was unaware there had been a murder until one of the hotel clerks told me the next morning as I was checking out."

"Did your friend check out with you at the same time?"

"No, he left earlier than I did."

"Did the police by chance interview him?"

"Not that I'm aware of."

"Very well. I thank you for your cooperation, Mr. Abbey. You may be certain I will soon identify Mr. Rafferty's murderer."

"Well, that is good to hear. He was by all accounts a fine man. Now, would the two of you be interested in a postprandial drink? I have some excellent Amontillado that would do quite nicely."

As we drank our wine in the parlor, Holmes said, "You have been a most delightful host, Mr. Abbey. I must say I am fascinated by your beautiful home. It must require a large staff to maintain."

"Yes, I usually employ five or six people."

"Mr. Rafferty, I know, had a particular interest in one of those employees, a young man named Johnny Riordan. He seems to have been a friend of Daniel St. Aubin. It has even been bruited about that he and Mr. St. Aubin were involved in a blackmail scheme of some kind. I should very much like to speak with Mr. Riordan. Do you know where I could reach him?"

The mention of Riordan appeared to cause Abbey some distress, and he began to drum the fingers of one hand on his knee, as though trying to dispel nervous energy building up inside him. But he did not relinquish his self-control.

"Mr. Riordan left my employ some months ago. It was in November, as I recall, and I have not seen him since. I don't believe he is in St. Paul anymore, but as to his present whereabouts, I'm afraid I can be of no help to you."

"I have heard he was in New Orleans for a time and that you sent him there."

"I did not send him anywhere, but it is possible he went to New Orleans of his own accord."

"I see. How old do you suppose he is?"

"I'm not sure. Perhaps twenty or so. Why do you ask?"

"Mere curiosity. If he were younger, say under eighteen, I imagine some questions might be raised about his activities here. You do enjoy intimate relationships with some of your servants, do you not?"

The audacity of the question stunned me, and Abbey as well. He rang a bell cord and then rose from his chair, a frozen smile on his face. "It has been a pleasure, Mr. Holmes, to meet you and Dr. Watson. Unfortunately, I have urgent business to attend to this evening."

The liveried servant who had greeted us at the door reappeared and Abbey said, "John, please secure a taxi for my visitors and then show them out. Good evening, gentlemen."

"Well, that was quite a final scene," I said once we were in the cab. "Abbey is obviously hiding something when it comes to this Riordan fellow."

Holmes responded with a heavy sigh. "That is the trouble with this business, Watson. Everyone involved has secrets."

18

The Priest

Pierre Jean Denis grew up on a dairy farm in the pale light of eastern Canada among wooded hills and rocky fields hard won from the wilderness. His father, a fun-loving man who played the fiddle every chance he could, claimed to be a direct descendant of a French adventurer who had sailed with Jacques Cartier to the New World. His Scotch-Irish mother was a soulful woman marooned in a place much too small for her dreams. She loved music and art and books, and when Denis was a boy she took time out of her harried life to read to him every night. He was her youngest son and her favorite, and because of her he grew up speaking English as well as French.

By the time he was twelve Denis understood that life on the farm promised little except endless drudgery steeped in the odor of manure and hay and lowing cows. His three older brothers and a younger sister seemed satisfied enough with their lives, but Denis longed for something more. He had also begun to feel spiritual stirrings, especially on those nights when he left his sleeping family to go out to what he thought of as his sacred place—a boulder-strewn hillock near the farm that offered a sweeping view of the night sky. The spectacle of the stars always amazed him and he wondered how they had come to be. He saw the aurora borealis on rare occasions, and the phenomenon seemed to him so profound and beautiful that only a God in heaven could have created it.

Every Sunday morning Denis and his family walked two miles to a little country church to attend mass. Denis loved the mystery and magic of the ritual, and he also found a friend in the local priest, a jolly man of faith who encouraged him to consider whether God might be calling him to serve. But how, Denis wondered, would he know what God wanted him to do?

Then one winter night, gazing at the stars from his perch, Denis felt a burning inside him despite the cold. He would later struggle to describe the sensation, but he likened it to a sharp, hot tongue of fire. It was painful yet also purifying, as though flames were burning away all the refuse inside him, clearing the way for some grand transformation. God had called.

Denis's parents, pleased to have a devoutly religious child in the family, supported him when he announced at age sixteen that he wished to become a priest. They were not as happy when he informed them that his vocation would take him far from home. His parents had assumed Pierre would attend the nearest seminary, in Toronto, but he had other plans. He wanted a complete escape from his existing circumstances, an entirely new beginning that would allow him to pursue his vocation free of filial distractions or duties. God and the priesthood would become his only family.

But how to effect his escape? His family had no money to send him beyond Toronto, and to go elsewhere would require resources he did not possess. Never lacking for boldness, Denis concocted a plan that on the face of it seemed ridiculous. But he believed God was looking out for him, and so he sat down and wrote a letter addressed to "James J. Hill, Great Northern Railway, Saint Paul, Minnesota, U.S.A."

Denis knew about Hill because his mother was related to the great man and talked about him often. "I am a cousin twice removed from Mr. Hill," she liked to say, "but much further removed from his fortune." Hill had grown up just twenty miles south of the Denis family farm in circumstances as rough and unpromising as theirs. Yet by sheer force of will he had managed to overcome his rude beginnings and make a magnificent mark on the world. Denis desperately wanted to do the same.

In his letter Denis pointed out how he had been raised near Hill's own family farm and had shared many of his experiences. "Just as you must have felt at my age, I believe I cannot stay where I am. I must move out into the wider world." He concluded by asking whether Hill, "out of Christian charity and a willingness to assist a poor relative, might help me go to St. Paul to study for the priesthood and so be of service to the faithful of your community."

When Denis told his parents about the letter, his father, skeptical by nature, laughed and said, "Well, I am sure the almighty Mr. Hill will get to it first thing. I am thinking, son, you might have been better off appealing to God directly and waiting for a message from heaven."

Yet Denis never lost hope, patiently awaiting what he blithely assumed would be a favorable reply. To the family's vast surprise, one arrived in the mail a month later. What Denis's father didn't know was that Hill, despite his lofty position, read or had read to him every piece of correspondence he received, without exception. After Hill's secretary read the letter from Denis aloud, Hill said, "Give it to Mary and see what she wishes to do with it." Unlike her husband, Mary Hill was a devout Catholic, and she was receptive to Denis's plea, providing train fare to St. Paul and a small stipend.

He arrived in St. Paul in 1894, just as the St. Paul Seminary was moving to a new campus largely funded by a half-million-dollar donation from Hill. Most of Denis's fellow seminarians came from Minnesota or nearby Wisconsin, and at first he felt out of place. But he met some fellow French speakers and he soon settled into the structured life of the seminary. His first sexual experience came a few months letter, with a seminarian he'd grown close to, and it left him confused and uncertain.

He confided his sin in the confessional and received a stern lecture. Sex was the enemy of divine love, the priest told him, and if he could not control his carnal impulses, he had no business in the seminary. Denis took the lecture to heart and held to his vow of celibacy thereafter, though not without difficulty. He found himself attracted to both men and women, but he learned how to ward off temptation through hard work and long bouts of prayer.

By the time his seminary days drew to a close and he prepared for ordination, Denis had come to realize that the priesthood was in its own way a worldly career like any other. Doing God's work was not without earthly rewards, as Denis saw whenever he was in the presence of Archbishop John Ireland, a figure of Hill-like drive and ambition who commanded a community of thousands of the faithful. Ireland exuded power, which Denis found to be a surprising intoxicant.

Denis had kept in touch with Mrs. Hill and found ways to insinuate himself into her good graces. He sent her notes on her birthday, alerted her to special prayers he'd said on her behalf, and frequently complimented her on her steadfast devotion to the church. Just before his ordination in 1902, he told her how he hoped to work one day as an assistant to Ireland, whom he described as "one of the greatest men of our time."

When Mary Hill talked, Ireland always paid strict attention, money being a great inducement to the art of listening. Denis's name came up in one of their conversations and before long the newly minted priest was assigned to the chancery office as an aide to the archbishop. Smooth and well-spoken, Denis quickly mastered the subtleties of archdiocesan politics. Within a few years he became Ireland's right-hand man and helped plan and raise funds for the huge new cathedral that was the archbishop's abiding dream. He also proved adept at dealing with city hall, and whenever the archdiocese needed some earthly accommodation to advance its heavenly mission, Denis could be counted on to get the mayor and city council in line. By age thirty-five, Denis had been elevated to monsignor, and there was talk he might be a bishop one day.

But there was other talk as well, and it was not as favorable. Denis had grown into a handsome man, tall and athletic, and he was known to have a roving eye. While an occasional, discreet lapse from celibacy was not considered cause for undue alarm by his superiors, there were boundaries and Denis eventually crossed them. A prominent Minneapolis businessman went to Ireland to report that his wife was having an affair with Denis, who had no choice but to admit to the archbishop what he had done.

Two weeks later, he was "loaned" to another bishop and then assigned to new duties as the pastor of a parish in the bleak muskeg country of far northern Minnesota. "We will find out now if you really want to be a man of God," Ireland told him. After much soul-searching and prayer, Denis decided he did, and in his "Siberian exile," as he called it, he became a beloved figure to his mostly impoverished parishioners, known for his kindness and compassion. He remained in his remote outpost for five years, until Ireland's death in 1918, and he assumed he would thereafter always lead a lost but devout life in God's backwaters.

But the church, he had long since learned, could be as mysterious as the God it served, and in 1919 he was reassigned, without explanation, back to the chancery office in St. Paul by the new archbishop. Mrs. Hill, he later learned, had been his angel once again. Denis threw himself into his new work. By 1927, when he celebrated his fiftieth birthday, Denis was newly installed in a plum job as rector of the cathedral. But before the year was done, troubles rained down on him like the wrath of God, beginning with a visit from Daniel St. Aubin.

St. Aubin appeared at the rectory at eleven and requested an immediate meeting with Denis to discuss what he called "a matter of the utmost urgency." Denis ushered the young man, who was strikingly handsome, into his office and asked how he could be of help. It was then he discovered that St. Aubin's good looks masked a deep and malevolent corruption of the soul. Staring straight at Denis with an insolent grin, St. Aubin removed a glossy photograph from a briefcase and set it on the table between them. "The lighting isn't the best," he said as casually as if he was talking about a photograph of a family picnic, "but you'll get the picture. It seems you've been a very bad boy."

The photograph, taken some months earlier at the Ryan Hotel, was shocking. Denis had no idea how or by whom it had been taken, but he knew it had the power to destroy his life in an instant. They were seated in a consulting room beneath a dour photograph of Pope Pius XI, whose quest for world peace, Denis thought ruefully, was of no use in his sudden predicament. Not even a papal blessing could save him.

"Pretty revealing, don't you agree?" St. Aubin said. "You're in a big jam, Mr. Priest. No vow of chastity for you, is there? Imagine the scandal if the public found out who you've been sleeping with at the Ryan. It would be awful, don't you think? The archbishop wouldn't be very happy with you, either."

As he spoke, St. Aubin twirled a rubber band in his hand, and to Denis it looked like a small noose. St. Aubin was bleary-eyed and sometimes slurred his words. He clearly had been drinking, despite the early hour, and he seemed to take pleasure from the pain he was inflicting.

"What do you want?" Denis asked.

"I'm a reasonable fellow, and there's a way to keep this nasty photo in the dark, as it were. Can you guess what it might be, Mr. Priest?"

"Money, I suppose."

"Exactly. Five thousand dollars would work."

"I don't have that kind of money."

"Don't you? I'm sure you could find it somewhere. I'll be back in two weeks. Have the money then or my next stop will be at the chancery office. The newspapers might be interested, too. You've been sleeping in beds where you shouldn't be, and you're a big phony if there ever was one. Get the money, you bugger. It's the only chance you have."

THE MOMENT ST. AUBIN had slithered away, Denis called Abbey to describe his frightening encounter. "I don't know how he got that photo. Somebody must have been hiding in the room or made a hole in the wall or something."

Abbey responded with a stream of expletives. When he'd calmed down, he said, "St. Aubin is a well-known blackmailer. He came after me, too."

"What did you do?"

"I got him off my back, but it appears he hasn't learned his lesson."

"Well, all I know is that he told me the archbishop, not to mention the newspapers, would be very interested in that photograph."

"How much does he want?"

"Five thousand dollars, if you can believe that. Where does he think I'd get that kind of money?"

"Maybe he figures you've been dipping into the collection plate."

"That's not funny."

"Listen, don't panic. The police have been bought and paid for. They'll take care of St. Aubin and get that photo."

"What about the newspapers? If they print a story—"

"They won't, believe me. For now, just ignore St. Aubin's threats. We can deal with him."

"What about God?"

"What about Him?"

"I fear there is a great punishment coming for my sins."

"Well, you take that up with the Almighty the next time the two of you chat," Abbey said before ending the call, "or maybe you'll just have to pray for forgiveness."

ON THE FIRST OF DECEMBER, two days after St. Aubin delivered his blackmail demand, Denis experienced another great shock. It came from Margaret O'Donnell in the confessional. What she revealed left Denis deeply worried, and barely a week later she was dead.

He'd first caught a glimpse of her a year or so earlier during Saturday afternoon confessions at the cathedral. She was waiting in the pews with the other penitents, and she was so beautiful Denis found it hard to keep from staring at her. She had a fine Irish face, long auburn hair that flowed down to her shoulders, and she exuded a dewy sexuality that Denis thought must have all but hypnotized any boy, or man, within sight of her.

Her confession that day had proved to be unremarkable. She'd sassed her father, been unkind to a classmate at school, used a bad word or two. Denis found her presence beyond the screen all but unbearable, a temptation sent straight from hell. But he quickly repressed such thoughts. She was, after all, just a child. Still, he wondered if she was aware of her effect on the young men who must have flocked around her.

"Do you have a boyfriend, my dear?" he asked.

"No, my father doesn't allow that."

"Ah, that is just as well. You are at an age when danger lurks, especially with boys. You understand the facts of life, don't you?"

"Yes, I guess so."

"Good. Then you must remain pure until the proper time comes and you have been joined with a man in the sacred bonds of matrimony. God expects that of you, and you must expect that of yourself as well. Do not succumb to temptation or let yourself be fooled by some boy who wants to commit an immoral act with you."

"Yes, father," she said but in a mechanical way that gave Denis pause. It was as though she was already bored by their conversation.

"Are you at Derham Hall now?" he asked, referring to the city's largest Catholic high school for girls.

"No, I left. I go to the Summit School now."

Denis wondered why she wasn't in the Catholic school system, as she should be, but he didn't pursue the matter. He gave her ten Hail Marys and five Our Fathers and sent her on her way, hoping he might see her again.

Now, after a long hiatus, she was back in the confessional, Denis's last penitent of the day, and she was in tears, choking back sobs, when he slid open the screen.

"I think I'm going to have a baby," she blurted out. "Sometimes I wish I was dead."

"Never say that," Denis said and did his best to calm her, offering all the pious platitudes he could muster and assuring her that everything would be all right. "It's not the end of the world."

"Maybe not for you," she said, "but what am I going to do?"

"Don't worry. I'm here to help. Do you know how far along you are?"

"I'm not sure."

"All right. But I presume you're not showing yet, is that right?"

"Yes."

"Well, that's good. There's time then to make plans. Have you told your father?"

"You know I can't tell him."

"I understand. But he'll find out when your condition becomes obvious."

"Maybe that won't happen."

"What do you mean?"

"An abortion. Girls have them all the time."

Although the church's position on abortion was clear, Denis found himself tongue-tied. Would she care if he told her abortion was a sin in the eyes of God and the church? So was extramarital sex, and yet here Margaret was, with child. What was to be done?

"You shouldn't make any rash decisions," Denis said. "Perhaps you need better advice than I can give you. There's a woman I want you to see. She understands what you're going through and can be of great help."

"And can she give me money, too?"

"What do you mean?"

"I have to get away from here. That's what Danny says, but I don't know."

"Who's Danny?"

"Danny St. Aubin? Do you know him?"

Denis was stunned. How could that snake Danny St. Aubin be involved with her? Denis debated whether to tell her what a vicious man St. Aubin really was, but he thought the better of it. Denigrating St. Aubin would be a bad idea if word got back to him about it. Better, Denis thought, to offer veiled hints that it wasn't wise to confide in a man such as St. Aubin.

"You must be very careful in whom you place your trust," Denis finally said. "You never know who has your best interests in mind."

"Well, Danny has been nice to me, which is more than I can say about most men."

Then, without prompting, she revealed a secret Denis could scarcely believe, and he saw at once that he was in danger. The secret was highly explosive, and if it ever detonated Denis was almost certain to be collateral damage. He had to be very careful. Still, he couldn't just leave Margaret dangling, so he instructed her on how to contact the woman he'd told her about. "But there's no need to mention my name. Just tell her about your situation, and she'll take it from there. I know you'll like her."

After he'd given Margaret a blessing and sent her off with a few Hail Marys and Our Fathers, Denis felt his heart sink. He knew what he should do, but the consequences would be terrible. Doing the right thing was doing the work of God, but at what cost? Would misery and shame be his reward? And why had God sent him so many troubles? That night, alone in his room at the rectory, he opened up the Book of Job and read it more carefully than he ever had before, but he found no consolation.

A few days later, Denis learned that Richard O'Donnell had sent his wayward daughter to the House of the Good Shepherd, indicating he knew of her pregnancy and wished to keep it a secret. But could he do so? Margaret had to be in a volatile state, ready to erupt with the truth at any moment, and if she did, there would be many casualties.

FROM THE TIME he was a seminarian, Denis had kept a notebook filled with what he called his "Meditations." These were gnomic observations about God and His relationship to sinful mankind. Like so many others, Denis maintained his faith despite regular assaults of doubt. The Meditations were a means by which he sought to reinforce belief through the contemplation of divine mystery.

In one of his Meditations Denis wrote, "God does not sleep, and His eternal wakefulness is both our burden and our salvation." Yet as Denis's troubles deepened, "the awful gaze of God," as he once called it, began to fade away, like a ship slowly disappearing over the horizon. Instead of a powerful presence, the Almighty grew ever more hidden and inscrutable, and Denis felt the very foundations of his faith being tested. He had sinned and sinned again, and God seemed ready to abandon him to earthly punishment and shame. And if God no longer cared, should he?

Before long, that question would become even more urgent because new troubles were in the wind. Daniel St. Aubin was back on the prowl, looking for the biggest payday of his life. He intended to demand a ransom of twenty thousand dollars, and he thought Denis was just the man to collect it for him.

19
"I Fear for Your Soul"

On the Monday following his eventful visit with Bertram Abbey, Rafferty caught up with Margo Sartell in her studio on Fourth Street, a block from the new public library overlooking Rice Park. Photographers were averse to high rent, and Sartell's studio occupied the upper floor of a decrepit brick building that dated to the pioneer days of the city. The building had no elevator, so Rafferty had to climb up a narrow set of steps to the studio. He was panting by the time he rang the doorbell.

Sartell greeted him with a smile. "Shadwell Rafferty! Well, I'll be damned. I thought you'd be dead by now, and then I started seeing your name in the newspapers, and lo and behold, you're alive and kicking. Have a seat and don't mind the mess."

Rafferty had first met Sartell, who was just shy of forty, during her brief stint as a newspaper photographer. Petite but fiery, with blazing red hair and hard blue eyes that showed no mercy, she'd been the first woman in St. Paul ever to hold that job. She only lasted a few years before something—word had it that it was a torrid affair with the newspaper's married city editor—got her fired. Undeterred, she set up her own studio, and her skill, along with a willingness to do just about anything to get a picture, won her steady work from divorce lawyers, private detectives, insurance agents, and anyone else interested in documenting bad human behavior.

"A seat would be most welcome," Rafferty said. He wedged himself into a rickety Windsor chair next to a slanted, north-facing window that admitted soft light into the studio, which was crammed with cameras, enlargers, shelves of chemicals, and all the other apparatuses of the photographer's art. Photographs were pinned up everywhere on the walls, and in one of them Rafferty recognized a certain well-known jurist, arm in arm with a young woman who most definitely was not his wife.

"Doesn't look like you're doing any weddings these days," Rafferty observed. "I see no blushing brides up on the walls."

Sartell responded with a gleeful snort and said, "Ha, I'm not exactly the type for that sort of crap. It's much more fun seeing people violate their vows than taking them, don't you think?"

"And more lucrative too, I imagine."

"A girl has to do what she can," Sartell said. She wore overalls over a plaid shirt and was fussing with an enlarger as she spoke. "Damn thing doesn't want to stay in focus. Something loose somewhere. So what are you looking for, Mr. Rafferty? Marriage is out of the question. An old bull like you would be too much for a poor young thing like me."

Rafferty managed one of his best roaring laughs, of the kind Wash Thomas had once described as "the universe being richly amused at itself."

"Ah, I do believe it would be the other way around, but I am not here bearing a proposal."

"You want some information, I suppose."

"I do. It concerns a photo I believe you took some months ago at the Ryan."

"I have taken many photos there, but of course my work is always confidential, at least until it appears in a court file."

"Or someone buys it. I have one hundred dollars in my pocket that is itching to be released if you can confirm you once took a photo, no doubt through a cleverly concealed wall hole, showing Bertram Abbey and a boy together in intimate circumstances."

"So that's what you're after. Interesting. Why is it any business of yours?"

"I'm investigating the death of Daniel St. Aubin. I have reason to believe he was a blackmailer and that Abbey was his intended victim."

"No kidding. That's very curious. Well, you can hang on to that hundred dollars. I'll tell you all about it, free of charge. As for who was being blackmailed, you may have it wrong, Mr. Rafferty. Abbey's bedmate was no boy, and I'd say he was the one in real trouble."

"What do you mean?"

"Abbey was with Monsignor Denis from the cathedral. How about that for a nice tasty scandal?"

Rafferty thought he was too old to be surprised by anything, but now he had to admit he was wrong. "Well now, Miss Sartell, you have caught me unawares. I did not expect to hear the monsignor's name in connection with such a business."

"In my line of work, Mr. Rafferty, you learn that everybody's just a secret waiting to be exposed. But if you're looking for the photo in question, you're too late. I don't have it."

"Why is that?"

"Good question. Do you know that big cop, Grimshaw?"

Rafferty's ears perked up at the mention of the detective's name. He said, "I know the man and how he operates all too well. Am I right in guessing you had an unpleasant encounter with him of late?"

"*Unpleasant* isn't nearly a strong enough word. That gorilla came barging in here back in November and he wasn't polite. He said I'd better cooperate with him or else."

"He wanted the photo of Abbey and Monsignor Denis."

"That's right. He said he knew I'd taken a photo and if I didn't turn it over along with the negatives, he'd shut down my business and in general make life miserable for me."

"Ah, and what did you say to that?"

"I told him to go to hell and get a court order along the way if he wanted to seize any of my photos. He didn't like that. He was still shaking his fist at me when he left. You'll never guess what happened next."

Old age and experience had made Rafferty a good guesser. "Someone broke into your studio, ransacked it, and stole the photo and negatives from your files."

Sartell looked at Rafferty with a kind of bemused respect. "Aren't you the clever old man? My studio was trashed the very next night. The photo and negatives were stolen."

"Could you describe the photo to me?"

"Two naked guys in bed. That says it all, doesn't it?"

"It does. When did you take the picture?"

"In October. The fifteenth, as I recall."

"May I ask who hired you for the job? Was it Danny St. Aubin?"

"No. I never met him, but I heard he had a regular blackmail business going. I guess you could say he was a competitor. Did he somehow get his hands on the photo?"

"Possibly. So if Danny didn't hire you—"

"It's no use, Mr. Rafferty. I won't tell you who did. I have a duty to protect my client's confidentiality."

"Would that hundred dollars in my pocket make a difference in your answer?"

"Afraid not. I have my principles, just like everyone else. I told you about the photo only because of what Grimshaw did. I'm sure he or one of his police pals staged the break-in here, but good luck proving it."

"It would seem so. But if Danny had a copy of the photo, which seems likely, I'm wondering where he got it. From your client, I'm guessing."

"Could be. All I can tell you is that he didn't get it from me."

"I will take your word on that, and I thank you for your help," Rafferty said as he struggled to get out of his chair. Sartell came over to help.

"Think nothing of it," she said. "After all, what good is dirt if you can't fling it around now and then?"

After Rafferty made his way back down the stairs and out into the street, he paused to think about the photograph. Who would have wanted such a picture and been willing to pay for it? With all the setup required, Sartell must have charged her client several hundred dollars. It had to have been ordered by someone with money who believed either Denis or Abbey was a cheating lover. And then St. Aubin had somehow managed to obtain a copy of the photograph. Rafferty let out a long sigh. Mysteries were piling up one after the other, jammed together like train cars after a derailment, and Rafferty was beginning to doubt he'd live long enough to untangle the mess.

Rafferty knew every employee at the Ryan, and after his talk with Sartell he began making inquiries about Abbey and Denis and their assignations. He discovered the two had been very circumspect, and he couldn't find anyone at the hotel who'd actually seen them together. So he decided he'd have to try extracting the truth from Monsignor Denis, however unpleasant that might be.

Denis had all but panicked when St. Aubin showed him the photograph, and yet he'd also feared for a long time that his sins would one day catch up with him. His relationship with Abbey went all the way back to 1907, the year Abbey's mother died. Although Florence Abbey was no one's idea of a devout Christian woman, she had been raised a Catholic and out of sheer habit regularly donated substantial sums to the church, all of which qualified her for a funeral mass at the old downtown cathedral. It was there, on a grim November afternoon, that Denis, who had been assigned to preside over the funeral mass, met Abbey.

Like Abbey, Denis had recently lost his own beloved mother and had just returned from her funeral in Canada. He was helpful and consoling to Abbey, who had adored his free-spirited mother, and in time they became close. Although Abbey presented himself as a hard-eyed man of the world ready to dismiss the notion of God as an old fairy tale, he enjoyed talking with Denis about the essential mysteries of the world, and their discussions often went far into the night. On one of those nights, after three bottles of wine, they first had sex.

Denis was torn by his sexuality in a way Abbey was not, and their lovemaking both repelled him and gripped him to the core. Afterwards, Denis insisted they must never have sex again, but it was a vow he couldn't quite keep. Denis was deathly afraid they'd be discovered together, exposing him to unendurable disgrace, and so they made love very rarely, no more than once or twice a year, usually in a room Abbey rented at the Ryan Hotel.

Between trysts, Denis rarely saw Abbey. He feared that if they were frequently seen together, people might start talking. But Denis did telephone now and then, just to see how Abbey was doing. As for their occasional meetings at the Ryan, they remained a well-kept secret until that late November morning when Daniel St. Aubin— the devil in human flesh if there ever was one—paid Denis a visit.

LATE ON THE AFTERNOON of January ninth, with snow softly falling, Rafferty took a cab to the cathedral's rectory to look for Denis. It pained Rafferty to think of the questions he would have to ask, but he saw no way around it. He liked Denis and respected him as a man whose faith seemed genuine. But the monsignor was neck deep in the St. Aubin affair, and Rafferty knew he had to interrogate him.

A secretary at the rectory said Denis was in the cathedral, and Rafferty soon found him there, puttering around the altar. Above him the cathedral's dome sprang toward the heavens, and under its vast sway even a man of Denis's holy stature seemed inconsequential, a speck before the eyes of God. Rafferty caught Denis's attention with a wave, and the monsignor, dressed in his usual black garb and Roman collar, came over to talk.

"Why, Shadwell, how nice to see you," he said, shaking Rafferty's hand. "How are you?"

"Old and slow," Rafferty said, "but not quite ready yet for the great beyond. Do you have a few minutes? There's something we must talk about."

"Of course. Let's take one of those pews at the back. It will be quiet there." Denis had already been tipped off by Abbey that Rafferty might pay him a visit. The monsignor's simple strategy would be to deny everything.

He did so, responding to Rafferty's questions with a tone of aggrieved disbelief. Yes, he knew Danny St. Aubin but had met him only briefly. No, he was not aware of any blackmail scheme. The disgusting allegation he had been sexually involved with Bertram Abbey was defamation, pure and simple, and Rafferty should be ashamed for even bringing up such a baseless claim. As for the allegedly compromising photograph taken at the Ryan Hotel, where was it? Nowhere, because it did not exist.

Rafferty was a well-practiced judge of lying in all its forms—he'd listened to men tell tall tales in his saloon for thirty-five years—and he knew Denis wasn't being truthful. It was also apparent Denis had been ready for him, no doubt after being alerted by Abbey.

"Monsignor, I am deeply disappointed," Rafferty said. "You have not been truthful with me. I have no interest in exposing your secret life, but a man has been murdered, and I think you know something about it."

"That is not true. Why would you say such a thing?"

"For one, because St. Aubin was looking for you outside the Ryan on the night he died. He asked the hotel's doorman if he knew you by sight. Why would he have asked that unless he expected to find you in the vicinity?"

"I really can't imagine why. I happened to be shopping down-town that night, but I never saw Mr. St. Aubin."

"God's truth?" Rafferty asked.

Denis said nothing.

"Monsignor, if you do not speak up and tell me all that you know of this business, you will have committed a grave offense in the eyes of God," Rafferty said. "I have always thought of you as a good and holy man. Perhaps you still are, but I fear for your soul."

Denis's head slumped and Rafferty thought he might break out in tears. Instead, he lifted his head up and said quietly, "We should all fear for our souls, Shadwell, but I do not think there is anything more to say."

WHEN DENIS CALLED ABBEY afterwards, he said, "It's as you feared. Rafferty knows about that photo of us together at the Ryan. What are we going to do?"

"We're going to stay calm. It doesn't surprise me that he found out. He's a sly old geezer and he seems to know pretty much everyone in St. Paul. But before you panic, let me ask you this: You said Rafferty is aware of the photo, but has he actually seen it?"

"I'm not sure."

"But he didn't show it to you, is that right?"

"Correct."

"Good. If he had the photo, he probably would have trotted it out just to get your reaction. And so long as he doesn't have it, he has no proof. I think everything will be fine."

"How can you be so sure?"

"There are protections in place. Your friend, the mayor, will see to it that everything remains under control."

"Oh God, I can't believe this is happening. The mayor must never know—"

"About what we do together? He probably doesn't. But if he

does find out, so what? Nothing will come out in public. The mayor controls the police, including Grimshaw, who is watching Rafferty closely. Besides, Rafferty is a very old man. He could die at any moment. All you have to do now is keep your mouth shut. This will all blow over and no one will be the wiser."

"I pray you are right."

"Praying is your business," Abbey said and hung up.

IN HIS MEDITATIONS THAT NIGHT, Denis wrote: "Is God still looking at me or has He finally turned away in disgust? Am I beyond salvation?" And yet Denis had to admit he was ready to jeopardize his eternal soul to save his life and reputation. What had happened—his role in St. Aubin's death, his trysts with Abbey, the terrible fate of Margaret O'Donnell—had to remain a secret. The alternative was simply too grim to contemplate.

He knew silence was the devil's bargain, and yet he could not bring himself to step forward into the light. If his sins became public knowledge, God could be of no earthly help to him. He would at best be exiled to some forgotten place and at worst defrocked. In either case, shame would envelop him like a cloud of soot, and he would never be clean again before the eyes of the world.

A life without faith or conscience would have been much easier, and Denis sometimes wished he had never gone to that hillock by his family farm and gazed out longingly at the stars. But he couldn't change who he was now, or could he? Perhaps, he thought, God could in the end turn back time, like rewinding a string in the opposite direction around a stick, and so undo all that had been done. It was a comforting thought, and Denis clung to it before he finally drifted off into a fitful sleep.

Rafferty was also busy that night, filling his notebook with detailed accounts of his interviews with Abbey and Denis. Both men had been dead-end alleys, closed off by lies Rafferty could not readily refute. Margo Sartell had obtained evidence of their sexual relationship, thereby providing an obvious source for blackmail, but her photograph—proof Rafferty needed—was gone. At the same time, she had refused to reveal who'd hired her, other than to say it wasn't St. Aubin. All of which left Rafferty without any solid evidence that St. Aubin was a blackmailer whose attempts to extort money had led to his murder.

Johnny Riordan was also on Rafferty's mind. Why had he left St. Paul so abruptly and what did he know about St. Aubin's various blackmail schemes? Supposedly, Riordan had gone to New Orleans, but finding him there was beyond Rafferty's means at the moment.

Just as Rafferty was about to finish up his notes, he received a phone call that brought vital new information. A scullery maid who worked at one of the mansions on Summit Avenue reported that she'd seen Riordan by chance in Minneapolis earlier in the day. Rafferty was smiling when he hung up the phone. Riordan, it seemed, wasn't out of reach after all. Rafferty added a quick note about the maid's report before he went to bed.

RIORDAN HAD RETURNED to the Twin Cities in early December following his "vacation" in New Orleans. He'd been packed off to the Crescent City without explanation, but he knew the real reason for his swift departure was that Abbey was being blackmailed by Daniel St. Aubin. Riordan, in fact, had helped set up the scheme.

He'd met Danny at one of Abbey's salons and was struck by his sheer physical beauty. But it turned out St. Aubin was interested in information, not sex, and Riordan eventually disclosed how he and other underage servants at Abbey's mansion performed regular bedroom duties. St. Aubin had then tried to exploit this intelligence by blackmailing Abbey. The fact that his employer was in trouble didn't bother Riordan in the least. In his view Abbey was just a bugger who happened to be rich and could afford to buy what he wanted. Love had nothing to do with it. If Abbey got himself in trouble because some of his bedmates were too young in the eyes of the law, so be it.

Riordan's time in New Orleans had been enjoyable enough, but he blew through Abbey's money on alcohol and clothes and parties until Abbey quit sending it. "You're on your own, Johnny Boy," Abbey told him over the phone. "You've had your little vacation, but it's time to move on. You're a resourceful young man, and I'm sure you'll land on your feet somewhere. But don't come back to St. Paul. Remember Grimshaw? He'll be looking for you if you do, and I'd hate to see you get hurt." That was the last time he'd spoken to Abbey.

Riordan knew he was taking a chance by coming back north but believed he'd be safe enough in Minneapolis, where no one from St. Paul, especially Grimshaw, would look for him. The two cities, Riordan knew, were separate, largely self-contained worlds. You were either from Minneapolis or St. Paul, but you couldn't be from both, and Riordan had heard stories about people who supposedly spent their entire lives in one without ever stepping foot in the other. There was also the convenient fact, from Riordan's point of view, that Grimshaw had no jurisdiction in Minneapolis.

Riordan had good reason to fear Grimshaw. He'd been at a club one night in St. Paul when Grimshaw came storming in, looking for someone. Riordan had gotten lippy and Grimshaw responded by shoving him up against a wall and hitting him so hard in the chest he wasn't sure he'd ever be able to breathe again. "Don't you ever mouth off to me, you little whore" had been the message Grimshaw delivered with his blow. Riordan never forgot it.

Once he reached Minneapolis, Riordan tracked down St. Aubin, who secured a job for him at the Munsingwear factory in Minneapolis and set him up with a cheap apartment in one of the mostly "colored" districts just north of downtown. Riordan soon realized, however, that St. Aubin had an ulterior motive for his generosity. St. Aubin had devised a new, "sure-fire" blackmail scheme, one that promised to bring in thousands of dollars, or so he claimed.

Riordan was skeptical—St. Aubin's attempt to blackmail Abbey hadn't met with success—but he agreed to serve as a middleman in the scheme because the money seemed too good to pass up. Living in a slum and working a stupid job held no appeal for him, and he desperately wanted a change of scenery. Except for the ridiculous costumed sex parties, Riordan had enjoyed his time in Abbey's mansion, feeling the moist, pleasant breath of wealth all around him. He still aspired to a life of ease, and he thought St. Aubin might help him attain it.

Then just minutes after Riordan had met St. Aubin on the night of December 16 in St. Paul, ready to consummate a twenty-thousand-dollar deal, St. Aubin lay dead in an alley. Riordan didn't believe for a second that St. Aubin had committed suicide, no matter what the cops in St. Paul were saying. Danny had been murdered and Riordan had no doubt who was responsible for the crime.

After Danny's death, Riordan's first thought was to lay low for a while or even leave Minneapolis out of fear for his own safety. But he soon had second thoughts. Maybe he could carry through the scheme that had cost Danny his life. Riordan was in possession of an envelope with some very interesting information, and there was someone who might pay him a lot of money for it. Exchanging the information for money would be extremely risky—as Danny's fate had demonstrated—but Riordan had survived by his wits all of his life, and twenty thousand dollars was a prize worth pursuing at any cost.

20

"We Are Tangled Up in a Web of Lies"

[From "Murder in St. Paul"]

Our meeting with Bertram Abbey in his ridiculous red house had seemed unsatisfactory to me, but Holmes took a different view when we discussed the matter later that night in his room.

"What a man hides is usually more interesting than what he reveals," Holmes noted. "For example, Mr. Abbey would not tell us whom he was with on the night of Mr. Rafferty's murder. Yet we can be all but certain it was Monsignor Denis, for the simple reason that had it been some other person—say an old lover with no obvious connection to the St. Aubin affair—then why bother to shield his identity? Rather, it would have made sense to identify the person, who could then have provided Mr. Abbey with an irrefutable alibi."

"I am not sure I agree. Perhaps Abbey simply didn't want to cause embarrassment to his partner, who could be someone prominent in the community."

"I will not deny you that possibility, Watson, but there is a way to find out, if we can force the truth out of Monsignor Denis."

"And how do you propose to do so? As we know from Rafferty's notes, he was not forthcoming when asked about his relationship with Abbey."

"True, but it has been three weeks since Mr. Rafferty talked with the monsignor. I believe his conscience will be gnawing at him by now, and that will work to our advantage. And if we apply the right sort of pressure, I am confident he will crack."

"What sort of pressure?"

Holmes responded by going over to his writing desk and removing a manila folder from one of the drawers. He handed it to me and said, "The incriminating photograph taken by Miss Sartell should loosen his tongue."

"Good God, Holmes, where did you get it?" I said, opening the folder. I expected to see a decidedly unpleasant image of Abbey and Denis in bed. Instead, I found a glossy eight-by-ten photograph of the Ryan Hotel.

"A thing known to exist but unseen can have a powerful effect," Holmes said with a smile. "We shall soon see if my little ruse will work."

By virtue of his worldwide notoriety, for which I can fairly claim some credit, Sherlock Holmes finds most doors open to him, and so it came as no surprise that Monsignor Denis agreed to an interview the next day. We met him late in the afternoon in the cathedral's rectory, a sober building of plain gray granite directly behind the mighty church. He escorted us into a consultation room with pale-blue walls and two high windows, which admitted the day's fading light. A large crucifix and a photograph of the Pope hung on the otherwise bare walls. Denis, all in black save for his white collar, sat across from us at an oak table as severe in its lines as the rest of the room, which felt like a cool sanctum far removed from the lush temptations of the world.

"I am honored to speak with you once again," Denis said. "Is there something in particular you wish to discuss?"

"There are several things," said Holmes, who had brought along the manila folder with the photograph inside. He set it on the table, making sure one edge of the glossy print protruded from the top of the folder. "Let us begin with the photograph in this envelope. I will not show it to you, unless you insist upon it, as I have no wish to cause embarrassment. But it should be obvious I know of your relationship with Mr. Abbey. I also know the two of you were being blackmailed by Daniel St. Aubin, and blackmail is always a motive for murder."

Denis stared down at the folder and began to reach for it before quickly pulling his hand back, as though afraid of being burned. Then he said in a quiet voice, "What do you intend to do with it?"

"I intend to destroy it when the time comes, providing you tell us the truth."

There was a long pause, which suggested Denis was thinking through his situation. Finally, he said, "Very well, what do you wish to know?"

"Tell us about how you were blackmailed."

Denis offered an account of the blackmail scheme, which was very much in line with what Rafferty had written in his notes.

After Denis had finished his rather lengthy narration, Holmes said, "You say you refused Mr. St. Aubin's demands for money, and yet, as you surely know, he did not commit suicide in December. Someone murdered him, and both you and Mr. Abbey must be regarded as prime suspects."

"I do not see why that would be the case, Mr. Holmes. St. Aubin's scheme failed and nothing came of it. There was no reason to murder him."

"So neither you nor Mr. Abbey ever paid him any money?"

"Not a cent. We agreed we could not give in to such vile demands."

"He did not threaten you with exposure after you refused to pay him?"

"Mr. Abbey and I concluded that his threats were as empty as he was. Mr. St. Aubin thought he could make some easy money, but once we resisted he simply gave up."

"I find that curious. Mr. St. Aubin was by all accounts a professional blackmailer. As such, he would not allow potentially lucrative victims to defy him and suffer no consequences. Instead, he would inflict public humiliation upon them, as a warning to others who might refuse his demands. And yet that did not happen in your case. Why do you suppose that was? Did you threaten him with criminal prosecution?"

"Not that I am aware of."

"So the matter wasn't brought to the attention of the police?"

"I really don't know. You would have to ask Mr. Abbey about that. I'm not sure what he may have done."

"Mr. Abbey denied contacting Detective Grimshaw or anyone else at the police department. Do you also deny doing so?"

"Yes."

"You are lying, Monsignor, and it does not become a man of the cloth."

"I am sorry you think that, but I am being honest with you."

Holmes's next question, which came as he picked up the folder and waved it toward Denis, surprised me. "Who hired the photographer to take this surreptitious picture?"

"I assume it was Mr. St. Aubin."

"Did he tell you that?"

"No."

"So, you do not know for certain."

"I cannot say that I do. But who else would have done it?"

"A very good question, Monsignor, for which I have no answer as yet."

Holmes, as was his wont, abruptly switched to a new line of questioning. Staring at the monsignor, he said, "Mr. Rafferty had evidence that you were in the vicinity of the Ryan Hotel on the evening Mr. St. Aubin was murdered. You denied it. Do you still do so?"

"Yes. I had nothing to do with his death."

"Yet you seem to have been a frequent visitor to the hotel. What were you doing there on the night of Mr. Rafferty's murder? A clerk said you spoke to him and then went upstairs."

Denis's reaction was swift and telling. His head snapped back as though he hoped to be as far away from us as he could, and he hesitated before answering. "Yes, I . . . I was there, but I know nothing of what happened to Mr. Rafferty."

"You went that night to see Mr. Abbey, is that right?"

"No, I most definitely did not! I was there to provide spiritual counseling to a parishioner who resides at the hotel."

Denis's denial was perhaps too emphatic, and Holmes took note. "I am an excellent judge of men, Monsignor, and in your troubled eyes I do not see the calm presence of the truth. However, let us move on. You were aware Mr. Rafferty lived at the Ryan, were you not?"

"Yes, but I was never in his apartment, if that's what you're asking. And as I told you, I most certainly had no involvement with his murder. I considered Mr. Rafferty a good friend."

"I am sure you did. What time did you leave the hotel?"

"It was around six, I believe."

"The desk clerk does not recall seeing you leave at that hour."

"The clerk, I'm sure, is often busy and might well have missed me going by."

"I see. Now, who is the parishioner you no doubt so ably counseled? I am sure he could verify everything you have told us."

"That is privileged information, Mr. Holmes. The gentleman in question has nothing to do with the matters that interest you."

"So you will not reveal his name?"

"No."

"Very well. Perhaps you can tell me on which floor of the hotel his apartment is located?"

"I do not see how that is of any consequence."

"It could be of great consequence, Monsignor. Did this gentleman of whom you speak by chance occupy room 652?"

"No, that was not the number of his apartment."

Holmes said sternly, "Are you sure? You were in room 652, were you not? And you met there with Mr. Rafferty to discuss evidence relating to the murder of Daniel St. Aubin. Did you talk about the death of Margaret O'Donnell as well? You must know what happened to her."

"You are greatly mistaken, Mr. Holmes. I was never in the room you mentioned, and I had no meeting of any kind with Mr. Rafferty that night."

"That is very peculiar because we have found a witness who states he saw you entering Mr. Rafferty's apartment." It was the same ploy Holmes had tried with Abbey and it met with a similar lack of success.

"Your witness, whoever he may be, is simply wrong," Denis said firmly.

"We shall see about that. Now, let us talk about the late Margaret O'Donnell. She was one of your parishioners, was she not?"

"Yes. I didn't know her very well, but she certainly was a lovely girl."

"I have been told she was strikingly beautiful."

"I suppose you could say that."

"Were you aware she was pregnant at the time of her death?"

"I, I was not aware of that," he said, but the hesitation in his voice suggested otherwise. "The poor child."

"Indeed she was. Did you preside at her funeral?"

"Yes."

"It must have been a very sad occasion. She was so young."

"Seventeen. Far too young to die, but God does not explain Himself, and we must accept that there are tragedies in this world."

"God did not make her pregnant," Holmes said sharply. "That was the work of a man. Do you know who the father was?"

"No."

"Margaret never told you, not even in the confessional?"

"I cannot speak of that, as you must well know."

"But Margaret is dead. Does that not unseal her words?"

"No."

"How did she die?"

"I have no knowledge of that."

"You never asked her father or heard whisperings about what happened to her?"

"No, it was not my business to ask."

"You are a most incurious man, Monsignor."

"I had no wish to add to her father's grief. But if you speak to him, perhaps he can answer your question. I have told you all I know, Mr. Holmes, and I must put my faith in your wise judgment as to how you will treat my situation. Now, if you will excuse me, confessions will be starting shortly."

AFTER DENIS LEFT, Holmes said, "We are tangled up in a web of lies, Watson, and there is more than one spider spinning it. Still, I believe Monsignor Denis may be the key to this case. He has a conscience, and that is the greatest danger to any criminal enterprise."

"And yet you believe he has lied to us. How can you induce him to speak the truth?"

"By learning all we can about Margaret O'Donnell's fate. Did you hear the monsignor's halting response when I brought up her pregnancy? I am convinced he knows what happened to the girl. Indeed, it is not impossible he fathered her child."

"Come now, Holmes," I protested, "he is a priest!"

"And a man, Watson, who is no more immune than any other to the temptations of the flesh. It is too bad Margaret didn't identify the father when she confided in the Forsyth girl. Our task would be much easier if that were the case."

"Well, I am of the opinion St. Aubin must have been the father, if she was in fact pregnant. We know he was a reprehensible character and would have thought nothing of seducing the girl."

"True, but we have no proof. We also remain in the dark as to the cause of her death."

"Perhaps she had a miscarriage or some other issue with her pregnancy and died as a result. That might explain why her father has taken such pains to cover up the cause of her death. It could also explain St. Aubin's murder as an act of vengeance."

"By the mayor, who presumably also ordered the killing of Mr. Rafferty? Yes, I have considered that possibility, Watson. But there is a problem with this theory. Mr. Rafferty's notes give no indication he was looking into Margaret O'Donnell's death until the very last moment. Indeed, the telephone number he left behind is the only evidence we have that he had become aware of a possible connection between the girl's death and Mr. St. Aubin's murder. As a result, we cannot be certain that the mayor knew what Mr. Rafferty had discovered."

"Perhaps Mr. Rafferty, having found the connection, confronted him at once here at the hotel," I said.

"And the mayor put a knife in Mr. Rafferty's back? No, I doubt that. The mayor, of necessity, is well known throughout St. Paul. He could hardly have entered the Ryan without being seen. His henchman Grimshaw, on the other hand, could have done so, assuming he possessed a master key. But it is all an arabesque at this point, Watson. We are in want of hard evidence, which is why we must locate Mrs. Coddington. Our friend Mr. Thomas has already set a trap for her, and we will see if she takes the bait. In the meantime, we will pay a visit tomorrow to the House of the Good Shepherd."

We left the cathedral at five and Holmes was silent on our taxi ride back to the Ryan. But as we reached the hotel's front door, he said, "That black sedan parked just down the street followed us all the way back here. The police, it seems, have become interested in our movements. Detective Grimshaw is undoubtedly behind the surveillance. We must be very careful, Watson. There could be real danger in this business."

During our usual breakfast the next morning, Holmes told me about two important telephone calls. The first was one he made to the home of Mrs. Muriel St. Aubin, on the chance she might have returned from New York. She had and agreed to meet us early in the afternoon in the Ryan's lobby.

The other call had come from Sergeant Logan in Chicago and offered intriguing news. "The sergeant learned that Paul O'Donnell was a ticketed passenger yesterday morning on a Milwaukee Road train to St. Paul. He is probably at a hotel, since I rather doubt he would be staying with his father. I have already checked the front desk and he is not here at the Ryan."

"I will start making inquiries at other hotels," I said.

"Excellent. But we will not need to find the son if the father will tell us the truth."

"What makes you think he will do so? From all we have heard, he has steadfastly refused to speak of his daughter's death."

"I am not without persuasive skills, Watson. I can even be quite charming if I have to."

"I have not seen great evidence of that," I said, "but shall take your word for it."

Holmes arranged a meeting with the mayor just before noon at his city hall office. Ensconced behind the sort of massive desk that signifies power and influence, O'Donnell rose to greet us in a friendly fashion, and there followed the usual exchange of pleasantries. But when Holmes introduced the subject of Margaret, O'Donnell grimaced as though the mere mention of her name was as painful as a poison arrow shot into his chest.

"I cannot speak of my dear daughter," he said. "Her death is my burden to bear and no one else's. I am sorry, Mr. Holmes, but that is how it must be."

"I have no wish to intrude upon your grief," Holmes said, "but the fact of the matter is that her death may in turn be linked to the murders of two men—Mr. St. Aubin and Mr. Rafferty."

"I do not believe that," O'Donnell said. "I do not believe that for one second. Maggie's death has nothing to do with your investigation."

Any point in trying to charm the mayor was now gone, and Holmes bored in on him with his customary intensity.

"You cannot hide your secret forever, sir. Your daughter became pregnant, quite possibly by Daniel St. Aubin, and you had her sent away to the House of the Good Shepherd. Shortly thereafter, she died suddenly. Why are you so afraid to say what happened? Do you not owe her the truth?"

"That is for me to decide. But I owe you nothing, Mr. Holmes, and I have nothing more to say to you. I am a busy man. Please show yourself out."

"The mayor is most adamant," I said as we left his office, "and I doubt you can pry his secret from him."

"I fear you are right, Watson. But it is a terrible thing to behold. The mayor is locked inside himself and cannot find the way out. It will kill him in the end."

MURIEL ST. AUBIN APPEARED for her interview with us fifteen minutes late, at quarter past two. There was no doubt as to her identity or her social status when she walked into the lobby. She wore a long mink coat, a dazzling pearl necklace with matching earrings, and she inspected the lobby as though she owned every inch of it before spotting us.

"It is kind of you to join us here," Holmes said as we rose to greet her. "I trust it was not an inconvenience for you."

"No, I was already intending to do some shopping downtown when you called. I am looking for some new furniture and that is always a trying task. So much of it is poorly made these days, like everything else, don't you agree? Besides, I wanted to examine the great Sherlock Holmes in the flesh. You are not quite as tall as I imagined you would be, but perhaps Dr. Watson is to blame for that. Now, I take it you have some news to share regarding my son's murder?"

"I have no great revelations to pass on, Mrs. St. Aubin, but we are getting closer to the truth every day."

"Mr. Rafferty made similar statements, and yet here we are with the murderer still on the loose. I must say, I expected more of you, Mr. Holmes, given your renown."

"Uncovering the truth, Mrs. St. Aubin, is a journey and there are always steep hills along the way. We are climbing now, steadily, and I assure you we will reach our destination before long. You can be of great help in this regard. We have learned from Mr. Rafferty's notes all that you told him, but there are two matters I wish to explore in further detail. The first concerns your son's accommodations."

"What do you mean?"

"Your son was living, I believe, at the Piedmont Apartments at the time of his death."

"He was."

"And you told Mr. Rafferty, if I am correct, that you went to your son's apartment afterwards and discovered it had been searched, presumably by the police. You also reported you found no possessions missing, except possibly for some photographs from his darkroom."

"Yes. What are you getting at?"

Holmes responded with a question of his own. "Do you know how your son made a living, Mrs. St. Aubin?"

"I am aware of Mr. Rafferty's claim that Danny was a blackmailer, but I am under no obligation to believe that."

"I am afraid you must, Mrs. St. Aubin. Blackmail seems to have been your son's full-time occupation, and he was quite good at it."

"So you say."

"It is true, I assure you. The evidence of his crimes is irrefutable, and I am convinced he was murdered because of his activities. The fact is he blackmailed many people, including some very prominent citizens of St. Paul. I suspect he even arranged to have secret photographs taken at this very hotel to entrap his victims."

Mrs. St. Aubin suddenly appeared quite alarmed, the color draining from her face. "Well, that is certainly a shock. Who was in these photographs?"

"That is not a matter I am prepared to discuss. I can only say they were photographs no respectable person would wish to be seen by the public."

"You mean bedroom photographs?"

"Yes."

At this point, I thought Mrs. St. Aubin might lodge another strong objection to the idea that her son was a criminal, but instead she lowered her head and said, "You have proof of all of this, I suppose, including the photographs?"

"Let us just say we continue to gather evidence. Watson and I have already talked to several of your son's victims."

"I see. It is terrible to hear of this, but I suppose I cannot claim complete surprise. I must ask myself where it all went wrong. I fear I failed Danny."

"No, Mrs. St. Aubin, your son failed himself, but that does not mean he deserved to be brutally murdered. And you can be of great help to us in finding his killer. I believe he must have kept incriminating material he gathered as part of his blackmail schemes. Yet I doubt he would have filed away such documents in his apartment, where the police or even one of his victims could have discovered them. Do you know if your son had a safe-deposit box?"

"I don't think so. He told me more than once he didn't trust banks."

"Could he have left the material for safekeeping at your home?"

"No. He had no more confidence in me than he had in the banks."

"What about entrusting the material to a friend? Was there one in particular he was close to?"

"My son had many people he called friends, but I have no reason to believe he was truly close to any of them. He was always his own best friend and no one else's."

"I see. What about the young man named Johnny Riordan, who used to work for Bertram Abbey? I know he called you once asking about your son. Did Mr. Riordan happen to mention where he was living?"

"No. I gave him Danny's address, that was all. I have not heard from him since. Does he have something to do with Danny's murder?"

"Possibly. Now, there is another name I am interested in. Have you ever heard of a Mrs. Bertha Coddington?"

The mention of her name elicited a long stare from Mrs. St. Aubin. "Why in heaven's name would you bring her up?"

"So you know her."

"I know *of* her, Mr. Holmes. She is a disreputable character as far as I am concerned."

"Be that as it may, I have been told she has been of service to some of the city's most prominent families. I should very much like to speak with her. Do you know how to reach her?"

"No."

"But you could find out, could you not?"

"Why would I do such a thing?"

"Because you want to find out who killed your son, and Mrs. Coddington may have vital evidence in that regard."

To my surprise, Mrs. St. Aubin grasped at once the implications of Holmes's statement. "Are you claiming that my son impregnated the O'Donnell girl? If that's true, what could it have to do with his murder?"

"It may have much to do with it or it may not, but it is a matter that must be investigated if we are to find our way to the truth."

"Very well, I will see what I can do. Now, if that is all you want of me, I must be going."

After Mrs. St. Aubin left to hunt for furniture, I said, "What do you make of the lady?"

"I am not quite sure. There can be no doubt she is a strong and highly intelligent woman and that she wants justice for her son. But I also think she is hiding something from us."

"Why do you say so?"

"Call it an impression, Watson. For example, when I mentioned the blackmail photographs, she seemed especially interested. I wonder why. And I cannot believe she had no inkling of her son's illegal activities. She is very much a member of this city's upper class, and it was among just such people Mr. St. Aubin plied his terrible trade. She must have heard rumors, at the least, of what her son was engaged in."

"Yes, but no mother ever wishes to believe ill of her child."

"Mrs. St. Aubin, however, is not just any mother. She strikes me as an exceptionally clear-minded woman who harbors few illusions. I think she knew all too well what her son was doing but nonetheless felt compelled to defend him. Blood runs thick, even where there is doubt."

Holmes paused, looking up at one of the long clerestory windows that brought daylight into the lobby, and said, "There is a bright blue sky today, Watson, but when it comes to this case we are in a London fog, stumbling along and trying to find our way. However, I have seen a shaft of sunlight."

"Ah, you must have a new idea."

"I do, and it concerns what Mr. St. Aubin did just before his death. We know from the letter to his mother that he believed he was in jeopardy. Yet he also wrote, as I recall, that 'if things work out as I expect they will, I will be fine.' This suggests he had a black-mail scheme in the works designed to protect him from all harm. In order for such a plan to work, however, he had to be certain that whatever incriminating material he had gathered would be safe while he arranged to collect his ransom, which I believe is what he set out to do on the night he was murdered. And so we are back to the question I posed to Mrs. St. Aubin. Where or with whom would he keep this essential material?"

I suddenly saw what Holmes was driving at. "You are saying he gave it to that fellow he met just before his death."

"Bravo, Watson! Yes, and that young man to whom he handed an envelope at the corner of Seventh and Robert Streets must have been his friend and perhaps co-conspirator, Johnny Riordan."

"Then it is more imperative than ever that we find Riordan."

"It is, but I suspect Grimshaw will be looking for him as well. Mr. Riordan is a loose end, and loose ends are usually cut away."

21

The Politicians

Montgomery Meeks told the story of his life in many different ways, depending on his mood of the moment and the gullibility of his audience. In one version, he hailed from a prominent Main Line family in Philadelphia and attended Yale, only to rebel against what he saw as a life of feckless wealth by heading west to carve out a career in politics. Meeks told others he had sprung from poverty in the Hell's Kitchen neighborhood of New York before clawing his way out to a better life. In still another account he claimed he and his parents had been members of a traveling circus in the Midwest, an experience that prepared him for a career in politics because, as he liked to say, "it's the biggest carnival of all."

The truth, with which Meeks never enjoyed a steady relationship, was far more prosaic, at least as it regarded his childhood. He'd actually been born only a few hundred miles east of St. Paul in Waukesha, Wisconsin. His Scotch-Irish father had fought with the legendary, black-hatted Iron Brigade in the Civil War and then returned home to operate a family drugstore. He eventually began sampling several of his products, including laudanum, to mask the pain of a war wound. He married late and was forty by the time Meeks was born in 1885. The boy was named Montgomery after a beloved comrade of his father killed on the first day of fighting at Gettysburg.

Meeks was just two when his father died and was raised by his strict mother, who was very German and very prim. She extolled a virtuous life of hard work and dedication to God and believed that smoking, swearing, and what she called "self-abuse" were all major way stations on the road to Hell. Meeks disagreed. By the time he was fifteen he had enthusiastically taken up all of those vices and several others. Handsome, cunning, and a wizard with words, he became known in high school as the boy who could talk his way out of any problem and into bed with any girl. He was just seventeen when he fixed his first election, removing and replacing enough ballots from a locked box in the principal's office at his high school to ensure that a friend became senior class president.

He left home a year later, much to the dismay of his mother, who had wanted him to take over the drugstore. But the dull, predictable life of a shopkeeper in Waukesha held no appeal. Instead, Chicago beckoned. A friend found Meeks a job selling Collier's encyclopedias door to door, a task at which he excelled. Part of Meeks's territory was in the infamous First Ward just south of the Loop, where vice flourished under the watchful eyes of "Bathhouse" John Coughlin, an alderman, and saloonkeeper Michael "Hinky Dink" Kenna.

Meeks found both men fascinating, and he soon quit his job selling overpriced knowledge in favor of running numbers for the two local kingpins. His intelligence, audacity, and unfamiliarity with ethics made him a rising star in the political machine, and by age twenty-six he was working at city hall as an assistant to the mayor. Opportunities for graft came with the job, and Meeks took his share of boodle on the theory, as he once told a friend, that "when it comes to politics, well-crafted dishonesty is always the best policy, because the last thing people are interested in is the ugly truth."

In time he became a highly regarded fixer for Chicago's Democratic Party, keeping wayward members of the political flock in check through bribery, flattery, and threats. At election time he also helped round up reluctant voters by the careful application of money to their wallets. His work for the machine proved increasingly lucrative, and he bought a fancy townhouse where he entertained many women.

Smooth, charming, and always impeccably dressed in the latest fashion, he was regarded as among the city's most eligible bachelors. He viewed marriage, however, as a particularly unpleasant form of imprisonment and never seriously considered it. He found it especially thrilling to link up with married women, who as he put it "are always discreet and usually grateful." Still, he kept a pistol by his bed in case an outraged husband paid him a visit in the dead of night.

By 1918, Meeks had every reason to believe that he was permanently ensconced as a Chicago operative. Then trouble arrived in the form of a group of reformers who began digging into the workings of city government and were shocked to discover rampant corruption. Meeks figured the reformers, who were mostly high-hats from the North Shore, would quickly fade back to their ballrooms after discovering Chicago politics were no more subject to improvement than human nature. But the do-gooders proved tenacious, and a grand jury that the machine somehow hadn't been able to fix began issuing indictments.

As the jury's investigators began to worm their way ever deeper into the corrupt core of Chicago politics, Meeks decided it was time to take an extended "vacation" rather than wait around for a possible indictment. His travels ultimately took him to Guatemala, a nation conveniently lacking an extradition treaty with the United States. When he returned a year later, with a nice tan and a pile of money he'd made trading coffee, he found that the situation in Chicago remained dicey and so determined to take his talents elsewhere.

It was said he ended up in St. Paul on the advice of a friend, who described the city as ripe with opportunity for graft. Meeks, however, claimed he was drawn to St. Paul "out of dedication to the sacred ideal of public service," an observation always accompanied by a knowing wink. Whatever attracted him to St. Paul, he quickly found the city to his liking. Its government was loose and tribal, and while outsized boondoggling was frowned on, there were plenty of opportunities for well-managed thievery. Better yet, from Meeks's viewpoint, the city was a tenth the size of Chicago, and that made it easy for him to become a big player in local politics. All he needed to succeed was a good candidate to back for mayor, and before long he found one.

TALL, RUGGEDLY HANDSOME, and unburdened by the weight of any profound ideas, Richard O'Donnell seemed tailor-made for a career in St. Paul politics. The son of a prominent lawyer, he grew up in one of the city's better neighborhoods, attended good Catholic schools that served as nurseries for the city's Irish political class, managed with some difficulty to earn a law degree, and made friends with the "right" kind of people everywhere he went. He was gregarious by nature, good at storytelling, backslapping, and drinking, and he saw politics as a profession that required no particular skill other than avoiding scandal.

He'd met Meeks in 1922 during his first foray into politics as a candidate for city council. Meeks attended a neighborhood event where O'Donnell gave a short speech, and afterwards the two men struck up a conversation. Meeks's first words were, "I believe I could make you governor one day, Mr. O'Donnell, if you would let me help you." A week later, Meeks was running O'Donnell's campaign.

Although he lacked Meeks's calculating guile, O'Donnell had an instinctual feel for the art of politics, and he knew how to project an image of rectitude and strength. His good looks—he had a fine head of black hair, warm brown eyes, and a pencil mustache always kept impeccably trimmed—enhanced his political aspirations, as did his oratorical skills. He had a gift for coating platitudes in honey, and his rich baritone made even the most jejune ideas sound profound.

After serving one term on the city council, O'Donnell ran for mayor in 1924 and won easily. He was reelected two years later. While O'Donnell became the public face of the city, Meeks operated behind the scenes. He made complicated deals, doused political fires, settled old scores, and saw to it that lucrative contracts were awarded to the right people. At the same time, he carefully cultivated the press, leaking embarrassing news about political enemies while deftly deflecting reporters away from any stories that threatened to cast the mayor in a bad light.

O'Donnell was popular with the electorate, and his political prospects appeared bright. By 1927 he was laying the foundations for a run at the governorship, with Meeks guiding the way. Then trouble struck, and all of their plans suddenly threatened to disintegrate into family scandal. Margaret's pregnancy was the problem, and it caused O'Donnell to regret, not for the first time, that he'd ever had children. O'Donnell was thirty when he married a secretary at his law firm he'd foolishly impregnated. He hadn't wanted to marry but knew he had no choice. The alternative was a scandal that might well lead to his banishment from the firm. His new wife's name was Kathleen Doherty, and she was beautiful but also tempestuous and demanding, or so O'Donnell told his friends. After their son, Paul, was born, Kathleen wanted another child. Two miscarriages followed before the successful delivery of a daughter.

O'Donnell worked long hours and drank for more hours after that, and when he appeared at home it was as though he was merely a boarder, seen in passing. He was content to view his children, six years apart, as untidy pets best cared for by Kathleen. The children did not turn out well, and O'Donnell blamed Kathleen, who seemed to enjoy conflict for its own sake and was forever stirring up turmoil. It did not occur to O'Donnell that his refusal to play a role in the family drama lay at the heart of the problem.

His son, Paul, was extremely intelligent but something of a ne'er-do-well from the beginning, lacking motivation or discipline.

While still in high school, he discovered alcohol, and by the time he graduated near the bottom of his class, he seemed destined for a life of disarray. O'Donnell was relieved when at age eighteen Paul left home and became a wanderer, supporting himself by odd jobs and, it was said, playing high-stakes poker aboard trains. But alcohol was his real passion, and those who knew him believed he would drink himself to death by the time he was forty.

Margaret had seemed a much sweeter child at first but began battling with her mother when she entered her teen years. Yet the two of them were close, in a profoundly tangled way, and when Kathleen died, quickly and painfully of metastatic breast cancer at the age of forty-three, Margaret went crazy with grief, or so it seemed to O'Donnell.

Still, O'Donnell assumed Maggie, as everyone called her, would settle down in the end and prove far less of a problem than her brother. So he kept his distance from her, as he always had, and hoped for the best. But hope did not serve him well, and in November 1927 he received a decidedly unpleasant surprise.

MONTGOMERY MEEKS bore the bad tidings. He stopped by the mayor's house late one evening, and O'Donnell could tell from his aide's unusually somber demeanor that something was wrong. They went into O'Donnell's study, its shelves lined with impressive-looking tomes the mayor had never read, and after generous slugs of bourbon had been poured, Meeks said, "I have some bad news about Maggie. I've been told she's pregnant."

O'Donnell stared at Meeks and said, "I hope you're not joking with me."

"I'm not. You know me, Your Honor. I hear things. Maggie apparently has admitted it to more than one person. But it gets worse. The father is said to be Daniel St. Aubin, and he's a nasty customer if there ever was one."

The mayor felt his stomach sink and he medicated with bourbon. "St. Aubin? Do I know him?"

"Probably not, but I do," Meeks said and then explained how he'd encountered St. Aubin in connection with a blackmail scheme. "I won't name any names, but a couple of St. Paul's leading citizens were among his recent victims, and at their request I stepped into help them."

"You never told me about this."

"No, and for good reason. If something went wrong, you couldn't be blamed. It would all be on me."

"I see. Well, what are we to do about Maggie? Are you sure she's pregnant?"

"Not a hundred percent, but close. I'm told she saw a rather disreputable doctor and he confirmed it. Apparently, she used a false name and claimed to be nineteen years old."

O'Donnell shook his head and said, "How could she do this to me? A professional blackmailer the father! She has no idea what kind of problems this could create."

"She's young, Your Honor, and she made a mistake. It happens. We have to focus now on what to do about the situation. We should begin by calling in Grimshaw to deal with St. Aubin, in case he tries to blackmail you. If he threatens to spread the word about Maggie, it will not look good in the public eye. Your career could be in jeopardy."

O'Donnell had campaigned on a platform calling for "a return to morality, decency, and honor," all the while roundly condemning the sins of the Jazz Age, including the scandalous behavior of "loose women in short skirts." The appeal to old-fashioned morality worked, and O'Donnell had been elected by a healthy margin in 1924 and reelected by an even healthier one in 1926. And it would be just the message, he thought, to propel him to the governor's office when the time came. But with his daughter pregnant by some low-life at age seventeen, what would the public think once her condition became evident? His carefully cultivated image as an upstanding family man would be hopelessly tarnished, putting his political career at risk.

"Christ, Monty, this is a goddamn mess," O'Donnell said. "Maybe I should have seen it coming. Maggie grew wild after Kathleen died and not even the nuns at Derham Hall could deal with her. She started skipping classes to run off and meet boys. I had to go over to Minneapolis once to pick her up after the police found her necking in a car. I confronted her about it, but she wouldn't even talk to me. She screamed it was none of my business. She's become impossible and now look what she's done. It'll make me look like the world's biggest hypocrite."

"There's another complication," Meeks said. "St. Aubin must be in his midtwenties, which means he could be charged with statutory rape, and that wouldn't be good for us. If the case goes to court, all kinds of dirt could come out."

"So what should we do? Maybe sending Maggie away would be a good idea, assuming I can get her to cooperate. She hates me, Monty, and I don't know why. Haven't I given her everything she ever wanted? I should go up and talk to her right now."

Margaret was upstairs in her room, the door locked as always against any and all intruders, including her father. O'Donnell wondered if he'd have to batter down the door to confront her, such was their state of alienation.

Meeks said, "I wouldn't do that, Your Honor. You're right. It's not fair what she's done, but here we are. Why don't you let me handle Maggie? I think I can talk to her. Sending her away is an excellent idea. Once she starts showing, there'll be no smoothing over the situation. I suggest we get her to the House of the Good Shepherd pronto. Once she's safely out of sight there, I can work on a long-range solution. My thought would be to send her down to Chicago, where there's also a Good Shepherd. I could make all of the necessary arrangements."

"I don't know about that. Maggie won't go willingly."

"Then she'll have to be persuaded. Grimshaw could help if need be."

"What about the baby?"

"That won't be a problem. The baby can be put up for adoption and no one here will ever be the wiser. There are, of course, other options available, if you know what I'm saying."

"An abortion? No, that I could not accept under any circumstances."

"I understand. Just leave everything to me, and it will all work out."

MARGARET MARY O'DONNELL was fifteen when her mother began to die, and seeing the pain on her face, as though some terrible beast was clawing at her insides, was more than Maggie could stand. Her father, stoic and cold, offered little consolation when Kathleen finally died, and by the time Margaret turned sixteen she felt she was on her own.

She found a willing crowd of friends, among them older boys who promised undying love. She had a hopeful heart and believed in fairy tales, and she soon lost her virginity to a boy she never saw again. Everything seemed different after that, as though she'd crossed over some high mountain pass into a world without enchantment. There were parties and alcohol and more eager boys buzzing around her, but her heart wasn't in any of it, and one night she cut her wrists with a razor blade and lay down in her bed, waiting to die. But the blood clotted before that happened, and when her father found the wounds, he sent her off to a locked hospital ward where nuns in long white gowns told her to pray for deliverance from her sins. If she found God, they said, He would fill her lonely heart with grace.

God didn't answer her prayers. Instead, disaster struck. When she found out she was pregnant, abused, and seduced by an awful man, all seemed lost, and she thought of throwing herself off the High Bridge, as so many other lost souls had done. But then she encountered Danny St. Aubin, who seemed as though he could be a true friend. He listened patiently as she poured out her troubles and feigned outrage at how cruelly she had been treated. Better yet, he promised to obtain justice on her behalf. "Trust me," he told her, and in what would be the ultimate misfortune of her life, she did.

MARGARET HAD NO WISH to go to the House of the Good Shepherd, which she called "the nun prison." Confronted with her recalcitrance, her father and Meeks had to resort to more forceful means, with the assistance of Grimshaw. Margaret was pulled from her classes one afternoon and told she needed to go home with the police, ostensibly because something had happened to her father. Grimshaw was waiting for her in a squad car, but he didn't take her home. He drove her instead to the House of the Good Shepherd after slipping a sedative into a bottle of cola he offered her.

She was deposited at Good Shepherd on December 2 and kept there in a locked dormitory with twenty other girls. Five days later, she was dead.

AFTER HIS TALK WITH THE MAYOR, Meeks considered what to do about Daniel St. Aubin. He'd known nothing of him before learning of his attempt to extort money from Abbey and Denis. Now, the young schemer's involvement with Margaret O'Donnell made him a threat to the mayor as well. It was time, Meeks decided, to let Grimshaw loose. Meeks had always viewed the detective as a revolting character, a thick-headed bruiser with a badge, but as such he had his uses.

Although Meeks had never been in a fistfight in his life, he held the art of physical coercion in high regard. In Chicago he'd seen firsthand how a hard punch to the stomach, followed by a few well-chosen blows with a sap, could persuade even the noisiest advocate of some misguided cause to adopt the virtue of monkish silence. As for more extreme measures, Meeks had always spoken against them but with his eyes carefully averted from the scene of the carnage. There were things in Chicago a man simply didn't want to know.

St. Paul, he'd found, was not much different from Chicago when it came to dealing with the likes of St. Aubin. The blackmailer needed to be put in his place and strongly dissuaded from future misconduct. He also had to be made aware that any more involvement with Margaret O'Donnell would put his life in jeopardy.

"Don't get carried away," Meeks instructed Grimshaw. "Just make it clear what a nasty boy he's been and where he'll end up if he doesn't mend his ways."

ON THE DAY HE DIED, Daniel St. Aubin awoke with the belief he was on the verge of the biggest deal of his life. He'd spent more than a week making the arrangements and the payoff—twenty thousand dollars—was at hand. It would be enough to keep him going for at least a year, and after that there would be a second installment, even if the man he was blackmailing didn't know it yet.

Nothing about the deal had been easy, however. St. Aubin had already suffered a beating at the hands of Jackson Grimshaw, and he knew who had sent the detective to teach him a lesson. But the beating hadn't deterred St. Aubin. Instead, it only served to confirm he was onto something really big. So he'd moved forward with his plans but also taken precautions by temporarily relocating to a safe place where Grimshaw and the police wouldn't be able to find him.

The deal promised to radically change St. Aubin's fortunes. Once he had the twenty thousand, he planned to leave St. Paul for good and start a new life in New York. The pickings there, he believed, would be lush for a man of his talents and striking good looks. He could see himself as a Park Avenue dandy, mixing with the upper crust of New York society and discovering all of their toxic secrets.

But first, he had to consummate the deal, and he knew it would be tricky. The money exchange was always the hard part—the mark would undoubtedly have the police hovering around—but St. Aubin had devised a clever plan to evade them by enlisting the help of an unlikely middleman in the person of Monsignor Pierre Denis. Once St. Aubin got the money, he intended to leave immediately on an overnight train to New York.

Still, there was always the possibility something could go wrong. St. Aubin was a fatalist who saw life as a game of chance and death as the wild card always lurking in the deck. So he'd made arrangements to pass on some documents to Johnny Riordan before the money exchange took place. If St. Aubin died, Johnny would send the explosive documents to all the right people, and it would reveal a scandal for the ages.

It was all very complicated, but as St. Aubin left his hideout late on the afternoon of December 16 and headed downtown toward Seventh and Robert Streets, he was confident he was in good shape. It was going to be a night to remember.

22
"We're Always Just a Step Behind"

After learning that Johnny Riordan was in Minneapolis, Rafferty began making inquiries across the river. But his sources in the Mill City weren't nearly as good as those he had in St. Paul, and the search for Riordan yielded no immediate results. At the same time, Rafferty was laid low for several days by what he thought must be another bad cold. Bowls of hot chicken soup from the Ryan's kitchen proved to be good medicine, and by mid-January Rafferty was feeling better.

Rafferty, however, was growing ever less certain he'd ever discover who killed Danny St. Aubin. "I have cast out my line," Rafferty told Thomas at one point, "and it has become so snarled I fear I may never catch the fish." Then, exactly one month after St. Aubin's murder, a surprise visitor showed up at Rafferty's apartment to tangle the line even more.

"I TRUST THIS ISN'T A BAD TIME for you," Montgomery Meeks said when Rafferty answered the knock, "but it would be lovely if we could have a little chat."

"It is as good a time as any, Mr. Meeks. Please, take off your coat and have a seat."

Once Meeks had settled in, Rafferty was reminded once again that the mayor's assistant was a very debonair man. He wore a navy blue pin-striped suit, a perfectly starched white shirt with gold cufflinks, and a subtly patterned burgundy tie matched in color by the handkerchief precisely folded into his breast pocket. His black wing-tipped shoes were polished to glossy perfection, and even the crease in his black fedora hat bore evidence of careful attention. By contrast, Rafferty was still lounging in his favorite robe, a ratty red affair that looked to have been last cleaned sometime during the World War.

"And to what do I owe the pleasure of this visit?" Rafferty asked before sinking into the old sofa that had become his island of refuge. "Something to do with Danny St. Aubin perhaps?"

Meeks's eager blue eyes, in which both pleasure and suspicion always seemed to lurk in equal measure, toured the apartment before focusing on Rafferty. "I suppose you could say that, in a roundabout way. I know you're looking into the matter of his death. Have you discovered some great plot yet?"

"Ah, there is always a plot. Whether it is a great one remains to be seen. But yes, I believe he was murdered, despite what the police are saying."

"So I have heard. And I must tell you I am beginning to believe you are right. Like many others, I at first thought he took his own life, but now I am not so certain. What I am sure of is that St. Aubin was not a very nice young fellow."

"Yes, he was a blackmailer, if that is what you mean."

Meeks nodded and said, "I don't know all the details, of course, but our mutual acquaintance, Detective Grimshaw, assures me St. Aubin all but made his living extorting money from others. And I will readily admit that as such, he was certainly a candidate for—how shall I put it?—early departure from this vale of tears. Yet Grimshaw, initially at least, found no evidence of foul play."

"Grimshaw finds what he is told to find, nothing more and nothing less. It's said, after all, that he's the mayor's lackey first and foremost."

"My, my, what cynicism, Mr. Rafferty! I imagine a man of your age has seen too much of the world to trust it anymore. I assure you, however, that the mayor had no involvement with St. Aubin. No involvement whatsoever. But as I said, I have begun to change my mind in the matter of St. Aubin's unfortunate demise because of certain circumstances in his life that have only recently come to light."

"Well, I am all ears, Mr. Meeks. What were these circumstances?"

"Let me preface by saying it is not my wish to malign the dead. Like you, I am only interested in the truth. Does the name Johnny Riordan mean anything to you?"

"Yes, I know of him."

"Good. Then you know of his sexual preferences, I take it. And I suspect you also know that Mr. Riordan made certain claims regarding his relationship with an older man."

"That would be Bertram Abbey."

"It would. Now, it so happens Mr. Abbey is a friend of mine, as is Monsignor Pierre Denis, whom as you know St. Aubin also attempted to victimize. As such, I suppose you consider them suspects in St. Aubin's demise. I find that to be preposterous. Be that as it may, I am here to tell you now that I believe, as do Mr. Abbey and the monsignor, that Johnny Riordan is the real culprit in this business. You see, he was Daniel St. Aubin's lover."

Rafferty had not seen this ploy coming but quickly suspected where it was going. "And how do you know that?"

"Let's just say I am privy to certain information in the police files."

"From Big Jack, no doubt."

"Yes. It is Detective Grimshaw's firm belief, based on eyewitnesses he interviewed, that Mr. St. Aubin and Mr. Riordan were out for a night on the town when they had a terrible quarrel. So terrible, I'm afraid, that Mr. Riordan killed his lover in a fit of rage and then ran from the scene. Indeed, you saw him, did you not, when you reached the alley?"

"I saw two men," Rafferty said. "Who do you suppose the other one was?"

"One of his many friends, I imagine. Riordan seems to have been a busy boy around town and slept in many beds."

Rafferty could only marvel at the brazenness of the tale Meeks had unfolded. Did he really expect Rafferty to believe it? Probably not. But it hardly mattered. There was now a new, carefully embossed official explanation for St. Aubin's death as well as an official suspect to be chased down and no doubt silenced before he could tell the truth.

"Well now, that is quite a tale you've spun for me, Mr. Meeks. However, I will wager on my last breath that Mr. Riordan was not one of the men I saw in the alley. Speaking of the lad, has anyone heard his side of the story? I suspect it will far different from the one you've just offered."

"Mr. Riordan is in the wind, as they say, and at last report was no longer here in St. Paul. But Grimshaw, I'm sure, will find him. He is out hunting as we speak."

There was something ominous about the way Meeks said "out hunting," as though Riordan was a wild animal being stalked. Rafferty said, "I trust he will be safely arrested and will not conveniently die in a police shooting or some other unfortunate mishap."

"Oh really, Mr. Rafferty, you're being a bit melodramatic, aren't you? No one wishes to harm the boy. The police simply wish to hear the truth from him."

"I'm certain they'll get it if they work him over long enough. You know as well as I how Grimshaw operates. In any case, it will all be a show. I very much doubt Riordan had anything to do with Danny's murder."

"Don't be so sure, Mr. Rafferty. You are a wise man who has seen much of the world, and you know that lovers' quarrels are as old as the Garden of Eden. It was just such a quarrel, and nothing more, that led to Mr. St. Aubin's unfortunate demise."

"I do not believe that," Rafferty said flatly, "and I wonder why you are so eager to pass on such an obvious falsehood."

Meeks smiled and said, "A falsehood must be proven false or it is simply one possible version of the truth, is it not? And therein lies your problem, Mr. Rafferty. You have many suspicions but they are as paper in the wind, anchored to nothing solid."

Meek was right, but Rafferty wasn't prepare to admit it. "We will see where all that paper ends up, Mr. Meeks. You may be surprised by what it reveals."

"Then I look forward to the day of revelation," Meeks said as he stood up, put on his fedora, and adjusted his tie so that the knot was straight and tight. "Enjoy the rest of your day, Mr. Rafferty. At your age, savoring each hour must be of the utmost importance, I'm sure. Don't bother to get up. I'll show myself out."

It had been quite a performance, Rafferty thought, but had Meeks written the script himself or had somebody written it for him? Rafferty typed up a few quick notes about his conversation with Meeks and set them aside in a folder, but he never got around to putting the carbon copies in his bank box.

"I DO NOT THINK RAFFERTY is cause for worry," Meeks later reported to Abbey. "I observed him closely as we were talking in that overstuffed dump of his. He was breathing heavily and had great difficulty moving about. He is not long for this world."

"Well, that may be, but even if he has only a few weeks or months of life left he could still cause plenty of trouble, especially if he manages to locate that little liar Riordan before Grimshaw does. Did he buy the story about Johnny murdering St. Aubin?"

"Probably not, but who cares? It's a story he can't easily refute. And I wouldn't worry about Rafferty finding Riordan. He can barely get out of a chair to find his reading glasses. Grimshaw will get his hands on Riordan. It's just a matter of time."

Meeks delivered much the same message to Denis, but the

monsignor did not seem reassured. "I think you are underestimating Mr. Rafferty. I know him better than you do. You are right that he is very old, but even an old bulldog can have quite a bite."

"Well then, we'll just have to avoid his jaws, won't we?" Meeks said. "But if he comes after us, we have a big, bad bulldog of our own we can sic on him."

WITH WASH THOMAS in Savannah, Rafferty had no reliable helpmate in his investigation, and he wasn't sure how long he could keep up the effort. His body had become a signalman, sending out urgent signs of what was to come in the form of ever more irregular pulses from his heart and increasingly painful attacks of angina. Death was approaching and Rafferty knew it. "I am inching out on the pirate's plank," he told Thomas on a long-distance call, "and it seems to be getting shorter by the minute."

The comment alarmed Thomas, but Rafferty tried to ease his worries. "I am not quite done yet, Wash, and this St. Aubin business keeps me going. Better to think of it than the inevitable. But unless there is some breakthrough, I do not see a solution in sight. I am awash in suspicion, but I have no ironclad proof that would convict any of the suspects."

"Well, just go slowly, Shad. Don't push yourself. Remember, I'll be back in a few days."

"That will be a blessing. I am still looking for that Riordan lad, and I will be grateful for your help."

LATER THAT DAY, as Rafferty pondered how to find Riordan, he had a flash of inspiration. There was, he knew, an underground community of homosexuals in St. Paul who lived secret lives. Fearing exposure and public shaming, not to mention legal prosecution, they'd built a private world of clubs and meeting places. Perhaps, Rafferty thought, that hidden realm might offer a means of tracing Riordan.

Rafferty's attitudes toward homosexuality had evolved over the years. He'd grown up under the sway of Catholic doctrine, which required him to despise homosexuality as a perversion in the eyes of God. During his war service, he'd first encountered a few "girlie men," as they were called, and saw them treated with uncommon cruelty. But over time, as religious moralism began to lose its grip on him, Rafferty grew more tolerant. He still regarded sex between a man and a woman as the right and proper way, and homosexuality made him uncomfortable. Even so, he could no longer bring himself to hate people whose nature led them down a different path.

The most prominent establishment serving homosexuals in St. Paul was Billy Baer's club on St. Peter Street, within eyeshot of the state capitol. Rafferty hoped a club patron, or perhaps even Baer himself, might have a clue as to Riordan's whereabouts. Rafferty knew Baer fairly well. Like Rafferty, Baer had operated a tavern for years, and so they'd run across each other now and then. After Prohibition took effect, Baer had the bright idea of opening a "gentlemen's club," and it had done well from what Rafferty knew. The club had no phone number, but Baer was listed at his home address, and Rafferty called there. Baer recognized Rafferty's voice at once.

"Shadwell Rafferty. By God, I haven't heard from you in ages! What are you doing these days?"

"Ah, Billy, that's a good question. The Grim Reaper is hounding me but I'm fighting him off as best I can with one hand. With the other, I'm going about some business. My last case, I like to call it. Do you remember the death of a young fellow named Danny St. Aubin last month?"

"Sure. You found the body, didn't you?"

"I did, and then I stepped right into a regular cow pie of a mystery. I have good reason to believe he was murdered and that a big cover-up is in place."

"Wouldn't surprise me. You can't trust nobody if the coppers are involved."

"I will not dispute that. Now, did you know Danny by chance?"

"Not by name. But he was at the club at least once. It must have been not long before he died. I only know because I recognized him after I saw his picture in the papers."

"So he wasn't a regular?"

"No. I don't think he was of the right persuasion, if you know what I mean. That's why I remembered him, because he seemed out of place."

"Was he with someone when you saw him?"

"Sure. A kid named Johnny Riordan. Funny you should ask, Shad. I had a copper in here the other day asking about him."

"Big Jack Grimshaw, I imagine."

"That's him. How'd you know?"

"An educated guess."

"Well, Big Jack's a real jerk, even for a copper. He promised to close me down if I didn't cooperate. Well, I said, you just try that and then who'll pay off your captain every month? We got into it, but I ain't afraid of nobody, and I didn't tell him nothing. I got no time for the coppers, and my customers know it. That's how I stay in business."

"You are a wise man, Billy. Now, about young Riordan. Has he been at your club lately?"

"Naw, haven't seen in at least a couple of months."

"I need to talk to him. He may know something about St. Aubin's death. I understand he's over in Minneapolis these days. Any idea where he might be living?"

"Well, Shad, the luck of the Irish is with you today. It so happens a young guy was in the club last week who works for that poof Abbey up on Summit. That's also where Riordan worked, but maybe you know that already."

"I do. Go on."

"Well, the gist is that this guy said he bumped into Riordan over in Minneapolis. Riordan didn't want to talk and told the guy to forget he ever saw him, or something like that. It was all very mysterious, or so the guy said."

"Where did the encounter occur?"

"Up on North Lyndale by the Munsingwear factory. The guy works there but comes over to my place because he says he likes the *ambience*, whatever the hell that is."

"Am I safe in betting you didn't tell any of this to Grimshaw?"

"Safest bet you'll ever make."

When Rafferty hung up, he felt his chances of locating Riordan had greatly improved. If Riordan was living near or perhaps even working at the Munsingwear factory, Wash Thomas—due back from Savannah in the morning—would be just the man to track him down.

THOMAS AND PATS ARRIVED at Union Depot just before noon on Wednesday, January 18, and stopped by Rafferty's apartment before heading home. Thomas was surprised to see how chipper Rafferty seemed.

"You are looking bright-eyed and ready for the chase," Thomas said with a smile as Rafferty poured out coffee.

"Amen," Pats chimed in. "Have you been sipping at the Fountain of Youth?"

"Ah, if that were true, I'd be dancing a jig before your eyes. But I have found out something that might lead us to the end of this St. Aubin business."

Rafferty recounted his conversation with Billy Baer, then said, "I am of a mind, Wash, that Johnny Riordan is within our grasp. I'm too old to go traipsing around Minneapolis, but if you could do a little snooping over there, maybe we'll flush him out."

"For sure, I can do that," Thomas said. "I know quite a few folks across the river."

Thomas had made friends in Minneapolis largely because of his membership in the local chapter of the NAACP. He'd been galvanized into action after the brutal lynching of three Black men in Duluth in 1920. Thomas had thought such a thing wasn't possible, at least not in Minnesota, and it made him both sick and incredibly angry. He and other African Americans had then pushed for an anti-lynching law, which the state legislature passed the next year. Among Thomas's fellow activists was a man named Warren Davis, who worked as a municipal court clerk in Minneapolis. His job gave him access to thousands of records. Equally important, he had a network of friends scattered across the city.

After Thomas arrived home with Pats, he put a call in to Davis. "I'm looking for a young white fellow named Johnny Riordan," he said. "Could you tell me if has a recent arrest record?"

Rafferty had suggested this line of inquiry because of what the Minneapolis police had been up to in recent months. "Judging by what I've seen in the papers, the coppers there like to raid the bathhouses every chance they get. There's an outside chance Riordan could have been swept up in a raid, assuming he patronizes such establishments."

Anyone charged in Minneapolis with offenses ranging from gross misdemeanors down to parking citations fell within Davis's purview. If Riordan had been caught in a raid, Davis would know about it. But he found no arrest record for Riordan, so Thomas tried another approach.

"I've heard Riordan could be working over at Munsingwear. Do you know anybody there?"

Davis did and said he'd make some calls. The next day Davis reported that a source in Munsingwear's personnel department confirmed that Riordan worked there. Better yet, the source provided

Riordan's home address. After consulting with Rafferty, Thomas made plans to call on Riordan early that evening in hopes of catching him at home.

"If you do find Riordan, approach him carefully," Rafferty said. "Try to persuade him to come here and have a nice talk with us. Even offer him some money for his time. We have to find out what he knows."

RIORDAN'S ADDRESS was on Highland Avenue in the Oak Lake neighborhood just north of downtown Minneapolis. Oak Lake had once been a tony precinct, its curving streets lined with tall Victorian houses sporting ambitious towers, shingled gables, and big porches laced with gingerbread. But the neighborhood's status as a genteel enclave had quickly faded, in part because of the construction of the huge Munsingwear factory just across Lyndale Avenue. By 1928, the neighborhood had devolved into a decrepit tangle town of cheap boarding houses and warrens of rental rooms carved out of tumbledown mansions. Its occupants were mostly poor immigrants and Blacks, two communities unwelcome elsewhere in the city.

The address Thomas had been given belonged to a huge old wooden house largely free of paint and maintenance. A sign on the sagging front porch advertised rooms for rent. Thomas went up to the porch and rang the doorbell but received no answer. He tried the door. It was open and he stepped inside, where he found a vestibule with eleven mailboxes mounted on the wall. Names were scrawled on most of the boxes, but Riordan's wasn't among them. Two boxes, for rooms 206 and 301, carried no names. If the address provided to Thomas was correct, one of them had to be Riordan's room.

At the far end of the vestibule a creaky staircase led to the upper floors. Thomas went up to the second floor and followed a narrow hallway that snaked through the subdivided house. Room 206 was at the far end of the hall. Thomas knocked on the door.

A burly man in a union suit, with a thick cigar mounted in his mouth like a dangerous weapon, came to the door. Clearly, he was not Johnny Riordan, and just as clearly he was not pleased to see a Black man.

"What the hell do you think you're doing here?" he said, adding a racial slur for good measure. "Get out or I'll call the cops."

Thomas had once been a decent amateur boxer, and in his younger days he might have knocked the man down right on the spot, but he was too old for that now and he couldn't afford a confrontation. If the coppers got involved, he'd be in trouble, because they usually enjoyed the opportunity to whale on a Black man.

"I must have the wrong room," Thomas said and turned to leave.

"Goddamn right you do, and don't come back, you hear?" the man shouted, then threw out more ugly insults as Thomas disappeared around a bend in the hall.

As he had for his entire life, Thomas wondered what was wrong with so many white people. Why did the mere color of his skin incite such anger and fear? It made no sense and it hurt, a wound that wouldn't stop bleeding. But he'd long since decided he wouldn't let racist jackasses ruin his life, no matter how maddening and tiring it was to have to deal with their blind hatred every day.

Thomas returned to the staircase and climbed up to the third floor, where there was another narrow, winding hallway. Room 301 was the first door he encountered. The door was badly damaged, as though someone had kicked it in. Thomas knocked politely, just in case. There was no answer, so he pushed the door open and found an upended mess of a room, its meager contents scattered every which way.

Riordan was nowhere in sight, but Thomas noticed a half-eaten clump of scrambled eggs on the room's only table. It appeared that Riordan had either left quickly on his own or had been dragged from the room before he could finish his meal. Whatever had happened, Riordan was once again in the wind—or worse.

JOHNNY RIORDAN had been living on his own since he was fourteen. That was when his father, a devout Catholic who worked in the Northern Pacific shops, caught him naked in his room snuggling with a boyfriend who had also shed his clothes. A brutal scene ensued, with yelling and threats and talk of perversion and sin and Sodom and Gomorrah. Later that night, Riordan left home and never returned, although he did stay in contact with his mother, who prayed daily that he might renounce his unnatural ways and return to the Christian fold.

Riordan was slim and handsome, and older men with money and secret desires soon discovered him. He put up with the sex because the money was good and he had no other source of income. By the time Bertram Abbey invited him into his household, Riordan was a seventeen-year-old without illusions, although he still harbored dreams.

When he met Danny St. Aubin, who was the most beautiful man he'd ever seen, Riordan fell in love and fantasized about a new life with him. However, blackmail seemed to be Danny's only real passion. Riordan held out hope that they would one day find true love. Now, that hope was gone. What was left was the opportunity to make a lot of money from Danny's final intended blackmail victim, if Riordan was clever about it. In the process, if he was extra clever, he thought he could also avenge Danny's death.

RIORDAN HAD LAID THE LAST OF HIS PLANS by the evening of January 18, with everything he needed in a satchel that rarely left his side. Fearful of the police, he remained extremely vigilant. At nine o'clock, as he was digging into a plate of scrambled eggs in his room, Riordan idly looked out the window. What he saw was terrifying. Caught in the glow of a street lamp was the hulking form of Jackson Grimshaw, and he was on a beeline toward Riordan's residence.

Riordan did not hesitate. He put on his winter coat and heavy boots, grabbed the satchel, and was out the door in thirty seconds.

He raced down to the second floor in time to hear Grimshaw coming up the stairs from the front vestibule. A dark alcove off the staircase provided a hiding place, and Riordan slipped into it as Grimshaw passed by on his way to the third floor, climbing fast. Riordan raced down the hallway to the rear staircase. Behind him, he heard the crash of a door being kicked in. Grimshaw had found his apartment.

Riordan went down the stairs and out the back door into the frigid night. After pausing to catch his breath, he ran through an alley lined with high wooden fences and zigzagged between a pair of vacant houses before turning toward the Gateway district of downtown Minneapolis, near the river. There he could find a flophouse or mission to shelter him for the night. On his way, he passed the downtown post office, where he dropped off an envelope addressed to a man in St. Paul.

Riordan found a flophouse called, apparently without humorous intent, King's Hotel and rented one of its less-than-regal cubicles for the night. Surrounded by tin, plywood, and chicken wire, with snoring derelicts and drunkards to keep him company, Riordan pondered what to do next. He had to find a safe hiding place, insulated from the police, and decided he would make inquiries in the morning at one of the Turkish baths on Hennepin Avenue.

Although he was exhausted, Riordan tried to stay awake. Flophouses were notorious for thievery, and he didn't want anything to happen to the satchel he clutched in his hands. Its contents—mostly clothes and toiletries—were hardly valuable except for one precious item. It was the envelope Danny St. Aubin had entrusted to him for safekeeping minutes before he was murdered, and it contained everything Riordan would need to collect a fortune.

After leaving Riordan's room, Thomas called Rafferty from a pay phone to report what he'd seen.

"Could be the cops nabbed Riordan or maybe he made a quick getaway. Hard to tell."

"I pray it's the latter, Wash. Otherwise, we'll have no chance of ever talking to the lad."

"Well, whatever happened, I just missed him."

"It's the story of this whole business, Wash. We're always just a step behind, and we are running out of chances. We could use some manna from heaven, but I have not seen Moses in the vicinity of late. I doubt he likes the cold weather."

To Rafferty's vast surprise, manna arrived the following night at his door, and everything he thought he knew about the St. Aubin case was suddenly upended. Twenty-four hours later, before he had time to share his newfound knowledge, someone put a knife in his back.

RAFFERTY WAS JUST PREPARING to go down to the Ryan's café for dinner when a bellboy brought the manna, in the form of a sealed envelope addressed to "Mr. Shadwell Rafferty, Ryan Hotel." The bellboy said it had been left at the front desk by an unknown messenger who disappeared as quickly as he had arrived. "But he said it should be delivered at once, and so here it is. I made a point of coming up to your room as fast as I could."

"Then you'll be wanting something for your exceptional effort," Rafferty said, knowing a plea for a tip when he heard it.

He sent the bellboy on his way with a silver dollar and then opened the envelope, which contained a printed message and a brief newspaper clipping. The message said: "Call Bertha Coddington at Colfax 2609 in Mpls. She can tell you what happened to the mayor's daughter. The girl was pregnant and St. Aubin died because of it. Powerful men do not wish the truth to be known. A friend." The clipping was an obituary notice from the December 9, 1927, edition of the *St. Paul Dispatch*. It read: "Margaret Mary O'Donnell, beloved daughter of Richard O'Donnell. Died suddenly on December 7. Services to be private. Memorials preferred to the Catholic Relief Society."

Rafferty puzzled over the message, wondering who had sent it and why. He knew nothing of Margaret O'Donnell's death or how it might be linked to the murder of Daniel St. Aubin. And who was Bertha Coddington? Rafferty decided to do some quick digging. On a hunch, he called a retired obstetrician he'd met some years earlier in connection with another investigation. Had the good doctor ever heard of a Bertha Coddington? He had but knew little about her, other than that she was said to operate in a shadowland where women with unwanted pregnancies sought a way out of their dilemma.

"And what exactly does she do?" Rafferty asked.

"Apparently she arranges abortions," the doctor said, "although I do not know that for a fact. If she does, it is highly illegal, of course."

"Is she a nurse?"

"I doubt that, but I really can't say. It's a business no one likes to speak of, myself included. Some things are best left in the dark."

"True," Rafferty said, "but murder is not one of them."

After a quick dinner, Rafferty returned to his apartment. He felt tired and lay down for nap, and when he awoke it was almost midnight, too late to call Bertha Coddington. But he would try to contact her first thing in the morning.

ON THE MORNING of Saturday, January 21, the final day of Shadwell Rafferty's long and momentous life, he placed a call to Colfax 2609 and reached Bertha Coddington. She was reluctant to talk at first, but Rafferty played his hand shrewdly, even though he was "flying without wings," as he liked to put it. Guessing that Mrs. Coddington did not wish to deal with the police, he brought up just that possibility unless she answered his questions. After much hesitation, she finally told him what she knew of Margaret O'Donnell and her death, all the while insisting she had done nothing wrong.

The big revelation came when Rafferty pressed her about who had fathered Margaret's child. She claimed not to know, but by means of persistent questioning Rafferty became all but certain who the father was, despite Mrs. Coddington's unwillingness to name the man. It was a stunning development. Daniel St. Aubin, Rafferty now believed, was in fact not the father. Even so, Mrs. Coddington said she had received a call some weeks earlier from St. Aubin, who apparently had stumbled on the truth. It all fit together, the baby and the blackmailer and the man who resorted to murder to cover up what he'd done.

After finishing with Mrs. Coddington, Rafferty called Thomas at the Chicken Delight. "I have come upon an astounding development, Wash, and I think I know who murdered Danny St. Aubin."

"Well, that's mighty sudden. Care to tell me all about it?"

"Ah, you know me. I like to keep my little secrets for a while before I spill the beans. But I will say it's as terrible a tale as you'll ever hear. I doubt Satan himself could outdo it. Why don't you meet me for dinner tonight at six and I'll give you the whole story."

"I can't wait to hear it. By the way, I just got a new tip about Johnny Riordan's possible whereabouts in Minneapolis. I was thinking of going over there pretty soon to check it out. But if you've got this business solved—"

"I wouldn't say that. We can always use more evidence, and Riordan might be able to confirm everything. By all means go over there and see if you can run him down."

"Will do."

"Good, then we'll talk tonight."

It was the last time Thomas heard Rafferty's voice.

23

"We Are on the Cusp"

[From "Murder in St. Paul"]

Snow fell in the morning, making a pretty scene on the busy streets around the Ryan, and I went out for a walk while Holmes remained in bed. Upon my return, I found him in the lobby, looking rather morose.

"What is it, Holmes? Has some new problem arisen?"

"No, it is an old problem that preoccupies me. The problem is young Mr. Riordan. It is unfortunate Mr. Thomas just missed him, or this entire case might have been resolved by now. Indeed, it is possible Mr. Rafferty would be alive today if Mr. Riordan had been captured."

Thomas had told us earlier how he'd almost managed to track down the elusive young man just two days before Rafferty's murder. Thomas had searched the apartment, but as the police had likely been there first, he found nothing of consequence. Holmes believed it was very probably a visit from Grimshaw that had prompted Riordan's swift departure.

"If Grimshaw did lay hands on him, then I fear Mr. Riordan is dead," Holmes said. "But there has been nothing in the newspaper about a body being found, and it is likely Mr. Riordan remains at large. If so, he has been on the run for several weeks without being detected, which suggests he is clever beyond his years."

"That may be, but I must say I am surprised the police in Minneapolis have not been able to find him by now. You have still heard nothing from them, I presume."

"They have proved entirely useless. If only we were in London, Watson! I can find a man hiding there within hours. But here I have no spies or informants or the Baker Street Irregulars to serve as my eyes and ears."

"Is it possible Riordan has fled Minneapolis?"

"I doubt it, for the simple reason he has an incentive to stay—money. I believe he inherited, as it were, Mr. St. Aubin's blackmailing business, and I believe he intends to use it to his advantage. But he knows from his partner's death that it is a perilous business and so he will have to be very careful. That is why he is in hiding at the moment."

"But won't he have to step out of the shadow at some point if he wishes to cash in from his *business,* as you call it?"

"He will, and then he will be in even greater danger, which is why we must find him before the police do."

Two DAYS LATER, with Riordan still lost to us, Holmes turned his attention once again to the fate of Margaret O'Donnell. Beneath a cold gray sky, we rode out in a taxi to the House of the Good Shepherd, where the girl had been sent just days before her death. Knowing little of the place, Holmes had done some research before our visit and found a valuable connection. The institution, Holmes learned, had received significant financial assistance over the years from James J. Hill and later his son, Louis. As we were well acquainted with the younger Hill, Holmes spoke with him and received assurances he would "strongly advise" the nun in charge of Good Shepherd to answer any and all questions we might put to her.

The institution stood amid large grounds on the slope of a small hill in the western part of St. Paul. Its main building, which had several satellites, was an irregular mass of dark red brick culminating in a haphazard ensemble of dormers, gables, towers, domes, and spires. An aspect of deep gloom seemed to inhabit the place, as though it were some cursed old castle, and as we approached the front entrance, which was sheltered by a grim Gothic portico, I mentioned my thoughts to Holmes.

"You have been reading too many stories by your hero Mr. Poe," he chided. "I rather doubt we shall encounter any fantastic events here."

But we did encounter, waiting for us by the front door, the mother superior of whom Louis Hill had spoken, and she was indeed a woman to be reckoned with. Attired in a flowing white habit offset by a long black headdress, she was extraordinarily tall, not much under six feet, and the firm line of her jaw and the cool severity of her blue eyes left little doubt as to her forceful character.

"I am Sherlock Holmes," my friend said with a slight bow, "and this is Dr. Watson."

"Yes, I know who you are," she said matter-of-factly. "I am Sister Mary Gallagher. Follow me."

She led us along a vaulted corridor lined with hissing steam radiators to a large office outfitted with a simple desk, a bank of file cabinets, several hard wooden chairs, and a photograph of Pope Pius XI, who gazed down on us with a look of stern godliness.

"I understand you wish to speak to me of some important matter," she said as we took seats on the remarkably uncomfortable chairs. "What might that be?"

Sister Mary obviously did not believe in idle talk, and so Holmes stated his mission directly.

"We wish to speak to you about Margaret O'Donnell. She was a resident here for some time before her death, was she not?"

"Yes, she was here for a brief time in December."

"How did she come to be in this institution? I am under the impression most of the girls and women you take in are sent here by the courts."

"That is not entirely true. We also take in orphans and girls whose families cannot or will not support them. We also endeavor to assist girls who are facing some great difficulty in their lives. Miss O'Donnell's father believed she needed our guidance and so we naturally agreed to be of help."

"Did the mayor explain why he felt compelled to bring her to you?"

"You will have to ask that question of him. I cannot speak for the mayor."

"I have reason to believe she was pregnant, and unmarried young women in that condition are frequently sent here, are they not?"

"I cannot discuss her condition. That is another matter best left to the mayor, if he wishes to speak of it at all."

In normal cases, Holmes would have pressed for an answer, but both he and I could tell at once that Sister Mary was a rock not easily moved.

"I am disappointed by your silence," Holmes said. "It appears there is no one who will speak up for poor Margaret. Why is that?"

"It is not my place to speak for her, Mr. Holmes," Sister Mary said with more than a hint of irritation. "I leave that to her father."

"I see. And yet he has been a tower of silence, as though he has tried to erase all memories of his daughter, who lies dead and buried at seventeen. How curious and sad that is!"

"Perhaps, but I know him to be a good Christian man, and I am sure he has his reasons. Let God be his judge, not you or I."

"I have found, Sister, that God is often called upon to judge a man when others are afraid to speak the truth about him. Let me ask you this: did the mayor personally deliver Margaret here?"

"No, she arrived with a police officer."

"Detective Jackson Grimshaw?"

"I believe that is his name. He was acting of course on orders from the mayor."

"Do policemen often bring girls to your doorstep?"

"It is sometimes the case. The girls we serve can be quite wild and disorderly when they arrive. However, we soon get them into line. Discipline is always the first step on the pathway to God."

Sister Mary stared unflinchingly at Holmes as she uttered these words, and I could readily imagine how even the most recalcitrant girl might succumb to meek obedience under the power of her gaze.

Holmes stared back and said, "But Margaret apparently did not take well to the disciplined life here. She escaped the first chance she could get, did she not?"

"This is not a prison, Mr. Holmes. She was not authorized to leave until her father was ready to take her back, but she left before that time."

"When did Margaret arrive here and when did she leave, as you put it?"

"She arrived on December fifth and left in the early morning hours of December seventh."

Holmes folded his hands under his chin, apparently lost in thought for a moment, then said, "She certainly was not here for long. Yet I have been told the dormitories here are kept locked so that girls will not run away."

"The dormitories are locked to keep the girls safe at night from intruders or anyone else who might wish to do them harm."

"How then did Margaret manage to leave?"

"She tied together sheets and went out a window. It was a dangerous thing to do, since the dormitories are on the second floor."

"Is it possible she had help from someone on the outside?"

"I would not know."

"Do the girls here have access to a telephone?"

"They are allowed to make one phone call a week to a relative or friend."

"Did Margaret call anyone before she left?"

"I am not aware of that."

"Did any of the other girls see her leave?"

"No, or so they say."

"I should like to talk to some of these girls," Holmes said. "Perhaps—"

"That would not be possible."

"Why?"

"Because I will not allow it. Now, I do not believe there is anything else I can tell you. I will be happy to escort you to the door."

She rose from her chair behind the desk, and I started to get up as well. But Holmes stayed put.

"You have not told us what happened to Margaret," he said in a stern voice. "She left your institution in the middle of the night and shortly thereafter she was dead. How did she meet her end so suddenly?"

"I have no knowledge of that."

"Her father never told you the circumstances of her death?"

"No. Now, I must ask you to leave. It is time for chapel with the girls."

We had instructed our cab driver to wait for us, and once we were on our way back to the Ryan, Holmes said, "The good nun, like everyone else in this affair, is not being truthful. I have no doubt she knows what happened to Margaret O'Donnell. Still, we learned something of value today. Margaret must have made a telephone call to make arrangements for her escape. Whomever she called, that person was very likely waiting for her when she came down those sheets in the middle of the night. And that same person must have been instrumental in her death."

"Are you thinking St. Aubin was the culprit?"

"It would certainly tie many loose ends together if that were true. But I have found, my dear Watson, that tidiness and the truth do not always go hand in hand."

WHEN WE RETURNED TO THE RYAN, a message from Declan Morrissey was waiting at the front desk. Holmes placed a call to the number Morrissey had left. After a brief conversation, Holmes hung up and said, "Mr. Paul O'Donnell has shown up unannounced at the speakeasy and apparently he is getting himself quite drunk. Mr. Morrissey said if we wish to speak to him, we best do it before he is too far gone."

It was but a short walk to Morrissey's establishment, and there we found the mayor's son, standing alone at the speakeasy's long bar and contemplating the double shot glass in front of him as though it might offer some clue to his life. Although O'Donnell wore a well-tailored suit, he had the look of a wild and disorganized man. He was small framed, with narrow shoulders and hips, and even though he was only in his midtwenties he had already gone to fat in the belly. His sallow, rounded face bore the stubble of beard and his bloodshot brown eyes lent credence to the stories he had led a dissolute life of drinking and whoring.

Morrissey was tending bar and gave us a silent nod before we took stools on either side of O'Donnell. He swiveled around to look at Holmes and did a double take.

"Well, I will be damned and damned again," he said, slurring his words slightly. "Mr. Sherlock Holmes!" He then turned to look at me. "And his faithful companion, Dr. Watson! Won't I have a story to tell the boys."

"Indeed you will," Holmes said, although we had no idea who "the boys" might be. "It is a pleasure to meet you, Mr. O'Donnell."

"Likewise, I'm sure. How about a drink for the two of you? Bourbon is my elixir, and I consume it daily to ward off the evil spirits who populate this cursed world of ours."

"Why not?" Holmes said and motioned to Morrissey to bring us drinks. When they arrived, Holmes hoisted his glass and said, "To you, Mr. O'Donnell. May I ask why you have returned to St. Paul?"

"I have some very important business," he said. "I must kill my father."

"And why is that?" Holmes asked, giving no hint that he was surprised by O'Donnell's murderous intentions.

"You know why. You got that message I sent, didn't you?"

Holmes had long suspected the anonymous message we'd received shortly after arriving in St. Paul—a message calling upon us to investigate Margaret O'Donnell's death—had come from her brother.

"I did receive your message," Holmes said, "and we have indeed been looking into the matter. Do you believe your father had something to do with Margaret's death?"

"Don't call her Margaret," O'Donnell said. "Nobody called her that. Maggie, she was Maggie. Not that it matters anymore, I guess. She's in her grave and that bastard of a father of ours put her there. I know it."

"How do you know?"

"Who else could it have been? She got knocked up, you know, and that must have made the mighty Richard O'Donnell furious."

"No doubt. When did you last speak to Maggie?"

"Six thirty-nine p.m., December 3, 1927. Don't be surprised that I have memorized the moment. I should have come up here to help her but I didn't. It is a dark stain on my soul, and it burns like acid. But I have a wondrous anodyne, God's own cure-all for all mortal ills. Speaking of which—"

O'Donnell suddenly stood up, like a man who had been startled out of a dream, and shouted, "Barkeep! Barkeep! Another round for the three of us!"

A man drinking to forget will not remember for long, and Holmes knew it. He said to Morrissey, who was standing nearby behind the bar, "I think Mr. O'Donnell deserves your very finest bourbon. Perhaps you should retrieve some of that special stock you have in the back. I am sure it will take some time to locate it, but it will be worth the wait."

Morrissey understood Holmes's delaying tactic at once and said, "Yes, I do have an exceptional bottle back there. It is some of Kentucky's finest. I'm sure I can find it."

Before O'Donnell could object, Morrissey left. Holmes said, "While we are awaiting that splendid bourbon, please tell me more about the talk you had with your sister. Did she say who had fathered her child?"

"No, she said it was a secret she had to keep. Whoever it was, he promised to help her out, or so she said. He was a big man, she claimed, and not who you would expect. But she was worried about what was going to happen. She thought our dear father wanted to send her away to that hellhole the nuns operate."

"You mean the House of the Good Shepherd?"

"More like a chamber of horrors, if you ask me," O'Donnell said. "They take the poor girls and shear them like sheep until their spirits are gone." He was growing agitated, his hands trembling as he held his empty shot glass. "Where is that damned barkeep? I need a drink right now."

"He is on his way," Holmes promised. "Now, do you recall anything else Maggie told you?"

"She was sad. Her life was going to hell. Or maybe I should say it was just going, except she didn't know it. Goddamnit, I should have come up here. Why didn't I?"

"It is of no use to blame yourself, Mr. O'Donnell. I believe Maggie was in the middle of circumstances she could not control, nor could you. Do you know how she died?"

"Why, somebody killed her, of course, and the baby, too. Father dearest knows but he isn't saying anything, is he? Now, where's that drink? I swear—"

Morrissey now appeared with a bottle and filled O'Donnell's glass. "To your health," he said, "but go slowly if you would. I wish no harm to come to you."

O'Donnell gulped down the bourbon and said, "The harm has already come, can't you see? My life, sir, is a fruitless enterprise and will always be so. I drink, therefore I am. The wise words of a French philosopher, I believe. Let us have another round."

Morrissey glanced at Holmes, who nodded, presumably because he believed alcohol was all that would keep O'Donnell talking. Morrissey poured another drink as Holmes asked about Daniel St. Aubin. But O'Donnell said he didn't know him, nor did he appear to be aware that he had been murdered.

"I travel," he explained. "I travel here, I travel there. I ride the trains. I play poker and I win more often than not. I should have come here sooner to avenge Maggie's murder. I should have, but I didn't. You may engrave that on my tombstone: 'Paul James O'Donnell, Traveling Man: He Should Have But He Didn't.' He, he—now where was I?"

O'Donnell was sleepy-eyed on the verge of drunken oblivion. "Maggie, Maggie, Maggie," he muttered. "God forgive me." Then his head slumped down on the bar and he went silent.

Morrissey said, "Looks like he's gone for the night. I'll fish through his pockets for a hotel key. One of my boys will make sure he gets tucked in safely. He seems like a lost soul."

"One of many," Holmes said.

Morrissey nodded and said, "Well, I wish him peace, though I doubt he will ever find it. Now, do you think he might actually try to kill his father?"

"No. His courage is of the liquid variety. I imagine he will not be here in St. Paul for long. He will need to keep moving. The trains are all he has."

As we walked back to the Ryan, Holmes said, "We are on the cusp, Watson. The endgame is now before us. This case began as a forest of possibilities, growing wildly in all directions. But Mr. O'Donnell has given us a clear view through all of the foliage. Blackmail is very much a part of it, as is the cold calculation behind Mr. Rafferty's murder, but at the center of it all is the Garden of Eden and a devil who seduces."

24

"I Pose No Threat to You"

A visitor to the Ryan Hotel in the late afternoon hours of January 21, 1928, would have detected nothing out of the ordinary. Saturday was usually busy at the hotel, and a dozen or so guests, all men, were scattered around the lobby, sunk into deep chairs as they read the afternoon *Dispatch* and worked on their cigars in a haze of blue smoke. At the front desk Donald Hobbs was already on duty, unaware he was on the verge of a night he would never forget. Nearby, in elevator number one, Henry Johnson moved up and down as he had for so many years, greeting passengers by name and remarking what a cold day it had been and how the night promised to be even colder.

By the time Johnson started his shift at three, Bertram Abbey was already in a corner room on the third floor, awaiting a visitor and taking what solace he could from a bottle of Cabernet Sauvignon. The poet-turned-mystery-writer was feeling anxious because of Rafferty's investigation into St. Aubin's death. Rafferty had already excavated plenty of dirt, and Abbey feared the pile was about to grow much larger. Abbey had done some unfortunate things and they needed to stay hidden. But now Rafferty, who had many friends in the press, was poised to bring the whole sordid story into the open. If that happened, Abbey knew, he would become an outcast to the bluebloods of Summit Avenue and might even face criminal prosecution.

Abbey believed his visitor could pose even more problems for him unless he acted decisively. Money was the universal solvent, able to clean up almost any mess, and Abbey had brought along a thousand dollars in cash. He hoped it would be enough to convince his visitor to do what needed to be done.

Two stories down from Abbey's room, just past the lobby, the Ryan's popular café was quiet, with only a few customers sipping on coffee or tea. Among them were Richard O'Donnell and Montgomery Meeks. The mayor and his aide had much to discuss, particularly when it came to Rafferty. The old man, they agreed, was becoming ever more troublesome as he continued to investigate Daniel St. Aubin's death.

"He appears to believe some vast conspiracy is afoot to cover up Mr. St. Aubin's demise," Meeks told the mayor. "He's suspicious because of all that blackmail business St. Aubin was involved in. But there really is nothing to it. The problem is that Rafferty is a persistent old codger and doesn't know when to quit."

"Well, I don't want to see any of this come to our door, Monty. That's the most important thing. I can't be caught up in a scandal."

"You won't be."

"What about Margaret? Do you think he knows about her and St. Aubin? It would be very embarrassing for me if that story got out."

"You have no need to worry on that score. Rafferty never brought up the subject when I talked with him. All he cares about is what happened to St. Aubin."

"I pray you are right," O'Donnell said, then glanced at his watch, which showed the time was three-thirty. "Well, I must be on my way. I have some work to do before I speak to the Civic Improvement Club tonight."

After the mayor left, Meeks finished his coffee before being summoned to one of the house phones to take a call. The conversation was brief, and Meeks left the hotel at quarter to four.

Monsignor Pierre Denis entered the Ryan at quarter to five. He spoke briefly to Hobbs at the front desk, then headed toward the cen-

tral staircase, bounding up two steps at once, eager to reach his destination. When he reached the second floor, he turned down the main
corridor in the direction of Rafferty's apartment. Neither Hobbs nor
anyone else at the hotel recalled seeing him again that night.

Denis had spent the day praying and fasting, fearful his trans-
gressions were about to rain down on him in a storm of shame.
How he wished he had been able to control his secret desires! He
wished, too, that he'd had the courage to come forward and confess
his sins. But the prospect of ruin—complete and abject ruin and the
loss of everything he held important—was more than Denis could
bear. His life, he believed, was in Rafferty's hands. They had been
friends once, but now he wasn't so sure. They needed to talk so that
Rafferty fully understood Denis's awful situation. There had to be a
way out, but would Rafferty leave the door open? Denis had to know
one way or another

A few blocks from the hotel, at the Union Depot, Jackson Grimshaw lounged on a bench in the waiting room, although he had no
intention of boarding a train. A plan was in place and his timing
had to be absolutely right. Just before four, he went up to the information desk, flashed his badge, and asked the agent on duty about
a man he was looking for. But the agent hadn't noticed the man in
question.

Appearing to be crestfallen, Grimshaw thanked the agent with
far more politeness than he usually displayed, then headed out
toward the depot's main entrance on Fourth Street. Before leaving, he undertook one more brief task in accord with the plan. Once
outside, Grimshaw walked two blocks west on Fourth, then turned
north on Robert Street, toward the Ryan Hotel.

At Fifth Street, he stopped to look at his watch and have a
smoke. He was a little early, so he stomped around in the cold for a
few minutes as trolleys rattled past on Robert. A few shoppers were
out but they paid no attention to the hulking man in the long wool

coat hunched over a cigarette, unaware he was a dark angel come to do the Devil's work.

THE TELEPHONE CALL, sent through to Rafferty's apartment early in the afternoon, took him by surprise. A murderer was calling. Only hours earlier, Rafferty's conversation with Bertha Codding-ton had produced a breakthrough, pointing him toward the man now on the phone.

"So you have been digging into things, I hear," the caller said. His voice was without inflection, a smooth but very deep and dangerous river. "We should talk. I think I could set your mind at ease."

"Could you now? I doubt that."

"I believe some people have been telling lies about me, and I simply wish to defend myself against such hurtful insinuations."

"Who are these liars you speak of?"

"Come now, Mr. Rafferty, don't be coy. You and I both know who they are."

Rafferty wondered if the man had spoken with Mrs. Codding-ton. That seemed unlikely, since she had demanded strict confiden-tiality from Rafferty out of concern for her own well-being. Or so she'd said. However it had happened, the man obviously recognized he'd become Rafferty's prime suspect.

The man continued. "I can prove I am the victim of terrible falsehoods, if you will let me. I will not require a great deal of your time, I promise."

Rafferty smelled a trap, but even if it was, what did he have to fear? There was already a ghost rattling in his bones, ready to escort him out of the world at a moment's notice. Why not have one final adventure, face to face with a cunning killer? A meeting with the man might even yield the proof needed to bring him to justice, and Rafferty believed every earthly reckoning was important, if only because the ultimate ledger book might well be a dream.

"All right, we can talk."

"Excellent. As it so happens, I'm leaving on a trip later this evening, so the earlier the better. How about five o'clock? I could meet you at your apartment, if that would be convenient."

A meeting at five didn't give Rafferty a great deal of time to prepare, but he agreed to it. "Come alone," he said, "or there will be no meeting."

"Of course. I will see you soon."

It didn't take long for Rafferty to have second thoughts about meeting in his apartment. His door lacked a good peephole, and if the man brought along an accomplice, that person would be hard to spot in the hallway outside. Once Rafferty opened the door, even with a gun in his hand, he could be overpowered. Nor did Rafferty have any reliable backup. Wash Thomas was in Minneapolis, still on the hunt for Johnny Riordan, and Rafferty had no way to reach him. Thomas was due back for dinner at six, but until then, Rafferty would be on his own. After some quick thinking, Rafferty formulated a plan. He would meet the man at the Ryan, only it wouldn't be in his apartment.

At precisely five o'clock, the man appeared at the door of Rafferty's apartment, where he made an unexpected discovery. A note tacked to the door said:

Go to room 652. Come alone. I will be aware if anyone is with you. —Rafferty

Rafferty had known about the room for years. Members of the hotel staff used it for a variety of purposes, few of them wholesome, and the door was usually kept unlocked. More important for Rafferty's purposes, the room was at the end of a long corridor that provided the only means of access except for a rear stairway door, which could easily be blocked shut. Anyone approaching the room would be in full view for a distance of forty feet down the corridor, making an ambush impossible.

At four-thirty Rafferty boarded an elevator operated by Henry Johnson and asked for the sixth floor. Rafferty was wearing a red jacket, a ruffled white shirt, and black slacks. Beneath the jacket were two heavy pieces of hardware. He'd also brought along a folder with his notes on the St. Aubin case. He'd debated whether to bring the notes along but finally decided they'd be safer with him than in his apartment, where a burglar might find them. Rafferty chatted a bit with Johnson, whom he'd known for years, and encountered no one else before being deposited at his desired floor. Once in the elevator lobby, he paused to make sure nothing was amiss, then slowly made his way around a corner and down the hallway to room 652.

The door to the room was open and Rafferty went inside. There, he found two chairs and dragged them out into the corridor near a rear stairway door. He propped one chair up against the door to keep it from being opened. He sat in the other chair, looking down the corridor to the point where it turned toward the elevator lobby. For protection, he carried his trusty old Stevens pocket rifle as well as a Colt automatic pistol. The Stevens rested on his knees, on top of the folder, while the Colt lay ready in his jacket pocket. All he had to do now was wait.

AT EIGHT MINUTES PAST FIVE, the man appeared at the far end of the hallway. When he saw the rifle, which Rafferty pointed directly at him, he thrust his hands out.

"There really is no need for a gun," he said as walked slowly down the hallway toward Rafferty. "I pose no threat to you."

"I will be the judge of that," Rafferty said, motioning for the man to stop about ten feet away. "After all, you have already killed twice."

"Not true, not true. Now, please hear me out, if you would. Am I not entitled to that?"

"All right, tell me what you wish."

The man spoke for a half hour, building a marvelous fairy-tale castle of lies. Rafferty had expected as much, but the story was presented with such apparent sincerity that he could only marvel at the sheer audacity of it. Daniel St. Aubin, the man claimed, had impregnated Margaret, who had then suffered a terrible miscarriage and bled to death before the doctors could save her. Later, Riordan murdered St. Aubin after being spurned by him. Or perhaps St. Aubin, dirty blackmailer that he was, had refused to share the proceeds of one of his foul schemes with Riordan.

"I know it is a disturbing story," the man concluded, "and Margaret's death in particular is a tragedy. It was her grave misfortune to become mixed up with a criminal like St. Aubin. But it is over now, and what more can be done? Margaret is gone and Daniel St. Aubin will have to face judgment in the next world, where there is unlikely to be much mercy for so terrible a sinner. For us, however, it is time to move on, don't you agree?"

"I wonder what Johnny Riordan would say if he were here," Rafferty said and then told a lie of his own. "I have a letter from him, and it is very revealing."

"Is that so? I would like to see it."

"I imagine you would. The newspapers are sure to find it very interesting as well."

"They would not publish such a document, assuming it even exists."

"The newspapers might surprise you. Now, why don't you stop lying? I know you impregnated Margaret and killed Danny, or had him killed, because he was blackmailing you. Nor do I believe Margaret died from a miscarriage. You murdered her because she threatened to expose you, and that would have meant your ruin. It is all as simple as that. Now you must stand up like a man and face the consequences of your actions. You have no other hope."

"Is that so? I had a talk with Mrs. Coddington today. She has come to greatly regret what she told you and in fact will deny every word of it."

"Ah, you put the fear of God in her, I imagine. I suppose you told her that if your crimes became known, so too would her illegal activities."

"It really doesn't matter what I told her. The point is, you have nothing against me and if you claim otherwise, you will be exposed to the world as a fool. Is that really what you wish your final legacy to be? After all, your days are numbered."

"Everyone's days are numbered, but I will take my chances. I do not like murderers and I have spent much of my life finding them out. I know who you are and what you have done, and I will expend my final breath if necessary to bring you to justice."

The man shook his head and said, "You're very wrong, about everything, but it doesn't look as though I can change your mind. I fear you're about to make a mistake you'll come to greatly regret. I will say goodbye now."

As the man turned to leave, Rafferty took out his pistol and said, "Wait a moment. I'm sure you won't mind if I accompany you, just in case someone is lurking around the corner. Be assured I will shoot you dead if I have to."

"Don't be ridiculous," the man said. "No one is lying in wait for you."

"We'll see about that."

Rafferty followed the man down the hall and around the corner to the elevator lobby and main staircase. The hall was deserted. Rafferty pressed the elevator button as the man stepped away and headed for the staircase.

"Perhaps we'll talk again soon," he said before disappearing down the stairs. "I really would like that."

WHEN RAFFERTY RETURNED to his apartment, he checked the door carefully for signs that anyone might have tampered with the lock in his absence. Nothing looked out of order, so he unlocked the door and went inside to prepare for dinner with Thomas in the Ryan's café. It was ten after six and Rafferty was running late. He set his pocket rifle and pistol on a table in the front parlor. They would go into his gun cabinet later. Then he went toward the study, where he wanted to jot down a few notes before he forgot.

The door to the study was ajar, as he had left it. He pushed it open and as he stepped inside, a shock of premonition struck him with the force of an electrical surge. But it was too late to avoid the knife. It sliced deep into his body, and his back erupted in searing pain. Rafferty crashed to the carpet. Almost immediately he heard knocking at his door, followed by the familiar voice of Wash Thomas calling his name. His final lucid thoughts were about why the murderous man with the knife had come for him. He remembered the phone number tucked away in his shirt pocket and reached for it. Perhaps it would be a useful clue for whoever investigated his murder. Yes, and perhaps he should also—

Then conscious thought gave way to a racing stream of memories. He saw a northern pike, its scales glinting in the summer sun as it leapt from Osakis's blue-green waters, thrashing against the hook and line. He saw a blond-haired soldier's head torn off by a cannonball at First Bull Run, a crimson fountain of blood pumping from the severed arteries in his neck. He saw a hillside in Vermont ablaze with fall colors and his brother Seamus shooting arrows into a maple tree and laughing every time he struck his target. He saw a tall glass of lager, foam cascading down its sides as Wash Thomas slid it along the bar to a thirsty customer. He saw a full moon hanging in the sky and stars glittering all around like souls on their way to heaven. And finally he saw Mary, plump flakes of snow melting into her white wedding dress as she came down the steps of the old cathedral on the happiest day of her life, and his. All gone now, all gone, to wherever people go. Rafferty's eyes closed, and there was a flash, bright as the dawn of creation, before the darkness came.

WASH THOMAS WOULD NEVER FORGET—could never forget—finding Rafferty's body, and it made him angry every time he thought about it. Rafferty had literally been stabbed in the back by a murderer so cowardly he dared not face his eighty-five-year-old victim. Worse, Rafferty had suffered in his final moments, alone. It wasn't right.

As he worked with Holmes and Watson in the days after the murder, Thomas maintained his usual demeanor and did all he could to assist with the investigation. But he was burning inside, and he knew there was only one way to douse the fire before it consumed him.

One evening, after the restaurant closed, Thomas helped Pats with the dishes, then they went upstairs to make gentle love and talk. He told her how he felt but she already knew.

"Don't let it take you to a bad place, honey," she told him. "You and Mr. Holmes will find the man who killed Shad, and justice will be done. I know it."

"Oh yes, justice will be done," Thomas said, but what he didn't say was that he intended to see to it personally. There would be no courtroom and no mercy for Rafferty's killer if Thomas had anything to say about it.

25

"We May Have No Other Choice"

The letter containing a hand-printed note from Johnny Riordan reached its intended recipient the day before Rafferty's murder. It said: I KNOW WHAT YOU DID TO MAGGIE. IT WILL COST YOU $20,000. INSTRUCTIONS TO COME. IF I SEE GRIMSHAW AGAIN, YOU ARE DONE.

The note came as a nasty surprise, and as the man read it he realized he was once again thrust into a crisis. He was sure Johnny Riordan had sent the note. The little weasel obviously believed he could make a killing. But it wasn't going to happen. He had to be stopped dead, literally.

The man was appalled the police hadn't been able to find Riordan. They'd been searching for weeks with no luck. The kid was only seventeen. How could he have eluded detection for so long? A call to Jackson Grimshaw was in order.

When Grimshaw answered, the man said, "I am in need of some good news. Please tell me you've found Johnny Riordan."

"Not yet, but we're close. He stayed in one of those flophouses on Washington Avenue two nights ago, so we are looking for him in that area. Trouble is, there must a hundred cheap hotels there. We're also keeping an eye on those bathhouses where the queers hang out."

The man didn't mention the note he'd received, saying only that he'd heard Riordan was making more threats, which suggested he'd somehow acquired Daniel St. Aubin's trove of blackmail material.

"Well, the little fag is a bold one, I'll give him that," Grimshaw said.

"Yes, and he can't be allowed to continue going about his dirty business. You need to do a lot better. How many men do you have looking for him?"

"Two."

"You should have more. If Riordan starts spouting off, he could send us all to hell in the proverbial handbasket. You know what to do when you find him."

"Yeah, I know. I'll put more men on it, but it won't be easy. The cops in Minneapolis don't like us nosing around in their territory, so we have to be cautious."

"Don't worry about that. If the cops over there cause any more problems, let me know. I'll handle them."

"What about Rafferty? Grimshaw asked. "I hear that colored pal of his is looking for Riordan. We could persuade him not to do that, if you want."

"No, for the time being concentrate on finding Riordan. And when you do, I want to be the first one to see everything he has. Do you understand?"

"Sure, you're running the show, but I'll expect to be well paid for my work."

"You will be. I've got money salted away. Just make sure you get the job done."

MAYOR RICHARD O'DONNELL liked to tell confidants, including Montgomery Meeks, that his life had been "smooth sailing" until marriage and children sent hurricanes his way. Kathleen had been more than he could handle, and so had their two children. And as problem upon problem compounded, O'Donnell began to feel extremely sorry for himself. How had a simple fling—the kind that might tempt any red-blooded man—led to so much misery?

"It just isn't fair," he told Meeks one morning as they talked over the latest developments in the St. Aubin case. They were in

O'Donnell's office, smoking Larrañagas from his private stash. The mayor always brought out his best Cuban cigars for important discussions. The rich tobacco helped him think better, or so he believed, and it was somehow soothing to watch the aromatic smoke drift through the air.

"I never should have had any goddamn children," O'Donnell continued. "They've never been anything except trouble. And now look where we are. I'll never be governor if any of this stuff comes out. We have to keep a lid on things. We have to! If the press finds out, they'll crucify me and that will be the end of my career."

"It doesn't have to come out," Meeks said. "You know where things stand. St. Aubin is already out of the picture. Once we have Riordan, our problems will go away."

"I'm not so sure about that. Rafferty is still stirring the pot, and we can't underestimate him. He could find out something if he keeps at it."

"He won't have the time. He's at death's door. We'll be rid of him soon enough."

"I hope you're right, Monty, I really do, or we're all cooked."

THAT SAME DAY, as Grimshaw intensified his hunt for Riordan, Monsignor Pierre Denis walked over to Bertram Abbey's mansion for a strategy session. Denis didn't like the idea of being seen with his very occasional lover. He suspected Abbey's staff of gossipy young men would quickly spread the word of his visit and probably make obscene jokes about it. But there was nothing he could do. Abbey had insisted on meeting in person.

Abbey wanted the meeting so he could gauge Denis's state of mind. The monsignor, he knew, was a man of secrets that ate at him like a worm in his belly, and he seemed vulnerable at any moment to a complete breakdown because of his silly obsession with God. The idea of sin had never taken root with Abbey, who saw life as nothing more than an opportunity to do what he wanted. But Denis had a conscience, and that made him a threat. If the good monsignor was starting to crumble, Abbey needed to know about it.

Denis wasn't crumbling, however. He was calculating, trying to find a way to avert disaster, and sometimes he was surprised by his own ruthlessness when it came to covering up his sins. He'd lied, burgled, and worse, and yet here he was, in the middle of the biggest mess of his life, even as his fervent prayers for divine guidance met with silence. Abbey, on the other hand, was blissfully free of scruples, and Denis often wished he could be the same way. Life would be so much easier without a conscience.

"I don't like meeting here," Denis said as Abbey escorted him into his library and closed the door behind them. "People might get the wrong idea about us."

"And what would that be?" Abbey asked, lighting a cigarette he'd removed from an elegant gold case stamped with his initials. "That we're lovers? At last report, that was true."

"I don't know that I'd call it love," Denis said, "but it's over. It has to be."

"You'll change your mind, you always do. That itch comes and you just have to scratch it. It's how God made you, if you believe that sort of thing. As it so happens, I'll be at the Ryan tomorrow on some business. Why don't you stop by, say around five, and we could spend some time together."

"No, no, I couldn't do that. Not now."

"Well, if you change your mind, you know where you'll find me. I'll be in my usual room. But we're not here to talk about the temptations of the flesh, are we? We have to figure out what to do about that little bastard Riordan. The police are looking for him, but if he manages to get away, he could cause us no end of trouble."

"How much do you think he knows?"

"He knows everything, my friend. It's been whispered in my ear that he's decided to become the new Daniel St. Aubin."

"That can't be good."

"No, it's not good at all. Apparently, he got in thick with St. Aubin at some point and now he's inherited the goods, as it were. The goods on us and who knows how many other people."

"What can we do about it? We're not the police. We can't find him."

"True. But guess who else is looking for him?"

"Rafferty?"

"That's right. The old man is becoming a big, fat nuisance."

"I take it you're afraid he might get to Riordan before the police."

"It's possible. Not likely, but possible. If Johnny Boy spills the beans to Rafferty, then all manner of ugly things could happen. I could go to prison and you could be disgraced."

"So what do you propose we do?"

"Let me think about that," Abbey said. "Perhaps the lovely Mr. Jackson Grimshaw can be of some help to us. We may have no other choice."

Although Denis had his doubts, he agreed to go along. He liked Rafferty as well as the next man, but self-preservation had to come first. He would do what needed to be done. As to how God would react, Denis shuddered to think of it.

JOHNNY RIORDAN KNEW he had to keep moving. He left King's Hotel in the early morning hours of January 19 and debated whether to spend the next night at another flophouse or try something else. He had become a burrowing animal with a sharp nose for trouble, and the deadly scent of predators was in the air. He suspected Grimshaw's men were canvassing every cheap hotel in Minneapolis looking for him, and the longer he stayed in such places, the more likely he was to be found.

He thought of trying one of the notorious bathhouses on Hennepin. He could get picked up there and then find shelter, possibly for weeks, in the home of some lonely old man. But Riordan feared the bathhouses were being watched, too, and he wasn't sure where to go next.

His fears only increased when, on January 22, he saw on the front page of the *Minneapolis Tribune* that a man named Shadwell Rafferty had been murdered in St. Paul. Riordan didn't know Rafferty and would have thought nothing about his death except for a subhead that said: "Had Been Investigating Mysterious Death of Daniel St. Aubin." Riordan quickly read the entire story and it was not good news. If Rafferty had been killed because of what he'd found out about Danny's death, then Riordan assumed he was next in line.

At the same time, Riordan still dreamed of raking in twenty thousand dollars in blackmail money. But the deal was beginning to look very dicey. Try as he might, Riordan couldn't figure out a safe way to collect the cash, assuming it was offered, without Grimshaw and his men pouncing on him. He knew he'd be a dead man if that happened.

An envelope in his satchel contained all the most damning material St. Aubin had collected relating to Margaret O'Donnell's death. It would be enough to send at least one man to prison for the rest of his life. It would be also be Riordan's ticket to the twenty thousand once he worked out a way to collect it from his mark.

Riordan believed he could elude Grimshaw and his men, but he was less confident he'd be able to collect his twenty-thousand-dollar prize in the end. But if he didn't get the money, he decided he would at least find a way to avenge Danny's murder. The *Tribune* story reported that Sherlock Holmes was coming to St. Paul to investigate Rafferty's death. Who better, Riordan thought, to secure justice for Danny as well, if and when the time came?

JUST AFTER TWO IN THE MORNING on February 7, the day after Holmes and Watson had gone to the House of the Good Shepherd, a grisly incident occurred on the tracks of the Chicago, Milwaukee, St. Paul, and Pacific Railroad in South Minneapolis. A freight train was heading west at thirty miles an hour along a sunken corridor with no pedestrian access when the engineer saw a body lying crosswise on the tracks just ahead. There was no possibility of avoiding the body, which the train ran over as the engineer looked on in horror. When the engineer and his fireman stopped the train and ran back to the scene, they found the mangled, decapitated remains of what appeared to be a young man. His severed head, its face torn away, lay to one side of the tracks. Both the engineer and fireman lost their dinners before they were able to summon the authorities.

26
"The Game Is Afoot!"

[From "Murder in St. Paul"]

"I have found a most interesting item in the afternoon newspaper," Sherlock Holmes announced when I joined him for a late lunch at a small downtown café where he found the tea to be "quite excellent." He had spent the morning in his room "lucubrating," as he called it, and I could tell by his eager manner that some grand plan was forming in his mind.

Holmes handed me the newspaper and pointed to the story that had caught his attention. It concerned an unfortunate young man who had been run over and decapitated by a train in Minneapolis. The story described the victim as "about eighteen years of age, with a slender built and wearing the clothes of a vagabond. Authorities said his features were left unrecognizable by the accident. No identification was found with the body, and it is thought the young man may have been a transient who had fallen off another train and was lying insensate on the tracks when he was struck."

I saw at once what Holmes was thinking. "You believe the dead man could be Johnny Riordan," I said.

"Yes, and if it is indeed Mr. Riordan, you may be assured his death was no accident."

"But we can't be sure."

"No, and that is the problem. Do we assume he is dead or do we continue searching for him in the hope he is still alive?"

"What have you decided?"

"We must move forward along other avenues, Watson, while

keeping an eye out for Mr. Riordan, just in case. It is the only course that makes sense for the time being."

"And what will these other avenues be?"

"I have been extremely stupid," Holmes said, words I was hardly accustomed to hearing from him. "Do you remember what I did with Mr. Rafferty's notes after we obtained them from his bank box?"

"Of course. You hid them away in a closet on the floor above our rooms."

"Yes, and it has belatedly occurred to me that Mr. St. Aubin might have employed a similar strategy at his apartment building to safeguard all of his blackmail documents, knowing as he did that the police might search his rooms at any time."

"But didn't he hand over all that material to Riordan just before he was killed?"

"I think not. Recall, if you will, that the newsstand operator who saw them stated Mr. St. Aubin gave a single manila envelope to Mr. Riordan. However, one envelope can hardly have been sufficient for all of Mr. St. Aubin's 'treasures,' if they can be called that. He must have collected quite a trove of material over the years, and I believe it may still be somewhere in the apartment building."

After lunch, the hotel doorman hailed a cab for us. When we got in, Holmes quickly engaged the driver in conversation, and I soon understood his intentions. The driver left us off at a large clothing store only a few blocks from the hotel. We walked briskly through the store and out a rear door to another street. Our driver pulled up moments later, and we were off again, this time toward the Piedmont Apartments, where St. Aubin had lived.

Holmes craned his head around as our cab sped away and pronounced himself well satisfied. "We have shaken them," he said. "Detective Grimshaw's men are as obvious as crows in a bevy of swans. Driver, how long to the Piedmont?"

"Five minutes. It's not far."

The Piedmont, located on a quiet street at the edge of the city's commercial quarter, was impressive in an old-fashioned way, sporting craggy brownstone walls and all the agitated effects common to buildings from the past century. Light shafts cut through it above the ground floor, and the size of the building—it rose to a height of six stories—suggested a thorough search would not be easy.

Holmes had called ahead to make arrangements, and the building's superintendent greeted us when we arrived. He was a short, bespectacled man named Laurence Barteau, and he was quite pleased to be in our presence.

"Sherlock Holmes and Dr. John Watson! Don't that beat all! My wife's read every one of the stories. She loves those deductions of yours, you know, where some fellow comes to talk and you say, 'I see you've been to Abyssinia recently and rode a camel with three humps,' that type of thing. Too bad she's out playing cards with her hens. She'd be beside herself, she would, if she knew—"

"Yes, but she is not here," Holmes said with some asperity. "Now, tell us what you knew of Mr. St. Aubin."

"Not much, really. He wasn't the talkative type. Kept to himself for the most part. But he was a good tenant. There was no trouble from him and he always paid his rent on time."

"It is nice to learn he had at least one virtue," Holmes said. "We should like to begin by seeing his apartment. I understand the police searched it quite thoroughly after he died."

"That very night. They didn't waste any time, I'll say that. A whole squad of them came to my apartment flashing their badges like they were a gift from God and demanding my passkey. Scared my wife, they did. Then they trooped up to St. Aubin's apartment and started tearing it apart. I was watching, of course, and I told the big cop in charge they'd have to clean everything up, but he just laughed at me and told me to mind my own damn business."

Holmes provided a precise description of Grimshaw and asked if he was the policeman in question.

"That sounds like the one who barked at me all right," Barteau said. "Not what you would call a friendly sort of a fellow."

"You have a gift for understatement, Mr. Barteau. Did Detective Grimshaw say anything else to you?"

"No. He just told me to get the hell out of his way and keep my mouth shut. When the baboons finally left, I couldn't believe the mess they'd made. No respect for private property. I called the mayor's office to complain but nothing happened, of course. St. Aubin's mother finally had to have the place cleaned up. That was kind of a funny business, too."

Holmes's ears perked up. "How so?"

"Mrs. St. Aubin wasn't the first one in the apartment after the cops went through it. She sent the monsignor over to look for some things, or so he said."

"Monsignor Pierre Denis?"

"Sure, from up at the cathedral. Have you met him? Quite the man. But like I said, it was funny because when Mrs. St. Aubin showed up the next day, I mentioned the monsignor's visit and she didn't seem to know a thing about it. She was even mad at me for letting him into the apartment. Sometimes you just can't make people happy no matter what you do."

"You are a font of wisdom, Mr. Barteau. Now, how long was the monsignor in Mr. St. Aubin's apartment?"

"Oh, at least an hour."

"Did you see him when he left?"

"Sure. I keep an eye on things around here."

"I have no doubt you do. Was he carrying anything with him on his way out?"

"Not that I noticed. Of course he had a heavy coat on, so he could have slipped something under it, for all I know."

"Did he say anything when he left?"

"Nope, he just nodded to me and went out the door."

"You have been most helpful," Holmes said. "Please show us Mr. St. Aubin's apartment now."

"Sure thing. Follow me."

Chattering all the way, Barteau led us up a staircase to the second-floor apartment and used his passkey to let us in. The four-room apartment had been cleaned and repainted after the police search but not yet rented to a new tenant. No personal belongings were evident.

"Nothing here, as you can see," Barteau said. "Clean as a whistle. I'm hoping to have a new tenant in here soon."

After we'd walked through the apartment, Holmes said, "I should like to speak to the resident of the apartment across the hall, if he or she is in."

"That would be Mrs. Monroe. A real busybody, she is. Knows everything that goes on here."

Mrs. Monroe, a dark-eyed wisp of a woman in her seventies, was indeed in, and very happy to answer the questions Holmes put to her. Holmes quizzed her in some detail about her neighbor. One singular detail emerged from the avalanche of largely irrelevant information she offered. She said St. Aubin kept very late hours, and she sometimes saw him leaving his apartment at three in the morning and returning not long thereafter with a handful of file folders.

"It was very strange, if you ask me," she said.

I thought it even stranger that she was at her peephole at that hour of the morning, but I did not say so.

Holmes then asked Mrs. Monroe when she had last seen St. Aubin. She said it had been about two weeks before he was murdered, adding, "I don't know where he went. He didn't confide in me, you know."

"Our elderly night owl has confirmed my suspicions," Holmes

said after we'd sent her back to her spying. He then asked Barteau
if there were any janitor's closets, storerooms, or the like near
St. Aubin's apartment. There were, and Barteau showed us three
such rooms, all small and all locked. As Barteau looked on with considerable bafflement, Holmes meticulously examined each room,
reaching up behind shelves, looking into boxes, and even tapping
the walls to sound out any hollow spaces behind. He found nothing.

Searches of similar rooms on the third, fourth, and fifth floors
proved equally fruitless. By the time we reached the sixth and uppermost floor, I was beginning to think Holmes had miscalculated.
Perhaps St. Aubin's stash of blackmail material, assuming it even
existed, was stored in another location.

It wasn't. As Holmes searched an unlocked and apparently
unused janitor's closet on the sixth floor, he found three thick file
folders lodged behind old cans of paint stored on a high shelf. What
was in the folders would help lead us at last to Rafferty's murderer.

THE NEXT MORNING, Thomas joined us for breakfast, and afterwards
we retired to Holmes's room for what proved to be a most enlight-
ening discussion. Holmes and I had stayed up much of the night
carefully examining the file folders discovered in the storeroom
at the Piedmont. St. Aubin was a very meticulous blackmailer,
and his files, organized by name, formed a stockpile of damning
information about some of St. Paul's leading citizens. There were
photographs of men cavorting with prostitutes, passionate love
letters not addressed to spouses, and financial documents suggesting arrant thievery, along with much other evidence of deceit and
wrongdoing.

St. Aubin's encyclopedia of untoward human behavior included
a thick file that contained a set of documents describing how he
had attempted to blackmail Bertram Abbey and Monsignor Pierre
Denis for their sexual indiscretions. Its most damning item was an

explicit photograph of the two men together at the Ryan, presumably taken by Margo Sartell. Rafferty had mentioned the photograph in his notes but indicated he had never seen it.

There was much more in the file. St. Aubin described how he had attempted to use the photograph for purposes of blackmail, only to suffer a beating at the hands of Grimshaw. St. Aubin believed Mayor O'Donnell and Meeks had orchestrated the attack. Both men, he alleged, were also engaged in a "vast conspiracy" designed to cover up "widespread criminality" at city hall. He offered no proof but vowed he'd avenge his beating by bringing down "the whole system" in St. Paul.

"We now have strong evidence that all five of our suspects had a motive to kill Mr. St. Aubin," Holmes said. "Indeed, he might be described as a murder waiting to happen. Still, the documents do not tell us who committed the crime. There are other questions as well. I wonder, for example, how Mr. St. Aubin learned of the intimate relationship between Mr. Abbey and the monsignor."

"Perhaps he suspected what they were doing and had them followed," Thomas suggested. "Then he hired the Sartell woman to take the incriminating picture, despite what she told Rafferty."

Holmes shook his head. "That does not seem likely, given Mr. St. Aubin's rather limited wherewithal. Following someone around the clock is usually the work of private detectives, and it is a costly proposition. I have no doubt engaging the services of Miss Sartell would also have been expensive."

"And yet St. Aubin had the photo," I noted. "If he didn't hire Sartell, who did?"

"I have an idea along those lines," Holmes said but would say no more. "In the meantime, there is one more crucial item in Mr. St. Aubin's files we must consider."

"You must mean that note regarding a woman named Ruth Merrill," I said.

"Who's she?" Thomas asked.

Holmes showed Thomas the handwritten note, which said: "Ruth Merrill (Mrs. Coddington), Birth Control League, 1610 Mt. Curve. Ask $2,000 to start?"

Thomas understood the note's significance at once. "The American Birth Control League. They're a client of that answering service with the phone number Shad left behind."

"Indeed they are," Holmes said. "Like all good blackmailers, Mr. St. Aubin was a detective at heart, and he must have found a connection between Ruth Merrill, who also seems to have gone by the name of Coddington, and Margaret O'Donnell. If the girl was seeking to end her pregnancy, she may have turned to the Merrill woman for help. The fact that St. Aubin apparently thought he could extort two thousand dollars from Mrs. Merrill suggests she may have been involved in arranging an illegal abortion. There is one other point to consider. I am beginning to think that 'astounding development' of which Mr. Rafferty spoke on the day of his murder may have had something to do with Margaret O'Donnell and the father of her child."

I saw Thomas's shoulders slump, and he said, almost in a whisper, "I still wish Shad had told me what he found out. I would have stood guard by him every minute of the day if I knew a killer might be after him."

"There is no blame to be had," Holmes said. "I think the killer simply moved more quickly than either Mr. Rafferty or you had reason to suspect."

"And do you now know who the killer is?" I asked.

"I will say only that the truth is close at hand. The many strands of this case are coming together and they will form a tight noose before long."

Thomas said, "Well, the way I look at it, we maybe can eliminate Abbey as a suspect if everything hinges on who fathered Margaret's child. I don't see that he could have done it, given his, you know, preferences."

"True, but I am not yet ready to rule out Mr. Abbey as a suspect. As Watson and I have seen, he presents a smooth veneer, but there is much rough-work underneath, and I would not put murder past him. It is possible he is strongly connected to the father. If so, he might have abetted in the crimes so as to prevent exposure of his illicit activities with underage boys like Riordan."

"So now you seem to pointing toward Monsignor Denis," I said, "since he and Abbey are obviously close."

"I should say they are extremely close," Holmes said with a sly smile.

"Then we must talk to Mrs. Merrill at once to find out what she knows," I said.

"Yes, but there is another woman I should like to speak to first. Let us see if we can find her at home."

EARLY IN THE AFTERNOON, Holmes ordered a cab and gave the driver an address on Summit Avenue.

"Where are we going?" I asked, for Holmes had been silent about his plans.

"You shall see soon enough."

The cab deposited us at the door of a stout house of buff brick and white stone that looked to have been built many years ago. I soon learned its owner was Muriel St. Aubin.

"This is a surprise," she said in a guarded voice after she led us to a small parlor outfitted with gilt mirrors, an oriental rug, and cream-colored furniture. "Have you something new to report about my son's murder?"

"You might say that," Holmes said.

"Very well. Please tell me."

"A matter has come up which puzzles me," Holmes began. "It

concerns a revealing photograph taken last year in a room at the Ryan Hotel."

Mrs. St. Aubin's large gray eyes betrayed a hint of concern, and she cocked her head slightly to one side. "And what of this photograph?"

"It was taken by a woman named Margo Sartell who specializes in such things, and it ended up in the possession of your son, who used it for purposes of blackmail. I believe you gave it to him."

I will admit I was astonished by this statement, but I was even more surprised when Mrs. St. Aubin made no effort to deny it.

"You have talked with Miss Sartell, I suppose," she said in an even voice.

"Yes," Holmes said. "She told us you hired her."

This was not true but Holmes sounded utterly convincing. He added, in a matter-of-fact way, "You wanted, of course, to know with whom your lover, Monsignor Denis, was having an affair."

I could scarcely believe what I was hearing, and yet Mrs. St. Aubin still gave no sign of contradicting Holmes. Instead, she said, "I see now why you are called the world's greatest consulting detective. Yes, the monsignor and I became very close, to use a euphemism. I make no apology for it. Men and woman have needs and always have. We satisfied each other for a time before I discovered, after hiring Miss Sartell, that he was not the man I thought he was."

"What kind of man did you think him to be? He is a priest, bound to celibacy, and yet he became your lover. Surely, you could not have believed such a relationship would last for long."

"Perhaps, but I certainly did not think a man to whom I'd given my heart would go off and have sex with a man behind my back. It was insulting and disgusting, and I told him so to his miserable face."

"How did you find out about his relationship with Mr. Abbey? Did your son tell you about it?"

"No. I found out by other means, which I prefer not to disclose. But you may be assured I was unaware at that time of my son's activities as a blackmailer, and I most certainly did not give him that photograph, as you seem to think."

"Then how did he obtain it?"

"I can only guess he stole it. It was kept in a locked box in my bedroom, and he may have come across it when he stayed here for a few nights in early December."

"Was that after he was badly beaten?"

"So you know about that, too. Yes, he said he'd run into some trouble over a debt and didn't feel safe in his apartment. I see now it was a mistake to let him in the house."

"I am curious, Mrs. St. Aubin, what you did with the photograph before it was stolen, as you claim. Did you threaten to expose Monsignor Denis, perhaps by bringing the picture to the archbishop's attention?"

"I am not a blackmailer, Mr. Holmes. Such a sordid business would be beneath me."

"And yet the monsignor appears to have been very worried about that picture. Is that why he went to search your son's apartment after his death, a fact you did not mention to us earlier?"

"I saw no need to mention it, as it is irrelevant to my son's murder. You will have to ask the monsignor what he was looking for in the apartment."

"I intend to. Was your son aware of your involvement with Monsignor Denis?"

"Of course not."

"So you were not one of his blackmail victims as well?"

"Really, Mr. Holmes, you are being ridiculous. I am not on trial here. The simple fact remains that someone murdered my son and thus far you seem incapable of finding the guilty party. I suggest you put your energies into your investigation instead of dredging up old dirt of no consequence. It hardly becomes a man of your eminence to be trafficking in idle gossip."

It was a bit of a tongue-lashing but Holmes took no offense. He said, "I have found, Mrs. St. Aubin, that gossip is usually quite busy rather than idle and that sometimes it can even point to the truth. However, I have no wish to embarrass you. Provided you have been truthful, your secrets will be safe with Dr. Watson and me."

"How kind of you. I believe we have said all there is to say. You may show yourselves out."

As we left, I asked Holmes how he had come to suspect Mrs. St. Aubin was having an affair with the monsignor.

"It was her extreme curiosity over the blackmail pictures I mentioned when we talked with her at the Ryan. She looked quite alarmed and asked at once who was in the photographs. This suggested to me she might know something about them, or perhaps even had hired Miss Sartell. I then devised a theory and placed it before Mrs. St. Aubin, who was good enough to confirm my suspicions."

"Well, it was quite brilliant of you, Holmes."

"Perhaps, but now we are left with yet more questions. I cannot allow myself to believe Mrs. St. Aubin would have been involved in the murder of her own son. However, Monsignor Denis is another matter. His affair with Mrs. St. Aubin and the incriminating photograph she arranged to have taken might have pushed him over the edge. He almost surely was looking for the photograph when he went to Mr. St. Aubin's apartment."

"But do you actually think the monsignor could be a cold-blooded murderer?"

"Any man can be a murderer, Watson, if he believes his own life is at stake."

We went to see Ruth Merrill on Mount Curve Avenue in Minneapolis the next morning. The street runs atop a low bluff overlooking the business district, and like Summit Avenue in St. Paul it is lined with mansions of varying size and splendor. The stately house at 1610 Mount Curve, a broad Georgian affair with red brick walls and a curving white portico, presented an image of sedate, well-founded prosperity. A young maid in gray-and-white livery answered our knock.

"Good afternoon," Holmes said. "Is Mrs. Merrill at home?"

"And who should I say is calling, sir?"

"Sherlock Holmes and Dr. John Watson."

The maid looked at us for a moment in apparent disbelief, but it soon became apparent that she recognized Holmes from the many photographs of him that had appeared in the local press.

"Why, it really is you!" she said, stating the obvious with great enthusiasm. "Oh, do come in. I will tell madam you are here. Won't she be thrilled!"

The maid took our coats and directed us to a large parlor expensively furnished in the Chippendale style. We took our seats as a tall corner clock chimed the hour of eleven. The clock had just gone silent when a short, stout, gray-haired woman of sixty or so came into the room and walked straight up to Holmes.

"I suppose I should not be surprised you have come looking for me," she said in a husky contralto. "It's about the O'Donnell girl, isn't it? Well, come along to the library and we'll talk."

The library was a cozy room, well stocked with leather-bound volumes. Sunlight streamed in from two tall windows, and we took chairs around a long table strewn with books and papers. Set amidst these items was a framed photograph, mounted in a stand, of an attractive middle-aged woman with a broad face, black hair, and riveting eyes.

"Please excuse the mess," Mrs. Merrill said. "This is where I work."

"And what exactly is your work?" Holmes asked.

Mrs. Merrill responded by pointing to the photograph. "Margaret Sanger's work is my work," she said. "You know of her, no doubt."

I suspected Holmes had never given much thought to Mrs. Sanger or her work as an advocate of contraception, but as a physician I was quite aware of her controversial ideas. "She has certainly made a name for herself," I said. "As I recall, she even moved to England for a time to escape prosecution here in the United States."

"Yes, and her travails tell you all you need to know about the absurd laws of this nation," Mrs. Merrill said. "To answer your question, Mr. Holmes, I am in the business of saving women's lives, in some cases quite literally. I have been associated with Margaret Sanger for many years. She and I believe women should not be condemned to lives of drudgery and poverty by virtue of constant pregnancies, nor should their lives be endangered by self-induced abortions or those performed in back alleys. Birth control is a means of making life better for women everywhere."

"You make your case most forcefully," said Holmes. "And yet I am curious why you also go by the name of Coddington. If your work is as high-minded as you say it is, why not attach your own name to it instead of using an alias?"

"There are people, Mr. Holmes, who take strong issue with what I do. Mrs. Sanger's life has been threatened many times, as has mine, by men whose only wish is to subjugate women for their own vile purposes. So I must take precautions. I prefer to think of Mrs. Coddington not as an alias but as my working name. I must also protect my dear husband, who supports what I do but whose business associates are not as enlightened as he is."

"I see. As to this work of yours, does it include arranging abortions?"

"Abortion is illegal in Minnesota," she replied evenly.

"So it is. Yet I have heard you are not above making certain accommodations to help girls, especially those from wealthy families, to deal with unwanted pregnancies."

"I provide counseling, Mr. Holmes. That is all I do."

"And you counseled Margaret O'Donnell, did you not?"

"Yes. She was lovely girl, intelligent and high-spirited, but the beauty that was her gift was also her undoing. Men buzzed around her from a young age, and in the end she could not resist one of them and became pregnant. As you may imagine, it was a frightening situation for her and I was asked to be of assistance."

"So she did not contact you herself?"

"No, I was approached by someone acting on her behalf."

"Who was that person?"

"I cannot say."

"No, you must say!" Holmes insisted. "Dr. Watson and I are investigating two murders, and I assure you anyone connected to them will pay a high price. I shall see to that. Are you prepared to pay, Mrs. Merrill?"

"I was not involved in any murders."

"But the man who fathered Margaret's child almost surely was. He may well have murdered her too. You would be ill-advised to protect such a man. His ship is sinking fast and the truth is your only lifeboat. Now, I will ask again: who approached you to help with Margaret's predicament?"

Mrs. Merrill stared at Holmes, and I could sense the workings of her mind. Was Holmes to be believed or was he bluffing? How much danger was she really in? What would happen to her if the ship Holmes spoke of did indeed go down?

"Very well, I will have to take you at your word. But I do not wish my name to be associated in any way with what happened to Margaret. It was all his doing, not mine."

She then provided the name of the man who had contacted her. Holmes nodded as though he had expected her response and said, "I thank you, Mrs. Merrill. Now, please tell us how your involvement with the girl came about?"

"It was in the usual way. He called in late November to explain Margaret's situation and that she was the daughter of the mayor of St. Paul. I told him I would do what I could for her."

"Did he tell you who the father was?"

"Not in so many words."

"What do you mean?"

"I mean, Mr. Holmes, that everything about the way he spoke suggested strongly to me he was the father. He never admitted as much, but I always know these things. The anxiousness in his voice was evident."

"How far along was Margaret in her pregnancy?"

"About two months, from what I could gather."

"Had she seen a doctor?"

"I was told she had, but I do not know the physician's name."

Holmes then asked how many times Mrs. Merrill had spoken with the man suspected of impregnating Margaret.

"Three, I believe. He was quite adamant that something needed to be done."

"An abortion, in other words."

"He did not say so. He merely wished to hear my best advice, and I gave it to him."

"Yes, I have no doubt you did. What about Margaret? Was she in agreement with him?"

"I spoke to her over the phone, and she told me in no uncertain terms she did not like the idea of having a child at her age."

"So she also wished to abort the pregnancy."

"She did not use that term."

"But it was implied, was it not?"

"I will leave you to interpret that."

I was beginning to think Mrs. Merrill might have had a fine career as a lawyer, since splitting hairs appeared to come naturally to her.

"I see you are cautious woman, Mrs. Merrill. In your line of work, I imagine that is a necessity. Now, you said you agreed to help Margaret with her pregnancy. What kind of help did you offer to provide?"

"I cannot be specific in that regard, for reasons which I'm sure you understand."

"Did you provide the name of a doctor who could terminate Margaret's pregnancy?"

"I admit to no such thing."

"Then let me put the question another way. To your knowledge, was any kind of medical procedure performed on her?"

"I am quite certain it was not."

"How do you know?"

"I will only say, Mr. Holmes, that I speak now and then with physicians who sometimes have interesting information to share. None of them treated Margaret."

"I see. And yet she nonetheless died suddenly only a few weeks later? What happened to her?"

Mrs. Merrill paused, her eyes dancing in their sockets. She was clearly holding a debate with herself. Finally, she said, "It was claimed to me she committed suicide by slitting her wrists, but I do not know if I can give the story any credence."

Holmes had told me only a few days earlier, during one of our desultory conversations, that he'd grown "too old to be excited anymore." But that clearly was a lie, for his face now took on the bright, eager look of a child on holiday at the beach. He said, "Who told you this, Mrs. Merrill?"

"I received an anonymous phone call from a man seeking to blackmail me. He demanded two thousand dollars and claimed my activities had somehow caused Margaret to take her own life. He also threatened to expose me as 'the abortion queen.' Those were his words."

"When did you receive this call?"

"The tenth of December. It is not something I will ever forget."

"I assume the caller did not identify himself."

"He did not."

"How did you respond?"

"I told the man to go straight to hell."

"I should not be surprised if your wish has been granted," Holmes said, for we knew Daniel St. Aubin had been the caller.

"Were you subsequently made aware Daniel St. Aubin was the man who attempted to blackmail you?"

"The name is unfamiliar to me," Mrs. Merrill said in a voice so free of inflection that she might have been reciting the alphabet. I thought she was lying and so did Holmes.

"I believe you know more than you are telling us, Mrs. Merrill."

"You are free to believe what you wish," she said calmly.

"I believe above all else in the truth, and I shall have it before this business is done. You say the blackmailer threatened to implicate you in Margaret's death, which occurred just three days before he called you. Speak the truth now and tell us how Margaret died. You do know what happened, despite your denials."

"I do not!" Mrs. Merrill said with great force. "I would swear to that in a court of law. You must understand I provided initial advice regarding Margaret's situation but nothing more, as I have already told you. Naturally, I was very curious when I learned of Margaret's death, especially after receiving that threatening phone call. Still, I cannot say to this day whether or not she took her own life. I said the same thing to your friend, Mr. Rafferty, when he got in touch."

Once again, Holmes was a child at the beach, his eyes flashing with excitement. Rafferty's notes had made no mention of an interview with Mrs. Merrill/Mrs. Coddington, and yet it was now apparent he had tracked her down.

"Did you speak to him in person?"

"No, over the phone."

"When was this?"

"I will always remember the date, I'm afraid. You see, I talked with him on the very day he was murdered."

"And did you tell him what you've just told us?"

"Yes."

Holmes thought for a moment, then asked, "Did you mention your conversation with Mr. Rafferty to anyone else?"

Her answer proved fateful, for she said the man who had asked for her help with Margaret O'Donnell's pregnancy called her only an hour or so after she'd spoken with Rafferty.

"I have no idea how he found out I had talked to Mr. Rafferty, but he demanded to know everything that had been said."

"What did you tell him?"

"As little as possible. But he clearly knew what Mr. Rafferty was interested in and seemed quite angry about it."

"Yes," Holmes said. "I imagine he was."

THAT EVENING, WE ACCEPTED AN INVITATION from Thomas for a late dinner at his restaurant. The establishment occupied a modest wooden building in the Negro section of St. Paul that had once been, as Thomas put it, "a notorious after-hours dive where shootings were as common as dirt." Thomas and his wife, Pats, had by dint of much hard labor turned the place into a successful restaurant that attracted patrons from every corner of the city.

A short, buxom woman with a vivacious smile and an accent that identified her birthplace as somewhere deep in the American South, Pats greeted us at the door and showed us to a table in the small but neatly kept dining room. She then retired to the kitchen to perform what Thomas described as her "culinary wonders." The dinner of fried chicken and "all the fixings" she prepared was indeed excellent, and she joined us at the table as Holmes held court in his usual manner.

His first topic was our revealing conversation with Mrs. Merrill. The news that Rafferty had talked with her just before his murder took Thomas by surprise, just as it had us.

"Mr. Rafferty, of course, didn't have time to make any notes about his talk with Mrs. Merrill, but we now know she told him what she told us," Holmes said. "We also know that the man who is now our prime suspect learned of their conversation and therefore must have believed Mr. Rafferty was about to break the case wide open. That is why he murdered him or had him murdered."

"I would like to have at him at this very moment," Thomas said. "A minute is all I would need."

"I understand, Mr. Thomas, but we must allow the law to take its course. Our man will face the bar of justice and very soon, I assure you. But there are other matters that must occupy our immediate attention. Tell us more, if you would, about your discoveries today in Minneapolis."

Thomas revealed it was by no means certain that Johnny Riordan was the young man whose decapitated body had been found next to the train tracks in Minneapolis. "My source at the coroner's office said the dead fellow was short, maybe five feet five or so, and had blond hair. That sounds like it could be Riordan. But the dead fellow also had a stocky build, whereas Riordan was slender judging from what I've heard."

"It's always possible he put on weight," Holmes noted. "In any event, it is too soon to assume he's dead. We need more information."

"Well, I'll keep nosing around, Mr. Holmes, but if he is alive, there's a good chance he's left Minneapolis by now."

"I fear so, and as he has proved as adept as the late Mr. Houdini in escaping the shackles of the law, we shall no doubt have a devil of a time finding him. In the meantime, we must consider how best to move forward so as to bring Mr. Rafferty's murderer to justice. It is all a matter of finding proof now."

"But we have Mrs. Merrill's testimony," I said. "Shouldn't that be sufficient?"

"I do not think so. Remember, she only suspects who fathered Margaret O'Donnell's child, and that is proof of nothing. We think we know our man murdered three people, if we count the O'Donnell girl, but at the moment we have little chance of making our case in a court of law. We need irrefutable proof, which like a vein of pure gold is rarely easy to discover."

"How will you find it?" Thomas asked.

Holmes smiled and said, "The best way to catch a dangerous animal is to set a trap, and that is what we must do. The only question is how to bait it."

As was his wont, Holmes maintained an air of mystery about his plans for the next day and a half, and it was only on Sunday morning that he revealed what he had in mind. I had stationed myself in his room, reading the newspapers, while he went on a long walk. With tobacco no longer available as an aid to contemplation, Holmes found that walking stimulated both his mind and body. He thought nothing of going ten miles or more while working out a problem, and so I was not surprised he was gone for several hours.

When he returned just before noon, he fairly burst into the room and said, "I have worked it all out, Watson. Here is what we must do."

The essence of his plan was to secure, by rather elaborate means, an admission of guilt from the murderer. To do so, however, we would need the help of one of the other suspects in the case.

"He will be our bait," Holmes said as he paced about the room like an expectant father eager to hear the first cry of his newborn child, "and he will draw the murderer into a perfect trap."

"But how do you know he will go along with your plan?"

"I shall give him no other choice."

Late that afternoon, Holmes called the man to demand his co-operation. What followed was a long, at times tense conversation as Holmes laid out what he knew in great detail and concluded by stating, "Your only hope is to do exactly as I say. Otherwise, you will be lost."

When the call was over, Holmes said in an exultant voice, "Success! He has agreed to everything, and he will be ready to do our bidding. To use that phrase you so love, Watson, the game is afoot! But we must be very cautious. The man we are after has already murdered and he will think nothing of murdering again, for no one fears being hanged twice."

Book V

Endgame at the Ryan

27

Convergence

On February 13, all of the figures in the murder case that had consumed Sherlock Holmes and Dr. John Watson for three weeks moved toward a final reckoning. The point of convergence, perhaps inevitably, was the Ryan Hotel, haunted by the ghost of Shadwell Rafferty. Later, Holmes would say the day was "like an intricate dance," one choreographed by his own hand but attended as well by the "whirling Fates, to whom all men must pay homage." And when the dance was finally done, a murderer stood revealed at last.

BERTRAM ABBEY WAS THE FIRST to arrive at the hotel. He checked into his usual room, fortified himself from a flask of whiskey he'd brought along, then considered his precarious situation. A thorny new problem had come up, and he wasn't sure how to deal with it.

Holmes was a big part of the problem. He was like a mighty lion on the prowl, looking for a kill, and Abbey feared he was potential prey. Yet the lion, for all of his strength and cunning, didn't know everything, and Abbey thought he still had a chance to extricate himself from the mess he was in. It would be a dicey business, especially if Holmes interfered, but Abbey saw no other choice.

He took another slug of whiskey, followed by a deep breath. It will all work out, he told himself. He knew he'd need a silver tongue, along with plenty of silver dollars, to accomplish his ends, but would they be enough? Abbey wasn't certain, and so he'd armed himself with more silver in the form of a gleaming, plated revolver. If left with no other option, he was fully prepared to use it.

WORRY ALSO WEIGHED HEAVILY on Monsignor Pierre Denis. As he walked down to the Ryan from the cathedral, the winter air a cooling balm for his charred heart, he thought back to his childhood in Ontario and the faith that had sprung to him from the stars. How had he lost his way? He knew the answer—he'd sinned and sinned again, putting his own dark impulses before the love of God—and he wondered whether salvation was even possible anymore.

And yet he had to go on—suicide would be the final, irreversible sin—but how? His life was unraveling. He could see it happening, feel the terrible force of his undoing, yet he saw no way to stop it. He'd spoken with Muriel St. Aubin and knew Holmes was aware of their affair. It was yet another black mark on his character. What else was Holmes aware of? He knew of Margaret O'Donnell's pregnancy, but how far had his inquiries taken him?

Before setting out for the Ryan, Denis had gone into the cathedral to pray for forgiveness and wisdom. But it had seemed an empty exercise, as though he was begging God to save him as he plummeted from a high bridge. Yet wasn't faith itself a leap? Denis clung to that hope as he walked into the Ryan's lobby, steeling himself for the terrible events to come.

LIKE THE MONSIGNOR, Montgomery Meeks was drawn to the Ryan by forces that threatened to destroy his life. He had always prided himself on being a man who by dint of clever dealing could iron out even the ugliest wrinkles in the human enterprise. There was always an accommodation to be made, an opponent to be bought off, or so he thought. Now he wasn't so sure. Sherlock Holmes had seen to that.

Holmes was a different sort of beast—immune to all the usual blandishments—and he had clawed and clawed and clawed until he was on the verge of digging out the ugly truth. Meeks had done his best to protect the mayor, not to mention Abbey and Denis, but it hadn't been enough. Now he was in jeopardy and so were they, their dirty secrets on the verge of exposure. What was to be done?

Meeks had thought the matter through, following every contingency as far as it would lead, until he had exhausted all the possibilities. In the end, he saw but one course of action to stave off disaster. As for the others, they would have do the best they could. Meeks couldn't save everybody.

MAYOR RICHARD O'DONNELL felt every bit as unsettled as his chief aide and confidant. The mayor was having dark visions in which he saw his life and career ground into the toxic dust of scandal. Margaret was to blame, of course, but what did that matter now? If only Holmes hadn't come to St. Paul! Without his intrusive presence, everything would have been tucked away and forgotten, like a suitcase of old clothes in the attic. But Holmes just wouldn't let that happen.

O'Donnell called in Meeks for a talk. Meeks offered encouraging words, insisting Holmes couldn't hurt them, but the promise rang hollow. Holmes was relentless. He'd somehow found Mrs. Coddington, and soon he would know everything. How could he be stopped? O'Donnell saw only one surefire solution, but he didn't like the idea of it.

Still, there was nothing to do but forge ahead and hope luck would be on his side. After Meeks left, O'Donnell glanced at his daily calendar. It listed only one event: "Speech, Elks Club, Ryan Hotel ballroom, 7 p.m." He was hardly in the mood to speak to a bunch of sloshed Elks, but he had to. Duty called.

JACKSON GRIMSHAW WAS THE LAST to arrive at the Ryan, after dark, when he turned into the long alley behind the hotel. He did not pause at the spot where Daniel St. Aubin had met his demise, nor did he give much thought to the bloody scene that had unfolded there in December. Grimshaw had business on his mind and nothing else.

The alley was deserted, as Grimshaw hoped it would be. He stepped up to the hotel's loading dock and used his master key to open the door there. He entered a back hallway, walked unseen to the freight elevator, and summoned it. When the car arrived, it was empty. Everything was going exactly as planned. After pressing the elevator's override button, Grimshaw ascended nonstop to the sixth floor as he felt the reassuring heft of the Colt automatic holstered under his left arm. Before the night was over, he knew, he might have to use it to kill Sherlock Holmes.

JOHNNY RIORDAN WAS ALSO ON THE MOVE after lying low for weeks in an apartment in Northeast Minneapolis. The apartment belonged to a friend from St. Paul who'd moved across the river and agreed to take in Riordan, provided there was no trouble. Fearful of Grimshaw and his men, Riordan had rarely left the apartment, but as the days dragged on he grew restive. He'd also come to realize that the twenty-thousand-dollar blackmail scheme inherited from St. Aubin was simply too risky to carry out in its entirety. A bullet in the head, he figured, would be the most likely result of any attempt to collect such a large ransom.

But what to do with the sensational blackmail material Danny had so skillfully assembled? If Riordan couldn't use the bulk of it to extort money, he could at least present it as proof of who had murdered Danny. At the same time, he wasn't ready to give up all hope of reaping a nice reward from Danny's stash of incriminating information. There was someone who still might be willing to pay up if Riordan played his cards right, and it was a chance he intended to take.

By February 13, all of Riordan's plans were in place, and that afternoon he walked to a small branch post office near his apartment to mail an envelope containing two items.

"Is this the only address you have?" the clerk asked.

"Yes, but it will be enough, don't you think?"

"I suppose so," the clerk replied. He placed the required postage on the envelope, tossed it into the outgoing mail basket, and then stared at it for a moment as Riordan went his way.

"Sherlock Holmes, St. Paul, Minnesota," the address read.

After returning to the apartment, Riordan gathered his meager belongings in a satchel and used his friend's telephone to make a call. Later, he was seen boarding a streetcar to St. Paul.

28
"You Are a Monster"

Monday, February 13, 1928, is a day I shall always remember. By the time the day was done, Holmes and I had confronted a heartless murderer and gained some measure of justice for Rafferty. Yet our success was not complete, and only later would justice for our friend be fully served, in a way that would shock the good people of St. Paul.

The day began with Wash Thomas joining us for breakfast at the Ryan's café. Holmes had already explained his plans to me in great detail, and over our meal he briefed Thomas as well. He explained that Thomas would have a critical part to play in apprehending our quarry.

"Your role will be to watch our backs," Holmes said. "I fully expect the murderer will not come alone. Do you still have that sawed-off shotgun you used to keep under the bar at the saloon?"

"Sure do."

"Good. Bring it along. You may have use for it."

After Thomas left, Holmes grew solemn and quiet. As I looked at my friend, who unlike the eager trenchermen all around showed little appetite for food, I knew we were at the perilous brink of our final adventure in St. Paul. Although he sat very still, Holmes conveyed a sense of pent-up energy, as though quietly summoning all of his strength from a reserve deep within. I had no need to ask what was on his mind, for the peculiar cast of his deep gray eyes told everything. He had become a hunter and nothing would deter him from his prey.

THE MAN WHO HAD AGREED to assist us arrived at the hotel in the early afternoon and came directly to a vacant suite on the third floor that Holmes had arranged to use because it was equipped with two telephones. The man was clearly nervous, and Holmes tried to put him at ease. "Just be yourself and speak as you normally would. I have written out a script, which will get you started."

The man nodded and said, "All right, I will give it my best."

"Good. You are doing the right thing."

"I hope so."

For the next hour, Holmes went over the script with the man, making sure he understood how he was to direct the conversation. Finally, just after two o'clock, Holmes asked, "Are you ready?"

The man said he was.

"Then go ahead and place the call."

As we listened in on the room's second telephone, we heard the murderer answer rather abruptly, "Yes, what is it?"

"Something has happened and I'm very worried," our man said.

"What's the matter?"

"Holmes is getting close to the truth, and I'm not sure what to do. He called today and claimed he has all the evidence he needs to convict me. But we both know I didn't kill anybody. You're the one he really wants."

"How do you know that?"

"I know what happened to Maggie because she told me. Then you had to silence St. Aubin and Mr. Rafferty, because they found out, too."

The man on the other end of the phone offered no denial but made no admission either. He said, "Listen, don't panic. That would be the worst thing you could do. Holmes is probably bluffing."

"Are you sure? Holmes is hardly a fool. Even if he's bluffing now, he'll eventually put everything together. He's relentless and he'll never stop. We have to figure out what to do. I don't want to be dragged into this, but if I am, I'll tell the whole story, and that won't be a good thing for me or you."

There was a long pause, and it was almost as if I could hear the murderer thinking and plotting. He finally said, "All right, let's meet before you decide to do anything foolish."

"Yes, that's a good idea. I can't get away this afternoon, but I'll be free later tonight. I have to see someone at the Ryan at seven, but I'm available after that. Why don't we meet at the hotel at eight? Is there a private room we could use?"

Holmes had made it clear to our man that the meeting had to be at the Ryan, in room 652 if possible. The killer, Holmes believed, was familiar with that room, where he'd in all likelihood met with Rafferty on the night of his murder.

"The Ryan would be a good place. Meet me in room 652. It's very quiet up there and no one will bother us."

"Very well, I'll see you at eight."

"Fine, but don't say a word to anybody in the meantime. Agreed?"

"Agreed."

"Good. Just stay calm. Everything will work out for both of us. Trust me."

"You were superb," Holmes said to our man after he'd hung up. "Now, I must inform you of the danger you will face when you meet at eight o'clock. He intends to kill you, and I cannot guarantee your safety. I can only guarantee that Dr. Watson and I will do everything in our power to protect you from harm."

"I understand. It is a risk I'll have to take."

THE REST OF THE AFTERNOON went by quietly, even as my anticipation of the night to come became as sharp and demanding as a knife held to the neck. The man who was helping us went to my room, where he stayed out of sight. Holmes, meanwhile, remained in his room, reviewing his plans to make sure he had missed nothing.

With Holmes a temporary hermit, I stationed myself in the lobby and tried to read, but the newspapers were a desert and I a thirsty man. I tossed them aside and stared up at the big clock over the main desk, counting off the slow seconds.

Donald Hobbs, the desk clerk who had provided us with so much useful information, was on duty and I talked with him for a time, hoping to while away the idle hours.

"How long will you and Mr. Holmes be staying?" he asked.

"Not much longer," I said.

"So he has solved the case, is that it?"

"We shall see."

"Well, what a lucky man you are to be with Mr. Holmes. It must be wonderful to have so many adventures together."

"It is, and you are right, Mr. Hobbs. I am indeed a lucky man."

AT SIX I WENT UP TO HOLMES'S ROOM to see if he was interested in dinner. He wasn't—starvation seemed to suit him—but he said he would meet me in a half hour in the lobby and that I was to bring along my outercoat and revolver. I fetched both items from my room, went back downstairs to eat a very quick meal, and was ready when Holmes appeared at six-thirty.

We went out the hotel's main entry on Robert Street and into the night. I had no idea what Holmes planned to do but guessed we might hail a cab. Instead, Holmes said, "It is a fine night for a walk, Watson, don't you think?"

"If you say so. Where are we going?"

"Why, around the block, where else?"

We went south on Robert and then east on Sixth, a route that took us past Rafferty's old saloon. It had been known as Shad's Place for many years, but after Thomas became a full partner, the name was changed to Shad and Thom's Sixth Street Saloon. Now, it was a men's clothing store called Eddie's.

"I have no doubt the saloon would still be as popular as ever were it not for the absurd experiment with Prohibition," Holmes said as we paused to look through the store's display windows. From what we could see, no traces of the saloon remained, its old rollicking life gone forever.

"*Tempus fugit,*" Holmes said, "as it shall ever do. Incidentally, there is a man across the street following us. He undoubtedly works for Grimshaw, but he is both obvious and incompetent. We will be rid of him momentarily."

I realized then that Holmes had not stopped to look into Rafferty's old saloon out of sentiment but to see if anyone might be reflected in the windows. And so he had spotted our follower. I will not describe all the maneuvers that followed, but after passing through two department stores on Seventh Street and then looping around another block, we lost the man.

"I wish to give the impression we have left the Ryan on some unknown business and have taken steps to avoid detection," Holmes said. "We can safely return now."

We soon reached the alley next to the Ryan where Daniel St. Aubin had been murdered. A short walk down the alley brought us to the hotel's rear door. To my surprise, Holmes opened the door with a master key. "On loan from our friend, Mr. Hobbs," he said. "It is vital we are not seen entering the hotel."

Once inside, we went directly to the freight elevator and up to the sixth floor, where Thomas was waiting for us in the elevator lobby. He wore a long gray coat, which was unbuttoned, and beneath it he held a shotgun in his right hand.

"All clear," he said. "Your fellow arrived ten minutes ago. He's waiting down in 652. There's a little spot around the corner where I can take cover. If there's trouble, I'll be ready for it."

"Excellent," said Holmes. "Now, let us see if our man has his nerve up."

He was seated at the room's writing desk and stood up as we entered. "I didn't hear you coming," he said.

"Precisely so," Holmes replied. "Please, be seated. We have some time yet."

The room was just as we had first seen it, furnished with a double bed, a chest of drawers, a nightstand with a wash basin, two wooden spindle chairs, and the desk. A shade covered the only window, which looked over the hotel's inner court. The room was as cold as I remembered it, and I was grateful to have my heavy coat on.

The man appeared to be anxious, rubbing his hands together and fidgeting in his chair, although it occurred to me he may simply have been trying to stay warm. His expression suggested a mixture of anticipation and anxiety, which was hardly surprising in view of the fact he would soon be face-to-face with a murderer.

"Are you prepared for what must be done?" Holmes asked.

"Yes. I will be your stalking horse, but you must keep your end of the bargain."

"I shall, if you do the same. Of course, I must remind you again there may be great danger."

"There is always danger in this life, is there not? Fear will not stop me from doing what needs to be done."

"Very well, but do not be reckless. Our guest, when he arrives, will be in a volatile mood and therefore unpredictable. He almost surely will be armed. I presume you know what you are to say?"

"Yes, we've gone over it."

"Good. One more thing: if at any point you see him reach suddenly toward his coat pocket, you must shout out 'Help' at once, and Dr. Watson and I will come to your aid."

It was now ten to eight, and we made our final arrangements. We had already cleared out the room's large closet, moving all of the items stored there to an adjoining room. We stepped inside the empty closet, closed its louvered doors, and awaited the arrival of a murderer.

THE MAN WE HAD BEEN HUNTING for more than three weeks entered the room at two minutes past eight and closed the door behind him. The conversation that followed was at once revelatory and unsettling, and I have done my best to report it verbatim.

"You look nervous," the murderer began. We could see his legs through the louvers as he slid a chair toward the desk and sat down facing the other man. "Holmes has you buffaloed, doesn't he?"

"I don't think so. I have every right to be afraid, and you should be, too. The way Holmes talked, it sounds like he knows the whole story."

"Be more specific. What exactly does he know? I want you to tell me everything he said."

"All right, but you won't like it. He said he knows you were the father of Maggie's child, and he thinks you killed her and made her death look like a suicide. He said he has proof that you, or perhaps Grimshaw, then killed St. Aubin because he found out about you and Maggie. Finally, you arranged for Rafferty's murder because he was getting too close to the truth."

"So Holmes told you all of this?"

"Yes."

"Did you ever wonder why?"

"What do you mean?"

"Well, if he knows everything, as he claimed, then why is he telling it all to you and not to me? I'll tell you why. It's because he doesn't have any proof. All he really knows for sure is that you're a weak link, and so he's pulling at you, trying to get you to come apart and blurt out the truth. Tell me, my friend, what do you really know as opposed to what you and Holmes are guessing at?"

There was menace in the murderer's voice now, and I tightened my grip on my revolver, well aware I might have to use it.

"I know more than enough. You can't fool me anymore. My God, you murdered three people. Three people! How can you live with yourself?"

"I live with myself because I have no other choice. I only did what was necessary. You should understand that as well as anyone. Look at all the lies you've told and the secrets you've kept. And now you're going to be smart and save your own skin, and mine, by keeping your goddamn mouth shut."

"I can't do that. I can't be a party to three murders."

"You will be a party to them if I say you are."

"It doesn't matter. I'm through lying. I intend to go to the chief of police and the newspapers if necessary to speak the truth. Your only hope now is to admit your crimes and plead for mercy."

"Oh, I think there is another option."

Then came frightful shouts of "Help, help!" and we burst out of the closet.

HOLMES LED THE WAY and I was right behind, my revolver cocked. What happened next was a kind of chaotic dance, punctuated by gunfire. The man at the desk dropped to the floor, shielding his head with his left arm and shoulder, just as a bullet smashed through the window behind him. The shot had come from a small, silver-plated pistol in the murderer's hand.

A look of astonishment crossed the man's face as Holmes went directly at him, grabbing the pistol and wrenching it upward as a second shot struck the ceiling. I couldn't fire my revolver for fear of striking Holmes and so joined the fray in the hope the two of us could overpower the man. But Holmes and I weren't young anymore and the fight did not go well for us. The murderer, who possessed surprising physical strength, regained control of the pistol and then put a shoulder to Holmes, knocking him backward before fleeing out the door. Holmes lost his balance, as did I, and we both tumbled over the man crouched on the floor.

"Have you been hit?" Holmes asked him as we struggled back up to our feet, apparently none the worse for wear.

"No. He somehow missed."

"Well, it is your lucky day. He will not get far."

We went out into the hall, but only after I had rather rudely elbowed Holmes aside to take the lead, since I was armed and he was not. I caught a glimpse of the murderer as he disappeared around the corner toward the elevator lobby. He was not the only man I saw. Grimshaw had come to help his master, and he and Thomas were engaged in a terrific fight halfway down the hall. Thomas, however, was no match for a man of Grimshaw's ferocious strength, and the detective had just managed to wrestle away the shotgun when I came up on him and put my revolver to the back of his head.

"Have no doubt I will shoot you," I said. "Put the shotgun down."

Grimshaw complied with a grunt as Thomas took back the shotgun, his hands still shaking from the struggle.

"I have him now," Thomas said, backing off from Grimshaw and leveling the weapon at his chest. "I will blow you to kingdom come if you try anything, Big Jack."

"Go to hell," came the reply, but Grimshaw made no attempt to come at Thomas again.

"Stay with him," I told Thomas. "I must find Holmes."

Holmes had already gone past me toward the elevator lobby. I followed and found him bent over by the elevators, trying to catch his breath.

"He went down the stairs," Holmes said. "I am certain he will leave by the rear door. With luck, we can get there first."

The elevator Holmes had called arrived. The operator was Thomas's friend, Henry Johnson.

"What are you doing up here, Mr. Holmes?" he asked. "Is something going on?"

"A great deal is going on. Take us down to the ground floor as fast as you can. No stops," said Holmes.

When we reached the lobby, we came upon yet another startling scene. Hotel guests were cowering behind chairs, tables, and anything else that might afford protection, and the pungent smell of gunpowder filled the air. So, too, did the blaring of a burglar alarm. Holmes did not hesitate.

"He is ahead of us," he said as we turned toward the narrow service hall leading to the freight elevator and rear door. But we immediately encountered an obstacle. A heavy door that had been open when we entered the hotel was now closed tight and we could not push it open.

"He must have locked it behind him," I said.

Without a word, Holmes turned back toward the lobby. We were rushing toward the main doors, at the far end of the lobby, when Hobbs popped up from his hiding place behind the front desk and said, "He shot at somebody, Mr. Holmes, and then ran back toward Eddie's."

"Is there an inside entrance to the clothing shop?" Holmes asked.

"Yes, and he must have broken in. That's why the alarm is sounding. The police should be here any minute."

Holmes was in no mood to wait for the police, nor was I. We left Hobbs and walked quickly past the elevators toward an overhanging sign that said Eddie's Fine Clothing for Men. Beneath the sign was a half-open glass door that had been shattered, triggering the alarm. A pair of overhead lights illuminated the closed store, which was filled with display cases and clothes racks.

"He probably went out the other door on Sixth," I said. "I doubt we'll catch him now."

"Perhaps not. But we must be certain he's not hiding inside," Holmes said. "Follow me."

As we stepped inside, I saw something that had not been readily visible when we'd peered through the store's windows earlier. Positioned in the far back corner of the store, like a museum display, was a portion of the bar from Rafferty's old saloon. The bar was equipped with a brass rail, spittoons, three stools, a lamp, and a back mirror framed by paintings of voluptuous women above rows of shelves. Carefully stacked shirts had replaced the bottles of liquor the shelves once held.

I was about to comment on this remarkable find to Holmes when I heard a noise behind the bar. The murderer, who had ducked behind it, rose out of the darkness and switched on the lamp. He was smiling in an odd sort of way that suggested a mixture of amusement and contempt. His hands, which held no weapon, rested atop the bar as though he was ready to serve a thirsty customer.

"I suppose this is what is meant by poetic justice, Mr. Holmes," he said in an unhurried voice. "This old bar was part of Mr. Rafferty's saloon, wasn't it?"

"Don't move," I said, "or I will shoot."

"Fear not, Dr. Watson. My criminal career is finished, thanks to Mr. Holmes and you. And so here we are at the endgame, about to talk of one thing or another as though it all must be very important."

"Murder is always important," Holmes said.

"So you say. I'm not so sure. Murder is death and death is what everything always comes down to, doesn't it? I'd offer a tearful confession and all of that, but really, why bother? The sun will come up in the morning and the stars will shine at night no matter what I say. I will admit it was too bad about Maggie, but she was a foolish girl, Mr. Holmes, a very foolish girl."

"Foolish to become involved with a man like you."

"True enough. Still, isn't it strange how one small thing leads to another and then another, and before you know it, you're in a big tangle? St. Aubin was to blame, of course. What a greedy fellow! I think you'll agree he got what he deserved."

"He did not deserve to be murdered. He deserved to be brought to justice for his crimes. Nor did Mr. Rafferty deserve to be stabbed in the back. Grimshaw, I assume, did the dirty work for you."

"You know, I admire Grimshaw. There are no complications for him. All he wants is money and the opportunity to beat up and kill people now and then. It must be pleasant to live so simply. As for Rafferty, well, he was an old man with one foot already in the grave. Anyway, it's better to die young than old, don't you agree?"

"Margaret O'Donnell was just seventeen, with much to live for. And yet you killed her, or had her killed, merely because you feared your indiscretion would become a matter of public knowledge."

"Ah, beautiful little Maggie! I fear her blandishments were too much for me. Would you believe it if I told you her death was an accident? If she'd just done as she was told and let me handle everything, she'd be alive today. Mrs. Coddington had made all the necessary arrangements. So I got Maggie out of Good Shepherd to take care of her unfortunate pregnancy, and that's when Maggie suddenly started having second thoughts."

"She didn't want to go through with an abortion after all," Holmes said, "and you could not abide that."

"No, she really couldn't be allowed to start showing. That would have been extremely messy. And yet there she was, talking about having the damn baby and wanting me to pay support for it. Well, that wouldn't look good for me, as you can imagine. So we argued. It was after dark and we were in my car. I tried to talk some sense into her, but it was hopeless. She grew very angry and began clawing at me. That's when my hands ended up around her neck, and before I knew it, she was unconscious."

"You are lying, as you have always lied. I believe you deliberately killed her to get her out of the way."

"Suit yourself, Mr. Holmes, but why would I lie about it now? In any event, the deed was done and there I was with a half-dead girl in my car. I had to do something, so I drove her back to Good Shepherd and set her down by a tree on the grounds. Then I slit her wrists to make her death look like a suicide. I'm sure she died quite painlessly."

"You are a monster," Holmes said.

"Yes, I suppose I am, but the funny thing is, it's never bothered me. I was perfectly content to live with what I'd done."

"But then Mr. St. Aubin came along to put a wrench in your plans."

"Yes, he'd wheedled his way into Maggie's good graces and discovered the truth. Then he tried to blackmail me, as he had so many others. He had to be stopped, and as I said, one thing led to another and then Rafferty became involved and, well, you know the rest of the story."

"I should like to know more. For instance, what exactly did Grimshaw do for you?"

I heard sirens and saw flickering lights on Sixth Street. The police were at hand, and I wondered what they would do. Would Grimshaw take charge and detain us while the murderer was allowed to slip away? It seemed entirely possible, and then what?

"Ah, the gendarmes have arrived, too late as usual," the murderer said. "There's little more for me to say. I wish I could tell you I greatly regret all I have done, but I don't."

"I should think you regret being caught," I said.

"All too true, Doctor, but I will not regret it for long. Farewell, gentlemen."

There was a commotion outside the door, and I heard someone say, "They're in the clothing store. Be careful. He has a gun."

At that instant, the murderer reached under the bar and produced his pistol. Before I could fire, he put the weapon under his chin and pulled the trigger. Several uniformed policemen, their guns drawn, came storming into the shop as the murderer dropped straight down behind the bar.

Holmes raised a hand to stop the policemen and said, "You will not need your guns. He shot himself."

We went over to the bar to look at the body. The man's jaw was all but gone and blood poured from the gaping wound. Daniel St. Aubin, by a peculiar twist of fate, had died in almost exactly the same way, except that his wound had not been self-inflicted. I got down on one knee to look for any evidence of life but found no pulse. The shot had been instantly fatal.

"I didn't think he was the sort who would kill himself," I said.

"A man who believes in nothing will do anything," Holmes said, staring down at the body. "Montgomery Meeks was just such a man."

I WILL NOT GO INTO GREAT DETAIL about the remainder of the night, other than to say our dealings with the police initially proved difficult because of Grimshaw. He came down to the clothing store, Thomas still guarding him, after Holmes sent a bellboy up with a message. With them was Monsignor Pierre Denis, the man who at Holmes's direction had lured Meeks to room 652. The monsignor nodded at us, then quietly slipped away amid all the commotion.

Once he was no longer staring down the barrels of a shotgun, Grimshaw hurled vile insults at Thomas, promising to "fix" him for good, and then tried to take charge of the scene. He succeeded in cowing the other policemen, all the while proclaiming himself to be an innocent victim of Holmes's perfidy, and he might well have arrested us had it not been for the timely arrival of Louis Peltier, Rafferty's old friend and confidant. As a police captain, he outranked Grimshaw and put him in his place at once. Holmes then explained all that had occurred as Peltier listened patiently.

"Well, this is one fine mess," Peltier finally said, "but how could anyone doubt the word of Sherlock Holmes?"

As we were talking with Peltier, Grimshaw slipped away briefly to make a phone call, and a half hour later Mayor Richard O'Donnell arrived, looking pale and shaken.

"Where is Monty?" he asked at once and was escorted to the body, which the coroner had not yet collected. He lingered over the body for some minutes, shaking his head in disbelief, before returning to speak with us.

"This is a great tragedy," he announced. "Monty was a good friend."

"But not a good man," Holmes said bluntly, adding, "Dr. Watson and I should like to have a few words with you in private. There is much you need to know."

We went to the front of the store, well away from the police, and there Holmes told the mayor how his daughter had died and how Meeks had also arranged, with Grimshaw as his henchman, for the murders of St. Aubin and Rafferty.

The blood drained from O'Donnell's face and he murmured, "No, no, that cannot be."

"Mr. Meeks admitted it to us," Holmes said. "He deceived you as he deceived everyone else."

O'Donnell choked back sobs and said, "God, what I have I done? Maggie, poor, little Maggie. I failed her in every way, didn't I? I should have known."

"Perhaps, but what has been done cannot be undone, and all you can do is try to gain some small measure of justice for your daughter. Mr. Meeks is beyond your reach now, but Detective Grimshaw is not."

"I will take care of him," O'Donnell vowed and then turned away, still fighting back tears. "You have my word on that."

Peltier and his men had many more questions for us, and it was almost midnight by the time we returned to our rooms. I fell asleep at once, too exhausted to do anything else. Holmes, however, took little rest, as I learned from the next day's newspapers.

ONLY A BRIEF ACCOUNT of Meeks's suicide appeared in the morning *Pioneer Press,* which was constrained by its evening deadlines. The afternoon *Dispatch,* however, offered a lengthy story that included an "exclusive" interview with Holmes, who had called the newspaper's offices at seven in the morning to make himself available. The interview was quite remarkable, for Holmes did not err on the side of circumspection. Instead, he named Meeks as the mastermind behind three murders and accused Grimshaw of carrying out at least two of the killings. It was, of course, sensational news, yet also the cause of great controversy, for Grimshaw vehemently denied any involvement in the crimes.

"Holmes is out to get me because I have found him out to be liar and a cheat," he proclaimed in the *Dispatch.* "He has no evidence against me but acts like he does. Let him try to prove anything in a court of law, and you will see what I mean."

29

"How I Wish He Were Still Here!"

[From "Murder in St. Paul"]

The night after Meeks's suicide, Holmes staged what he called "a final meeting" at Declan Morrissey's speakeasy. Thomas joined us, along with Peltier and Morrissey himself. I had wondered whether Holmes might also invite the two cleared suspects in the case, Monsignor Denis and Bertram Abbey, but he saw no purpose in doing so.

"They are sinners," he told me, "but not murderers, and I will leave them to deal with their own consciences."

"Still, I wonder what the great versifier was doing at the Ryan last night," Morrissey said. "He must have met somebody up in his room."

"So it would seem," Holmes agreed. "It is well known he uses a room for assignations, but I suspect sexual intrigue wasn't what brought him to the Ryan. I had a brief conversation today with the desk clerk, Mr. Hobbs, and he informed me that a handsome, blond-haired young man was seen in the lobby last night."

"Johnny Riordan," I said at once.

"Yes, I think he met Mr. Abbey and that the two of them made an agreement regarding certain incriminating information in Mr. Riordan's possession, after which money changed hands. Mr. Abbey, of course, will not be inclined to admit to anything, while the elusive Mr. Riordan, we may safely assume, has already left for points unknown. In any event, I doubt either one of them knew that Mr. Meeks would also be at the hotel with the intent of silencing Monsignor Denis."

As we sipped Morrissey's best Scotch, Holmes then launched into a full account of what happened. "Three murders wound together like the strands of a rope, but with a single devious mind behind them all. I wish to begin with the case of Mr. St. Aubin, for his murder was the central strand. His demise arose out of Margaret O'Donnell's death and led in turn to the murder of Mr. Rafferty. The St. Aubin case, as both Mr. Rafferty and I found, was an exceedingly complicated affair. Even so, I was quite certain from the start that Jackson Grimshaw shot Mr. St. Aubin in that alley. For reasons which I will explain later, I became equally certain Grimshaw also murdered Mr. Rafferty. But what was much more difficult to establish was who had ordered the killings."

"Why did you suspect Big Jack from the start?" Morrissey asked.

"For the simple reason that I did not see how any of the other prime suspects in the case would have had the sheer physical strength to overpower a strong young man like Mr. St. Aubin, put a gun to his jaw, and pull the trigger. Nor did I believe the other suspects possessed the stomach for knifing a man in the back. Now, let us go back to the night outside the Ryan when the blackmailer met his end. I believe Grimshaw was tailing Mr. St. Aubin at the behest of Mr. Meeks and was looking for an opportunity to kill him."

Peltier said, "All right, I can believe that, but why was he tailing him on that particular night in that particular place?"

"An excellent question, Captain Peltier, and the answer is this: Mr. St. Aubin was on his way to collect a huge blackmail payment from Mr. Meeks, who in fact had no intention of paying up. Murder, therefore, was on his agenda, with Grimshaw assigned to do the dirty work."

"Wait a minute," Peltier said. "How can you be so sure of that?"

"Monsignor Pierre Denis—I am sure you know of him, Captain—filled in many of the details."

After describing how he had persuaded the monsignor to help

us set a trap for Meeks, Holmes said, "This past Sunday, Dr. Watson and I interrogated the monsignor at great length. I asked him then, as I had earlier, about Mr. St. Aubin's curious conduct on the night of his murder, when he approached the Ryan's doorman and wanted to know if he recognized the monsignor by sight. This strongly suggested that Mr. St. Aubin was looking for the monsignor and expected him to be in the vicinity. After much prodding, the monsignor finally admitted that Mr. Meeks had enlisted him to act as the middleman in the money exchange that was supposed to occur that night."

"Well, that's mighty peculiar," Morrissey said. "Why would Mr. Meeks want the monsignor involved?"

"Because he calculated, rightly, that Mr. St. Aubin would not view the monsignor as a threatening figure. After all, would a man of God try some dirty trick or, for that matter, pull out a gun? Mr. Meeks, I am sure, gave the monsignor no choice but to cooperate with his plans."

"Ah, so he had something on him," said Morrissey, who appeared to relish the idea of a priest gone wrong. "What was it? A sex thing, I imagine."

"I will only say the monsignor had committed certain improprieties known to Mr. Meeks. Mr. Meeks therefore was in a position to make the monsignor do his bidding. The monsignor was instructed to appear across Robert Street from the Ryan at the appointed hour and make his presence known to Mr. St. Aubin. He was then to proceed to the Golden Rule Department Store, a half-block away, where the actual exchange was to take place."

"Obviously, that didn't happen," Peltier noted.

"No, but the monsignor did arrive on the scene, carrying a satchel supposedly containing twenty thousand dollars, not long after St. Aubin had inquired about him. He said he nodded at St. Aubin, who nodded back, after which they both started walking

toward the Golden Rule on opposite sides of the street. The monsignor went into the store and up to the men's shoe department
on the second floor. There, he was to meet with St. Aubin and
hand over the money. But the monsignor told me St. Aubin never
showed up."

"So how did St. Aubin end up as dead as a flushed quail in that
alley?" Morrissey asked.

"We will never know for certain, but I suspect he was indeed
flushed by someone who managed to drive him into that alley.
It is likely Grimshaw hired a local hoodlum for the job. Whoever
he was—and he is probably long gone from St. Paul by now—he
accosted Mr. St. Aubin as he passed by the alley on his way to the
Golden Rule. Once he had been dragged or forced at gunpoint into
the alley, Grimshaw did the rest. This accounts for the fact that
Mr. Rafferty saw two men running from the alley after he heard the
gunshot and found St. Aubin's body."

"It seems like an awfully risky business," Peltier noted. "If Meeks
wanted St. Aubin dead, why not just stage the suicide at his apartment, for example?"

"I agree that would have been much easier. However, a very
nosy neighbor of Mr. St. Aubin reported she saw no sign of him
for at least a fortnight before his murder. I believe he had gone to
live somewhere else during that time, fearing another attack from
Grimshaw. With St. Aubin in hiding, Mr. Meeks concluded that an
offer to hand over the blackmail money would be the only way to
draw him out into the open. And since Mr. St. Aubin undoubtedly
chose the site of the money exchange, Mr. Meeks and his henchman Grimshaw had to arrange for his demise as best they could,
despite the risks. Yet even in death, Mr. St. Aubin had one last ace
up his sleeve."

"Johnny Riordan," Thomas said. "I guess you could say he was
the unofficial keeper of secrets."

"So he was," Holmes said. "Before Mr. St. Aubin arrived outside the Ryan, a news vendor on Seventh Street observed him handing an envelope to a younger man. That man could have been no one other than Johnny Riordan. The envelope contained all of the incriminating information Mr. St. Aubin had gathered regarding Montgomery Meeks and his involvement with the mayor's daughter."

"Exactly what kind of fragrant dirt did that snake St. Aubin have?" Morrissey asked.

"He had all that would be necessary to destroy Mr. Meeks and very probably send him to prison for the rest of his life. Margaret O'Donnell, of course, was his downfall, but through no fault of her own. She was like Helen of Troy in some respects—a beautiful young woman whom men lusted after—and yet I am convinced she was also an innocent. She did not seduce Mr. Meeks. Instead, it was he who, out of uncontrolled desire, attacked and impregnated her."

I wondered at once how Holmes knew this, for Meeks claimed to us in his last moments that he succumbed to Margaret O'Donnell's "blandishments." I said, "Are you saying, Holmes, that Meeks left behind a statement of some kind regarding his involvement with the girl?"

Holmes smiled and said, "No, my dear Watson. It is Margaret herself who told us what happened."

So it was that Holmes sprang a surprise, producing an envelope from his jacket pocket. "This arrived in the mail this morning, addressed only to 'Mr. Sherlock Holmes, St. Paul.' The postal service is to be commended for its efficiency in locating me. The envelope contains a ring and a most interesting document, both obtained by the industrious Mr. St. Aubin for purposes of blackmail."

I guessed at once who had sent the envelope and said, "It must be from Johnny Riordan."

"An excellent deduction, Watson. Mr. Riordan is a most resourceful young man, and he seems to have escaped the clutches of the police. I suspect he hoped to use these items for his own blackmailing scheme but finally decided it would be too dangerous. And so he kindly sent the ring and the document to me."

"I take it you think these are the same items St. Aubin entrusted to Riordan just before he was murdered," Thomas said.

"Yes."

"Well, let's see what you have," Peltier said with a trace of impatience.

Holmes showed us the ring first. It was a signet, with tiny diamonds and the words "Chicago 75 Years of Progress" circling a miniature city skyline.

"What is its significance?" I asked.

"You will see soon enough," Holmes replied as he removed a document from the envelope and set it down next to the ring. The document, which consisted of two sheets of yellow legal paper stapled together, proved to be quite extraordinary.

Looking very somber, Holmes said, "We have testimony from the grave, as it were. This is a statement dated November 30 from Margaret O'Donnell, in her own hand and no doubt prepared at the urging of Mr. St. Aubin. The rather formal language suggests he provided much of the wording. Even so, I am convinced the statement is truthful in all of its essentials."

Holmes read the document aloud. Dated November 25, less than a fortnight before Margaret's death, it was deeply disturbing, for it showed the full extent of Meeks's cruelty and perfidy:

My name is Margaret Mary O'Donnell. I am the daughter of Richard O'Donnell, who is the mayor of St. Paul. Today is November 25, 1927. I am writing this statement of my own free will, and I assure anyone who may read it that every word of what I am about to say is true.

I have known for some time a man named Montgomery Meeks, who is my father's assistant at city hall. He was always very friendly toward me and would give me small gifts of jewelry and tell me how pretty I am. I know now he was preparing to seduce me in the most wicked way imaginable, but at the time I viewed him much like a kindly uncle who was looking out for me, since my father was too busy to take any interest in my life.

On September 17 of this year, when my father was out of town for the weekend, I was invited by Mr. Meeks to one of the salons held by Bertram Abbey at the University Club in St. Paul. As I knew Mr. Meeks and thought the salon might be interesting, I agreed to go. Afterwards, we talked for a while. He told me he had an overnight room at the club and wanted to show me something "very important" there. I did not think much of it but said I would go with him.

What happened next was the work of a demon. I believe Mr. Meeks put some substance in a glass of Coca-Cola he offered me in the room. I quickly became sleepy and confused. I have only vague memories of what followed, but I do recall lying down on a bed and him touching me. When I awoke hours later, feeling very groggy, I was alone and naked on the bed. I felt something touching my feet and found a ring I had seen on Mr. Meeks's finger. I knew something terrible had occurred.

After I got home, Mr. Meeks called and wanted to know if I had found a ring, which he described to me. I asked him what he had done to me, but he acted as if he didn't know what I was talking about. I pressed him but he denied he had taken any liberties with me and claimed I must have had a bad dream. I knew this to be untrue but was uncertain what to do next. However, I decided not to tell him about the ring, which I saw as evidence of his crime.

I did not tell my father or anyone else what Mr. Meeks had done, for I feared no one would believe me. But I kept the ring in a safe place just in case. I decided I would try to put what had happened behind me. I avoided Mr. Meeks, who called me several times and tried to act as my friend. It is disgusting to think any man could be such a foul liar.

Last month, after feeling ill for some time and observing other signs that led me to suspect the worst, I went to a doctor on my own and learned I was with child. This was a great shock to me, and evidence that Mr. Meeks had indeed raped me while I lay defenseless. My father somehow found out about my condition, but his only reaction was to insult me while demanding to know "which stupid boy" I had slept with. I wanted to tell him about Mr. Meeks, but as he and my father are very close, I saw no likelihood I would ever be believed. As for Mr. Meeks, he has promised to help me, but I am now convinced those promises are all lies and that he only wishes to get me out of sight as soon as he can.

I have now decided, with the help of a good friend, to state the facts of my situation and seek satisfaction. I have proof of what was done to me and I am prepared to go to the police, the newspapers, or anyone else to tell my story. I will do so unless Mr. Meeks admits to his crime and takes steps to recompense me in the amount of $20,000 for all he has done.

Margaret Mary O'Donnell

"That poor girl," I said. "First she is violated by Meeks, and then she falls into the clutches of a cad like St. Aubin."

"Yes, she was used again and again by men for their own cruel purposes," Holmes said. "I do not know precisely how she came to confide in Mr. St. Aubin, but she probably believed he was her savior and would run off with her once they received the blackmail payment from Meeks. It is safe to say he had no such plans. The money was all that mattered to him."

Morrissey said, "If only the girl had found a true friend, everything might have turned out differently for her."

"Monsignor Denis did try to be of help," Holmes noted. "He said he gave her the name of a woman from a Catholic social agency who could provide counseling. Margaret, however, never contacted the woman. Nor could she confide in her father, who had never really cared about her. Instead, Mr. St. Aubin turned on the charm and she fell in with him. However, I believe no blackmail demand was made immediately because Mr. St. Aubin, who seems to have been very careful about his business, wanted some time to consider how best to proceed. Meanwhile, Mr. Meeks found out Margaret was pregnant, and that obviously created a grave problem for him. His immediate response was to arrange, no doubt with the mayor's blessing, to send Margaret off to the House of the Good Shepherd. Grimshaw, I imagine, all but kidnapped her to accomplish that end. With Margaret safely in the hands of the nuns, or so he thought, Mr. Meeks weighed his options and decided to contact Ruth Merrill, or Mrs. Coddington, as she calls herself. Mr. Meeks told us the rest of the sad story."

"Speaking of Mrs. Merrill, I wonder how Meeks found out so fast that Shad had talked to her," Thomas said. "From what you've told me, Mr. Holmes, he was on the phone to her in no time asking about Shad's call."

"An excellent question, Mr. Thomas. I wondered the same thing and so made a few inquiries at the Ryan. It turns out Mr. Meeks, clever fellow that he was, convinced one of the hotel's switchboard operators to notify him of any calls placed to Mrs. Merrill. It was simply a precaution on his part, since Mrs. Merrill was the one person who could expose his terrible secret. The operator, of course, had no way of knowing the information she provided would lead to Mr. Rafferty's murder."

Holmes then went on to describe how Meeks had arranged for Margaret's escape from the House of the Good Shepherd only to have her balk at his plans to take her to an abortionist. "He claimed to us that he killed her by accident, but I think it just as likely that he intended to murder her all along. She and her baby would have been a problem to him for days and years to come."

"How did he convince the mayor to cover up his own daughter's death? I can scarcely believe such a thing would be possible," Peltier said.

Holmes said, "It was possible because the mayor is a cold-hearted, calculating man who seems to have never loved or cared for his daughter. His ambitions mattered much more to him than Margaret. Remember, the mayor presented himself as a great advocate of morality and decency. When Mr. Meeks told him Margaret was pregnant and had committed suicide, the mayor saw at once that any public disclosure of her tragic fate might well prove fatal to his political aspirations. So he did not hesitate to take Meeks at his word and do all in his power to cover up what had happened to Margaret."

"I have lost all respect for the man," Morrissey said. "It's a crime how he treated his own flesh and blood, and the Almighty will surely hold him accountable in the end. Still, I suppose he and that slithering creature Meeks thought they were free and clear of any more trouble until another snake by the name of St. Aubin came along."

"You have a nice way of putting it, Mr. Morrissey," Holmes said. "Yes, Mr. St. Aubin's blackmail demand probably came only days after Margaret was buried. And so events began to spiral out of control for Mr. Meeks, who ended up arranging for two more murders to cover up his original crime."

The drinks were flowing freely now, as was the conversation, when Morrissey addressed the question that remained on all of our minds. "And what of our dear friend Rafferty?" he asked. "Will his murder be avenged? You say Grimshaw did the awful deed, and if you can prove it, Mr. Holmes, there are people in this city who might just want to send Big Jack to Hades once and for all."

Holmes said, "I cannot advocate vigilante justice, yet in Grimshaw's case the courts may not be able to provide the justice we all want for him. Along with his rude and violent ways, he possesses much animal cunning, which can sometimes be of more use than high intelligence. It pains me to say so, but he may well go free, for I see no obvious way to convict him of murder now that Mr. Meeks is dead."

"But we overheard Meeks implicate him," I protested.

"Not in so many words, Watson, and in any event it is hearsay at best. Of course, it is as clear as day he murdered Daniel St. Aubin at Mr. Meeks's command. But where is the evidence?"

"This gun surely counts for something," Morrissey said, reaching into his jacket pocket and producing an old revolver with a portion of its grip missing.

"Why, that must be—"

"Yes, Watson, it's the antique Colt Thunderer Grimshaw confiscated from Mr. Delray, the well-known burglar, and used to murder Daniel St. Aubin. Certain gentlemen of Mr. Morrissey's acquaintance liberated it during a recent visit to the detective's home."

I was irritated Holmes had not informed me of the burglary and told him so, although I was all too used to his habit of springing surprises on me at the last moment.

"I should have told you earlier, my dear Watson," he now admitted, "but as the gun proved to be a disappointment, I saw no reason to bring it up. I had hoped I might find fingerprints on the grip, but it had been wiped clean. Nor were ballistics of any help, for I learned the bullet extracted from Mr. St. Aubin's brain had somehow 'disappeared' from the coroner's office."

"But if Grimshaw had the gun, isn't that proof he murdered St. Aubin?" Thomas asked.

"Unfortunately, it demonstrates only that Detective Grimshaw is a thief," Holmes said. "It would be of use as evidence only if we could prove he was in possession of the weapon prior to the murder. As it is, we have only Mrs. Delray's word that he confiscated the gun, and I doubt her testimony would stand up in court, if indeed it ever came to that. And of course, Mr. Delray is gone, presumably never to be seen again. Moreover, no one saw Grimshaw with Mr. St. Aubin on the night of the murder, except for Mr. Rafferty himself. One of the men he glimpsed running from the alley was surely Grimshaw. But Mr. Rafferty did not have a good enough look to identify him."

"What about Monsignor Denis?" Peltier asked. "He was on the scene."

"Yes, but he told us he did not see Grimshaw. Remember, he was across the street. From his vantage point, it would have been very hard to make out what happened in the alley. In the case of Mr. Rafferty's murder, hard evidence against Grimshaw is also lacking."

"And yet you told us you're sure he wielded the fatal knife," Morrissey said. "What has convinced you of that?"

"It is largely a matter of keys," Holmes replied. He explained how he had come to conclude Grimshaw possessed a master key to the Ryan. He went on to say there were no signs the lock on Rafferty's door had been forced. He also noted that Rafferty invariably carried his one door key with him whenever he left the apartment. Finally, he described how Rafferty had gone up to the hotel's sixth floor just before his murder to confront Meeks with evidence of his crimes.

"And so you're telling us that gave Big Jack his chance to sneak into the apartment," Morrissey said.

"Yes. While Mr. Rafferty was away, Grimshaw used his master key to enter Mr. Rafferty's apartment. He searched it, took Mr. Rafferty's notes from the St. Aubin case, and then lay in wait for his victim to return. He stabbed Mr. Rafferty in the back once and probably would have done so several more times had not Mr. Thomas come along. I suspect Grimshaw's plan was to rifle through the apartment to make it look as if Mr. Rafferty had been surprised by a burglar, but once Mr. Thomas disrupted his plans, he decided to leave at once."

"You make a fine case, Mr. Holmes," Peltier said, "but as you've said, there doesn't seem to be much proof, unless you're holding something back."

"I only wish that were the case, but you are correct, Captain Peltier, I am short of compelling evidence. No one has been found who saw Grimshaw enter or leave Mr. Rafferty's apartment. Indeed, no one seems to have seen him anywhere in the hotel before he conveniently arrived to investigate a murder he himself committed. No fingerprints were found on the murder weapon, or so Grimshaw told us. And if there were any prints, he would have made sure to wipe them off. Nor have Mr. Rafferty's stolen notes been located, and it is safe to assume they have been destroyed."

Peltier said, "Well, from what I hear, Big Jack has already hired a lawyer and a very good one at that. He will deny to the bitter end he had anything to do with any murders. Besides, he knows a lot of secrets that give him leverage over people in power. They'll protect him, if they can. The worst that can happen is that he'll get kicked off the force, but I wouldn't even bet on that."

Thomas, who had been quiet for most of the evening, suddenly spoke up. "Grimshaw will pay," he said, with the certainty of a man predicting the sunrise. "I do not believe he is long for this world."

Holmes read the look on Thomas's face and said, "It would not be wise to seek revenge on your own, Mr. Thomas. It would only put you in great danger."

"I will do what needs to be done," Thomas said, "but I can wait. I have the patience of Job."

"Yes, I believe you do," Holmes said softly.

It was two in the morning by the time we walked back to the Ryan. The streets were all but deserted, and snow flurries danced in the air. "We have done all we can do here," Holmes said. "It is time to go home."

THE NEXT DAY we made our preparations to return to England. We secured train tickets to Chicago and then New York and booked passage on the *Mauretania* to Southampton. In less than a fortnight, we would be back in London at last.

The St. Paul newspapers, meanwhile, were filled with additional stories about the death of Montgomery Meeks and its consequences for the mayor and Jackson Grimshaw. O'Donnell faced many questions about his daughter's death as well as his relationship with Grimshaw. A state prosecutor, it was announced, would be opening an investigation, and there were calls for both men to resign.

"It will take time for the drama to play out," Holmes noted after he had gone through all of the stories, "and I am not ready to predict what the final act will be. But I believe Detective Grimshaw will receive his just deserts in due time."

Holmes was in a pensive mood for much of the day, as was I, for we both knew it was unlikely we would ever return to America, where we had experienced so many remarkable adventures. The terrible forest fire that claimed hundreds of lives. The severed head in a palace of ice. The mysterious runestone. The anarchists bent on assassinating a president. The old nemesis in the lost town of Eisendorf. They were all memories now, and yet still vivid in my mind, as was Rafferty and his outlandish outfits and roaring laugh and undaunted courage.

Holmes and I were reminiscing about these and other cases over dinner at the Ryan's café when Bertram Abbey made an unexpected appearance. Dressed in his usual mauve suit, he came up to our table and without being invited to do so, took a seat.

"I thought I might find you here," he said. "Don't worry. I won't stay for long. I merely wish to tell you that your work in this recent nasty business was quite extraordinary. It's given me a marvelous idea for a new book that's sure to be a best seller. I intend to dedicate it to you, Mr. Holmes."

"I am flattered," Holmes said. "However, be aware that Dr. Watson has exclusive rights, as it were, to my cases."

"Of course. Vincent St. Germain will handle the detective work in my book, even if he can never be a match for the mighty Sherlock Holmes."

"I see. Will your detective be investigating the case of an older man having relationships with underage boys?"

Although it was a stinging remark, Abbey managed a wan smile in response. "No, that will not be the subject. Well, I will keep you no longer. Have a pleasant day, gentlemen, and look for *A Blackmailer's Tale* next year. I think you will find it to be an interesting read."

"It looks as though Abbey intends to profit from his troubles," I said once he was gone.

"Yes, but I wonder for how long. His vices will catch up with him one day and profit will turn to loss. Speaking of literary endeavors, I assume you plan to write an account of what might be called Mr. Rafferty's last case?"

"If I can find the time. I have much work to do when we return to London. I must resuscitate my practice. I can only hope my patients will not abandon me as I abandoned them."

"Perhaps you should retire, Watson. There are plenty of other doctors on Harley Street."

"As I recall, you retired for a time and it did not suit you. No, I will keep at it as long as I can."

THE NEXT MORNING, a day before we were to take leave, Thomas stopped by for a final farewell and expressed his gratitude for all we had done in hunting down Meeks.

"And we are grateful to you," Holmes replied. "Your help was essential to our success. Mr. Rafferty always knew he could rely on you, and even in death you proved to be his greatest friend."

"How I wish he were still here!"

"Yes, but he had an extraordinary life. We were all fortunate to be part of it."

Thomas began to tear up. "Well then, it is goodbye."

"So it is," said Holmes, who rarely showed much sentiment but was obviously moved. We all shook hands as Thomas wished us a safe journey home.

"A wonderful man," I said after Thomas left.

"Yes, and a very strong one, too. We have not heard the last of him."

Holmes, as usual, was right.

30
"May He Rest in Peace"

[From "Murder in St. Paul"]

That evening, as soft powdery snow swirled down from the heavens, Holmes suggested we take a cab ride. He did not indicate our destination, and so there was a final note of mystery in the air as the hotel doorman hailed a taxi and we climbed inside. Holmes gave the driver specific instructions as to our route, and I knew then that were going to say our final goodbye to Rafferty.

After passing through a tangle of streets, the taxi climbed the short, steep hill to Summit Avenue. Traffic was light, and as we moved along, the big houses loomed up like giant shadows pierced with shafts of light. There was, I confess, something gloomy about the scene, for even great wealth seems no match for the power of darkness on a cold winter night.

"There is Mr. Abbey's place," Holmes said as we rolled past the dreadful old mansion, a light shining from the uppermost room of its tower. "Perhaps he is at work on his new mystery, which will then be added to all the other mysteries of the world."

Next we passed the house where Meeks had lived. It was completely dark, as though all the lights had been extinguished by his death. "He was a most interesting if loathsome man," Holmes said. "He had no bedrock of belief on which to found his life, and so for him everything, even murder, was merely a matter of convenience."

Another mansion—that of Mrs. St. Aubin—soon showed itself, and I wondered if she understood how her cold emptiness of spirit had infected her son. Yet I doubted she had given it much thought.

She was too hard and self-possessed to look deeply into herself or make apologies.

James J. Hill's reddish-brown mansion was next in view, and its rockbound presence reminded us of the powerful man who had first summoned us to the New World in 1894. We had learned that the mansion no longer belonged to the Hill family, having been given to the Catholic archdiocese a few years earlier. Yet I had no doubt Hill's ghost—surely a most formidable specter—still roamed the halls, for the memory of a man in time becomes more real than the man himself.

Across the avenue I finally saw the cathedral, its gray granite walls turned to charcoal shadows in the darkness. The dome was dark too, except for a soft light illuminating the lantern at its summit. Next to the church a few people huddled at the upper end of the tunnel on Selby Avenue, waiting for the next streetcar. Otherwise, the streets were all but deserted.

"Let us off at the cathedral," Holmes instructed our driver.

We went inside and I marveled once again at the cathedral's daunting size. The few worshippers in evidence were dwarfed by the towering dome, larger even than that of St. Paul's in London, and its immensity suggested that God must indeed be all powerful, if very distant.

We walked down a side aisle toward the altar. Along the way, we passed the confessionals where Monsignor Denis, as he later told us, received Margaret O'Donnell's confessions. He would never reveal everything she had told him from behind the screen. But he did learn of her pregnancy and that Meeks was responsible. Yet he made no immediate effort to intervene on Margaret's behalf because he was frozen by fear that Meeks would reveal his indiscretions with Abbey.

It was only after her death, with his conscience gnawing at him like a worm in his skull, that the monsignor finally took action. He told us he sent an anonymous message to Rafferty informing him of Margaret's death and its connection to St. Aubin's murder. In the same message, he provided a telephone number to contact Mrs. Merrill in her guise as Bertha Coddington. How the monsignor had learned of Mrs. Coddington he would not say, but Holmes suspected Margaret brought up her name during the course of a confession.

The monsignor had hoped his anonymous message would point Rafferty to the truth. It did, but it also sealed Rafferty's fate. Once he learned of what had happened to Margaret, he became an immediate threat to Meeks. And so Grimshaw was dispatched to silence Rafferty forever.

Because the cathedral was still relatively new, it was far from complete, and as we ducked under some scaffolding we encountered, quite by chance, the monsignor himself, who was talking to a workman. When he saw us he was as surprised as we were.

He came up to greet us and said, "I did not expect to see you again. Are you here to pray?"

"We are here to honor the dead," Holmes said.

"You mean Shadwell?"

"Yes."

"It is only right you do so. I wish I had been a better friend to him. I should have told him everything I knew, face to face, instead of sending him that anonymous message. I took the coward's way out. If he'd known the whole story, he could have taken greater precautions, and maybe he'd still be alive today."

"We do not know that," Holmes said. "You are not to blame for Mr. Rafferty's murder. The blame lies with Mr. Meeks and his henchman Grimshaw."

"It's kind of you to say so, Mr. Holmes, but the worst blame is always that which comes from our own hearts, and it cannot be made to go away. It will be with me until my dying day. Still, I'm most grateful you didn't mention me when you talked to the press after Meeks killed himself."

"I saw no need to."

"That was very considerate of you. Will you be going back to England soon?"

"We are leaving tomorrow."

"I see. I'll be leaving St. Paul soon myself. I've decided to go to a quiet place to think and pray and do penance. I am hoping God will forgive me."

"I have no doubt of it," Holmes said.

"If only I could say that. But doubt seems to be my constant companion these days. Well, I'll let you go about your business. May you both travel safely with the blessing of God."

We continued now to a side chapel where rows of votive candles flickered in the dim light of the vast church, their small flames precious vessels of memory and prayer. Here Rafferty had gone weekly without fail to light a candle in memory of his lost wife and son. Holmes put a twenty-dollar gold piece in the offering box. Above it dozens of candles in red glass holders formed a testament to faith.

Holmes lit a candle in the front row and said, "In memory of the late Mr. Shadwell Rafferty, a man for the ages. May he rest in peace."

Epilogue

There Were Reports of His Death

After Sherlock Holmes publicly accused Jackson Grimshaw of murder, the detective came under intense scrutiny, both in the press and from state prosecutors. But as Holmes had foreseen, firm evidence of his crimes was lacking, and Grimshaw gradually slithered off the barbed hook Holmes had tried to set. Grimshaw also managed to hang on to his job, despite frequent calls for his resignation, and the word around city hall was that he had "something" on the mayor, who therefore felt compelled to protect him.

Exactly what sort of information Grimshaw possessed never became known, but while it proved sufficient to keep him on the police force, his goal of becoming chief was clearly beyond reach. By mid-April, two months after Holmes and Watson had left for England, Grimshaw appeared to have rebuffed all of his critics and was back to business as usual. "I beat that pansy Holmes at his own game," he liked to brag, but his boasting did not last for long.

On the night of April 18, he left his home at ten o'clock, telling his wife only that he had to "take care of a problem." An hour later, after someone heard a shot, Grimshaw's body was found sprawled in a dirt alley in the Badlands, barely a block from where he'd grown up. The shot had gone through his forehead, directly above the nose, killing him instantly. There were no witnesses to the crime, since in the Badlands no one ever saw anything. A tepid investigation ensued—Grimshaw was no more beloved by his fellow policemen than anyone else—and the assassin was never identified.

A few hours later, as fog rolled in along the Mississippi River, an old Model T chugged up the High Bridge not far from downtown St. Paul. Halfway across the long span, the sedan lurched to a halt and George Washington Thomas emerged from the driver's side door. In his hand was an antique .44 caliber Smith and Wesson revolver of the same type Wyatt Earp had used in the gunfight at the O.K. Corral. Thomas had received the gun many years earlier as a gift from Shadwell Rafferty. Once he was sure he had the bridge to himself, Thomas dropped the gun into the dark, flood-swollen waters of the river eighty feet below. Later, when the police got around to questioning him about Grimshaw's death, Thomas stated he had been home all night, and Pats agreed that had indeed been the case.

Thomas never spoke of Grimshaw's death during the remaining years of his life. But after he fell dead of a stroke in 1931, he left behind a brief statement admitting he'd pulled the trigger on that April night in the Badlands. "Grimshaw received his due," Thomas wrote, "and the world was a much better place without him." Thomas also left behind a gift to history—all of Rafferty's notes from the "Last Case"—which were discovered by chance decades later in the possession of a member of his sister's family in Georgia. Thomas's funeral, at Pilgrim Baptist Church, drew hundreds of mourners, mostly from the Black community. Among the handful of whites in attendance were Declan Morrissey and Captain Louis Peltier, both of whom had suspected all along how Grimshaw met his end.

When news of Grimshaw's death reached Holmes in London, he expressed no surprise. "The circle has come all the way around," he told Watson. "And I have no doubt Mr. Thomas is the one who completed it." Thomas's final statement only served to confirm Holmes's initial judgment. After Thomas went to his grave, Holmes sent a long letter to Pats, expressing his fondness for her late husband. She cherished it until she, too, was struck down by a stroke, in 1933.

Former mayor Richard O'Donnell was the next to die, in 1934, succumbing to liver cancer. He hadn't run for reelection after Meeks's death and gradually seemed to give up on life. His last years were marked by long bouts of depression, alcohol his only consolation. Angry at himself and the world, he could not suffer anyone to mention his daughter or her fate. He was buried next to her at Calvary Cemetery, perhaps the closest they had ever been.

Paul O'Donnell outlived his father by only a few months. Aboard the Union Pacific's *Overland Limited* bound for San Francisco, he won a high-stakes poker game and then headed toward the bar car with five hundred dollars in his pocket. He never got his drink. His body, minus the cash, was found beside the tracks twenty miles west of Omaha, and it was never determined whether he fell, jumped, or was pushed from the speeding train. No one claimed the body, and he was buried, at public expense, in a nearby potter's field.

That same year, Muriel St. Aubin, on holiday at the Ritz Hotel in London, was struck by a taxi after she stepped into St. James's Street and by force of habit looked to her left rather than her right for oncoming traffic. She never regained consciousness and died three days later. Her funeral in St. Paul was not well attended, but in death she proved more munificent than in life, leaving her entire multimillion dollar estate to charity. She, too, was buried at Calvary, beside her wayward son.

Bertram Abbey lived until 1937, but only after suffering a precipitous fall from grace years earlier. It happened in 1929, just as his thinly disguised account of the murders, *A Blackmailer's Tale*, became a best seller. Then the stock market crashed, and so did Abbey, brought down by what he'd done at the Ryan Hotel on the night of Rafferty's murder.

Abbey had taken a room that evening in order to deal with a

troublesome sixteen-year-old bellboy he'd seduced some months earlier with the usual trifecta of money, liquor, and lies. The boy felt ashamed, but Abbey managed to talk him out of doing anything foolish, such as going to the police, and paid him five hundred dollars to keep quiet. But matters didn't end there. Growing ever more distraught, the boy eventually told his mother what had happened. She went to the authorities at once. Charges of sodomy and corruption of a minor soon followed, and the story became national news. By the time Abbey was ready for trial in early 1930, his publisher had abandoned him, as had St. Paul's version of high society. But Abbey still had plenty of money and good lawyers, and the charges were ultimately dismissed after the boy refused at the last minute to testify, possibly because he and his mother had been paid a very large sum for their silence.

Despite going free, Abbey's problems weren't over. He became a pariah in St. Paul, even though all of his supposed friends had long known of his taste for boys. With his life and career in ruins, he left the city forever after ordering the demolition of his mansion. Where he went was a mystery, solved only in 1937, when a report filtered back to St. Paul that he and a seventeen-year-old boy had died in a violent car crash just outside of San Francisco.

Johnny Riordan was also in California at the time, living in Los Angeles. He'd made his way west with the aid of a five-thousand-dollar "gift" from Abbey, secured from the poet at the Ryan Hotel on the night Meeks met his end. Abbey had wanted to be rid of Riordan once and for all, and the payoff suited both men.

Under the golden California sun Riordan felt at home at last, and with his good looks and winning manner he found odd jobs around the movie studios. He met a rich film producer, who cast him in minor roles, including as a castle guard in *The Adventures of Robin Hood*. One thing led to another, and Riordan soon became the producer's partner, happily ensconced in a Beverly Hills mansion, where he would live for decades to come.

Far from Hollywood, on the high, lonesome slopes of the Coteau des Prairies in eastern South Dakota, Monsignor Pierre Denis also forged a new life as a Benedictine monk at the Blue Cloud Abbey. Work and prayer became his daily ritual, and on warm summer nights he would go out to look at the sweep of the stars, just as he had as a boy in Canada. He was still searching for answers when his heart gave out on a bright June day in 1940. He was buried with all the other hopeful souls in the abbey's cemetery, awaiting resurrection.

By that time, Dr. John Watson was also gone. Vigorous to the last, he was still working at age eighty-five when England went to war with Germany in 1939. Watson stepped forward immediately to volunteer his services. He fell dead of a heart attack a month later while tending to an injured airman at a London hospital. Obituaries printed in newspapers around the world hailed him as the author of the finest series of detective stories ever written, a judgment unaltered by time. The funeral was at Westminster Abbey, where Holmes delivered an unforgettable eulogy that concluded with these words: "There are few certainties in life, but there is one I know to be true beyond any shadow of a doubt, which is that Dr. John Watson was the best friend a man could ever have."

As for Holmes, he continued his career as the world's greatest consulting detective to a very old age. During the war he undertook a series of risky spy missions behind enemy lines in France and also assisted in breaking the German Enigma code. In the years that followed, there were reports of his death in England and India and Argentina, among other places, but they have never been confirmed.

Larry Millett was a reporter and architecture critic for the *St. Paul Pioneer Press* for thirty years. He is the author of twenty books, including eight other mystery novels in the series featuring Sherlock Holmes and Shadwell Rafferty, all available from the University of Minnesota Press.